Kate Quinn is the *New York Times* and *USA Today* bestselling author of historical fiction. A native of Southern California, she attended Boston University, where she earned bachelor's and master's degrees in classical voice. A lifelong history buff, she has written four novels in the Empress of Rome saga and two books set in the Italian Renaissance before turning to the twentieth century with *The Alice Network*, *The Huntress*, *The Rose Code*, *The Diamond Eye*, and *The Briar Club*. *The Astral Library* is her first foray into magical realism. She and her husband now live in Maryland with their rescue dogs.

◼ /KateQuinnAuthor
𝕏 @KateQuinnAuthor
◉ @katequinn5975

Also by Kate Quinn

The Alice Network
The Huntress
The Rose Code
The Diamond Eye
The Briar Club

The Empress of Rome Series
Lady of the Eternal City
The Three Fates (novella)
Empress of the Seven Hills
Daughters of Rome
Mistress of Rome

The Borgia Chronicles
The Lion and the Rose
The Serpent and the Pearl

Collaborative Works
A Day of Fire
A Year of Ravens
A Song of War
Ribbons of Scarlet
The Phoenix Crown

KATE QUINN

HarperCollins*Publishers*

HarperCollins*Publishers* Ltd
1 London Bridge Street,
London SE1 9GF

www.harpercollins.co.uk

HarperCollins*Publishers*
Macken House,
39/40 Mayor Street Upper,
Dublin 1, D01 C9W8, Ireland

First published in the United States by William Morrow,
an imprint of HarperCollins*Publishers* 2026

This edition published by HarperCollins*Publishers* 2026

2

Copyright © Kate Quinn 2026

Kate Quinn asserts the moral right to
be identified as the author of this work

A catalogue record for this book is available from the British Library

ISBN: 978-0-00-880404-6 (HB)
ISBN: 978-0-00-880623-1 (TPB)

This novel is entirely a work of fiction.
The names, characters and incidents portrayed in it are
the work of the author's imagination. Any resemblance to
actual persons, living or dead, events or localities is
entirely coincidental.

Printed and bound in the UK using 100% Renewable Electricity by CPI Group (UK) Ltd

All rights reserved. No part of this publication may be
reproduced, stored in a retrieval system, or transmitted,
in any form or by any means, electronic, mechanical,
photocopying, recording or otherwise, without the prior
written permission of the publishers.

Without limiting the exclusive rights of any author, contributor or the publisher
of this publication, any unauthorized use of this publication to train generative artificial
intelligence (AI) technologies is expressly prohibited. HarperCollins also exercise their
rights under Article 4(3) of the Digital Single Market Directive 2019/790 and expressly
reserve this publication from the text and data mining exception.

*For my mother and all librarians everywhere—
this is for you, Book Dragons.
Keep on breathing flame.*

PROLOGUE

Have you ever wanted to live inside a book?

I saw that written on a library wall once, in curly purple script over the doors to the children's section. Complete with a mural of an annoyingly adorable little girl crawling between the covers of an oversize book, pulling the pages up like clean sheets over her annoyingly adorable ringlets. She looked so smug, I wanted to slam the book on her head . . . but the curly scripted question lingered.

Have you ever wanted to live inside a book?

I began seriously contemplating this particular life choice eighteen years ago, on the day eight-year-old me was ushered through the front door of my third foster home in six months. I peered through my ragged bangs as I stood clutching a plastic trash bag full of all my clothes and a battered paperback copy of *The Voyage of the Dawn Treader*, and my new foster mother barely shifted her attention from her iPhone, on which she was thumb-tapping away at some candy-colored game.

Better than my last one, who'd been so hungover when I arrived that she could barely grunt a greeting when the social worker ushered me through the door. "You'll sleep in the back with the other kids," the new one grunted, not looking up. "Dinner's over, but there's Cheerios if you're hungry."

I lugged my trash bag to the back room, curled up on the cot in the corner, which was clearly meant for me, and inhaled stale cigarette smoke and even staler microwave popcorn as I peeled open my book. A book where a girl not much older than me was falling into another world, a world filled with dragon-crested ships and warrior kings and sapphire-blue seas dotted with golden islands like gems.

Have you ever wanted to live inside a book?

For God's sake.

Why would someone like me ever want to live anywhere else?

I was doing poverty math the day my life fell apart. To be fair, my life had already been falling apart for most of the twenty-six years I'd been alive, but that particular Tuesday was the day it fell spectacularly, conclusively to pieces, and it really all started in the checkout lane at the grocery store.

Maybe you've never done poverty math. If so, lucky you. It's the Olympic sport of the working poor, the mental gymnastics performed by a woman with $36.82 in her checking account and an empty fridge at home, desperately trying to calculate just what shopping-basket Jenga will stave off both bankruptcy and malnutrition in the ten days to go before payday. I stood there rubbing my chronically aching jaw and surreptitiously ditching items from my basket before the cashier could ring them up: nix the fresh strawberries ($5.99 saved); sub two apples for the tub of salad greens ($2.99 saved); add in the Massachusetts sales tax—better put back the skin cream I'd been hoping to afford this week because that giant red spot on my chin would have to go away without it. You get giant red spots on your chin because you can barely afford fresh fruit much less skin care, and you get jaw pain because doing poverty math in every checkout lane gives you a lifetime habit of grinding your teeth in your sleep. And forget the dentist, because you're too fucking broke.

"Giving a party, dear?" the motherly looking clerk asked, ringing up all my eighty-nine-cent cans of tomato sauce and corresponding $1.29 packets of spaghetti.

"No." Make a huge vat of cheap spaghetti and eat out of it for the next week of dinners—that was my go-to when it was a real death march till payday.

"Hmm." She gave me a certain look, ringing up all that pasta. A look I was used to. "You know, I used to eat spaghetti like there was no tomorrow, and goodness, but my hips showed it!" A flick of her eyes at my lower half. "Then I went Paleo and those pesky pounds just *fell* off."

I gave her a thin smile, swiping my debit card. Paleo, right. *See how much fresh meat and fresh veggies thirty-six bucks will buy you, lady.* Maybe starches stuck to these hips but at least they were cheap—or sometimes, if I got lucky at the coffee shop where I worked, free. If I could take home a few stale bagels and muffins at the end of my shift today, maybe I could avoid another shop until Friday. The sheer *waste* of what got thrown away every day at the shop still astounded me after a childhood spent fighting six or seven foster siblings for every piece of toast at breakfast.

"Just a few lifestyle changes is all it takes," the cashier kept yammering. "Maybe you should think about it, dear."

"Think about what? Not being fat?" I popped my eyes open wide, all overdone Disney-lashed innocence. "You know, I *never thought about it until now*. Not *once*. My *God*, what have I been doing? Praise the

Lord, my eyes have been *opened*!" I gave her my widest, sweetest smile, preparing to pick up my sack of groceries and sashay out swinging my ample ass like a bell. A perfect exit.

"Your card has been declined," she said frigidly.

And that's how it all started.

The sky was spitting icy flecks of early April sleet, and I had a feeling I was going to be late to my shift at the coffee shop, but I'd had a text last night about the possibility of some data entry work, so I cut down the lower end of Newbury Street and shifted into a jog until I found myself staring up at the display window of Brummell's. It was a place I liked to cruise for the eye candy: a little jewel box of a shop specializing in exquisite hand-stitched custom costumes featured by an increasing number of fashion blogs and YouTube influencers. You never knew if the mannequin in the big bay window would be sporting a Belle Epoque ball gown embroidered with blue-green beetle wings, a silvery replica of Cate Blanchett's Galadriel outfit from *Lord of the Rings*, or a *Bomkai* saree starred with tiny mirrors, but it was always going to be jaw-dropping.

Today it was a frothy white gown with drooping shoulders and enough tulle to tent a big top. The shop owner was putting the last touches on the mannequin, adjusting a towering brown wig decked in crystal stars, and as he straightened to give me a wave through the glass, I felt my stomach flutter.

(I don't cruise Brummell's just to ogle the clothes.)

"Hey there, Alix," Beau called, opening the shop door and aiming one of his easy cheek-creasing grins down at me. He was decked out like a Jane Austen hero today, wine-red frock coat and brocade waistcoat and tall riding boots, everything fitting like a glove. The owner of Brummell's, and the hands behind every stitch on that gown in the window as well as that coat on his back. "You got my text. Come on in—"

"Can't, I'm late for work." I bounced up the stairs to at least come in under the blue-striped awning and out of the sleet. "But I can do data entry for you whenever you need me. How many hours?"

"Four or five, sometime next week? I haven't entered in any of my receipts for months."

"Beau, do not tell me you got my beautiful, organized QuickBooks account into a mess. I left it absolutely pristine."

He looked shifty. "It's been two years . . ."

"That long already?" I had to think back. He'd been just getting the shop off the ground and had hired me to get his accounts set up online. For a week I'd had the pleasure of working out of Beau's back room, tabulating receipts and trying not to stare too obviously. It was tough not to stare at Beau Sato-Jones, and not just because he dressed like an extra from *Bridgerton*. He had a face forged somewhere among Japan, Pakistan, and South Africa, and I guarantee you've seen it on Instagram: Beau's shop handle, @beaubrummellsofboston, had north of half a million followers, all panting to see Beau lounging in supple Victorian pinstripes, Beau strutting in Sun King silver coat and embroidered stockings, Beau lotus-positioned in a *yukata* of hand-painted cotton with flying cranes . . . I cleared my throat, getting rid of the delectable mental image. "How about next Monday? I'm off from the coffee shop on Mondays."

"Deal." He leaned against the doorjamb, smiling as though I were an old friend and not just an acquaintance to say hello to whenever he caught me window-shopping his mannequin displays. "You still flogging away at that place on Boylston?"

I mimed throttling myself. "Unless I got lucky and it burned down in the night. How's the girlfriend—Isabelle?"

"Ysabel, with a *Y*. Broke up with me, went off to LA to be a model."

"She doesn't know what she's missing. Maybe you can get back together with your ex, what was his name? The one with the cheekbones, dropped by twice when I was getting you set up on QuickBooks?"

"Deryk, also with a *y*. Went to LA with Ysabel."

"Next time date somebody who can spell," I advised.

"Okay there, Alix-with-an-*i*." He laughed, not looking too heartbroken. He was probably consoling himself with one of the endless beautiful clotheshorses that paraded in and out of his Instagram reels: doe-eyed girls with endless legs, handsome boys with even more endless lashes. "When are you going to let me make *you* a dress?"

"When I win the lottery, Beau." Everything in that store would have been out of my reach even if the $36 in my bank account had been sporting a couple more zeros. Everyone knows that if you need a Marie Antoinette costume for the Versailles Masked Ball or an *Outlander* wedding gown for a high-end Halloween party, you shop the racks of Brummell's on Newbury Street or mail-order off its sleek blue and silver website . . . but only if you have a few thousand to spend. Definitely out of reach for someone whose brain was stutter-stepping sickly with the words *card declined, card declined*. I shoved those stomach-churning words away, gesturing at the window mannequin in the huge white gown. "Queen Victoria?"

"Empress Sisi. A replica of the gown she wore in the 1865 Winterhalter portrait, and let me tell you, appliquéing all those silver foil stars by hand was a bitch," Beau said candidly.

"Worth the effort. It positively scintillates."

"You and your vocabulary. You'd make a killing at Scrabble, czarina." His nickname for me since I'd originally introduced myself two years ago as Alix-with-an-*i*. *Very Romanov empress of you*, he approved. *I like it*, czarina.

"Hey now, ordinary life does not offer enough opportunities to use words like *scintillates*." I had whole lists of words I'd picked up from books that I was just waiting for a chance to use—always with a little feeling of triumph whenever I checked one off. "What scrumptious sumptuous splendiferous thing are you whipping up on that sewing machine next?"

"Got a special commission to finish. After that, I was thinking a replica of the emerald-green dress in *Atonement*—"

"Please tell me you will at least read the Ian McEwan book and not just copy the dress from the movie!"

"What do you take me for, a himbo? I do have a library card, as you know."

I did know. The only reason Beau had hired me two years ago was because we'd bumped into each other quite literally at the Boston Public Library—he'd been very nice when I tripped and spilled half my water bottle over his stack of historical fashion books. One spirited argument later about the best costumes in movies versus the best clothes described in books, and I'd been hired to do his data entry. "Haven't seen you at the BPL lately," I continued.

"I'll be there later this week. Some YouTube influencer rented the garden and the Abbey Room out for her twenty-fifth-birthday bash. I doubt anyone there will pick up a book, but it'll be swank. You should come—there'll be a whole group of us, we can squeeze you in under the velvet rope. We're heading out to Vox II afterwards for cocktails—"

"Maybe some other time." I wasn't going to go on one of those self-deprecating, *Oh, I'm not worthy of him* inner monologues that the heroines in bad books always seem to do when a beautiful man looks their way, but I was a realist: I didn't have the legs, the time, or the budget to hit the town with Beau Sato-Jones and his flock of swanlike friends at $24 per artisanal cocktail. Maybe in another life.

The Astral Library

"Don't you dare tell me you don't have anything to wear, because you've still got my IOU. At least I hope you do."

"In my wallet." He'd paid me for my last week of data entry with a chagrined look, an admission that he was more cash-strapped than he would have liked (which I knew, having just gotten his bank account in order), and a scribbled note on the back of a brand-new business card: *IOU—Beau Sato-Jones owes Alix Watson the unconditional loan of one (1) fabulous outfit for the event of her choosing. Redeemable whenever, wherever.* Signed with a dash, and jammed in between my ID and my grocery store discount card, now all creased around the edges. In my more cynical moments I wanted to toss it in the trash, because when would I ever go somewhere glam enough to need an outfit from Brummell's? But I never did, because if your life is Cinderella pre-ball, it's nice to think your engraved invitation and your monogrammed pumpkin are out there somewhere.

"C'mon, I've got a *robe à la française* with your name on it," Beau tempted me. "A nice long back like yours was made for Watteau pleats. Or if you want something more on the fantasy side, and I know you do because I saw the latest George R. R. Martin in your bag when you went by last week, I can kit you out as the Mother of Dragons. Dragon-scale smocking, attached cape, knee boots—what do you say, gorgeous?"

"I'd say I'm already late for work, and my boss is definitely going to look at me funny if I show up to make espressos in a *robe à la française*," I said, shoving down the pinch of regret that I'd never been called gorgeous in my life by a man who wasn't trying to sell me something, and slogged off to my shift at the coffee shop on Boylston.

Whoever thought to name a coffee shop The Bump 'n' Grind should have been gagged, bound, and thrown in the Charles River, because it meant that three quarters of the male clerks thought it was hilarious to grind up on the women clerks while saying *Bump and grind, geddit?* but it was the least crappy of my three crappy jobs, and let's face it, a woman with $36.82 in her bank account (*card declined, card declined*) can't afford to be picky.

"Late again," my boss Cody said sorrowfully. He never got pissy with his staff, he just sounded sorrowful. "I'll have to dock you." He sighed, laying a moist hand on my shoulder. He probably thought that made him less of a prick for cutting a full half hour of my pay when I was thirty seconds late. "You know that chronic tardiness is not in line with the company mission statement here at The Bump 'n' Grind, Alix."

I wanted to ask Cody if the company mission statement had anything to say about that man bun stuck on his head like the back half of a wasp, but I didn't. I just smiled tightly, putting on my apron with *Alex* embroidered on the tit. I'd tried pointing out that wasn't how I spelled my name, but he very kindly explained that my name was Alexandria, and therefore the correct nickname was Alex. I'd never liked Alex with an *e*; it sounded like the hard-boiled chick detective in every half-baked *Law & Order* spin-off, the one who runs around cleaning up the mean streets of Los Angeles by going undercover as a stripper. But Cody Man Bun had decided it was irrelevant how I actually wanted to spell my own name, so my left tit perpetually said *Alex*.

"Why Alexandria and not Alexandra?" My last foster mother asked me that, ten days, nine hours, and forty-two minutes before my eighteenth birthday, when I could finally exit her basement bedroom and the entire foster care system, not that I had an app on my phone counting it down or anything. "Alexand*ria*. Wasn't that like one of the Real Housewives?"

"Sure," I said. "*The Real Housewives of Alexandria*. Drink chardonnay and bitch about the invasion of Rome."

She'd given me a look that said I wasn't the only one counting the minutes till my exit from her house, and I didn't bother explaining I'd been named after a library in Egypt, not a Real Housewife. My mother loved books, almost as much as she loved shitty boyfriends, and when I was three years old she worked as a page in the local branch library. She used to push me around sitting on her book cart, which she'd decorated with a flamboyant bumper sticker—tacked down, since they wouldn't let her stick it on permanently: *They Got the Library of Alexandria—They're Not Getting Mine.*

She'd untacked it and taken it with her when we left town to follow Mom's latest boyfriend, the drummer of an indie rock band thisclose to a recording deal, and that bumper sticker was still around (tacked over my bedroom door) when I turned eight and my birthday present was the news that Mom was headed to LA with a tech bro who swore his start-up was the next TikTok. "He's not so big on the whole kid thing," she'd told me, wrinkling her nose affectionately as if to say, *Isn't that just the cutest.* "I'll be back for you the minute I bring him around, mmkay?"

I guess she never brought him around on the whole kid thing, because I ended up going into the foster system with nothing but that frayed, curling bumper sticker, a few tattered paperbacks, and a name no one spelled right.

I pushed Mom out of my head, but I didn't have any better thoughts today to replace her. I made a batch of cold brew and began taking drink orders, and all the time my brain kept blinking: *card declined*. And underneath that, the bills.

"Caramel macchiato for Lauren."

The bill for my phone with the cracked screen. The rent I owed my roommates. The dentist appointment I'd been putting off for four years—

"Flat white for Shawn."

The crappy $22 pleather boots with the disintegrating soles, which wouldn't survive another spring rainstorm—

"Pumpkin spice latte for Kayla."

Because I couldn't afford hundred-dollar boots that would actually last, which meant that two months from now I'd have flapping soles again and be looking at twenty-two more bucks for *another* pair of crappy pleather boots, and by the end of the year I'd have spent $132 plus Massachusetts sales tax on boots that didn't do shit to keep the rain out, all because I never had $100 in my bank account to spare at any point in time for a decent pair. I'd end up spending *more* money to have wet, aching feet, and that's another facet of poverty math: how expensive it is, how frustratingly, ruinously expensive, to be broke.

"Four quad-shot Red-Eyes for Allyson, Bonnie, Ashleigh, and Jazmin." A gaggle of college girls in Boston University sweatshirts and expensive Uggs (*Uggs?* I could imagine Beau side-eyeing. *Oh, honey, no*, but at least those glossy bitches had dry feet) took their espresso concoctions without thank-yous. They'd be up till three in the morning in their dorms, jittering and giggling as they crammed for their chem lab or their art history midterm, and I envied them with a bitterness that verged on despair. When I was eighteen and fresh out of that final foster home, getting my first grimy studio apartment and my first job at Dunkin' Donuts, I still thought college was a possibility—I'd be that inspirational story that racks up views on social media, the girl who waited tables or worked a stripper pole to put herself through night school (#FemaleEmpowerment! #ByTheBootstraps! #YasQween!)—but eighteen turned to nineteen turned to twenty without my managing to save even a third of what I'd need for college courses, even at the cheapest college in a city full of them. And here I was at twenty-six, and it probably shouldn't have taken me so long, looking at Allyson/

Bonnie/Ashleigh/Jazmin with their sleek ponytails and Coach totes full of $900 textbooks, to realize that the dream was done: Alix Watson wasn't going to college, ever. She'd be lucky if she got to her thirties with a full fridge and dry fucking feet.

Card declined. Card declined.

"No-foam cappuccino for Charlotte." I pushed the drink across the counter, and the brunette with the PTA bob frowned after one sip.

"This wasn't made with skim milk."

"Yes, it was, ma'am."

"I can *taste* the dairy fat in there. And did you use the sugar-free vanilla flavoring?"

"Yes, I—"

"You weren't paying attention. Head in the clouds the whole time you were making my drink."

I looked at her diamond stud earrings, her salon-frosted highlights. *Card declined.*

"What if I was lactose intolerant? I could have a reaction from full-fat milk, you know. You don't *know* someone else's life. You just looked at me and assumed I was a basic bitch on a diet, didn't you?" Her French-manicured nails drilled the counter. She wore Lululemon yoga pants that had probably cost $120, and her butter-yellow shirt said *Life isn't about waiting for the storm to pass, it's about learning to dance in the rain!* Of course it did.

I exhaled slowly. "Are you lactose intolerant, ma'am?"

"No. But you didn't know that."

"Ma'am, I'm not quite sure what you want me to—"

"Make it again, please."

I could feel Cody Man Bun watching me, so I made it again. Skim milk. Sugar-free vanilla flavoring. Shake of cinnamon.

"I said two shakes of cinnamon."

I added another shake, wishing it were arsenic. "Thank you for coming to The Bump 'n' Grind."

She motored off with a warning I-still-might-speak-to-your-manager sniff. "Your shirt has a comma splice," I muttered under my breath, and moved on to the next drink. *Card declined.* "Large Americano for Brent."

"Thanks, babe." Brent was young, slim, Hugo Boss suit. He took his cup and held a single dollar bill over the tip jar, dropping me a wink. "Only if you give me a smile!"

I stared at him. The words just fell out of my mouth, quiet, completely unplanned. "Fuck you."

Not quiet enough.

Just like that, I was fired.

"I'm afraid we don't have any more hours for you this week, Alix." Elizabeth's voice through my phone was apologetic; I could hear her tapping on her keyboard as she looked through the library schedule. "Sorry about that."

I sighed, hovering at the T-stop stairs just outside The Bump 'n' Grind. Shelving book returns at the Boston Public Library was the nicest of my jobs, but it paid the worst and gave me the fewest hours. "Anything next week?"

"Afraid not." Elizabeth was one of those rare bureaucrats who sounded honestly sorry rather than robotically bland if she had to tell you no, and I tried to muster a smile in my voice for my boss at the BPL as I gave her my well-thank-you-for-checking. Definitely the coolest of my bosses: thirty-five-ish with funky purple-framed glasses and a full sleeve of flower-vine tattoos, looking about as far as you could get from the stereotypical gray-bunned, cardigan-wearing librarian who shushed people, thank God. "I can give you four hours the following

Tuesday, though," she added with some more clicking. "One of the other pages has a baby shower to host and needs to go shopping—I was going to sub in Vicky but if you want the hours I can swap you two around. Will that help?"

My mind computed four hours at $17.19 an hour. That plus the cash from Beau's data entry might be enough to get my roommates off my back about my share of the rent. "I'll take the four hours," I told my boss, wondering in the back of my mind if I was ever going to get to the stage in life where a) my friends were having baby showers, and b) I could afford to buy presents for my friends who were having baby showers. Hell, if I was ever going to get to a stage in my life where I *had* friends. If my life were a book—some gritty award-winning lit-fic about former foster-care kids who make good—I'd have an inseparable pack who had my back through thick and thin, but real life wasn't like that. Ordinary kids I'd gone to school with wrinkled their noses at the ones who were in homes, and I'd moved around too much to bond with anyone else in the system alongside me. I had work friends now, sure, but with the kind of crap jobs that were all I could get, coworkers were always coming and going—and it's hard to keep up the closer kind of friendship when you're always working flat out to make ends meet.

Besides, friends are just more people who let you down. Who needs that?

"If any more pages drop out on me, I'll put you in for the extra hours," Elizabeth said, sounding encouraging. "You know we always have last-minute cancellations. Things will work out, you'll see."

Easy to say when you have a degree, a job, and more than forty bucks in the bank, I managed not to reply. Because she was practically vibrating encouragement down the phone at me, I muttered a quick "Thanks" and hung up, massaging my jaw again before I could resume grinding my teeth. I really, really needed that dentist appointment.

Thumping down the stairs to the T station, I hopped on the next car, knowing I should head home, wishing I could head to the library instead even though I didn't have any hours scheduled. It was just about my favorite place in the world, and I'd visited my share of libraries since I started getting ditched at the local branch at age five. A library is the one place a harried mom headed off on a lunch date with the latest guy who isn't keen on the whole kid thing can park her child for a couple of hours, without needing to make some kind of purchase. I started ditching myself in libraries as a foster kid, because even the worst roach-infested library branch was better than sitting around a shared basement room wondering if my latest foster sister was going to set my hair on fire because she was bored. At eighteen, libraries were the best place to cruise want ads and submit online job applications.

And when I found the Reading Room of the Boston Public Library, I felt a thrum of angelic song in my bones.

The old part of the BPL was beautiful, from the Italianate garden at its center to the great double staircase guarded by a pair of majestic stone lions to the Abbey Room with its murals of Galahad questing for the Holy Grail . . . but the Reading Room was something really special. A huge, barrel-vaulted room with an endless stretch of tall windows like a cathedral, a double row of long tables where laptops and research books were stacked between lamps with green glass shades like a scatter of emeralds, marble busts and book-lined niches on the wall facing the endless windows. You could sit at any of those tables, get out your book, and read as long as you liked, the only sound in the vaulted space the susurrus of laptop keys and the rustle of pages. For me it had been home since about the age of twelve, when I'd been plowing my way steadily through my sixth foster home and all the adventures of Camp Half-Blood, Alanna of Tortall, and Westeros (sure, I was too young for all the sex and gore, but who was around to care?).

Fantasy. That was where I always wanted to live, since I first crawled between the pages of *Voyage of the Dawn Treader* at age eight. I never wanted to star in some dystopian teen hellscape; I never wanted Pemberley and Mr. Darcy—what I wanted was ESCAPE, all caps, not just back in time but off to another *world*, preferably one where women rode dragons and flame-roasted the men who told them to *smile*. I wanted second breakfast in Tolkien's Middle Earth; I wanted L. Frank Baum's Yellow Brick Road under my feet and C. S. Lewis's lamppost lighting my way through snowy forests. I wanted gunpowder-scented winds in my hair as I walked the decks of Jeannie Lin's Chinese junks; I wanted to challenge a queen to single combat on G. R. Macallister's desert sands; I wanted to make the earth tremble alongside N. K. Jemisin's rage-filled orogenes. I wanted to hatch one of George R. R. Martin's dragon eggs, only I wouldn't get dragged down to my doom—I'd ride off into the sunset in a flash of emerald-green wings, and the only thought in my head wouldn't be *Card declined*. It would be *Fly, fly, FLY*.

I pulled out my battered copy of *Dawn Treader*—the third book in the Narnia series, my security-blanket book, the one I still dove into whenever the world's dice rolled me a bad day—and stared at it blankly. My head ached, I was grinding my teeth again, I'd just lost the steadiest of my jobs, and I'd be lucky if tonight's dinner was anything more than a bowl of instant ramen. I put my head down on the tattered paperback, fighting my stupid useless tears as the T rumbled along, and mumbled, "Fly, fly, fly."

But every time I checked, my feet in their leaking pleather boots were still ground-bound.

Still only two in the afternoon—sure, so far I'd gotten fired and had my card declined, but that meant the day had nowhere to go but up, right?

Never hand the universe a straight line like that.

"Everything looks in order," the bank cashier assured me. "No reason your card should have been declined, Ms. Bibb."

I blinked. "My name isn't Bibb. It's Watson—Alix Watson, Alexandria."

Clicking keys. "The name on the account is Libby Bibb."

"What kind of name is Libby Bibb?" I could feel a throb start up between my temples. This was supposed to be a quick stop at the bank branch around the corner from my apartment; a fast unscramble of whatever was wrong with my debit card. "I'm not Libby Bibb."

"According to this you are, dear. It lists Libby Bibb as the account holder for the last eight years."

"*I* opened this account eight years ago. Look—" I started digging through my frayed nylon wallet for ID. "It's me, Alexandria Watson. How can somebody else's name be on my account?"

"Do you have any paperwork from when you opened the account?"

"Are you seriously asking if I still have a piece of paper from eight years ago?"

She gave me a cold look. "If you are alleging account fraud—"

"You're damn right I'm alleging account fraud, if someone named Libby Bibb has put her name on my bank account." *Thirty-six dollars and eighty-two cents*, I kept thinking. It wasn't much, but it was a whole lot more than zero. "When can I access my account again?"

"You'll need to return with a minimum of three forms of identification. Passport, social security card, birth certificate—"

"Sure you don't want a blood sample? Retina scan? Shoe size?" Another cold look. "Look, I don't have three forms of ID. I've never had a passport"—because I'd never gone anywhere, and the way things were looking, I never would—"and I don't have a birth certificate or a social security card either." My mother didn't exactly pack up all my documents for me when she skipped town with her dead-beat tech bro.

"You can apply for a copy of your birth certificate, dear. Twenty-dollar fee for those applying in person—"

"How am I supposed to pay a twenty-dollar fee"—*out of thirty-six, Jesus Christ*—"when I can't access my account?"

She went off into a long drone, but what it came down to was *I can't help you*. I reclaimed my debit card and mumbled something, stomach roiling sickly.

"Are you sure you aren't Libby Bibb?" the idiot cashier called after me brightly as I turned away. "Things would be a lot easier if you were!"

I looked at her over one shoulder. "Lady, things would be a lot easier right now if I were anyone but me."

"Alix, I want you to know I'm sorry." My roommate Brandon looked nervous, and I paused in the act of unzipping my boots. Nothing made Brandon nervous. Normally he was too stoned to rise above torpid. "Really, I am."

"Did you drink my milk again?" Trying to hold on to my temper. If you'd lived in as many foster homes as I had, you got possessive about your food real fast. "Goddamn it, Brandon—"

"No, that was Laurel." He blinked at me, still looking nervous. The three of us shared a two-bedroom in Southie: Laurel had one bedroom and waited tables at the Union Oyster House; Brandon had the other bedroom and alternated between working tech support and delivering pizza; I had the couch in the combination living room/kitchenette. We weren't exactly friends—I'd gotten to know Brandon only because he'd delivered my discount calzone three Fridays in a row when I was living in the apartment before this one—but things had worked out okay, minor kitchen thievery aside.

"Did you eat my Pop-Tarts when you got the munchies, then?" Much as it pushed my buttons when people helped themselves to my food, I hoped he had. If my roommates owed me one, they'd have a hard time bitching when I came up late with my share of the rent this Friday, which I was certainly going to do.

"No." Brandon chewed his lip. "I'm sorry, Alix, but you're gonna have to find another place to live."

I stared. "You're kicking me out?"

"Taylor found out about the time you and me hooked up. And she's not cool with you still living here, so—"

"Brandon, it was *once*, before you even knew Taylor, and it was so lousy we both agreed it was never going to happen again. Did you tell your idiot girlfriend that?"

"She's not an idiot," Brandon said stiffly. "And it wasn't that lousy."

You kiss like a dying flounder and you went at me like you were pumping gas, I thought but didn't say. Because my stomach was roiling all over again, and my eyes were taking panicky little stutter-steps all around this shitty apartment with the curling lino and the stove with only two working burners and the cracked windows that wouldn't open because thirty years of paint layers had sealed them shut. This apartment, this couch with the wire coils that poked into my back no matter how I shifted—it was shitty but it was home. And right now, it was all I had. "Brandon, you can't kick me out."

He shuffled his feet. "Um," he said, and didn't have to say anything else because he could—his name was on the lease. Me crashing on his couch was a strictly off-the-books arrangement.

I tried to take a deep breath, but I felt like I'd been sucker punched in the diaphragm, and the breath only went about halfway down. "How long can you give me?"

"A week?" he mumbled. "Taylor's, um. She's really mad."

"Come on, Brandon, a *week*? How is that enough time to find a new place?" With only thirty-six dollars and eighty-two cents in an account I couldn't even access.

"Just stay with friends, or . . ."

Friends? Who did I know who would happily open their door if I turned up in a week's time with a duffel bag over my shoulder? No one, that's who.

Brandon was making puppy-dog eyes at me. "Don't make this hard, Alix."

"Oh, sure. I'm sleeping in a cardboard box next week because your bottle blonde thinks I'm angling for her man." I zipped my boots back up and rose. "She's even dumber than I thought, and I already figured she had two brain cells fighting to the death for third place."

"Hey—"

"I'll come back for my things." Grabbing my purse and slinging it over one shoulder. "Feel free to call Taylor and have two minutes and twenty-four seconds of tepid missionary on my couch while I'm gone."

"*Hey!*"

But I'd already slammed out.

Homeless. I'd never been entirely homeless—come close sometimes, close enough to feel the icy chill at my back, but never quite. Even the time my last boyfriend and I broke up (an argument about whether or not his making dinner two nights per week and pushing a vacuum around once a month counted as *50 percent of the chores*; he smacked me; I slugged back and then stormed out because as far as I was concerned my mother was the very last Watson woman who was going to accept *but he's so sorry!* as a reason to put up with *that* kind of shit) I managed to couch surf with a neighbor for a few nights till my next paycheck hit and I could negotiate the living room deal with the stoner who delivered my calzones. I had always, always managed. I'd never had to go to a shelter or sleep on a bench.

You won't this time either, I told myself, heading back into the teeth of the snapping wind with hands buried in pockets. It wasn't even five; there was still light in the sky—this day felt a hundred years long, but it still wasn't over. *You'll come up with something, Alix.* But my stomach was churning so hard I could barely breathe, and I stopped in the middle of the crowded sidewalk (commuters heading for the T, office drones in suits, Amazon drivers in vests pushing and shoving in all directions) and had to brace my hands on my knees. I could barely catch my breath—it felt like a landslide had come to rest on my lungs. *You'll come up with something.*

"Goddamn drunks around here," someone mumbled, rebounding off me, and I lurched into motion again because it was move or fall. I stumbled onto the T more because the crowd carried me there than because I had anywhere to go, feeling the lurch of the car as it headed inbound. Scrolled through Instagram—I had an account, but I hardly ever posted anything. @beaubrummellsofboston had a new post; I clicked on it, hungry to see a gauzy ball gown or an embroidered coat or *something* pretty just to steady my mind and my breathing—was it just that morning Beau had dropped a flirtatious wink at me and said, *C'mon, I've got a* robe à la française *with your name on it . . . What do you say, gorgeous?*

The new post was Beau's long-fingered hand caressing a square of gold silk in an embroidery frame, captioned simply: *Guess who's finishing up the commission for his very first movie premiere? Can't wait till you see this gown on the red carpet—stay tuned!* Eighty comments already, heart emojis and smiley faces and *OMG what movie?!* and *What actress are you dressing?!* and *Did they choose you or did you choose them?!* and it wasn't till the entire post blurred that I realized my eyes had filled with tears.

Did they choose you or did you choose them? What I wanted to know was, What if no one *ever* chooses you? If it came down to you and Dead-Beat Tech Bro and your mom didn't choose you; if it was you and an entire foster system full of lonely kids and not one prospective parent chose you; if it was between you and Two-Brain-Cell Taylor and your roommate didn't choose you . . . What if it's *never* you?

I mean, isn't that why we read fantasy? The perennially unchosen, dreaming that this time the magic wardrobe opens for *you*, the Yellow Brick Road unrolls in front of *you*. You're finally chosen. *You* get the adventure.

But you never do. Because that's not real life.

Because if you're me, if you're Alix Watson, no one ever chooses you.

"Alix?" Elizabeth paused as I came trudging up the stairs past the stone lions and toward the Boston Public Library Reading Room, which was technically called Bates Hall, though I'd never heard anyone refer to it that way. "Remember we don't have any more shifts for you this week," my boss said, juggling a stack of clipboards.

"I know. I just—" I'd switched to the Green Line and gotten off at Copley, the library stop, more by habit than anything else. The vaulted Reading Room was almost empty, a few studiers hunched over laptops at the long tables, green lamps gleaming in the soft dimness like dragonflies. I stood there in the choired hush, gulping a little, inhaling the smell of books like it was going to save me. "Adding to your tattoo?" I blurted out, because Elizabeth was looking at me with concern, so to head her off I pointed at the neat bandage over her flower-vine-inked forearm.

"No, just getting the flowers filled in gradually. I want the whole arm looking like a riot of color, but I don't have the patience to sit in the chair and get it all done at once." She peeled up the bandaging to show me the new pinks and purples filled in on a section of twining roses and violets, and normally we'd have had a whole lively conversation about it—I'd have told her about the little stack of books flying like birds that I'd always wished I could get tattooed on one shoulder, and she'd remind me to think hard about anything I wanted on my skin or else I might end up like her: *Remember me telling you about my first ink, the little Chinese symbol on my ankle? I thought it meant* magical *and I found out later it meant* weird. *How white-girl-embarrassing, right?* We'd both have laughed at that, and I'd have reflected again that librarians had come a long way from the bun-wearing, glaring-through-glasses stereotype—but I didn't have any laughter in me, or any banter about bad tattoos. I just stood there silently, choked up and halfway to a panic attack, and Elizabeth was looking more concerned than ever, but then my phone chimed with a notification, saving me.

"Email," I managed to say, turning away a little to look at my phone and giving my eyes a surreptitious swipe. A message from the data-entry company that was my third job. Data entry, not exciting but reliable, and I could even do it here at the BPL Reading Room . . . Maybe they had a job for me?

Elizabeth headed off toward a patron calling for help with the wi-fi, and I thumbed open the email.

> Automated notification: All future paychecks have been placed in the name of Libby Bibb. Thank you for using our company portal to update your account information!

I stared at it as if the words would magically start making sense. Libby Bibb. Who the hell was Libby Bibb? In order to get targeted for identity theft, didn't you have to have a life worth stealing? Could I really not keep hold of my measly thirty-six dollars and eighty-two cents, my goddamn data entry job, without someone mugging me for it?

My third job—gone. Or at least stuck in limbo, frozen like my bank account. Nothing bringing any money in—a little cash from Beau for a bit of under-the-table organization of his receipts and QuickBooks account, but that wouldn't be much. And maybe I'd never been homeless, but I had a sudden crystal-clear image of the women's shelter near Downtown Crossing, where supposedly they made you listen to a sermon before you could eat a cup of SpaghettiOs, and wondered if that was where I was going to be next week, me and my copy of *Dawn Treader* and my frayed Library of Alexandria sticker.

The sob burst out of me so loudly, it echoed in the barrel-vaulted space. I clapped a hand over my mouth as if to stuff it back in, but the tears I'd been able to choke off on the T came pouring down over my hand.

"There a problem here?" an officious voice demanded behind me. "No excess noise in the library, you know that."

"Oh, for God's sake, Chester," I snarled, swiping my eyes on the back of my hand as I turned to face Library Security. As always, Chester had knife-edge creases in his uniform shirt and a thumb hooked in his belt, where I was positive he daydreamed about carrying a gun. His aviator shades were down even indoors, because Chester had seen way too many episodes of *Law & Order*. "Will you get off my case?"

He looked pleased at my rudeness, probably because it gave him the opportunity to raise the shades and unleash his patented steely-eyed glare, which I was certain he practiced in front of a mirror. Probably with finger guns. "It's my job to maintain the order and security of the Boston Public—"

"It's a library, not the Pentagon. Haven't you got a Klan meeting or something?" Normally I enjoyed a good dustup with Chester, because a Jack Bauer wannabe with a walkie-talkie is just the guy to sharpen your claws on after a bad day, but I still had tears welling in my eyes and they weren't going away, and if Library Security saw me cry I was going to wreck the place. "Just leave me alone," I snapped, which was the wrong thing to say because there's nothing a Jack Bauer wannabe wants more than to see you cry.

"I'm afraid I'll have to escort you out. Disturbing the patrons of the Boston Public—"

"Listen, it's not my fault you failed out of army boot camp, so stop taking it out on—"

"Missy, I oughta—"

"Dial it down, Chester." Elizabeth again, this time minus the stack of clipboards. I could have kissed her. She fixed him with a stern look through her purple-framed glasses, not one bit intimidated by his patented steely-eyed glare. "Aren't you supposed to be manning the front desk?"

"I do my rounds," he said with a dark look as if he'd caught me trying to dynamite the place. "And let me tell you, I've got my eye on this one—"

"Left or right?" I asked, but Elizabeth was already making a *shoo* motion at him.

"Off you go," she said briskly, and turned back to me with a faint eye roll as Chester strode off like he was headed for the O.K. Corral. "I know he can be a bit overzealous—"

"If he's lucky he'll get to go Wyatt Earp on the next patron with an overdue notice," I said, but my voice wobbled and Elizabeth zeroed in.

"Is something wrong, Alix?" Putting a hand on my shoulder. "How can I help?"

I don't know where to go, I thought. The momentary irritation that was Chester had faded, leaving me with the stark realization: I had no idea where to go, not an idea in the world. The studiers were starting to look up from their laptops, frowning at me, and any minute now I was going to brim over again and start weeping like a fountain. I couldn't bear that, just couldn't bear it. So I swiped my eyes and gave a bright blind smile, saying, "Just fine, I'm just fine," and started off farther into the Reading Room.

"Alix?" Elizabeth called after me.

The tears flowed over again. All I could think was that I didn't want her to see them, didn't want anyone to see them, didn't want anyone to see *me*. Glancing blindly to my left, I saw a door standing open—just an ordinary wooden door set in the long wall of books, and I didn't stop to think if it led to the Elliott Room or the Guastavino Room or just a storage closet, or what my exit was going to look like to poor Elizabeth, who just wanted to help. I didn't think, just reversed away from her, brushed between the long study tables and the rows of emerald lamps, and stepped across the threshold.

Some Chosen One I am. Fate sounding a trumpet in my ear, *Here's your call to adventure!* And I blow right through it.

3

Lucy Pevensie, going into a wardrobe and finding a snowy forest on the other side, said, "This is very queer" (cue the snickering for post–baby boom readers for whom the word *queer* meant something different than in C. S. Lewis's day). Dorothy Gale, stepping out into Oz, gave a cry of amazement and did *not* say anything about not being in Kansas anymore (that was the movie, and Alix Watson is always ride-or-die for the book over the movie, thank you). But a lifetime of reading about girls who get dropped into strange new worlds evidently didn't prepare me adequately, because when I stepped through the door into mine, I didn't say anything profound or poignant. I stopped dead and sputtered, "Holy shit."

The vast room unrolling before me could have been a twin to the Boston Public Library Reading Room, only . . . more. The same intricately carved barrel-vaulted ceiling, but stretching out so far into the distance I couldn't see the room's end. The same tall arched windows lining the walls, but these weren't darkening toward night; they were deep green glass and glowed like blazing daylight through an emerald sun. The same rows of long polished tables and green lamps, but every one was empty—not a laptop or coffee cup or open textbook to be seen. The same tall shelves of books reaching down each wall and up toward the ceiling, but these books *rustled* on their shelves somehow, almost rippling.

"The books are moving," I heard myself say aloud. "The books are moving. Okay." I pursed my lips, nodded. "Okay."

There wasn't a single thought in my head along the lines of *Am I going crazy?* or *I must be dreaming.* I wasn't dreaming. I wasn't crazy. I wasn't high either (you need serious cash to afford the kind of drugs that will get you *this* messed up). I was here, wherever here was, standing at the top of an ornate mahogany staircase that spilled a velvety green carpet down before me like a forest sward (this situation definitely called for a word like *sward*, another off my "words rarely called upon for boring modern life" list) and then branched off right and left like two embracing arms down to the floor of the . . . library? Yes. This was definitely a library.

"Can I help you?"

A woman's voice, somewhere around the vicinity of my right elbow. Too low and raspy to be Elizabeth's, and I had to wonder what Elizabeth was thinking right now—that I'd just disappeared into a Reading Room storage closet and vanished?—but I couldn't make my head do the one-quarter turn necessary to see who the voice belonged to. I was still stuck somewhere on *The books are moving*, still drinking in the room below and finding new details to gawk at.

Halfway down the right-side shelves a book was hovering midair, and every so often a page turned as if someone invisible was reading it. "Okay," I said aloud. At the foot of the staircase where I stood was a massive globe in a bronze stand, only the continents weren't the standard Earth continents and the carved waves on the globe were actually *rippling*. "Okay," I said to that too. The enormous clock didn't seem to have hour *or* minute hands, so what was it actually counting off—

"I said, can I help you?"

And the smell. The book smell that was my favorite smell in the world, the smell that all libraries had, the smell that said *home* to me more than any home I'd ever actually had. Most people had a different set of smells that made them feel at home: some mixture of Mom's lasagna, the jasmine their dad planted at the front door, the floor wax their grandma always bought, the dog they'd had growing up. I'd lived in too many places as a child to associate any smell with safety and security, so I'd latched on to the smell of books instead... But the book smell in my local run-down branch libraries was usually overlaid more prosaically with roach killer or mold or the sweat of too many patrons in summer. This smell here, this *ambrosia* I was drinking in, was a pure library smell: not just books but everything good in the world that went with books. Old paper and beeswax and ancient polished wood, yes, but also the leathery smell of your favorite comfy reading chair; the delicious wafting aroma of the tea sitting at your elbow as you dove into your favorite book; the buttery deliciousness of the just-baked chocolate chip cookie you crammed into your mouth as you turned the pages faster and faster. The smell of woodsmoke because you were reading in front of a cozily crackling fire; the smell of lavender laundry soap from the lambswool blanket tucked around your knees; the smell of a cat because in a perfect library you'd have a cat purring at your feet as you read the best book in the world in front of a crackling fire with tea and chocolate chip cookies on the arm of your perfect reading chair.

One delirious inhaled breath of that smell—the smell that somehow eased the perennial ache in my jaw and the faint throb in my temples, the smell that calmed my pulse, which had been anxiously humming all day ever since I heard the words *card declined*—and I was gone. I didn't care that the books were moving and the clock didn't appear to be counting actual time. I took another hit of that smell and I never, ever wanted to leave.

"Look, kiddo," said the voice at my elbow. "Are you in or out?"

I finally managed to tear my eyes away from the spectacle laid out before me and look down at the woman at my elbow. Look down quite a ways, because she was short: plump and seventy-ish, iron-gray hair in a bun, glasses on a chain around her neck, green cardigan. "In or out?" she repeated, sounding impatient, and I realized one of my feet was still paused on the threshold from where I'd halted mid-step. Back in the BPL Reading Room? Was Elizabeth going to come grab me by the elbow and make this whole dazzling space disappear? "I'm in," I gasped, lurching forward as if I'd been electrocuted, taking three more steps for good measure. "In, in, in, I'm in."

All in. Right there. None of this "hero refuses the call to adventure" bullshit—I had no idea where I'd landed, but I was in with both feet.

"Pleased to offer you sanctuary," said the woman, swinging the door shut behind me. I expected some sonorous clang, but there was just a quiet click. "Welcome to the Astral Library."

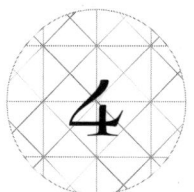

The Astral Library. The words echoed around the inside of my head as I stood there, heart thudding like a cannon. Smart-ass Alix Watson for once utterly speechless as I looked at the woman in the cardigan.

"Um," I finally managed to say. *Brilliant.* All the words at my disposal, and the best I could manage was *um.* "Um," I said again, like a moron. "Astral Library? Astral Library. Okay. Gotcha." I blinked, feeling a smile starting to break over my face. A dazed, blitzed, utterly ecstatic grin. "Who are you, exactly?"

"I'm the Librarian." Her voice implied a capital *L*.

"Obviously." Her appearance only included every single librarian cliché in the book. "Is that a title here, or a calling?"

She shrugged. "I've been petitioning the Library Board to change it to Book Dragon for a hundred years or so. Maybe in another hundred they'll get around to a vote."

Ageless guardian of magical space; got it. "All right, let's hear it," I said, suddenly dizzy with delight. I nearly bounced on my toes in my eagerness. "Monologue time!"

She stared at me over her rectangular spectacles. "Excuse me?"

"This is where you lay it all out, right? The world, the mission, what I'm supposed to do. Is there a quest?" Now that the words had started, I couldn't stop them pouring. "Do I get to be a queen? Are there dragons? Please tell me there are dragons—"

"Oh, shut up," said the Librarian.

I snapped my mouth shut with an effort. I really wanted to know if there would be dragons. I'd been reading a *lot* of Rebecca Yarros lately.

The Librarian pushed her glasses farther up her nose. "Are you under the impression that this is *your* world, and I'm some sort of wise mentor figure?"

"Um," I said again. I'd dated an aspiring screenwriter once, not one of my better choices—the entire six months we were together I hadn't been able to watch a single movie without him pausing nearly frame by frame to mansplain the story beats, no matter how many times I tried to tell him that I just wanted to watch the damn film straight through for once. He broke up with me to head to Hollywood with his *Matrix* knock-off script, but he did leave me with an excellent understanding of the Hero's Journey. And yes, this was the point when the wise mentor figure (Obi-Wan, Aslan, Glinda) shows up to shepherd the hero onto their path. So— "Aren't you?" I managed to ask.

"For gods' sake," the Librarian muttered, and marched straight around me and down the stairs. I hesitated a moment and then plunged after her, feeling a lot more like a lost duckling than a hero. "I'm not anybody's wise old mentor, least of all yours," she called back over one shoulder. "I'm not going to pat you on the head, stuff your rucksack for the road, or offer sentimental little aphorisms."

"I wasn't—"

"I'm not finished. Please divest yourself of the idea that you are the main event around here, Miss Watson."

"Wait, how did you—"

"Hundreds pass through the Astral Library every year, and you are just the latest. There is no *quest*."

"I can work with that," I told her, still trying to catch up. For someone so much shorter, she moved fast.

"Kind of you," she said dryly. Her voice was a raspy alto, with a tinge of an accent I couldn't place. Less like she came from somewhere I didn't know; more like she came from *everywhere* I didn't know.

"Hey, I don't mean to sound ungrateful here. I'm in a new world. That's enough for me." Tipping my head back to look at the tall greenglassed windows, nearly tripping over the last stair. "I don't need a quest. I don't need to be the capital-*H* Hero. I mean, isn't it better if I'm not? Heroes tend to get killed in battles or eaten alive by magic rings." If I was one of hundreds who'd come through here, didn't that up my chances for survival?

Even if she'd said no, I don't think I'd have tried to go back. I didn't have anything to go back *to*.

"How do you know my name?" I asked as she marched up to a wide oak counter tucked against one wall. The kind where you checked out your library books, only there was no computer here to log your library card, just an old-fashioned stack of cards and stamps—and a tablet in an emerald-green case, sitting in a long-armed frame clamped to the counter's edge. I jumped a little as the tablet turned on its frame to *look* at me. "What the—"

She ignored me, plucking the tablet out of its clamps and swiping through the touch screen. "You infernal machine," she muttered, and it beeped spitefully at her. "Kick her name up, I know she's here—ah." She turned the tablet around, and there I was, picture and all. For an instant I wondered if it was going to say Libby Bibb, but— "Alexandria Watson of Boston, yes?"

I swallowed. "Yes."

"I know your name because the Astral Library invited you in—" The Librarian paused, swiping her glasses off as a sob burst out of me. "You're not going to start blubbering every time I try to impart information, are you?"

"No," I gulped, wiping my eyes. "The Astral Library—it invited me? Chose me?" Because the first thing that came to my mind was that small, perennially bleating voice insisting, *There must be some mistake—no one chooses me.*

How broken and pathetic was I, that *that* was the first thing that came to mind as I stood in the middle of a demonstrably magic library?

"This place chooses a great many booklovers," the Librarian said, looking as if she knew every jumbled word going through my head. "The lost and the desperate. Is that you?"

In a goddamn nutshell. I wiped my eyes, realizing I didn't give a crap if I wasn't *the* chosen, as long as I was *a* chosen. I'd been invited. A door had opened. Someone had finally *picked me.*

I smiled, gazing down at the Librarian, who wasn't looking too patient. "What is this place?"

Okay, I thought, now *it's monologue time.* But no. The huge brass clock on the wall chimed a mellow tone, and the Librarian glanced up at the staircase. "Masako should be here any minute," she murmured.

"The rundown will have to wait, Miss Watson. If you wouldn't mind entertaining yourself for the next hour—"

"What should I do?" Because bad things tend to happen to characters in books when they go wandering off into new worlds before they learn the rules. Just ask Edmund Pevensie in *The Lion, the Witch and the Wardrobe*.

"You're in a library." The Librarian waved a hand, heading back toward the stairs. "May I suggest you read a book?"

"Fantasy section?" I called after her.

"Shelves 422 through 698," she called without looking back. The door at the top of the stairs opened, the same door that had admitted me, but this time I didn't see the Boston Public Library Reading Room behind it. This time I saw what looked like shelves of scrolls, a sliding screen, and then a woman strolled in who could have stepped right out of a scroll herself: tall, fortyish, a book tucked under one arm. She was swathed in wafting layers of embroidered silk robes in shades of green and pink, her hair drifted to her hips in a sheet of black satin, and she addressed the Librarian in a warm flood of Japanese, bowing. The Librarian bowed back, answering in the same language, and my God, did I have questions, but I knew I wasn't getting answers yet.

So I browsed Shelf 533, and somehow I wasn't surprised to see that alongside all the Song of Ice and Fire books was the next one in the series, the one that hadn't even been published yet. And I was in a fantasy world myself but I was still a bookworm, so what did I do? I let out a tremendous yelp of delight, yanked the book off the shelf, and sank right down on the floor. The book seemed to nearly sigh as I cracked the cover open, pages giving a little shimmy along their edges as I stroked them. "I think you want me to read you," I whispered.

The books along their shelves, the book in my lap, all gave a rustle as if to say, *Of course, you silly thing.*

It took another mellow chime of the huge clock to bring me out of Westeros. I blinked, looking up to see the Japanese woman taking her book back from the Librarian, who was tapping away at her tablet. "Renewed for another year," the older woman was saying in English. "Do tell Genji hello for me. He's a darling boy even when he's being annoying. Which he usually is."

The two women bowed again, the Librarian reversed for the big oak counter, and I scrambled upright. "Wait—" I called to the Japanese woman as she began to glide up the staircase in her butterfly-wing layers of silk. Beau would have swooned over her court robes—he'd have pounced on those trailing sleeves in a heartbeat, turning them over to examine the back side of the embroidery: *Oh, honey, you are nailing it. Couching stitch or long-and-short stitch here . . . ?*

The woman turned toward me, rice-powdered face serene as a moon, and I realized I had no idea if she spoke English. The Librarian had addressed her in both languages, but was there a translation spell or something going on? Jesus, I needed a manual. "Um. *Ohayo gozaimasu,*" I said, trying to remember the few words of Japanese I'd learned from a fellow coffee-shop clerk last year.

"Don't stress, I was born in Detroit." The Japanese woman grinned, and I saw that her teeth were black—not bad nutrition, I realized with a closer look, but because they'd been meticulously painted with some kind of cosmetic. A little startling at first, but then I realized it was to set off her ivory-pale skin. "Let me guess," she went on, her flat American English at stark odds with her elegant scroll-painting appearance. "You've only just come through the door?"

The Astral Library

"Yeah." I let out a breath. "My mind is pretty well blown." I wanted to ask her a thousand things: why she sounded like Detroit and looked like medieval Japan; what door she'd walked through and why she was here; what business she'd just concluded with the Librarian...

"I'd fill you in on all the details, but the Librarian will do that. Besides," the Japanese woman added, "I'm due at a moon viewing."

"Moon viewing..." I echoed, mind still blown.

"Yep. I'm a lady-in-waiting and poet to Lady Fujitsubo at the Imperial court, so I'll be expected to kick out some top-notch verses tonight." My entire face must have been a question mark, because with a flutter of her billowing silk sleeves the woman showed me the book tucked under one arm—an extremely modern HarperCollins paperback, but with a woman in multilayered robes on the cover, looking very much like her.

"What—" I looked at the Librarian, back at my elbow with her tablet. She turned it around and I saw the data entry: *Yoshida, Masako; first checked out* The Tale of Genji *(Murasaki Shikibu) on 2/26/2014; renewed one year.*

"Masako here lives inside a book," the Librarian explained as the Detroit-born poet/lady-in-waiting gave a wave and floated up the stairs toward the door for her moon viewing. "And if you want, Miss Watson, so can you."

"First of all, why is it called the Astral Library?"

"Because it can open from any library in the world." The Librarian was leading me through the Library now, her sensible brogues going *slap-slap* against the polished hardwood floor. "For you it opened at the Reading Room of the Boston Public Library. For Masako, it originally opened in the back shelves of the Henry Ford Centennial

Library on Michigan Avenue in Detroit. Four months ago, a gentleman in a great deal of cold weather gear ambled in from the McMurdo Library in Antarctica." She indicated the barrel-vaulted space around us. "It can open a door from any library it needs to."

I blinked, sidetracked by the idea of a library in Antarctica. I guess it stood to reason. What else were the scientists going to do down there when they weren't counting penguins? "So the Astral Library exists everywhere, all at once. Doesn't that violate physics?"

A wave of her hand. "Oh, we're well past that."

"Gotcha." I had a feeling my head was going to hurt if I thought about that too much, so I plunged on. "Are the books here, um. Alive?" I had the new George R. R. Martin book tucked under one arm, finger firmly marking my place, mainly because I had a feeling it *wanted* to stay with me. I'd never had a reading sensation like it, perusing a book so eager to be read it practically flipped the pages for me. *Just one more chapter!*

"Whether books are actually alive or merely enchanted is a matter for some debate among the Library Board," said the Librarian. "I can tell you that the books here most certainly have opinions."

A smug rustle rippled along the bookshelves at that. The book under my arm nipped my fingertip like a frisky pony.

"How do you have copies of books that haven't even been published yet?" Giving the volume a light smack: *Stop that.*

"Naturally the Library stocks books that haven't been written yet," the Librarian said as if it were obvious. "Though sometimes the story changes if whoever's writing it can't make up their mind how it all ends. *Authors,*" she muttered.

"The story changes?"

She indicated the book under my arm. "Flip back to chapter two."

I flipped. Sure enough, a chapter that had started in Essos when I first read it now started in King's Landing. "Um. Okay." I had a feeling I was going to be saying that a lot. "So what's the Astral Library's purpose?"

"Sanctuary," the Librarian said briskly, still walking. It felt like we'd been walking for ten minutes, and I still couldn't see an end to this space—the shelves, the high-arching ceiling, the emerald windows just went on and on and on. "The Library offers—will you get off that ladder?"

"Sorry." I'd scrambled onto the long rolling library ladder the moment we passed it, barely managing to keep my squeal of delight silent, because what bookworm doesn't fantasize about library ladders sliding along bookshelves on polished wheels? I certainly did, having spent half my childhood imagining myself as Belle from *Beauty and the Beast*. I gave the ladder a pat and hopped down. "I promise I'll behave," I said, dizzy with delight all over again.

"As I was saying, the Library offers sanctuary to booklovers who are desperate."

"Desperate for what?" I didn't entirely enjoy hearing myself described that way. Maybe it was true, but no one likes to hear it out loud, do they?

"For anything. For everything. Love, hope, joy, security. All of the above, sometimes, as in your case. It picked you, I help you, you escape into a new life. If that's what you want."

"It's what I want," I said immediately, falling back in at her side.

"I thought so. Now, when it comes to choosing the book you want to escape into—"

"Narnia," I said. "Narnia. Please, Narnia." *Alix, Queen of Narnia, Chatelaine of Cair Paravel*—I liked the sound of that. I could already see myself setting sail on the *Dawn Treader*, heading out over sapphire waters for horizons unknown. Dragging Prince Caspian off to my bunk the minute it was sunset . . .

"You cannot go to Narnia," said the Librarian, exasperated.

"Why not?"

"The rules are—" she began, but my brain was already running ahead of the explanations.

"If not Narnia, what about Middle Earth?" If Cair Paravel and the *Dawn Treader* were off the table, I'd take a hobbit hole with a round green door and a cozy pantry loaded with seed cakes and pork pies and apple tarts. My mouth watered, and I thought of that grocery store clerk who advised me to go on Paleo. *Second breakfast, here I come!*

"I'm afraid Middle Earth is out."

"Earthsea, then? Pern? Tortall? Ravka? Eshoza? The Stillness? The Five Queendoms?"

"No—"

"What about magic *schools*, then? I can see myself at Brakebills or Camp Half-Blood—"

"No! Will you shut up and listen?"

I snapped my teeth shut with an effort.

"The Astral Library only offers escape into books that have passed into public domain." Seeing my blank expression, she elaborated. "Libraries and librarians are gatekeepers, protectors of the written word. If you aren't allowed to copy, reproduce, quote, or print an author's book without legal permission, why on earth would you be allowed to *live* in it?"

"I am positive this particular situation is not covered by copyright law," I stated.

"Maybe not, but the Astral Library doesn't use books unethically." More rustling from the shelves around us, as if the books were harrumphing. "If you wish to lodge a complaint, contact the Library Board."

"What's the—never mind." I pinched the bridge of my nose. "Okay. What kind of book *can* I pick? What are the rules?"

The Librarian waved me to a chair—I hadn't even noticed there was a chair there, but suddenly here was an entire little reading nook in the endless stretch of shelves: two deep green armchairs in ancient worn leather, fleecy lambswool blankets tossed over their arms, a table between with a Wedgwood teapot issuing the smell of just-brewed Darjeeling, not to mention two teacups in robin's-egg blue and a variety of perfectly plated snacks. This time I didn't even blink. Of course the Library would provide tea and reading chairs. It could open doors simultaneously into Boston and Antarctica if it was in the mood; was it supposed to blink at a few blankets and a fully laden tea tray? I poured out a cup, adding sugar with the kind of lavish abandon I couldn't usually indulge in since a box of Sweet'N Low in Boston would set me back $6.49, and gulped blissfully as the Librarian sat down and consulted her tablet.

"All right," she said. "The rules. Say you want to go live in *Pride and Prejudice*—"

"I don't." I'd read it, but I didn't fantasize about going there. No dragons, no magic, and those high waists weren't really a good look on me.

"No interest in *Pride and Prejudice*? Well, that's a change," she muttered. "You know how many women I've shepherded into Meryton with their bonnets and reticules? I'm all for Austen, but read another book, ladies. Anyway. Using *P&P* for an example: it's in the public domain so yes, you can choose it. I drop you into the world of the book at the beginning, when Netherfield Park has been let at last. You do *not*," she said with a glare, "get to be Elizabeth Bennet. Or any of the Bennet sisters, or any named character from the book. The book inserts you as a background character—imagine a neighbor to Lady Catherine de Bourgh, or a cousin of Aunt Gardiner. You'll be at the Netherfield ball, you'll be watching the militia march into Meryton, you just won't be part of the heroine's life. You'll be leading your own, as she leads hers."

"Would I be bumping into everyone else who decided to come live in *Pride and Prejudice*?" Seemed to me like an Austen novel could get crowded pretty fast.

"No. You're all in your own version. Every reader's experience of a book is different, after all."

"So it's kind of like fan fiction?" The Librarian gave me a withering look, which I answered with a grin. "Not to sound elitist here, but what are the chances I walk into a book world and turn into the chambermaid?" I eyed the platter of snacks the Library had provided seemingly without any chambermaid at all: everything from buttered popcorn to cucumber tea sandwiches, Girl Scout Samoas to fresh-baked berry scones. "Because I don't think anybody dreams of waltzing off to *Pride and Prejudice* so they can end up scrubbing Elizabeth Bennet's petticoats when they're six inches deep in mud," I said, snagging myself a scone.

"The Library is generally quite good about matching our Patrons to the kind of lives they've been aching to have." The way the Librarian said *Patrons*, it was clearly a noun with a capital *P* and a great deal of weight. "To a point," she added, pouring herself some Darjeeling. "Just because you're a side character in Elizabeth Bennet's life does *not* mean you can bump her out of the way and marry Mr. Darcy yourself. You don't get to change the course of the story as it's been written. And for gods' sake, don't assume the book will mirror the movie," the Librarian added. "Head off to *Pride and Prejudice* all you want but do *not* come crying to me when Mr. Darcy looks nothing like Colin Firth or Matthew Macfadyen."

"Got it." I took another gulp of hot sugary tea to wash down my perfectly buttered, piping-hot scone. "No non-public-domain books, no movie versions, you don't get to be the heroine, and you don't get to change the story." That made me think of something else. "What happens when the story ends, though? There I am in the church crowd with everyone else, Aunt Gardiner's neighbor or whoever, watching Elizabeth Bennet marry Mr. Darcy—what happens to me after that? After *The End*?"

"You can return your book to the Library and either try a new book or rejoin your old life," said the Librarian. "Or you can keep living in that world . . . Only the Library can't guarantee what happens, once you've lived past the last page. Stories take on a life of their own after the author sets down the pen."

"They—they do?"

She smiled, and I saw it was a smile with an edge to it. A smile that had teeth, and not the pearly whites kind. "Think of a map, Miss Watson. Once you leave charted waters, there's only the warning: *Here There Be Dragons*. It's the same with a book, if you continue to live in it. The story will take its own direction, because just by living there you've brought change. You can stay . . . but be aware of the dragons."

"Bring it on. I want dragons!"

"I was being," she said in exasperated tones, "metaphorical."

"Right." I made a mental note to choose a book with a reasonably long time span—no sense heading off into uncharted waters sooner than I had to, picking a story that got told in three days. Which made me think of another potential snag. "Being literal instead of metaphorical, can you die in a book world? Get hurt?"

"You can die or get hurt in this world, can't you? Of course you can die or get hurt in a book world. But you have to take into account when you choose, just how dangerous is the world you've chosen?" she added. "How many people in a Jane Austen novel get stabbed, as opposed to an Agatha Christie? How likely is death by tuberculosis in Mark Twain as opposed to Victor Hugo? Choose carefully," she advised.

I nodded. So this world I'd stepped into had its dangers; that seemed fair to me. What world doesn't, including the real one I'd just left? "How many, um, Patrons stay in their books for good?" I asked, hearing the capital *P* in my own voice now that I was about to become one. "In your experience."

"I'd say about one-quarter," the Librarian answered without hesitation. "It's quite a thing, walking away from your whole life and building another in a completely new world, isn't it? Some get tired of living in a book and hop out when the story's over. Some know from the start that all they want is a respite—I've got a woman living in *The Great Gatsby* with her two children; they're all slotted in as West Egg neighbors of Gatsby's, and she said from the start they'd stay till her children hit eighteen, when she could take them home without losing custody to the husband, who was threatening to take them in the divorce."

"Won't she be in a hell of a lot of hot water as soon as she reappears?" I couldn't help asking. I'd known more than one foster kid embroiled in the middle of a nasty custody battle.

"She's desperate enough to risk it. You have to be willing to accept the consequences," the Librarian said, "when you let magic into your life. It's not a cure-all, Miss Watson."

I absorbed that for a moment before thinking of something else.

"Wait, if she brings her kids back into the real world at eighteen, do they walk back home into the same moment they'd left? Just suddenly looking years older?" Time travel logistics. Man, did they get complicated quickly.

"Mmm." The Librarian raised her blue teacup, and a massive ring on one finger caught my eye—an emerald, big as a chunk of broken glass. "Time *here* inside the Astral Library stands still—no one ages inside these walls no matter how much time they spend here, and the Library clock doesn't tell time; it tells me when someone's coming. If you stepped out of the Astral Library back to the real world without any intervening stops, then yes, you'd step right back into whatever moment you left."

A little after 5 p.m. on a wet April evening in Boston, in my case. A bank account frozen by Libby Bibb, a near-empty BPL Reading Room, a concerned Elizabeth hovering at my elbow. I nodded.

"But if you go from here into a book," the Librarian continued, "time moves forward as usual—in the book, and in the world you left behind. Go from here to a book, spend a year in the book, then come back to the Astral Library, you're about a year older. Not to the minute, perhaps, but close enough. And if you go back to your original life in what you call the real world, that time will have advanced just a year as well. No Rip van Winkle effect."

That seemed like a double-edged sword. On one hand, I wouldn't be walking back to the world I knew and finding out time had sped on a hundred years without me, or that I'd sped on a hundred years without it. On the other hand, if I went to a book and stayed there five years, I'd walk back to a Boston where everyone who knew me assumed I'd gone missing for half a decade . . . But since when was magic not a double-edged sword?

Consequences, as the Librarian said. I rubbed my jaw, realizing that I hadn't ground my teeth in over an hour. "So maybe three-quarters of your Patrons leave their books eventually. What about the others?"

"Some prefer the life they build inside." The Librarian nodded back in the direction of the staircase where I'd talked to the Japanese poet with her copy of *The Tale of Genji*. "Masako, for example—she renews her book every year on the dot, and heads straight back to the Imperial court. I've got a fourteen-year-old boy in Neverland, ran from an abusive mother straight to Peter Pan and the Lost Boys; he says he's staying for good. One of my *Pride and Prejudice* ladies married Colonel Fitzwilliam a few years back and now has a baby—naturally she's staying." The Librarian smiled, and this smile had less of an edge. "You never know who's going to be a lifer."

I already knew. What the hell did I have to come back for? Thirty-six dollars and eighty-two cents, if I ever got it out of the clutches of Libby Bibb?

No. When Alix Watson headed into her book, she wasn't *ever* coming back.

"What if I pick a book and don't like living in it?"

"Don't stay. It's not a jail."

"Can I try another book? How many—"

"You may try up to three books."

"Why three?"

"Ask Collection Development."

"Who are they?"

"New committee put together by the Library Board."

We were trekking back through the Library in the other direction now, back toward the staircase and the huge clock and the bronze globe. The Librarian clickety-clacked along like an exasperated bird, and I still felt like a duckling waddling in her wake.

"Will the people in the book know I'm not from their world? Will I have to pass as an insider or else get arrested or—"

"No. They'll automatically accept you as one of them."

"Why?"

"Ask the Ethical Resources Committee."

"Who are *they*?"

"New committee put together by—"

"Right. What if I go to a book world where the language isn't English?"

"You'll be able to speak it too."

"Why?"

"Accelerated linguistic osmosis. Works much better than Duolingo."

"What if I get injured in the book world? Can I come out and go to a doctor here, or—"

"You have a lot of questions, Miss Watson."

"How does anyone not have a million questions?" I exploded, not out of anger but because there was still *so much* I wanted to know. "There are all these rules and it's a whole new system and isn't there a *manual*?"

"If there was a manual, nobody would read it. Nobody ever reads the manual."

"I would read the manual if—" I paused. "Okay, I have to ask, what are those?" It was the fourth time I'd passed a book floating open in midair all by itself next to the shelves, a page periodically turning.

"Those are the ghosts," the Librarian said, checking something on her green tablet.

"The *what* now?"

"People who die with too many books on their To Be Read stack sometimes end up here. The ones who don't feel they can pass over until they catch up on their reading. After a few decades you get to know them. Dennis, really," the Librarian called to the nearest floating book, making me squint—in the sunlight coming through

The Astral Library

the emerald windows, was that the faintest outline of a plumpish man in spectacles? Or was I just going crazy? "Dennis," the Librarian repeated, sounding stern, "you've been reading *War and Peace* for a decade now. Just acknowledge the fact that you are never going to finish and *pick something new*."

The ghost turned a page, stubbornly.

"Fifty years on Tolstoy alone," the Librarian muttered, marching on. "He's still going to be here when I'm finally tipped into my coffin. Dear gods, but I miss the Middle Ages when there were only so many books out there for *anyone's* TBR."

"Just how old are you?" I couldn't help asking. "If time doesn't pass in here, are you immortal? Where are you *from*?"

"Qom."

"What world is that?" My imagination was already conjuring up porcelain cities and jade rivers, djinns in brass lamps, possibly flying carpets. "I suppose it makes sense the Library touches on other worlds entirely. Is Qom a kingdom, a continent, an empire, or—"

"It's a city in *Iran*, you moron." The Librarian stopped to glare. "Are you an utter ignoramus outside the complete works of Tolkien and C. S. Lewis?"

"More or less," I had no problem admitting. "I got shuttled between nine schools in ten years, all of them abysmal and mostly designed to funnel us foster kids straight toward prison or the army."

"At least you can correctly use words like *abysmal*," the Librarian muttered, and started walking again.

"How did you come to work here, anyway?" I persisted. "I mean, how exactly does the interview process go for 'semi-ageless guardian of astral-plane book sanctuary'? I tell you, if I'd ever seen that on LinkedIn when I was job hunting—"

"Ask Bibliographics. They're a new committee formed by—"

"Don't tell me: the Library Board." I broke into a jog to keep up with her as she veered toward the huge oak counter near the foot of that sumptuous swirling staircase. "I think you just make up new Board committees every time I ask a question you don't feel like answering."

The green tablet in her hand let out a rude blat as if it was laughing. The Librarian slapped it into its frame on the counter, warning, "Don't make me shush you."

"Me? Or the tablet?"

"Both." Ominously. "You do *not* want me to shush you."

I swear the windows darkened for an instant, and the book under my arm gave a little shiver. "Or what?" I couldn't stop myself asking. "Should I just ask the Library Board?"

The Librarian sorted through a stack of mail, squinted over her rectangular glasses at a notification marked ANNUAL BOARD MEETING: FOUR DAYS! and sent it sailing into the trash can. "Now you're getting it."

What book would *you* choose? Because you've thought about it, right? Everyone with a library card has daydreamed along those lines at some point. Except when it becomes real, something you can *do* and not just daydream about, you realize the catch: most of the books you love aren't peaceful places. You love them because of the drama, the gore, the heartbreak . . . But how many of us want to live with that kind of drama, gore, and heartbreak? I thought about that, sitting at one of the long library tables beside an emerald-green lamp, tracing the cover of the new George R. R. Martin book. Did I really want to go live in Westeros, even if it had been in the public domain? With all that rape and famine and war?

No. But I didn't want to go live in *Horton Hears a Who!* either.

The Astral Library

Science nerds talk about Goldilocks worlds: planets that are just the right distance from their suns to potentially nurture life, not too far away to freeze water and not too close to boil it. What was my Goldilocks book? One peaceful enough to live in but exciting enough for adventure?

The Librarian seemed to understand my dilemma. Why wouldn't she; she'd been here at least five hundred years or something. "Take your time," she said, wrestling with one of those ancient paper cutters with a huge arm that crunches down like a guillotine. "You won't exactly run out of it here." *Crunch.*

That relieved me, because I was half convinced someone was going to turn over an hourglass and tell me that *whence the sands run out your choices end* or something like that, and back on my ass in the BPL I'd be. But I had time.

The only thing is, others didn't seem to need time. A little while later—a few hours? Impossible to tell in this huge space where time didn't move—the mellow chime of the clock announced an arrival, and I looked up from my browsing to see a girl of maybe eleven come stumbling huge-eyed through the door at the top of the stairs. "Pleased to offer you sanctuary," the Librarian said, looking up from where she was still wrestling with the paper cutter. "Welcome to the Astral Library—" and she launched into her welcome spiel, but the girl barely seemed to need more than a third of it.

"*Anne of Green Gables,*" she gasped in a West Virginia twang, starting to cry. "I want to go to A-Avonlea and drink r-raspberry cordial—" Skinny chest hiccuping with sobs now. "And find a b-b-bosom friend and have a dress with puffed sl-sleeves—"

"Of course we can send you to *Anne of Green Gables*," the Librarian said, not reaching out with hugs and pats, not telling her to stop crying, just matter-of-fact. *L. M. Montgomery's Avonlea; what a good choice,* her tone said. *Of course we can do that.* A librarian's voice, the good kind of librarian—not the type who harangued kids for refusing to join story hour or for making any sound over a peep, but the type who knew all a bookworm kid really wanted was someone to point the way and let them head off into this afternoon's adventure between the pages. "Here's your library card, child; try not to lose it. Follow me, and let's get you kitted out . . ."

That skinny West Virginia girl with bruises on her arms, she knew. She knew her book instantly, right away, and I wondered if something was wrong with me that I didn't. You get a door that opens into a magic world, you aren't supposed to be sitting around on your hands vacillating. *Make a choice, Alix,* I thought as I watched the Librarian bring the girl back dressed in a gingham frock and pinafore, her hair now in two plaits and her face one huge beam, and walk her up the steps to the door. *Just make a choice.*

"Is she really off to Avonlea just like that?" I asked, as the girl darted through the door and it closed behind her with its undramatic click. "Who's going to meet her on the other side?"

"The Library makes that decision. She'll have a place waiting for her, people—she'll be pulled right in and probably find herself sitting down to fruitcake and cherry preserves within the hour. I imagine the Library will insert her as one of the little girls Anne and Diana play with; lots of cake baking and games by the Lake of Shining Waters." The Librarian made a satisfied-looking double tap on her tablet. "I have a feeling it'll be a good fit."

The books around us rustled agreement. But— "What about her family?" I couldn't help asking. "She's just a kid. If her parents go crazy searching for her—"

The Librarian gave me a cool look. "If the Library offers a child a door, it's because that child has nowhere else to go. Or because whoever might come looking for them is not someone who should be trusted with a child."

I swallowed a wave of unexpected bitterness. Sweet Jesus, what would it have meant to me to come to this place at eight, instead of heading off to that series of foster homes with my clothes in a trash bag? Why couldn't the door have opened then? I'd have picked some nice kid-lit world like Oz, grown up among Dorothy and the Munchkins...

Or, the thought whispered, suggestive as a Garden of Eden snake in the grass, *if your mother was so desperate she was ready to ditch you and run off with her tech bro, why couldn't a door have opened for* her? *Why couldn't she have escaped into her favorite book, and taken you with her?*

I wondered what book she would have picked—Sherlock Holmes, maybe? She'd always loved good old Sherlock... but no, I was pretty sure she'd have chosen a battered historical romance by an author I couldn't even remember, so old it was probably public domain by now. One of those lurid vintage covers with a beautiful maiden swooning off the prow of a ship into the arms of a shirtless man. *I love historical romance*, I remembered her saying, laughing to a friend. *It's the past, but it's prettied up just enough. No one stinks, everyone has white teeth, and the heroes might be pirate captains and dukes, but they somehow don't make their money from rape and pillage or colonial plantations.*

She could have escaped into that book and taken me with her. I could have grown up stalking the decks of the hero's pirate ship and swimming in crystal-blue seas and learning to fence, while she seduced the pirate captain's hunky second-in-command and got all the great sex and financial security she'd never been able to find in her string of shitty real-life boyfriends.

Maybe, that insinuating little voice suggested, *that's exactly what she did. Only she didn't take you with her.*

Was that what had happened to my book-loving mother? She'd told me she was headed to LA with her latest true love, but that could have been a lie concocted for an eight-year-old. Had the Astral Library chosen her, and she'd escaped into her book . . . without me? Was that better or worse than running away to Los Angeles with a tech bro?

Better, I thought instantly. You could hop a plane from LA; you could send an email or make a phone call from LA. There wasn't any excuse for dropping off the map when you'd only gone to LA. But there wasn't such an easy way to stay in touch when you were on a fictional eighteenth-century pirate ship.

And I could almost—*almost*—understand if my mother had found herself able to escape into her favorite book world and then was too scared she'd lose it if she came back for me. I knew what it was to feel desperate (even if I didn't like admitting it, to the Librarian or anyone else). Desperate people make desperate decisions—like deciding your daughter was better off without you, maybe.

Making excuses, are we? This voice sounded a lot less insinuating and a lot more tart—more like the Librarian's, in fact. *Didn't I just finish telling you a book isn't a jail, and you can leave whenever you like? Haven't I just finished showing you that my Patrons come back once a year to renew the loan of their book?*

But maybe for my mom things felt different . . .

I *was* making excuses, pretty feeble ones at that, and I was well aware I was going to back myself into a corner and get really uncomfortable if I thought about this much longer, so I was almost relieved to look up and see the Librarian standing there with her tablet and her glasses and her cardigan, not looking at all like the semi-ageless guardian of an astral-plane book sanctuary. She just looked like an ordinary librarian, no capital *L*. That was the magic of it.

Is my mother here in one of your books? I desperately wanted to ask. *Did you help her find a new life, the way you're helping me? If she's here, could I—*

"Have you decided on your book?" the Librarian asked briskly, breaking my confused swirl of thoughts.

I took a deep breath, swallowing down the spiky question of my laughing, book-loving mother and what had really (maybe, probably not, but maybe?) happened to her. "I think so."

"Which one?"

I told her.

"Then you need a library card." Heading back to the broad counter, the Librarian threw the words over her shoulder. "And a dress."

It was the first time I heard the Librarian sound defensive. "I must admit our Wardrobe Department is a bit lacking. We used to have a proper staff for costuming, but budget cuts—"

"You get budget cuts?"

"Do you know of any library in this world, or the entirety of the multiverse for that matter, that doesn't?"

The room marked WARDROBE opened just off the big oak counter, and it was crammed: rack after rack of clothes, most looking decidedly tatty. I picked up a yellowing lace cuff on what looked like an eighteenth-century chemise, dubious. "Why do I need to be kitted up in a new outfit *before* going into my book? Doesn't the Library do that part? It's already supplying a character and a home and a new world and possibly a whole new language, and it balks at a dress?"

"Only someone with Librarian-level access gets an automatic wardrobe change on stepping through. Because the Library knows me," she said, forestalling my *why*. "With new Patrons, it's better to give the system a jumping-off point. I had a gentleman heading off to swashbuckle villains in *The Count of Monte Cristo*, and somehow instead of a doublet and bucket boots he ended up in quasi–*War of the Worlds* spandex tentacles. Cataloging error," the Librarian muttered. "Now we try to dress everyone to fit in at least a bit before they enter their book. You're looking at an 1870s rig, I believe? Nineteenth century is back that way, see if anything fits."

I went over and began rummaging through the musty rack of what looked like costume-department remnants and theater trunks, thinking optimistically that it had only taken about fifteen minutes to fit the little girl from West Virginia in gingham pleats and hair ribbons . . . But I only had the vaguest idea of what 1870s clothing looked like, and most of what I saw patently wouldn't fit me. All I could really find was an old serge skirt and a blouse that gapped at the bust. I scowled down at myself, my old stained Walmart bra with the stretched-out elastic showing through the blouse's straining buttons. I had to admit, I'd been looking forward to the whole magical-makeover part of this process: fabulous gown, zap of a wand. When Lucy walked into Narnia, at least she got a fur coat to put over her London Blitz togs.

"I suppose it'll have to do." The Librarian looked as dubious as I did when I came out tugging on the uneven black skirt. "You'll find your way into something better once you're inserted. Unless you've got something to supplement at home?"

I had a sudden, dazzling idea. "You know, I think I might."

It made me nervous, leaving the Astral Library. Some atavistic terror in my gut was convinced that if I walked out the door back to the *real* world, the one that held only my own deeply shitty little life, currently being ruined by Libby Bibb, I'd never find that door again. But there's nothing like an old lady in rectangular spectacles saying "Rubbish" with a truly epic snort to make you feel stupid for applying words like *atavistic terror* to what was essentially preflight jitters, so I gulped and put out my hand meekly for my library card. Just an ordinary paper card, the old-fashioned kind where you'd write your book in with a stub of pencil and get a stamped due date. "You keep that on you," the Librarian dictated, "and you can always come back. So don't blither around daydreaming about dragons and drop it down a grate, Miss Watson."

"What happens if I do that?" I couldn't help asking, just so I could chant right along with her: *"Ask the Library Board."*

"Smart-ass," she growled, stamping back to the broad counter.

"Better than a dumb one," I caroled back over my shoulder, bounding up the stairs and out the door—straight into the shadowy coolness of the Boston Public Library Reading Room. I stood a moment just breathing, wondering why the space felt so dead, and then realized it was the books. The books here weren't moving. I had a bizarre urge to cup my hands around my mouth and call out, *Wake up!*

"Alix?" A concerned voice, a hand on my arm. I blinked and saw my boss Elizabeth, tattoo sleeve and purple-framed glasses and all. "Are you okay?"

Right. I'd walked straight back into the moment I'd left, running in tears through the Reading Room on a Tuesday evening.

She was eyeing my skirt and blouse with a puzzled look, probably wondering if her eyes were playing tricks since I'd been wearing old jeans and a coffee-splashed T-shirt just a few apparent minutes ago. "Did you change just now?"

"In the closet just there. Gotta run," I said hastily, and dashed for the stairs.

"Hey there, missy, no running in the library—" Chester tried to stop me, Chester the wannabe tough guy on Library Security who thought he was Wyatt Earp, but I didn't have time for Library Security today. I flew around him and out of the BPL into a cool, damp April evening.

One street over and down a block, and in no time at all I was waltzing through the shop door of Brummell's. A voice floated out from behind the vast metal horse of an industrial sewing machine before I could speak: "Bespoke or off the rack?"

I blinked, rummaging through my wallet and peering over the machine at the most fashionable man in Boston. "Sorry?"

"I've got a special-commission gown to finish for a movie premiere, and until that's done I'm open by appointment only—at least if you want something bespoke. But if I can help you with something off the rack, something needing minimal adjustment—" Beau Sato-Jones finally looked up, lean brown hands still flying as he fed some sparkling fabric through the sewing machine, and blinked at the sight of me. "Hey there, czarina."

"Help me, Obi-Wan Kenobi." I held up a certain engraved business card, soft around the edges from being carried for so long in my wallet, scribbled across the back with a man's elegant writing: *IOU—Beau Sato-Jones owes Alix Watson the unconditional loan of one (1) fabulous outfit for the event of her choosing.* "You're my only hope."

"I'll say." His eyes traveled over my fusty skirt and yellowing blouse. "Oh, honey, serge? No. Absolutely not." From anyone else it would have sounded snide but the smile that put a crease in his lean cheeks was cheerful, not jeering. It wasn't a *You're not wearing that, are you?* sneer; it was a *We can fix this!* smile. "Come on in," he said, rising from behind the sewing machine, and even at the tail end of a long day he looked like a page out of *Vogue* if they published *Vogue* in 1810: taut pearl-gray breeches, silver brocade vest that hugged like a glove, and one of those white shirts with billowy sleeves that men always wear in period movies, striding out of ponds or banks of mist. "I have been *waiting* for the chance to sling some silk around you, Alix Watson. What are you looking for?"

"Um . . ." I pushed my frizzed-out hair behind my ears, feeling more and more out of place in this jewel box of a shop. When I'd come here two years ago to set up his QuickBooks account, the space had still been unpainted and heaped with boxes—now it was all creamy whites and silvery blues and dove grays, silver-framed mirrors everywhere to double the space, lush blue velvet drapes and dressmaker forms with sumptuous clothes on them: a Japanese kimono embroidered with mountains and clouds; an Elizabethan doublet in chocolate-brown brocade paired with a shirt covered in blackwork stitching; a Greek chiton in flame orange with gold key patterns rippling around the hem. "I'm going to a book-themed costume party." The excuse I'd prepared in advance. "I was wondering if you can help me spruce up this outfit I'm wearing? Put a nice cloak on top or—"

"What's your book?"

I took a deep breath. My book, the book I'd be headed into as soon as I was done here. *"Around the World in Eighty Days."*

A book I'd read around age fourteen, rolling my eyes at the more colonialist aspects but envious down to my bones of the whole idea of throwing a few belongings in a satchel and heading off for the ends of the earth. A good Goldilocks book, I thought: adventurous, but everybody comes through unscathed. I didn't see myself staying in Jules Verne Land forever, but that was all right: the Librarian said I could try up to three books, and until I found my forever book, I wanted an *adventure*. I'd never left Massachusetts in my life, and now I was going to go around the world with Phileas Fogg, or at least live adjacent to his adventures in some way. I was going to cross the Red Sea in a steamer, I was going to go up in a hot air balloon (all right, he didn't ride a balloon in the book, only in the movie, but maybe I could nudge the plot just a little?), and if I couldn't ride a dragon I could at least ride an elephant.

So what dress did you need to go elephant riding in the nineteenth century?

"Jules Verne, that's 1870s." Beau's eyes narrowed thoughtfully, scrutinizing my outfit. "You going steampunk Victorian here, or historically accurate?"

"Historical," I said, and his eyes lit up.

"A girl after my own heart." He beckoned me as he turned on his booted heel and strode back behind a painted screen where the real work of Brummell's was clearly done: bolts of fabric lining the walls, a worktable strewn with pins and swatches and bits of trimming. "Eighteen seventies British fashion," he rattled off, sweeping a tape measure up from the table and stringing it around his neck like a strand of pearls. "One of my favorite eras for clothes. The heyday of the bustle and *loads* of trim: pleats, flouncing, ruching, ruffles, ribbons, tassels. Tight waists, leading toward the more fitted princess line in the latter half of the decade, based on the then Princess of Wales . . ."

He went rummaging along the shelves and I wondered for a moment why he didn't seem to have any clerks or assistants, but then he was back with a big coffee-table book, flipping pages to show me various full-color plates. "Evening dress or day dress? We're talking square or V neckline, sleeves with a slight flare at the wrist, some fairly major corseting . . ."

I looked at the pictures he was showing me with a sinking feeling. How was I supposed to ride an elephant in all those ruffles? And I did not see my size 22 fitting into that particular silhouette no matter how much whalebone was involved. "You do realize there's no way you're squeezing me into Scarlett O'Hara territory, right?" I indicated my own midsection, trying to stretch tall because someone as long and lean as Beau probably hadn't had to work around a waist roll like mine in a long time. Nothing but model types named Deryk and Ysabel for him, and with a sudden flush of embarrassment I realized what a bad idea this was. "Look, maybe I should just go—you probably don't have a thing that will fit me, and you've got that red-carpet dress to finish. I'll just—"

"Not so fast." He stopped me from going by tossing his tape measure around my shoulders like a lasso, bringing me to a halt. "First thing, czarina: it's true I haven't got a lot of spare time right now, thanks to that movie premiere commission, but if I don't get a break from couch stitching crystal beads the size of protons onto raw silk, I'm going to strip naked and run screaming down Newbury, so you're the one saving *me* here."

Frankly I enjoyed the thought of Beau running naked anywhere, and I tried my best to banish that thought, considering he was stepping closer to take a measurement along the line of my shoulders.

"Second thing, I promise you I can get you rigged out in half an hour flat, period appropriate to the last detail. Arms out—"

"In something like that?" I raised my arms so he could measure, nodding at the coffee-table book where a flock of Tissot beauties promenaded on a yacht in huge gowns that exploded out from their tiny corseted waists like upside-down flowers. "Nothing like that is going to work on me."

"I thought we'd go a different angle." Taping around my rib cage now, touch featherlight and expert. "Have you heard of the Victorian fashion called artistic dress?"

I shook my head.

"Kicked off, among other things, by the Pre-Raphaelite artists and their craze for the medieval. A softer style, no corseting. Very flowing, very romantic, very King-Arthur-and-the-Round-Table—"

"You're saying even the Victorian era had high-fantasy nerds?"

"Bingo. And you're the girl who always has the latest George R. R. Martin or N. K. Jemisin in her bag when she comes by to ogle my window displays, so I'm guessing a fantasy angle is both right up your alley *and* historically accurate." He stood back, making a picture frame around me with his fingers. "You'll be a dish."

I could feel my cheeks heat. "I'm hardly a clotheshorse." I wasn't running myself down; really, I wasn't. It was just something I'd learned to do, reflexively: get in the *yes, I know I'm not exactly slender!* and get it in with a chuckle before someone else (the barely listening doctor at my very infrequent checkups, the annoyed saleslady pulling plus-size jeans down from the top rack) got there first. It stung less if I was the one who put it out there, and it wasn't like I didn't know people weren't thinking it. So it surprised me when Beau tilted his head, giving me a long, thoughtful once-over.

"A clotheshorse," he said, "is exactly what you are. Long back with a gorgeous arch to it, good shoulders with presence—there's nothing like trying to tailor a strong silhouette around droopy little pigeon shoulders. A nice flare from waist to hip; good for most historical fashion shapes. And there's what you've really got going for you, which is that coloring."

I blinked. No one had ever said my fairly average white-girl coloring (medium-brown hair, medium-brown eyes) was anything out of the ordinary. Because it wasn't.

"What I mean," he clarified, still sounding meditative, coming back from the worktable with another armload of fabric swatches, "is that skin of yours. I'm trying hard not to creep you out here, because it's difficult to compliment a woman's skin without sounding like something from *The Silence of the Lambs*. But sincerely, that skin of yours is like a tea rose crossed with a pitcher of double cream. Skin like that begs to have all kinds of satins and velvets thrown across it." He started matter-of-factly holding various strips of silk up to my face, which probably looked less like a tea rose and more like a tomato right now. "I don't think there's a color you *can't* wear," he mused, "but for your Jules Verne party I'm thinking midnight blue. Because I've got just the thing . . ."

Right. My supposed costume party. I bit my lip as Beau disappeared into a back room and returned a few moments later with an acre of dark sapphire moiré over one arm. "I made it in an offseason after taking a class on Historical Stitching and Decorative Techniques on Leather, when I was dying to make something with material I didn't have to punch through with an awl. Based on the gown in a Rossetti painting called—" Beau paused mid-flow. "I'm boring you, aren't I? Occupational hazard with historical-fashion nuts. Give us an inch and we'll talk your ear off about boning channels and double-plait stitching."

"You're not boring me at all," I said honestly. "People who turn what they love into a living? That's the dream. I mean, look at all this." Waving my hand at this exquisite shop he'd created out of what was once an empty, soulless retail space. "You're what, thirty? And you built all this."

"Twenty-nine." That dimple reappeared in his cheek as he showed me to a plush, curtained changing booth. "Though considering the hours I'm putting in getting that premiere gown finished, I'll look a hundred by the time the red carpet goes live."

"Can you at least give me a hint what the movie is?" There was a sheeted dress form half concealed behind a screen at the back of the room, but I couldn't see so much as a scrap of hem.

"Depends on whether you can keep a secret. Can you, czarina?" I mimed zipping my lips, and he leaned in to whisper in my ear, which I enjoyed far too much. "*Belle.*"

"What, the *Beauty and the Beast* remake coming out next month? The one that got all the online hate from outraged soccer moms—"

"Because it's a gritty feminist retelling, yep. The Beast is scary, the villagers are witch-hunting bigots, and Belle has sex in the library instead of singing Disney ballads in it. Cue the hate storm."

"How's the movie?" I asked, fascinated. Belle is every book girl's favorite fairy-tale princess, after all, and the Beast is every book girl's favorite Disney hero. Sure, he's a monster, but he gives her a library!

"Who knows? I didn't hang around the set or anything; I'm just designing the premiere dress for the lead actress. The movie could be terrible and I'd still be over the moon. First red-carpet commission; that's a bucket list item for any designer."

"The lead actress, is that . . ." I couldn't remember her name, only that the movie poster for *Belle* showed her tiptoeing through a vast shadowy library not unlike the Astral Library, and that she'd also gotten a lot of online hate because she wasn't a size two.

"Her, yep." Beau mimed zipping his own lips. "Not much I can tell you about her because of NDAs but I got the job because her assistant follows me on Instagram. That and because my first question on getting her measurements wasn't asking how much weight she was planning to lose by premiere night. Here, step back behind there and you can get changed—"

"*Belle*. Wow." I could see his silhouette on the other side of the curtain as I shucked out of the black serge skirt and yellowing blouse. "Look at you, rubbing shoulders with A-listers."

"Eh, it's a small movie. Not quite indie, but not a mega-blockbuster either. Still . . ." His voice sounded dreamy as he passed the armload of blue moiré under the curtain, and I began shimmying into it. "One dress of mine in the fashion photo gallery with all the Versace and Valentino dresses on the other stars at the premiere, and a guy like me can catapult right up the ladder."

"You're already at the top of the ladder," I said, sliding my arms into the billowing sleeves. "You've officially Made It."

"No, I know how to *look* like I've Made It. If I knock the *Belle* dress out of the park, I will have *actually* made it."

I thought about that as I twisted to get at the fastenings of the blue dress. If Beau really had Made It as much as I'd assumed he already had, it would be an assistant fitting me into this dress, wouldn't it? And there'd be clerks and salespeople all over this shop; he wouldn't be doing it all solo with bags under his eyes. "I guess it's all more fake-it-till-you-make-it than I thought," I ventured.

"Can be." His tone turned from wistful to brisk. "Come on out, czarina, and let's see how that dress fits."

It's hard to stand there while a man in skintight breeches laces you into a dress without imagining him unlacing you back out of it, but twenty minutes of tucking and basting and tweaking later, there I was in front of a triple-paned cheval mirror, dumbstruck.

"Oh man." Beau gazed at my reflection, looking smug. "Am I good, or am I good?"

"You're good . . ." I agreed, still staring at myself.

"Hair up in a high knot for maximum authenticity, none of this loose-hair BS you see in costume dramas. Real Victorian women pinned everything up. I can loan you some slippers, gloves, a hat—"

I shook my head, still staring. "This is more than enough." I didn't want to take *too* much advantage of his IOU, and there was no way I could pay for extras considering the chokehold on my finances by the mysterious Libby Bibb.

"At least take this. No 1870s lady would ever step out without her handbag." Beau held up a beautiful jet-beaded bag of the same blue moiré, dangling from a silver chain. "And if you put any pics on social media, tag me."

"Thank you." I slid the chain over my arm, realizing as soon as I tore my eyes away from the mirror that it was full dark outside. He should be closing up soon, and I needed to get back to the BPL before it closed for the night and shut off my access to the Astral Library till morning. "I'll just wear it out. Thank you again. You . . ." I trailed off. He'd made me beautiful, but I didn't know how to say it without choking up. I couldn't remember the last time I'd had a dress that made me look like this, feel like this. I couldn't remember the last time I'd felt beautiful. If I ever had, at all, in my whole life.

"I should be the one thanking you." He smiled as he walked me to the door, a bit less gleaming of a smile than that cheek-creasing stunner he usually greeted me with, and for an instant I saw that behind that polished tailored exterior Beau Sato-Jones was tired. Very, very tired. "Not just for a break from red-carpet-dress embroidery, but for giving me something historical to do. I end up working on a lot of costume stuff, movie replicas . . . not that I *mind* whipping up elf dresses from *Lord of the Rings*, it pays the bills, and besides, it can be downright interesting seeing which historical eras put their stamp on film costuming. I could talk all night about how Natalie Portman's gowns from *Star Wars* were inspired by everything from a traditional Mongolian *deel* to a fifteenth-century houppelande to a Korean *wonsam*—" He cut himself off. "I'm droning again."

I smiled, wishing he could have seen all those embroidered court silks on the woman who'd gone to live in *The Tale of Genji*. "As far as when you need the dress back—because there's no way I can afford to keep it . . ." Not when I had Libby Bibb all over my credit score.

"Whenever your party's over, I'm not fussy." *That'll be a lot longer than you think*, I thought guiltily. Once I was all set in Jules Verne Land—new name, new address, something else to wear—I'd have to see if I could return this gown to the Librarian to send back here. I didn't want Beau thinking I'd taken advantage of his IOU with a flat-out theft. "And if you do want to keep it," he went on, unaware of my guilty thoughts, "I've got payment plans."

"The day I go into debt for couture . . ."

"Hey, couture is the *only* thing worth going into debt for. I lived on ramen for a solid two months once because I found an 1803 Weston frock coat on a vintage fashion site. Blue facecloth, silk velvet collar, M notch and revers, gilt buttons by Charles Jennens . . ." He sighed. "Who cared about food when I could swan around in that coat feeling like Brummell himself?"

"Look, who *is* Brummell?" I wondered. "I never got around to asking that."

"Beau Brummell was a socialite and fashion arbiter of the Regency period, largely credited with turning menswear away from overly ornate excess to a look both understated yet perfectly tailored," Beau rattled off.

"Were you actually *named* after a Regency fashion icon?"

"No, originally I was Bo for Bomont—after the little one-stoplight town in Texas where my dad grew up." Making a face. "By the time I hightailed my ass east for fashion design school, I decided I'd rather go for the Regency spelling. And by the time I graduated fashion design school, I knew my dream shop was going to be named Brummell's."

"Is it everything you imagined?"

"Ask me after the fashion sites drop the reviews for my very first red-carpet look." He walked around to open the shop door for me, giving a sweeping bow. "Come back after your costume party, tell me how your ensemble went over."

I won't be seeing you for a long time, I thought. *At least not till I get back from* Around the World in Eighty Days. Which I regretted, because I'd have loved to hear him talk more about Mongolian and Korean influences on *Star Wars* costuming, and try to figure out if he had a replacement for Ysabel or Deryk yet and if he didn't, would he consider me as a temp even if I didn't have legs like a giraffe and spell my name Alyx. But I just curtsied in answer to his bow, very badly, and went swanning out onto Newbury Street, collecting quite a few stares from all the early evening shoppers, not caring. Where I was going, I wasn't going to stick out at all.

"Not bad," said the Librarian, looking over the top of her rectangular glasses as I came bursting through the Astral Library door in a storm of blue moiré. No trouble finding that door; I'd stalked straight down the row of reading tables at the BPL Reading Room (ignoring all the double-takes my new outfit was attracting) and *felt* the lively, rustling breeze off to my left between shelves where an astral plane's worth of books lived just a breath away, murmuring, rustling, dozing. The door had practically flown open in front of me as I reached for my library card, and I'd had that feeling again that made me nearly gulp down tears: chosen. Finally chosen. "Not bad at all," the Librarian continued. "Artistic dress?"

"Based on a Rossetti painting," I said, twirling for her. All that rippling blue moiré cascaded out around me like streaming water, supple and clinging wherever it hit my legs, foaming and sliding where it fell loose. The long sleeves covered my upper arms, which I'd always felt a bit self-conscious about, the skirts came down from a line at my lower ribs rather than my waist, which hid every roll of belly a girl ever had, and that low, square neck—well, I could see what Beau meant about my skin. I looked like I had absolutely acres of creamy white breast and neck and shoulder. I looked like the Lady of Shalott, like a fantasy-world heroine heading out on an adventure. Hearing a little phantom clapping in the corner from the ghost reading the still-floating copy of *War and Peace*, I curtsied in his direction. "Thank you, Dennis." Amazing what you can get used to, given enough exposure.

"Quite period-appropriate," the Librarian decreed. "The Library should know what to do with you based on that. Now—" She had another of those notifications in hand—*ANNUAL BOARD MEETING: FOUR DAYS!*—but she crumpled it up and sent it sailing into the nearest trash can. "Are you ready to go?"

I nodded, accepting the copy of *Around the World in Eighty Days* she took from the big oak counter and held out in one gnarled, emerald-studded hand. I hadn't bothered to head back to my apartment to grab anything, realizing there wasn't a single thing back there I wanted to carry into my new life. No friends I wanted to say goodbye to; no exes I'd miss; no keepsakes I treasured. I already had my ancient *Dawn Treader* paperback and *Library of Alexandria* bumper sticker stuffed into the jet-beaded bag; I didn't need anything else from my sad, soiled little life. "I'm ready."

"Library card, please." The Librarian started to scribble on it, and I realized with a tremble of excitement that I had no idea how this worked. Was there a portal, a gate, a leap of faith? I was just opening my mouth to ask when the clock chimed and the Librarian's head jerked up.

Because this wasn't the mellow single chime that meant *Someone's coming*. This was a series of fast, urgent strikes: *bong bong bong bong*, over and over, getting louder and louder. "What is that?" I called over the sound, realizing I nearly had to shout. It wasn't just the clock; it was the books: they'd gone from their whispering rustle like contented pigeons billing and cooing on a roost to an anxious flapping flutter.

The Librarian ignored me. She was still staring at the clock, but her eyes flicked from one side of the Library to the other, and I saw the flare of her nostrils as though she'd smelled blood. "No," she murmured. "It's not possible—"

Something flew out of the book-drop slot next to the big oak counter. It dropped to the glossy wood floor and slid nearly to the Librarian's shoe. It looked like a card from an old-fashioned card catalog, but I'd never seen one that was *red* before.

"What is it?" I asked as the Librarian picked up the card. Something was printed on it, but I couldn't make out the words—and the *bong bong bong* of the clock was only growing louder.

"It's a warning," she said tersely, "sent by the Library Board—" And she took off straight down the length of the Library, nearly running. With one hand she clutched the tablet and the red card; she ran the other along the nearest row of book spines. The books calmed at her touch but it was one row in an infinite space: the rustling of pages was growing louder now, almost louder than the *bong bong bong* of the clock.

The books were panicking.

"What's happening?" I shouted, running after the Librarian with my blue skirt billowing after me. From the corner of my eye I saw Dennis's ghostly outline as he dropped *War and Peace* and dove into the nearest wall. *"What's happening?"*

The Librarian came to a stop and pointed at the top shelf. A book flew down into her upraised hand, a hawk soaring to a falconer's arm. She threw it open, eyes glittering as she searched feverishly through the pages—I had no idea what she was looking for but I knew when she found it because she opened the book wide and flung it down on the floor. Another moment to tap something into her tablet, and the books on the shelves were nearly *screaming* now—I saw two or three take off toward the ceiling, crashing into the corners in blind panic. "Please," I begged, heart slamming up into my throat, "please just tell me—"

The Librarian snapped the tablet's green cover shut, looking up at the endless shelves around us. "I'm sorry, my lovelies," she said to the books. "You know this is the only way. You'll be safe till I get back—"

And then—I yelped at the sacrilege of it—she stepped forward, straight onto the open book lying on the floor.

Only she wasn't stepping on it. She was stepping *into* it.

And as soon as I saw her fall through, I grabbed her elbow and brought myself tumbling along for the ride.

7

I took my first gulp of air inside the world of a book and promptly began to cough, stumble, and rub at my eyes all at the same time. Some sort of city street—the air smelled like smoke and sewage, and I could barely see a yard in front of me. I gripped the Librarian's arm for balance, and realized that the wool of her green cardigan had changed under my fingertips to a balloon sleeve in some sort of smooth worsted or gabardine (*Beau would know which*, my brain told me unhelpfully). "Where—are we?" I coughed, blinking my watering eyes.

"The great cesspool into which all loungers and idlers are irresistibly drained," said the Librarian, coming to a halt at the nearest corner.

"Florida?" I guessed.

She barked a laugh. "London, you ignoramus. What are you doing here?" she demanded before I could get a breath to marvel at the fact that I, Alix Watson who had never owned a passport or crossed the lines of her home state, had apparently just one-step-traveled into *London*. Some version of it, anyway. "You aren't supposed to be here, Miss Watson."

"Somehow I didn't think it was a good idea to stay in the room where the books were panicking and the ghosts were running for the hills," I retorted. "What the hell happened back there? Why did we abandon the Library?"

"The Library can protect itself," she said grimly, peering around in the foggy gloom. "The threat lies elsewhere."

I followed her gaze, hunting through the murk. The streetlamp at my elbow cast a feeble circle of yellowish light down on the slimy cobbles under our feet; I stepped back hastily as a hackney coach rattled past with a whinny of its tired horses and nearly bumped into a gentleman hurrying by with an umbrella. He glared, muttonchop whiskers waggling as I stammered an apology. On the other side of the street I saw a flower seller in bright petticoats like something out of *My Fair Lady*, a gaggle of street urchins pelting past playing some game, and a woman in a bustle gown like the ones in Beau's art book crossing the street on the arm of a top-hatted gentleman. London. Victorian-era London, without a doubt. I'd done it, *I'd traveled into a novel*—

"What book are we in?" I whispered, but the Librarian wasn't paying attention to me.

"Ah, Upper Regent Street." She nodded at the dim outline of a castle-like building across the way: sandstone facade adorned with wrought-iron balconies, columned portico, fog clinging gummily to the French windows. "The Langham hotel. Means we've a short walk ahead of us. Margin-traveling, never the most precise means of transportation—" And she set off down the street at a brisk pace. I hurried to keep up, belatedly realizing that her cardigan and knee-length skirt had somehow been swapped out for a balloon-sleeved bottle-green walking suit, a sealskin muff, and a huge hat complete with half a dead bird in flight on the wide brim. The only thing about her that still said *twenty-first century* was the green tablet clutched tight in one gloved hand.

"Nice threads," I said, remembering her telling me that the Library costumed its Librarian for inter-book travel, unlike the Patrons. "What exactly is margin-traveling?"

"Normally one makes a more formalized transit to and from books. Through the Library door, on scheduled passage. But for quick travel, Library staff can move through a book's margins." She peered each way down a foggy street corner before choosing a direction. "It's never very exact, though . . ."

"Why?"

"That's a question for the Logistics Department."

"Who are *they*? You know what, never mind." My loose hair, I realized, was getting glances from the passersby—every woman on this street had an updo and a hat. Nothing I could do about the hat, but I hastily coiled my hair up into a knot at my neck and jabbed it through with a pencil from my beaded bag. So much for all those period movies where Keira Knightley runs all over the moors without a hairpin in sight. "What was that red card? You said something about a warning from the Library Board."

"The Board issues cards as warnings when something has gone wrong with one of my placements," she said without slowing down. "A blue card when a Patron is due to return or renew their book. A yellow card when the book they've chosen isn't a good fit and intervention is required."

"What's a green card?" I couldn't help asking.

"We don't have green cards, this isn't Immigration," she snapped. "Though the way some of the Board talk..."

"Never mind," I said again. "What's a red card, and why did it send you into such a panic?"

"Don't be ridiculous, I never panic."

I did an end run around her and planted myself in her path, stopping dead. *"Answers, please!"* I nearly shouted. "And don't just tell me to *ask the Library Board!*"

"A red card is a warning that someone is attempting to break in from the outside," she said, surprising me. "Trying to force their way into a book's world *without* being invited by the Library."

I blinked. "How is that possible?"

"It shouldn't be. There are safeguards, ever since—" She broke off, glaring around the foggy street as if looking for an enemy to skewer. "According to the bylaws no one can find the book worlds unless they find the Library, and they can't find the Library unless it invites them in. The fact that someone has found a workaround"—waving the dark red card—"is quite frankly disturbing. And should be impossible."

"But it isn't." I nodded at the red card in her gloved hand. "You wouldn't have safeguards in place without a precedent. It's happened before, hasn't it—an attempted invasion?"

Her lips pressed together into a flat hard line. "Once."

She looked so forbidding I didn't dare ask how it had turned out. "I don't understand *who* would be trying to break in," I said instead, shifting tack. "Why would anyone intend harm to the Library?"

"Not the Library. The *people*." Her gaze whipped back to meet mine so abruptly that any further words withered in my throat. Her black eyes were pools of pitch—I'd taken her rapid words and rapid pace for fear but it wasn't. It was fury. "The Library offers sanctuary to people who are desperate, who have nowhere else to go but between the pages. Quite often that means they are *fleeing* something—or someone. How many bruised, battered, and broken people over the decades do you think I've assisted into book worlds where their abusers can't find them? How many children do you think I've helped hide in fiction, far away from the adults exploiting them? How many refugees have I pulled through that door away from enemies wishing them harm?" She paused. "Or allow me to put it a different way: How many violent people in the world outside have lost a favorite target because this Library stepped in?"

I gulped. No one was looking for me with violent intentions or otherwise, but I thought of the little girl from West Virginia with the shadow bruises on her arms. What if someone—the wrong someone—wanted her back? Would do anything to get her back?

"The Patron I helped hide in this world is in danger, Miss Watson." The Librarian resumed her brisk pace up the foggy London street, slapping the card into my hands. "*This* is a warning that someone is coming, specifically, for her."

Finally I saw what was printed on the dark red card stock: *Sarah Ross/Sarah Hudson; TAoSH by ACD; orig. checked out 2019.*

I was too busy trying to decipher the initials to renew my question about what book we were in until we were mounting seventeen rather slimy steps toward a Georgian terrace house and I saw the number on the door. "Wait, I thought there *was* no actual 221B Baker Street in London," I said as the Librarian knocked.

"This is Sir Arthur Conan Doyle's London, not *the* London. It's always the author's world and operates according to the author's rules, not the real—hello, Mrs. Hudson," the Librarian broke off, addressing the motherly looking middle-aged woman who answered the door. "We're here to see Sarah."

✦

I'm not sure any of the Sherlock Holmes stories ever bothered taking the reader downstairs into the kitchens, but that cheery well-scrubbed place with its warm fire and copper kettle was a dream. Ushered in to sit at the scarred oak table where the ingredients for a lamb stew were laid out like a Dutch still life, I could see why a desperate person would choose to live here.

"I can't leave," the woman named Sarah burst out almost before the Librarian was done with her explanation. I'd been half expecting a Chosen One type, someone doe-eyed and haunted who looked like she'd plausibly have a sinister stalker tracking her across astral lines, but the mid-thirties brunette sitting across from me looked utterly ordinary. In her rose-printed twill dress with the cameo at her throat, she looked like she had been born to this world rather than mine. "I just can't," she went on, twisting her fingers together. "I'm Miss Hudson here, Mrs. Hudson the housekeeper's niece from America. I help her run the boardinghouse and I live on the top floor. I sometimes get to consult with a mystery or two. I go to the British Museum with Dr. Watson's wife and we take tea afterward at the Palm Court in the Langham hotel. I make scones, I've got a cat—" Looking over at the purring mound of calico fur curled up in a wicker basket on the hearth. "I've got a life here," she said, low-voiced. "I've got a *life*."

"And what if your husband bursts in on it?" the Librarian asked.

"There's no way he could—"

"But what if he does?"

The silence stretched. Mrs. Hudson—Sherlock Holmes's landlady in the flesh; I found it hard not to stare—came bustling in with a platter of piping-hot crumpets. "For your visitors, Sarah dear, take as long as you like. If you start smelling acid, it's just Mr. Holmes doing another chemical experiment upstairs." Out she bustled again, seeming to have very little curiosity about these two strangers who'd turned up out of the blue to visit her "niece." I reckoned that was more of the Library's magic. If it could insert this woman in her rose-printed dress into the world of 221B Baker Street without anyone batting an eyelash, it stood to reason that the Librarian could sail right in and be accepted as part of the scenery: vaguely familiar, somewhat expected, certainly unthreatening. If Mrs. Hudson cast any glances, it had been at me: the girl in artistic dress who'd waltzed in here *without a hat*.

"You really think Tyler is trying to find me here?" Sarah said, voice almost inaudible.

The Librarian held up the red card. "It doesn't tell me who's coming for you, but . . ."

Sarah's hand rose to cover her throat almost involuntarily. Protecting it, like someone had once wrapped his hands there and thrown her around like a rag doll. One of my foster fathers had done that to his wife in front of all the kids—I got very good at walking around the edges of the walls in that house, to avoid him.

"We can hide you," the Librarian went on. "And we can bookmark your place here—you can come back when the danger's past. But you need to come with me now."

Sarah's hand came down from her throat, slowly. "Let me gather a few of my things."

"Where are you planning to hide her?" I asked the Librarian as Sarah disappeared down a dark Victorian corridor. "Another book?"

"No. If he could track her to one book, he could track her to another. That isn't supposed to be possible, but none of this is. After the previous attack, there were safeguards put in place to prevent—Come on, you," she muttered, jabbing at her green tablet. "Oh, wonderful. Arbitrarily change the password on me, very mature."

"It arbitrarily changes the password on you?"

"Have you ever met an electronic device that didn't? This one's just a bit more up front about the fact than most." The tablet blatted, sounding somehow smug. "You're just in a snit," the Librarian told it. "Stop sulking and let me in, I need to send the Gallerist a quick email—"

Another rude electronic noise drowned out my "Who's the Gallerist?"

The Librarian sighed, glaring at the tablet, and recited: "'I have always imagined that Paradise will be a kind of library.'"

The tablet remained stubbornly blank.

"Moved on from Borges, have we? What about: 'Libraries store the energy that fuels the imagination.'" The tablet gave a purring sound and its screen lit up. "Sidney Sheldon, really?" the Librarian scolded.

"That's its password?" I blinked. "Quotes about libraries?"

"It changes the quote on me when it feels unappreciated. I have to guess until its ego is sufficiently stroked." The Librarian's fingers flew as she tapped out an email. "In the old days we propitiated deities. Nowadays we propitiate technology. In my experience they're about equally capricious."

"Are we heading back to the Library now?" I ventured, reaching for a crumpet. They were steaming hot, slathered in butter, and my stomach was suddenly snarling with hunger. One little snack tray scone aside, I hadn't really eaten since . . . Was it this afternoon when I'd stormed out of the bank branch in Southie, cursing about the phantom Libby Bibb locking me out of my checking account? I didn't seem to get hungry in the Astral Library, which stood to reason since time didn't actually pass there. But here I could see that the shadows of the streetlamps outside the kitchen windows had moved since we'd arrived, and my appetite was awake with a vengeance.

"Yes, temporarily." The Librarian thumbed another tab open

expertly. For someone hundreds of years old, she was certainly tech-savvy. I said as much, and she snorted. "Even libraries must do a certain amount of moving with the times. I have no use for these tech snobs who wish we were all still using quill and parchment—"

A clattering of boots in the hallway interrupted her. "Mrs. Hudson," a man's impatient voice called. "The fire's gone out upstairs, I need a steady stream of heat for—" He broke off as he came in, and yep, it was the man himself. Tall, lean, hawk nose, piercing gray eyes that seemed to skip right over the Librarian to settle on me.

"Artistic dress in the style of fifteen years past, clumsily dressed hair, lacking gloves and hat," Sherlock Holmes summarized. "Are you presenting me with a case?"

"Afraid not," I managed to squeak out.

"American, East Coast, similar inflections to Mrs. Hudson's niece." The eyes flared. "Would you mind pronouncing the word *charter*? Her *r*'s have always intrigued me; if yours are the same—"

"Now, Mr. Holmes, don't be alarming our guests." Mrs. Hudson reappeared in the kitchen doorway at her employer's shoulder. "Were you going to wait for Sarah, then?" she added, moving to the fire, where the teakettle was whistling. "She ran out in such a hurry, I wasn't sure."

The Librarian and I exchanged glances. "Ran out?" Sherlock Holmes said, beating me to the punch. "Your niece typically moves at a serene pace; locomotion at speed would indicate some kind of alarm."

"Well, I wouldn't know about that, but she went straight past me out the door without even collecting her coat." Mrs. Hudson wrapped a dish towel around her hands and lifted down the steaming-hot kettle. "Not bad news, I hope?"

The worst, I thought in dismay.

Our Patron in danger had just gone missing.

"Once and for all," the Librarian said in exasperated tones, "I do *not* need you coming along."

"Yes, you do." We were back outside 221B Baker Street in the pea-soup fog; I took a step back from the street to avoid a spray of mud from a passing cart. "London's a big place, and you've just lost your Patron. I can help you search—"

"Mr. Holmes has agreed to pitch in." He was still inside, rummaging for his coat; he'd be flying out the door in a deerstalker any moment. If the real Sherlock Holmes (could you call him the *real* Holmes?) even wore a deerstalker—I wasn't sure if that was just a movie affectation or actually came from the books. "I feel quite certain that the aid of one of literature's greatest detectives renders your assistance superfluous, Miss Watson," the Librarian finished crisply. "And I cannot have you putting yourself in danger. Conan Doyle's

London can be a dangerous place, and you are not used to navigating your way around book worlds."

I appreciated the concern, really, I did, but I was damned if I was getting left behind with Mrs. Hudson, the crumpets, and the cat while the Librarian went off on a search party with Sherlock goddamn Holmes. "You're operating out of your comfort zone here," I cajoled. "Centuries you've worked in the Astral Library with only one attack on the place—you said it shouldn't be able to happen again, but now you've got a red card, a potential invader, *and* a Patron missing?"

She glowered from under her enormous bird-decked hat. "And how exactly are you planning to help with that?"

"I've worked in a library before. I was a page at the BPL, so why can't I be your page? Assist you with whatever—"

"I have never required the services of a Page. You will stay behind while I—" she began, but I pointed at her muff, where she'd buried the red card with Sarah's name.

"You've got a problem, and now you want us to split up? Have you never seen a horror movie? You know what happens when the characters split up: they get *picked off*."

"And I imagine you're seeing yourself as the heroine in this scenario?" The Librarian winged a devastating eyebrow upward.

"No, I see myself as a survivor. I have no problem being the sidekick rather than the heroine, or maybe the plucky comic relief, but I want to get out *alive* and that means sticking with you. My name is even Watson, for God's sake. Let me be your Watson and let's *Study in Scarlet* this bitch." Behind me I could hear the door of 221B Baker Street rattle, and rushed to finish before Sherlock Holmes joined in and made me entirely superfluous. "Just—please don't split us up.

Please don't leave me sitting here in a fictional kitchen like a kid sitting in detention. I *need* to help."

I stood there, heart thumping. *Please, please, please* . . .

Looking dour, the Librarian opened up her tablet. Tapped on it for a moment. It beeped; she turned it around. "Sign there to accept provisional status as a Page."

I scrawled with one fingertip, feeling giddy. "Does this mean I get automatic costume changes too?"

"It does not." The Librarian looked up as Sherlock Holmes came flying down the steps in a slightly decrepit frock coat. "Extraneous library privileges are strictly limited—Ah, Mr. Holmes. Where do you recommend we begin?"

"A head start of sixteen minutes would give an approximate radius of one mile, possibly a mile and a half given a very brisk pace, which would seem to be indicated by Miss Hudson's haste in departure," the great detective said, clapping a battered top hat to his head. No deerstalker. Should have known the movies would get it wrong. "Allow me to alert my Irregulars; they can be counted on to pass along any sightings."

"The game's afoot!" I couldn't help crying out, earning a swat from the Librarian and a quizzical glance from Sherlock Holmes. "You say it a lot," I couldn't resist telling him.

"You confound me, Miss Watson, which proves you are no relation of the good doctor, as he never confounds me. But as puzzles go, you shall have to wait for another day," he said, and whirled into motion down Baker Street, the Librarian at his elbow.

"Elementary," I replied with a little salute and fell into step behind them, trying to keep my moiré hem out of the mud, not quite able to keep a smile off my face. Sure, we had a Patron missing and a mysterious enemy, and maybe I was only the comic sidekick in this story so far. But I was still off on an adventure. I was on a case with *Sherlock Holmes*. Who was I going to meet next?

Well. I wasn't expecting *her*.

I saw her walking by the river, east of London Bridge. Not Sarah—we hadn't seen hide nor hair of our elusive Patron yet, after a methodical search through the British Museum (her favorite haunt, according to Mrs. Hudson) and Hyde Park (her habitual walk, according to Holmes). No, it was someone very different who wandered into my view.

Our little trio had paused in one of the seedier sections of Conan Doyle's London: the high wharves lining the north side of the river. A grimy street urchin darted into our path and accosted Holmes in a Cockney patois that lost me at the third word. Apparently even *accelerated linguistic osmosis* or whatever it was threw up its magical hands at Cockney rhyming slang. I let my gaze drift over the pageantry of the wharves in all their grimy colorful bustle, thinking that this world might be dirty and sinister and odorous, but it was growing on me. Maybe all book worlds had the same crackle of potential, of plot, of *things about to happen* . . .

And that was when I saw her. A medium-tall woman with a smooth knot of brown hair the same shade as mine, hatless like me, walking along the street in a blue bustle gown with her head bent over a book, walking and reading at the same time but somehow not bumping into anyone. The same way I'd learned to do at age six. She'd taught me to do that.

My mom.

And here she was.

I didn't stop to think. I didn't pause to remember the Librarian telling me Patrons didn't inhabit the same world even if they chose the same book—that this was Sarah's book world and therefore couldn't be my mother's. The rules were already suspended, weren't they? The rules had changed when someone came after Sarah in what should have been her sanctuary, and I'd just seen my mother for the first time since I was eight years old, and I didn't stop for anything. I just cried *"Mom—"* at the top of my lungs and bolted toward the wharves.

"Miss Watson—" I heard Sherlock Holmes call behind me, and more distantly the Librarian's exasperated "Oh, for gods' sake," but I never looked back. I plunged into the crowd after my mother.

"What's the rush, luv?" a porter leered as I bumped past him, heart jackhammering away somewhere in the vicinity of my tonsils. She was there, she was *right there* ahead of me, and I'd been right all along in my suspicions: my mother hadn't abandoned me for a tech bro in LA, she'd escaped into a book. And I wanted to know why she hadn't come back for me, but she'd have a reason, surely she would—

"Mom!"

But that meandering figure in blue ahead of me never looked up. I plunged into a crowd of drunken dockworkers, shoving my way through them with elbows jabbing, hearing a variety of Cockney insults fly at my back, clutching my handbag tighter when I felt the tug of acquisitive, pickpocketing fingers.

"Mom!"

But when I pushed my way past the last of the dockworkers and skidded to a halt, nearly falling under a passing hackney and startling its tired horse, I'd lost her. No figure in blue, no brown head bent over a book.

No. No, I was not losing her now. I plunged into a narrow alley on my right, the first place she might have turned off the main thoroughfare. Something slippery and rotted squashed underfoot, and the alley's stench—coal, sewage, manure, overlaid by something acrid and sweetish—crawled up my nose like a living thing. Hand over my mouth, I ventured to the grimy window of the gin shop at my left and peered in. No sign of her, or at the slop shop on its other side. But there—a set of bowed and buckling stairs leading downward to a black gap like a cave, and at the bottom a flash of blue.

I plunged down in pursuit, throwing my moiré skirts over one arm to keep from tripping. "*Mom*—" Because wasn't it just like her to wander accidentally into the seediest part of town because she had her nose in a book? I began to cough as I came into a long low room choked with sweetish brown smoke, terraced with sagging wooden bunks on all sides like the steerage compartment of a ship.

"Help you, missy?" a skinny old man leered, lurching up from a dully glowing brazier. "Come for a trip to dreamland?" If I wasn't mistaken, I'd just wandered into the opium den from *The Man with the Twisted Lip*. I didn't see even my feckless mother lingering in a place like this, but I ventured one more step inside, craning my gaze through the fetid smoke, past the languid groping hand of a man on a pallet clearly lost in poppy-fueled dreams—but the spot of blue I'd been pursuing turned around, and I saw a bleary-eyed washerwoman in a blue skirt handing over a few coins with eager trembling hands, and getting a pipe in return.

Not my mother. My heart sank down into my shoes.

"Excuse me—" I took a step back, swallowing my disappointment, but the skinny old man had a fierce hold on my arm and refused to let go.

"Just a puff," he whispered, waving a gummy ball of something brown and sticky under my nose. "Just a puff, missy—"

"No, thank you," I tried to say, yanking at his grip, but those gaunt fingers bit into my arm like a python, and a hulking bruiser in a tattered waistcoat was pressing up on my other side with a feverish gleam in his eye.

"Pretty pretty," he crooned, fingers sliding into my hair, and I was revising my opinion on how much I liked this world. Conan Doyle's London had maybe a bit too much grist and grit for me, and now there was another set of grimy fingers insinuating themselves around my handbag, and I felt panic clawing at my throat.

"Get away from me," I shouted, shoving back against all these hands. Was I really about to get robbed and assaulted by fictional London underworlders? Because they felt real enough, one of those hands working its way from my hair to my neck, and I hiked a knee against the nearest set of ribs with all the force in me, but that only made one of them fall back. "Get *away from me*—"

"Women are never entirely to be trusted," an irritable voice remarked. "Forever haring off like frightened rabbits, all emotional impulse, entirely antagonistic to clear reason—" And I found myself plucked free by an irascible-looking Sherlock Holmes.

"Th-thank you," I gasped, as the last of those grimy hands was dragged off my arm. "I didn't mean—I thought I saw someone I—"

"Some trifling intrigue, to be sure, but I cannot break my other search for the sake of it." Holmes applied some sort of efficient martial arts chop to the throat of the skinny man who was still attempting to latch on to my handbag; the man folded and nearly fell into the glowing brazier, and I found myself propelled briskly back toward the alley above. And I nearly wished myself back in the opium den, because the Librarian was waiting with a face like a thunderclap. I cringed before she said a single word.

"Is this your idea of helping?" she snapped, and then I didn't just cringe, I shriveled.

"I'm sorry—"

"I thought I had made it clear to you that the dangers faced inside a book world are very much *real* dangers."

"You did." Sherlock Holmes was already whirling up the alley back toward the wharves, dusting off his hands; the Librarian set off after him at a ferocious clip but that didn't stop the diatribe pouring down on my head.

"I do not have time to haul you out of dens of iniquity like some hapless damsel, Miss Watson. Hapless damsels are of singularly little use when one has a crisis to deal with."

"I know." I winced, following. Some sidekick I was. What's the first rule when you go into a fantasy land and get instructions from the wise old mentor? *Follow* those instructions. And here I'd plunged off the path at the first opportunity and nearly gotten myself murdered in an opium den. *Well done, Watson. Really good show.* "Are—are you going to revoke my Page status?" I managed to ask, heart knocking and thudding all over again.

"Is there a reason I shouldn't?" the Librarian asked in return as we made our way back through the thronged wharf toward London Bridge.

"I wasn't just . . . being rash. Running off to have an adventure like an idiot. I thought I saw my mother," I whispered. "I would never have run like that if I hadn't seen her."

Had I seen her? I'd been so sure it was her: the set of her head, the color of her hair, her gaze bent on that book . . .

"Was it her?" I blurted out. "Is—is my mother here?"

"This is Sarah's world," the Librarian said in a slightly less acid tone. "Sarah is the only Patron here; that is the way it works."

"I know, but—" I took a deep breath. "Can you just tell me if my mother is one of your Patrons? If she—if she escaped into a book when she left me?"

The Librarian stopped, looking at me from under the broad brim of that huge feather-laden hat. My heart thudded even harder. "No," she said. "No, I couldn't tell you that. The privacy of my Patrons is paramount, Miss Watson. I am not allowed to disclose their whereabouts to anyone."

"But she's my *mother*." I fought back the stupid, stupid rise of tears in my throat. Why was I on the verge of crying, here on a Victorian street corner in a pea-soup London fog with horse-drawn drays rattling past and Cockney voices flowing around me like a river? Why had I even come to a fantasy world if I was just going to end up crying about my goddamn mother like the eight-year-old I'd long left behind?

"I'm sorry," the Librarian said.

"No, I don't think you are," I replied, my voice unsteady. "But I understand why you're not."

There was nothing more to say as we made our way back to 221B Baker Street. Where one of our problems at least was solved, because Sarah was sitting at the top of the steps, hugging herself in the chilly fog, her face pinched and resolute.

"Excellent," Sherlock Holmes greeted her. "I may return to the analysis of my acetones—" And he disappeared inside with a flick of his greatcoat, clearly already mentally back in his lab. Sarah didn't look surprised at his brusqueness, just rose to her feet as the Librarian and I mounted the steps.

"I didn't mean to lead you on a chase," she said, her voice thin but determined. She looked scared but capable; I highly doubted *she'd* have needed to be rescued from an opium den. "I just—I had to be on my own a moment. I needed to think what I wanted to do."

"And have you decided?" the Librarian asked, more gently than I'd ever heard her speak before.

"Yes." Shoulders squaring. "I'll go with you."

The Astral Library

✦

I had one last glimpse of the Great Detective before we left Baker Street. Sarah, carpetbag in hand, was in the front hall giving Mrs. Hudson a fast and fluent lie about needing to visit a sick cousin in Brighton when Holmes came stalking back through on his way to the kitchen, several bubbling glass vials in hand. "I doubt the existence of this cousin in Brighton, Miss Hudson," he remarked to Sarah in passing. "Changes to the dilation of your pupils would indicate a fib."

"Not now, Mr. Holmes," Sarah said firmly, and the Librarian drew her Patron outside before we had to field any more investigative probing.

"There is a mystery here, dammit." Holmes's voice floated behind me as we all clattered down the seventeen front steps. "And at some point I would appreciate a clue..."

"He is going to be all questions when I get back," Sarah said as we set off down Baker Street, the two of us falling in behind the Librarian. "I swear, half the reason he sleeps with me is trying to figure out where my accent *really* comes from."

"You're sleeping with Sherlock Holmes?" I nearly tripped over my blue moiré hem. "I thought he hated women." And having to haul my ignorant, careless butt out of an opium den probably hadn't done much to raise his opinion of my gender.

"He hates matrimony and domesticity," Sarah corrected. "So do I. Had quite enough of that with Tyler"—a shadow passing across her face—"so frankly, being fuck buddies with the genius upstairs when he's between cases is perfect all around."

"How is he?" I couldn't help asking. Because really, who hasn't read Conan Doyle and *wondered*?

She grinned. "Anyone who pays that much attention to detail

knows exactly what to do with his hands. And other things." But her smile faded as she looked at me. "You got into some trouble trying to find me? I'm sorry."

"Don't be." I winced all over again inside. "Entirely my own fault."

"You shouldn't beat yourself up. It takes time getting used to a book world."

Her smile was so wry and encouraging, I couldn't stop myself from blurting out, "I thought I saw my mother here. Stupid, right?" Kicking at a loose cobblestone, then cursing as the stone just hurt my toes through my worn pleather boot. "I walk into the world of a book, just like every reader has wanted to do since the dawn of time, and all I can do is fantasize about finding my *mother*. How much of a bad Freudian cliché is that?"

"I don't know." Sarah sounded thoughtful, shifting her carpetbag from one hand to the other. "I think these book worlds are very good at showing us what we really want."

I didn't much like the sound of that. I'd always thought what I wanted was capital-letters ESCAPE, to fly high, fly fast, and find a door to something magical. At least as far as dreams go, that was a fairly grand one. Now that I'd actually found the magic door, was it really showing me that what I wanted was my *mother*? That wasn't even a bad Freudian cliché; that was pathetic abandoned-child bullshit. "Well, who cares anyway?" I said with a shrug. "My mother left me when I was eight, so screw her."

"I certainly don't miss mine," Sarah said. Her face took on a hard sheen, as memory moved over it almost visibly. "Whenever I came home to her crying, showing her the latest bruises from Tyler, she'd get me ice packs and then tell me it was my responsibility to fix the marriage. Nice, right? Black finger marks around your daughter's neck, and all you can say is *Have you thought about buying yourself some prettier underwear and learning to be a better cook?*"

"I'm sorry." My own complaints seemed pretty pathetic by comparison; I started kicking myself all over again. "You—you don't ever have to see her again. Or your husband," I added awkwardly, trying to be comforting. "I promise. The Library, it gave you sanctuary."

"Whatever the hell that's worth." Sarah quickened her pace to catch up with the Librarian. "Can I really come back here once the danger's past? If Ty's going to ruin this for me too—"

"He won't. Not while I've got breath," the Librarian said grimly. "That, I promise." She was about to say something else, when a rustling sound from above made us all pause and look upward. My first thought was a bird, but this was no bird: it was a dark red card spiraling down out of the fog and landing on the damp cobblestones. The lettering caught the dim light of the streetlamp overhead: *Stephanie Scopelli/Sophie Dent; JE by CB; orig. checked out 2023.*

"Another one?" I whispered, at the same time as the Librarian whispered something almost inaudible. Something that sounded like *Just like last time . . .*

"What happened last time?" I asked, watching as she picked up the card.

"What does this mean?" Sarah said at the same time, looking between us. "Is it Ty?"

"No." The Librarian turned the card over, answering Sarah's question rather than mine. "It means we have another Patron in danger."

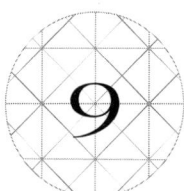

9

"*C*harming dress," drawled the Honorable Blanche Ingram, giving me the full eyelash-sweeping up-and-down glance all Mean Girls are so good at. "Very *exotic*. How is it you are acquainted with Mr. Rochester, Miss Watson?"

"One of his American friends, from his last journey overseas." I swirled my blue skirts. "I suppose artistic dress hasn't made its way across the water yet, at least not to such a *provincial* outpost as this." She smiled, all teeth. I smiled back, even more teeth, and I have to say my twentieth-century choppers really knocked me up a level in the looks department in this drawing room full of pre–dental care cavities. Not to mention armpit sweat stains. *Fluoridated water and powder-fresh deodorant for the win, Blanche Ingram.*

The Librarian had margin-traveled our little trio direct from Arthur Conan Doyle's London to Charlotte Brontë's Thornfield Hall in search of our next Patron-in-distress. I was firmly back in helpful-sidekick mode: I'd read *Jane Eyre* any number of times so I was well up on the plot, and after my opium den debacle I was determined to be an absolutely *model* Page. "Keep an eye out for our Patron," the Librarian had told me as we split up in the drawing room of Thornfield Hall. "Blond, late thirties—if she responds to the name of Stephanie, just bring her to me, quietly." And I'd nodded like a good soldier, not even asking if I was allowed to pull Jane Eyre aside for a little advice about falling for men who stash wives in attics.

No sign of our Patron yet. We'd landed smack in the middle of the book when Thornfield Hall is full of drawling party guests, and though neither the guests nor the servants batted an eyelash as we joined the throng, it did complicate our exit. "I'm not going to fit in with these clothes," Sarah had said, looking down at her sixty-years-fashion-forward 1890s rig. "I'll look around discreetly downstairs in the servants' quarters, see what I can find. The servants will think I'm odd-looking too, but they won't ask questions the way the drawing-room set will."

"Good thinking," the Librarian said, sounding considerably more approving of Sarah than she had yet to sound of me, but I was going to change that. I'd marched obediently into the drawing room after my boss (who was now dressed up to match the other guests in huge lace-tiered sleeves, green ribbon–banded skirts, and an Apollo knot) and started looking for our missing blonde named Stephanie. Only I hadn't caught sight of her yet, and now I'd somehow gotten myself cornered by one of the biggest bitches in English literature.

Fortunately I can out-bitch any bitch out there, fictional or not. "I don't see Mr. Rochester this evening—wait, is he over by the fire? Goodness, one would have thought he'd be hanging on *your* arm, Miss Ingram. Of course, one hears he's been quite distracted lately by . . . others."

Her smile hardened. "Where did you hear that?"

"Oh, a little bird. Excuse me—" Because I'd just seen another dark red card slide itself across the highly polished floor from under the door to the music room, and I hastily picked it up and stuffed it into my bag, but not before seeing the newest name. *Larry Barr/Lawrence Douglas; TAoTS by MT; orig. checked out 2025.* "Another one?" I muttered. Just how many infuriated astral-plane-crossing assholes were out there trying to find us?

"What was that?" A tall dowager in red velvet swished up to inspect me through a lorgnette—clearly Blanche the Bitch's mother; she had the same gimlet eye. "I don't remember seeing you arrive. Are you with Colonel and Mrs. Dent's party?"

I put her off with something or other, wondering why anyone would choose this particular world to live in. Maybe Sherlock Holmes's London had been a touch *too* eventful, but this just seemed like a snore. Even if the Librarian's Patron hadn't gotten herself stuck in the servant class doing all the work in this grand house—the maids unobtrusively whisking around the edges of this bustling party, the liveried footmen trimming the wicks on all these sputtering wax candles—it seemed to me that it wasn't all that much more fun being a titled guest: perspiring in this overheated drawing room in too many layers of clothes, droning small talk about the weather and being bitchy to your social inferiors. *Wearing a wedding cake like that too*, I could imagine Beau hooting if he could get his eyes on Lady Ingram. *Tasseled red velvet* and *a gold brocade turban? Oh, honey, no.* I sipped the glass of the nasty sweet hock some footman had blandly handed me, wishing Beau was here. He'd have had a blast making fun of all the giant leg-of-mutton sleeves at this party.

"Do be careful of your skirts, ma'am," a quiet voice said, and I turned to see a slight figure in dove gray sitting at the edge of the room, watching the bright birds-of-paradise that were the fashionable people. Jane Eyre, keeping her eyes away from Mr. Tall Dark and Brooding, currently a little bit heartbroken—but not for long. By chapter 38 she'd be off to *Reader, I married him*, not that she knew that yet.

"I do hope you're enjoying yourself, Miss Eyre," I said, because I'd always thought we'd be friends. Book-loving orphans the pair of us, who'd rather curl up with a novel than go for a walk. I wanted to pull up a chair beside her, but the Librarian was giving me a look across the room, making for the door where I could see Sarah discreetly beckoning. "Best of luck to you, Miss Eyre—Jane—and if you don't mind a tip? Mr. R's a dish, really, he is, but before he offers to put a ring on it, ask for a tour of the attic."

I left her startled face behind me, whisking out behind the Librarian. "What did I say about trying to nudge the plot?" she murmured with one of her dark glares.

"Look, you just don't leave one of your favorite book BFFs on the hook with a man keeping secrets. You just don't."

"Remind me not to take you to *Rebecca*," muttered the Librarian, pulling us into the oak-paneled corridor, where Sarah stood with a worried-looking blonde in pink satin swagged with ribbon loops.

"I found her in the library reading, away from all the other guests," Sarah said, casting a glance back at our second Patron. "She started hyperventilating the moment I told her what happened."

"Is my father really coming to find me?" gasped the woman in pink, latching on to the Librarian like a drowning woman. On closer inspection she looked maybe ten years older than I was, and her English accent sounded like the recently acquired variety. Like maybe she'd picked it up from *Downton Abbey*. "You told me no one could find me here, you *told* me—"

"You will come to no harm," the Librarian said with that reassuring implacability of hers, but the woman continued to gasp.

"I can't let my father find me, I *can't*—" She sank down on the carpet in a billow of pink satin skirts, shaking, her face ashen, breath coming in sudden gasps as if she were choking.

"Are you having a fit, Miss Scopelli?" the Librarian asked sharply, but I shook my head.

"Panic attack." One of the girls I'd shared a foster home with used to get them—hers lasted a good half an hour at a stretch, and I didn't think we had that kind of time here. Sarah was already crouching down by the blonde, rubbing a hand in reassuring circles between her shoulder blades; I crouched down on the other side. "Breathe," I said, "just breathe. Focus on your breath, in, out, in, out—"

"Can you tell me what color the carpet is?" Sarah asked quietly. "Blue and red, that's good. You've got this. What did you have for dinner last night?" Simple questions, grounding questions designed to pull someone out of the daze of panic and back into the world around them—clearly this wasn't Sarah's first rodeo either. She kept asking questions and I took over rubbing the blonde's back until the panicked race of her breathing slowed.

"Do you think you can walk now?" Sarah asked, as the Librarian gave her a nod and then moved to the end of the long corridor to see if the coast was clear.

"My father can't find me here," the woman whispered. "He *can't*. He told me if I ever moved out from his house and left him on his own—" A gulp. "He's going to be so angry."

"Did he hit you?" There was a particularly taut look on Sarah's face.

"No." The blonde looked startled. "He said men who hit women were no better than animals. He said women have to be protected . . . he just . . . I had to ask permission for *everything*. The money, the house schedule, my shopping; I had to get approval for everything I bought, every book I took out of the library. I wasn't allowed to move out, wasn't allowed to get a job—"

I cut her off because she was dialing herself right back into another fit of hyperventilation. "He won't find you here," I said in my most reassuring tones. Sarah signaled me with a look, and between the two of us we eased the blonde to her feet. The Librarian was returning from the end of the corridor in a rustle of green taffeta.

"Too many carriages and servants milling around out front to make a quiet getaway," she decreed. "We'll head up to the rooftop. Can you walk now, Miss Scopelli?"

I gave her shoulder a reassuring squeeze, and she made a jerky little nod, managing to follow as the Librarian headed for the grand staircase. "You've dealt with a few panic attacks before," I murmured to Sarah as we brought up the rear.

"Used to get them myself," she said. "I certainly don't miss *that* particular roller coaster. You've clearly handled your share."

"Foster kid." Sarah gave a nod at that, and I thought that maybe, just maybe, I'd acquitted myself a little better in this book than the last.

We tiptoed our way up to the very top floor of the house, toward the roof and along a certain corridor that anyone who has read *Jane Eyre* knows is trouble. As we passed That Door, a long malicious chuckle floated out from the other side just as I was pulling out the latest dark red card. I jumped a little, but managed to hand it over to the Librarian.

"Third one," I said as she fingered the crimson edges. "It came whizzing at me in the drawing room . . . What exactly are we dealing with here? It's supposed to be impossible for even one uninvited person to break into the Astral Library system, and now we've got a coordinated attack?"

"That," she said, not sounding one whit surprised, "is exactly what happened two hundred years ago."

I really wanted to know exactly *what* had happened two hundred years ago, and more important, how the Library had beaten it, but the blonde in pink paled as if she was on the verge of collapsing and I didn't want to send her over the edge. That ripple of eerie laughter came through the door to my left again, this time with a soft scratching sound on the other side of the oak panels, and we all jumped.

"You don't belong here," the first Mrs. Rochester's voice floated through, and my spine damn near clawed its way out of my blue moiré as I saw the doorknob rattle, as the blood-colored card looked up at me from the Librarian's hand like a baleful eye.

But I just linked arms with the two women the Librarian had hidden away from the people who would hurt them, and followed our guide onto the roof. Where she grabbed us by the hands and pulled us after her into another book.

The Library system was apparently under siege, because another card swirled up to meet us on the waters of the Mississippi when we margin-traveled to *The Adventures of Tom Sawyer* to snag a sixteen-year-old boy who'd been living in a white clapboard house in Missouri as a cousin of the Widow Douglas, the one helping to raise Huck Finn. And we had not one but two cards swirl down lazily on a sea breeze when we margin-traveled to a pier in a town the Librarian said was called Whitby; dark blood spots on a sunny summer evening (*what book was this, anyway?*) where Englishwomen in white 1890s muslins and parasols promenaded the beach below and men used their walking sticks to point out the seagulls swooping overhead, the fishermen throwing lines out into the bright water, the children with their pails and shovels.

"I think we need to go back to the Library," I said, low-voiced, to the Librarian as she picked up the new warnings. "This isn't just one or two potential incursions we're dealing with, it's—" I didn't want to say the words *an army*, but wasn't it?

"Hmm" was all the Librarian would say. Her hair had changed from the *Jane Eyre* Apollo knot to a *Tom Sawyer* bun to a frizzed front fringe and a low chignon; her skirts had shrunk down to the narrow silhouette I remembered from Beau's historical fashion book. "Nothing I haven't dealt with before." But a furrow of worry had carved itself between her dark brows all the same, and Sarah and I exchanged glances.

"Two hundred years ago, right?" I took a deep breath. "What exactly happened two hundred years ago?"

"A coalition of angry, self-righteous men happened," said the Librarian. "Who else is responsible for so much of the world's violence?"

"What happened to them?"

That sharklike smile reappeared. "They lost. And they will lose again this time, I assure you." She looked down at the two new red cards and tucked them into her sleeve. "Still, we may as well go back to the Library before getting these next two," she said. "We've got too much of an entourage now to move fast, so we'll take these Patrons back and get them settled. Let me make some arrangements . . ."

We. She was saying *we*, and quietly I hugged myself over that as she began tapping at her tablet. She wasn't wrong about the entourage: *we* were now a group of five, attracting a certain number of covert stares for the mixed costumes. This nervous little group needed coaxing and comforting, which I figured fell into the scope of my duties as Page, though I wasn't as good at it as Sarah—the blonde in the pink dress had attached herself to Sarah like a limpet, requiring a constant stream of quiet reassurances, and I found myself with the boy from *Tom Sawyer*, who shuffled along with a taut face, undoubtedly missing his world of fence whitewashing, river rafting, and hijinks. "Don't be scared," I told him, doing my best to sound confident. "The Librarian's done this before; she knows how to keep you safe."

"I'm not scared, I'm pissed off." A scowl as the boy crossed those bony arms across his chest. "I promised myself I was done running when I left Montana, and here I am on the run again."

"What were you running from?" I asked diffidently. "I'm not saying you have to tell me, but if it helps to talk—"

"My family," the boy said, jaw jutting. "They are all goddamn nutcases. The fire-and-brimstone kind."

"The kind who like burning books instead of reading them?"

"More or less. And who don't believe that girls can actually be boys even if they don't have the right plumbing."

"Got it." I started to pat his shoulder but he looked too prickly to welcome it, so I went for a soft reassuring punch on the arm instead. "Well, you know the Librarian. She won't let anything happen to you."

"What if they make her? There's only one of her and she's saddled with four of us plus whoever she picks up here."

It was a fair point, and I looked worriedly at the Librarian, who had stopped mid-pier to wrestle with the green tablet. "Where are we going to hide them all?" I asked, approaching her to speak quietly.

"That depends on if the Gallerist has answered my email. Oh, you goddamn machine," she swore. The tablet was clearly in a mood again, repeating PASSWORD INCORRECT when she recited "'Libraries store the energy that fuels the imagination.'"

"I'm not going to stand here on a fictional boardwalk guessing flattering book quotes," she snarled at it, giving the screen a good shake.

It gave one of its electronic squawks, sounding somehow smug. *Oh yes, you are*, I could imagine it saying. It was almost a relief, knowing for certain that inanimate devices were in fact both alive and actively malicious. I mean, we all know they are, but finally: confirmation.

I leaned over the Librarian's silk faille sleeve and cooed at the tablet in my sweetest tones, "'Libraries are full of ideas—perhaps the most dangerous and powerful of all weapons.'" It gave a little purring sound and the screen unlocked. "What?" I shrugged at the Librarian's slanted look over her glasses. "I'm not without skills."

She snorted, clearly thinking of my damsel-in-distress jaunt to the opium den. "You mean, you're not without book quotes. That seems to be your primary skill as far as I can see, Miss Watson."

"Yes, but I'm stuffed to the gills with book quotes and that's what you need right now."

"Hmph." She began swiping at the screen. "What's that quote from, anyway? Not that tedious Erasmus, he could be so everlastingly *precious* about libraries—"

"Nope, *Throne of Glass*. So don't you look down your nose at my reading habits, because my taste in popular fantasy just opened your email account."

"I never look down my nose at anyone for what they read. As long as they're reading, at least they aren't watching reality television." Her fingers flew over the tablet. "Well, the Gallerist is waiting back at the Library for me, so we'll head back there once we've collected the latest Patron—" And she headed off down the pier again, completely ignoring my "Who's the Gallerist?"

Of course she did. Maybe I was part of the *we* now, but that wasn't netting me any more answers.

"Ms. Ferreira?" the Librarian called to a short woman standing near the end of the pier. The sun was starting to slant in long brilliant rays and even longer shadows; all I could really see was a flood of garnet-red taffeta flounces at the back of the woman's dress and a jet-handled parasol angled over one shoulder. (*Chic*, I could hear Beau approving.) Then she turned and smiled: mid-fifties, dark chignon, frothing black lace up to the throat and black kid gloves down to her fingertips even in the warmth of the summer evening.

"Ms. Ferreira?" she said. "Do make it Elaine. I haven't heard 'Ms. Ferreira' in a dog's age."

"What book is this again?" the boy from *Tom Sawyer* wondered. I wasn't sure—what classic novel was set in a Victorian seaside town? I tried to remember as the Librarian launched into her little explanation, and I'd heard her give it enough times by now that I could admire her delivery. She was matter-of-fact without being cold, empathetic without being emotional, efficient without being rushed. Just what you want in a Librarian: a keeper of information who knows exactly how to dispense it.

"I don't think I'll be going," said the woman in red at the end of the Librarian's recitation, sounding utterly unworried. "No need to hide me. I'm safe where I am."

"Are you?" The Librarian put a hand to her hat, a wide-brimmed straw with a green-striped ribbon to keep it from whipping off her head into the sea below. "I remember you were very anxious, when I placed you here, that your brother not be able to find you."

"Mmmm." The woman angled her sunshade so not a ray of the setting sun could fall on her face, and her smile widened. "A few things have changed since then."

That's when I remembered just what classic work of English literature happens to be set in the charming seaside town of Whitby during the 1890s. The second half, anyway. The novel begins in Transylvania, with a young lawyer named Jonathan Harker . . .

"I've made some friends since the days I was Mark's scared little sister," the woman in red went on mildly. "The days when he pushed me around, helped himself to my money, told me I was stupid to read so much. That books were a waste of time and wouldn't do anything for me." She started back down the pier toward shore, but she smiled over her shoulder. Her teeth were very white, and very sharp. "If he wants to come looking for me? Let him."

Meeting my first vampire rattled me sufficiently that I didn't track the details of how the Librarian brought us all back home. It was some complicated process involving the tablet and the copy of *The Adventures of Sherlock Holmes*, where we'd made our first jump. Eventually the Whitby pier dissolved around us, re-forming into the endless shelves, the barrel-vaulted ceiling, and the emerald-green windows of the Astral Library.

Despite the Librarian's assurances that the place could protect itself, I was still dreading that I'd see it all in ruins—books burning, clock shattered, windows broken. But everything looked more or less as we'd left it; if anything, the atmosphere had quieted. The clock's terrifying *bong bong bong* had halted; the hands were spinning round the clockface as though they were on fast-forward, but that terrible *abandon ship, here there be monsters* tolling had ceased. The huge door at the top of the sweeping double staircase was still closed, and there was no sign of intrusion. The ghosts had even calmed down enough while we'd been gone to return to their endless TBR stacks—in the corner I saw the spectral outline of Dennis with his floating copy of *War and Peace*.

But when I looked upward, I could see all wasn't entirely well after all. Hundreds of books had flown from their shelves and were clustered along the ceiling like frightened birds, making that anxious fluttering sound as their pages ruffled.

"I hate seeing books afraid," Sarah said.

"I know what you mean," I agreed. "Books aren't supposed to quake at the thought of invaders. Invaders quake at the thought of books, or at least they should."

"I think they do." Sarah sounded thoughtful. "What that woman Elaine said about her brother making fun of her for reading . . . Tyler used to do that to me. If I picked up any women's fiction or romance, I was a shallow bitch for reading chick-lit. If I read a classic, I was a pretentious bitch showing off how smart I was. If I chose a mystery or a thriller, I was a stupid bitch who couldn't figure out a whodunit if her life depended on it. And I never saw him read a single book himself the entire time we were married." Shaking her head. "I think it scares people like that, the sight of other people reading. Reading *anything*."

"I had a few foster parents along those lines," I said. "Some adults think it's cute, a kid with her nose stuck in a big book, but some—"

"Think she's a little know-it-all?"

"Bingo." I looked at Sarah, her smooth hair and composed face. If she was afraid, she wasn't showing it anymore. "You okay?"

"Furious." She said it quietly, a river of rage running through that one word. "How dare that bastard ruin this for me? The one good thing I ever managed to get for myself . . ."

"He won't," I said, wishing I had something more reassuring to tell her.

"I know." She gave a mirthless smile. "There's nothing I wouldn't do to go back to my book. I don't care who I have to throw under the bus to get back there safe. I don't care. I'm *getting back*."

Her face was granite hard. It occurred to me that Sarah, despite all her soothing words and comforting hugs in handling the other Patrons, was not entirely a nice person. I understood that. Survivors don't tend to be nice people; niceness gets crushed out of them like juice out of a grape. A lot of it had been crushed out of me too.

"Just don't throw me under that proverbial bus," I said, not really joking, and then we both looked up as the Librarian moved out into the middle of the polished floor, commanding every eye in the room. She was back in her green cardigan and brogues, gazing upward at the anxious, rustling books clustered near the ceiling.

"Come down," she called out in her brisk voice. "There's nothing to be afraid of. Everyone will be calm now."

They didn't all come at once. A few fluttered down; she gave a reassuring stroke along each spine the way you'd stroke a cat, and they went off to their shelves with a relieved flap of pages. More came down then; some had to be held a moment before they'd go back home, but she coaxed the last one out of its corner with nothing more than a long, stern look. The kind of sternness that reassures rather than reproves. I could *feel* the Astral Library exhale a long sigh of relief.

"I've never seen the books in such a state," a low-pitched voice said, and for the first time I realized there was a stranger here—a long lean figure rising from the armchair by the huge oak counter. Very tall, black turtleneck, knee-high black boots. I felt a lurch of alarm, but the Librarian came forward and the two of them exchanged cheek kisses. "I got your email," the newcomer went on in a faint French lilt. I wasn't sure about gender, so mentally I went with *they*. "Goodness, you've got quite the entourage of lost ducklings here. Four Patrons to hide?"

"Three," I volunteered. "The last one, um. She stayed behind as a Bride of Dracula or something. Frankly, I hope her brother *does* break into her book, because she'll just eat him. I'm Alix," I added as the newcomer shot me a bemused look. "I'm the new Page."

"And I'm the Gallerist." They looked at our nervous group of four in our assorted book-world costumes. "I think I can find paintings to hide you all in until the danger is past—"

"Wait, people can go live in *paintings* as well as books?"

The Librarian gave me a *Can you truly be this dense?* look. "Why not?"

I opened my mouth. Closed it again. Bookworms disappearing into their favorite books, art lovers disappearing into their favorite paintings. Why not, indeed? "So there's an Astral Gallery and you're the head of it?" I asked our newcomer.

"*Bien sûr*," said the Gallerist with a faint smile, and turned back to the Librarian. "More Patrons in trouble?" they asked, and I saw the Librarian stoop to pick up another red card.

"I know you said this all happened before," I said, fighting my own unease. "But was it this many? The—the men who were trying to break in two hundred years ago?"

"It was nearly a dozen men, back then. We aren't quite that badly off yet, Miss Watson."

I took a deep breath. "Who were they?"

"Slavers," she said, spitting the word like a nail. "The Library provided escape for many, *many* of the enslaved during America's age of plantations, shackles, and the transatlantic slave trade. One Patron tried to go back, to bring more of her family through—she was caught by the man who fancied himself her master, and he forced the story out of her. Once he realized it was all true, he formed a coalition of his friends to find out if any of their 'missing property' were hiding in other book worlds." Her words dripped disgust.

"You said they failed?" I heard my voice quiver. "How?"

"The slavers forced the woman they had captured to open the door into the Library," the Librarian said, "and then the books ate them. Before escorting her back to her book world with the rest of her family."

A certain silence fell at that. Until the Gallerist gently cleared their throat, looking at the little trio of Sarah, Larry, and Stephanie. "Can you come with me while I place them? With this many to transport I could use someone to help row."

"Row?" I asked, but the Librarian was already answering.

"Afraid I can't. Not with more Patrons to pick up."

The Gallerist frowned. I stepped forward, trying not to sound tentative. "Um. Can I help?"

How do you travel from an Astral Library to an Astral Gallery? Through a book of paintings, of course.

"Let's see..." The Gallerist walked unerringly to the nearest shelf as though they knew exactly what they were looking for, pulled down a book, and began paging through it. One of those big coffee-table art books with huge color plates of famous paintings—I saw the *Mona Lisa* and a self-portrait of Van Gogh flip past, blank painted eyes staring at me as the Gallerist moved past them to a landscape of some kind. "There it is. Link up now, ducklings, link up—" And before I could ask what painting we were traveling to, I felt their cool-fingered French-perfumed hand clasp mine. I hastily clasped Sarah's, Sarah reached for Stephanie and Stephanie for the boy from *Tom Sawyer*, and we were stepping through.

Traveling into a painting was slower than jumping into the world of a book—it wasn't the falling sensation of stepping on a page and dropping straight into the book's world, but something more deliberate, as if the Library around me was blurring into an Impressionist slurry of colors and re-forming into an entirely new palette. I had enough time to wonder if I'd done the right thing here, volunteering to help the Gallerist: Should it be a Page's duty not to abandon her Librarian or her Library? But I felt a little less panicked about the flurry of red cards now that I'd heard how the last attack on the library had been defeated; a little bit less like I had to hunker down for a fight—clearly the Library knew how to defend itself, and so did its mistress. Besides, I so very much wanted to make a better impression on the Librarian after my Sherlockian debacle. Surely if I helped her colleague out in a pinch, I'd get that approving nod she'd bestowed once or twice on Sarah, but not so far on me?

No nod when I volunteered to go with the Gallerist and get the Library Patrons settled and hidden in their temporary painting sanctuaries, just a distracted *yes, all right* and a wave of the hand with that big emerald ring, but I'd take what I could get. Ideally, a glowing reference from the Gallerist when we came back: *Alix is the most helpful Page imaginable . . .*

And then the Impressionist swirl around me resolved itself, and I gasped aloud.

The five of us were in a boat—a wide rowboat with a squared-off stern and a high pointed prow, and we shouldn't have all fit but we did. All around us was the vast sweep of a glassy lake, its shores lost to sight, the bluster of piled clouds arching overhead. Somewhere in front was the shadowed outline of an island, its rocky cliffs climbing toward the sky, but my attention was arrested by something a little closer to hand. "What—what's that?" I asked, and I couldn't quite keep a quiver out of my voice as I pointed to the long rectangular box laid across the prow, lurking under a canvas drape and looking suspiciously like— "Please tell me that's not a coffin."

"*Bien sûr que non.*" The Gallerist tossed back the drape and opened the lid. No corpse, just a pile of folded blankets. "It gets cold here on the lake—who wants *une couverture*? Of course, Böcklin certainly *implied* it was a coffin when he painted the scene, but artists take creative license with everything. If someone can assist me in taking the oars . . ."

We all draped blankets around our shoulders, and then it turned out that Larry (the boy who had fled to *Tom Sawyer*) had done a fair amount of rowing with Tom and Huck and the gang out on the Mississippi, so he took one oar and the ever-capable Sarah took the other, and soon we were stroking through the lake's calm waters toward the distant island. *I'm in a painting*, I kept thinking, pulling the folds of a plaid wool throw around me, and the whole landscape had a different quality than a real ride on a lake would have had. Not that I had a lot of real-life lakeside jaunts to compare it to, but the ripples of the water below spread just a touch too slowly for real water; the blue-black of the lake and the blue-gray of the clouds were just a touch more vivid to my eye than the colors of any real lake or sky; and though I could smell the iron tang of lake water and the boat's pine planks, both those scents were underlaid with something stronger, something resinous . . . I put my fingers in the water, feeling the cool slide that was somehow thicker than ordinary water would have been, then sniffed my fingertips. Paint.

"Um." The blonde named Stephanie spoke up, voice uneasy. "That island . . ."

It was drawing nearer through the quiet plash of the oars and the shifting mists: a rocky islet half encircled by slate cliffs (just as the Astral Library had merited a word like *sward*, this definitely called for something like *encircled*), and thickly spired with tall ink-dark cypress trees. At its front was a small seawall, with steps leading down into the water; behind I could see stone-linteled doorways cut directly into the cliff face, looking at us like dark eyes.

"Creepy," said Larry from his oar.

"It's supposed to be the Isle of the Dead," said Stephanie, voice still wobbling. "Art books were one of the only things my father let me check out—well, as long as they were only landscapes and still lifes because he didn't think women should look at nudes, but I've *seen* that island before, in a painting. Are we—are we—dead?"

"No, we're merely in *The Isle of the Dead*, as painted by Arnold Böcklin," said the Gallerist, standing up at the prow with their French tweeds now overlaid by a decidedly chic white cotton-gabardine raincoat that had been whisked out of the coffin-shaped locker after the blankets. "Böcklin's art dealer was the one who put the title on, and admittedly Arnold leaned into the whole ethos—draped the boat in garlands, made my raincoat here look like a monk's robe so I might as well have been Charon the Ferryman. But it's not the Isle of the Dead at all." The Gallerist put up a hand as we drew up to the water-lapped stone steps, and Larry raised his oar just in time for us to glide up alongside. "It's the entrance to the Astral Gallery. Or one of them, at least," they added, scrambling nimbly out and throwing a loop of rope from the prow around a stake on the bottom step. "I use this one if I'm escorting a group. Or if I'm looking to make a real *statement* entrance . . . certainly Arnold was agog."

"Wait, so you bring artists here?" I discarded my plaid throw in the boat, managing not to fall into the lake as I made the awkward step across to the mossed-over stone stairs. "You brought a painter here during the Victorian era and he painted the place?"

"I've been known to inspire an artist or two with a visit to the

Astral Gallery." The Gallerist looked demure, helping Stephanie and her bulky pink satin skirts make the jump out of the boat. "Come along, ducklings."

And I thought maybe Arnold Whoever had it right, because the Gallerist in their sweeping white raincoat *did* look a bit like some sort of pagan priest as they led the way up the cracked and mossy steps into the shadowed path between the cypress trees, toward an ancient leaning lintel over a cliff-carved doorway. Behind me I could hear Stephanie gulping and Sarah soothing her—I felt Larry's rough paw slide into mine and gave it a reassuring squeeze as we followed.

Into the Astral Gallery.

It was all light, light from every side, dazzling light . . . And there was no smell of oil paint or acrylic paint or any other artist's medium. This place had not been painted; this place was *real*.

Imagine an infinite high-ceilinged passageway, black-and-white-checkered marble underfoot, an endless row of crystal chandeliers overhead. One long side nothing but floor-to-ceiling windows draped in velvet and tasseled in gold, pouring light in like a river of honey. The other long side simply an unending tapestried wall hung with pictures from floor to ceiling: pictures in acrylic and oil and chalk, pictures in mixed textures glued together into three-dimensional pieces, pictures that were little more than sketches in pencil or charcoal. Between the paintings and pictures were alcoves with sculptures, marble and wood and porcelain and majolica and plaster, every medium you could imagine. Sometimes arched doorways in the wall of paintings led to other rooms: an entire chamber of Byzantine mosaics across floors and walls and ceiling, all leaping dolphins and solemn-eyed empresses and grave saints; a room of exuberant street art that looked like it had been spray-painted on the sides of a warehouse; a room full of

Vermeers. I peeked into that one and saw the paintings were *moving*: in his landscape of Delft, the tiny figures along the river were actually walking; his *Girl with a Pearl Earring* didn't stay static and glassy-eyed within her frame but met my gaze and turned her head with a little smile so I could see the pearl flashing and gleaming in her other ear.

"Welcome to the Astral Gallery," said the Gallerist, with more than a hint of pride in their voice.

"I—I don't know much about art," I confessed, suddenly feeling very out of my depth. I barely recognized any of these paintings on the endless wall—peeping through another archway into a room of what looked like Renaissance paintings, I caught a glimpse of what I was fairly sure was a rendition of *The Last Supper*, but couldn't remember if it was a Michelangelo or a Leonardo. Either way, I didn't see the point of going to visit it. Stuck at a dinner party that never ends with a lot of religious types? Pass the water-into-wine, please.

"I don't know much about this either," said Sarah, and I was glad I wasn't the only one overwhelmed by all the beauty on display in this vast space. "I'm a book girl, not a gallery girl. Library cards, not museum memberships."

"Me too," I said. It occurred to me that here, I wouldn't be hallucinating any visions of my mother—she hadn't been a museum-membership type either. More a "My toddler could paint that, and you're putting it on a wall and charging admission to look at it?" type. I could almost hear her snort.

"Art is for everyone," the Gallerist said, very much making an Eleventh Commandment out of that statement. "It is not only for collectors, snobs, experts, college graduates, or the well-informed. If you can see it, touch it, or in any way appreciate it, it is for you. Do not ever let *anyone* make you feel out of place for looking at a work of art. Canapé?" Waving to a plinth where there sat a silver tray of smoked salmon canapés, mini crab cakes, little quiches, and deviled eggs, and I started laughing because of course. The Astral Library was replete with book snacks, everything from fresh-baked cookies to finger sandwiches; stuff you'd eat when cozying up with a book—naturally the Astral Gallery was stocked to the skies with food you'd find at a gallery viewing. I helped myself to a crab cake, took a glass of champagne from the tray next to it because of course there was champagne too in slender crystal flutes, and turned to toast Sarah. "Cheers," I said.

"I think you'd fit into a Monet landscape nicely," the Gallerist was telling Stephanie, drawing her little satin-gloved hand through their white-coated elbow. "Impressionist painting worlds are very gentle, very soothing to the senses. And who doesn't like a trip to Giverny this time of year? The hyacinths should be in bloom, and the tulips."

"I've never been to France," Stephanie said, looking cautiously anticipatory.

"If you wouldn't mind staying with the others, Alix," the Gallerist called to me, drawing Stephanie through a doorway where I could see an entire lily-padded room full of Monets, "I'll just nip through and get Stephanie settled . . ."

"I'm on it," I said, saluting with my champagne flute, and felt pleasantly useful as I turned back to the little gang of Patrons. "Come on, ducklings. Let's find you all paintings to hide out in."

Larry was easy to place—by the time the Gallerist returned sans Stephanie, trailing the scent of French hyacinths, I was delighted to show them that the boy in the Huck Finn overalls was standing transfixed before a painting of a knight in silvery armor and sweeping red cloak, pale horse champing beneath him. "What's the painting?" I asked, fascinated. The knight's visor was raised, and he looked tenderly upward at the golden-haired woman in white samite (how often in the ordinary course of life do you get to use a word like *samite*!) leaning over a castle parapet to tie her favor around his mailed arm. The colors were as rich as wine, the figures moving ever so subtly: I saw the pale stallion's ear twitch, the maiden's gold hair flutter as she leaned forward.

"*God Speed* by Edmund Blair Leighton," the Gallerist told me. "Painted 1900, after the heyday of the Pre-Raphaelites but very much in that style. Often dismissed as being a bit chocolate box, but I've always thought of him as a painter with a fine sense of story. What does it say to you, Larry?" So often that kind of question sounded pretentious, I thought: *Does the art* speak *to you?* followed by a condescending side-eye if your answer wasn't high-brow enough. But when the Astral Gallerist spoke those words, they sounded entirely serious and matter-of-fact: *Yes, the art is talking; what are you hearing?*

And maybe I was a book girl rather than an art girl, but I found I had a new opinion here, fast and firm: art *should* talk, and it does. These paintings were still stories, after all, just like books. Only the medium of telling the stories was different.

The Gallerist was still waiting on Larry's answer.

"I—think it's saying I could go on a quest like a knight?" Larry whispered, still staring at the painting. "I'm not sure I'd want to go around questing all the time, I mean, but I could do it for a little while?"

The Gallerist smiled. *"Bien sûr."* And held out an elegant hand.

I hadn't seen Stephanie enter her Monet garden (where I hoped she was wandering among the hyacinths breathing in a little French peace and listening to the frogs croak on their lily pads) but I watched at Sarah's side now, enthralled, as the Gallerist took Larry by the hand and simply stepped into the frame of the painting. A moment of that Impressionist blurring as the colors swirled, and then they were gone and it was just the knight and his damsel. I took a step forward, hunting among the richly painted figures . . .

"There." Sarah pointed, and I saw. In the shadow of the castle gate beyond the knight, under the raised portcullis, there had previously been the colorful outlines of more knights marching off into the world outside, vivid-hued pennants on sharp-tipped spears snapping over their heads in the breeze. Now there was a half-visible figure in white slipping through those serried ranks, and an even less visible figure of a young squire behind them wearing the same colors as the knight on the pale horse.

"He's off on a quest," I said softly, feeling my throat get thick. "Have fun storming the castle, Larry."

"Hope he doesn't get killed in a siege or eaten by a wyvern before he can go back to Tom Sawyer territory," Sarah said.

"In a world like that?" I nodded at Leighton's painting. "That's not the real Middle Ages with all the famine and plague and war. It's the nicer, prettied-up version where the kings are always good and just, the knights actually fight for the common people instead of crushing them underfoot, and the maidens always get saved before anything horrible happens to them."

"You're a real believer in all this, aren't you?" Sarah waved a hand, encompassing the Astral Gallery, the Astral Library, the Gallerist and the Librarian—all of it.

"Aren't you?" I smiled. "You had what looked like a pretty near perfect life in Conan Doyle's London."

"Until I learned my husband can maybe still get to me there." Her face was hard. "What's the point of these places if they offer sanctuary but can't actually deliver it?"

"They're trying," I said gently. "The Librarian moved you here, didn't she? Doesn't that tell you something?"

"It tells me what I already learned from being married to Ty. That you can't count on *anyone*. Including them." Her voice was rising, nearly a shout. "In the end, it's just you. It's always just you." Sarah looked at me, hazel eyes burning hard and bright with betrayal. "Don't sell your soul to the Library, Alix. It's nothing but a pretty space. It's not going to look after you, so look out for yourself."

"Is that what you're doing?"

"Yes," she said without hesitation. "I'd let that entire place burn down, and this one too, if it meant keeping myself safe from Ty."

I didn't quite know what to say to that. I wanted to argue with her for being so self-centered; I wanted to sympathize because I knew what it was to have to be self-centered because no one else was ever going to center you. I wanted to wipe that hard look off her face, and part of me wanted to do it with a slap and part of me wanted to do it with a hug. I wanted to tell her she didn't understand, and I wanted to tell her I understood exactly what she meant. But I didn't get a chance to do any of those things, because the Gallerist stepped back out of the Leighton painting, smiling.

"Our last duckling," they said, looking at Sarah. "I understand you come from the world of Monsieur Conan Doyle, yes? I can place you inside one of the drawings by Sidney Paget if you like; his illustrations ran alongside the stories when they were originally published in *The Strand*—"

"No," Sarah said decisively. "If Ty found me in Sherlock Holmes's world one time, that's the first place he'd look if he somehow tracked me here. I need something as far as possible from anything he associates with me." She about-faced and did a march down the long line of paintings, looking from frame to frame. I followed, getting distracted by a wall of Pre-Raphaelite portraits—one of them, I could have sworn, was the Rossetti painting Beau had modeled my blue gown from. Beau, I thought, even as the dark-haired beauty in the painting saw my dress and gave a tiny approving quirk of a smile, would have been entranced by this place.

"This one," Sarah said, bringing me out of my brief reverie as she came to a stop in front of a huge, exuberant canvas. "Roman Empire, right? Ty knows I hate Roman Empire stuff. Mostly because he never stopped playing *Rome: Total War* at top volume when I was trying to sleep."

I looked at the painting, so big and bright it nearly pulsated with life. A vast shining city, all columns and porticoes and temples in gleaming white marble, in the full throes of celebration: a parade of soldiers behind a man in a red-purple cloak riding along in state in some huge victory parade. Betasseled elephants and golden canopies; a queenly woman watching from a dais surrounded by leaping fountains; a harbor thronged by silken-sailed gilt barges; crowds of onlookers in togas and tunics, cheering themselves hoarse beneath the statues of their blind marble gods. Looked like ancient Rome to me.

"*The Consummation of Empire*, Thomas Cole," the Gallerist said. "He's better known for inspiring the whole Hudson River School of American landscape painting, all those sweeping vistas of mountains in the Catskills, but he does like his allegorical narrative works as well. This is third in the 'Course of Empire' series—it traces a civilization from an unsettled wilderness to a village to a great empire, and then its violent fall and eventual decay. I recommend you don't go shopping in the next painting for a safe haven; that's the one where the empire burns down." The Gallerist looked over their glasses at Sarah. "You're sure you want this one? Quite a change from Victorian London."

"I'm sure," Sarah said firmly. "Ty would never in a thousand years look for me there."

"Can I come too?" I blurted as the Gallerist took her by the hand and began drawing her toward the frame. "Not to stay, just to look while you take her through . . . I wouldn't mind a peek at ancient Rome."

"Just for a few minutes," the Gallerist warned, taking my hand in their free one. "Don't fall under an elephant—" And we stepped through a swirl of colors into ancient Rome.

If a book world felt more vivid, more gripping, more crackling with possibility than the real world, then the world inside a painting was in every way *brighter*. The colors punched me right between the eyes so I nearly reeled: the sapphire sparkle of the harbor, the vivid pinks and golds of the sails on the many-oared barges, the jewel-like green of laurel wreaths and palm branches, the pristine marble gleam of all those columns and temples and statues . . . I tilted my head back to take in the arch of a vast dome, then the parade with its majestic elephants and caparisoned horses (*caparisoned*! Another word coming off my Rarely Used list).

And not just the colors, but the *smells*. The smell of paint underlying the mud-and-water tang of the harbor, the spice of incense rising up from a thousand temples, the scent of sweat and perfume and beer as an entire city went mad with celebration. A man in a toga pushed past me, cheering lustily as the elephants lumbered past, followed by the godlike regally cloaked figure (emperor? victorious general?) with his handsome bearded profile that looked just like it belonged on a coin. The woman on the dais (empress? queen?) watched him with a cool shield of a face over her imperial purple stola, and I wondered if there was a story there, if Thomas Cole had painted one into this scene or if the story developed beyond the scope of the painting just as stories in book worlds continued on past the point of the author's *The End*. "What's the occasion here?" I called out to the nearest throng of cheering women in colorful tunics, like a bouquet of bright wildflowers.

"Emperor Hadrian's returned at last from the eastern provinces," one of them shouted back, looking tipsy and ecstatic, and I realized she wasn't speaking English at all. Latin? Regardless of what it was, I was perfectly able to follow along. Apparently the Astral Gallery had *accelerated linguistic osmosis* too. "Our emperor, back in the Eternal City at last!"

"His wife doesn't look so happy to see him," one of the other women snickered, sounding even tipsier—these ladies had clearly passed an amphora or two of wine around before all the festivities started.

"Is *any* woman when her husband's been away for months? Empress Sabina's no different!" They shrieked with laughter and kept pressing on toward the bridge, where a column of horses now pranced and trotted and tossed their heads in the descending showers of rose petals.

"Right." Sarah was looking around with a businesslike expression, and with a start I saw that the Astral Gallery had provided her with a costume change. Gone was the late-Victorian twill dress and the cameo pinned at her throat, replaced by a rust-red linen tunic and flat leather sandals and a string of Roman glass beads. I looked down at myself to see that I was still wearing Beau's blue moiré, which like the Gallerist's gabardine raincoat somehow attracted no stares in this crowd, but if we didn't look the part here, Sarah already did. She blended right in as though she'd been painted here. "I can get lost in a citywide party of thousands," she went on briskly, looking inside what had been her beaded Victorian handbag and was now a drawstring leather pouch—I could see that the wad of British pound notes inside had been replaced with a rattle of coins.

"Be careful," the Gallerist warned. "A world like this one has its sharp edges." At their nod, I saw the rows of slaves stumbling along behind the triumphant emperor, chained and terrified; heard the roar of what sounded like wild beasts in the nearby arena, probably locked in combat against spear-jabbing gladiators; saw sacrificial blood spilling crimson across the steps of the huge Doric temple. The dark ribbon of fear and violence running underneath all this gaudy imperial splendor.

"You sure you want to stay here?" I asked Sarah. "It might be the *Consummation of Empire*, but something tells me it's not the consummation of peace and equality." Another roar from the arena, and I wondered if a lion had just been slaughtered, or maybe had done the slaughtering. This place was starting to leave a bad taste in my mouth.

"Art doesn't exist to make you feel good," the Gallerist said as though reading my mind. "Art exists to make you think. Great art, now—it will often make you uncomfortable."

"Are you going to tell me to sit with that feeling?" Now that I was looking for it, I couldn't stop seeing the darker sides to the thousand different stories being told in this glittering spectacle all around me—the two boys tussling by a fountain over a toy barge, their tussle getting mean; the big Praetorian Guard almost out of sight behind the empress's throne who was staring at the parading emperor with a loathing so palpable it practically shimmered in the air like heat from a forge. "I should explore what it makes me feel?"

"You'll feel it whether you explore it or not," said the Gallerist. "That's the other thing great art does."

"Well, you two sit and feel things," Sarah said, sounding brisk again. "I'm off to hide in the crowd."

"If you're sure." The Gallerist frowned, looking down at their tablet, which had just lit up with a notification. "I've had a message from the Librarian; she's brought two more Patrons back to the Library for hiding, and now she's gotten *more* warning cards."

"More?" I blinked, disquieted. Even if she'd had to fend off a coalition of pissed-off slavers two hundred years ago, why hadn't the safeguards put in place since then worked better? What was happening here that the threats just kept coming?

"Whatever it is, I'm glad of it," Sarah said. "Makes it less likely Tyler can find me if there's a whole flock of us being moved around and muddying up the waters." And she disappeared into the throng of joyous Roman citizens without a backward glance.

"Goodbye and good luck to you too," I muttered, not able to stop from thinking that Sarah was being just a little heartless here. *Scared*, I reminded myself, *she's just scared*—but then a flash of blue caught my eye and I just stared.

A woman in a blue tunic, drifting along in the crowd oblivious to the parade or the delirious celebration all around her. A woman in blue, reading a scroll as she walked.

No, I thought. No, I was *not* seeing my mother here. Why would my mother ever show up in a Thomas Cole painting? I doubted she even knew who Thomas Cole was, any more than I did before hearing the Gallerist's little lecture. She wasn't here; it was my imagination. But my feet jerked me in the same direction anyway, after that mesmerizing spot of blue. Just a single step.

"Alix?" the Gallerist called, sounding distracted. "I think we must go back; there will be more Patrons to place."

I took a deep breath, willing myself not to go charging stupidly into the crowd again like I'd done in Conan Doyle's London. I'd fall under an elephant this time rather than into an opium den, and then the Librarian really would yank my Page status. My mother wasn't here. She *wasn't*. I was just imagining things. "Yes, let's go," I called, searching despite myself for one last glimpse of the woman in blue. Gone. "I'm ready."

11

"There you two are." The Librarian stood frowning at another pair of red warning cards as the Gallerist and I stepped out of the art book and back into the barrel-vaulted splendor of the Astral Library. Strange how it was already starting to feel homey to me—I headed right for the big oak counter where the blue Wedgwood teapot sat issuing the smell of hot, fresh-brewed Darjeeling, and poured myself a cup. That glimpse of my mother (*not my mother*, I reminded myself, sugaring up my tea) had rattled me more than I really wanted to admit. She'd been gone from my life for longer than she'd ever been in it; why couldn't I seem to escape the thought of her now, of all times? I took a long gulp of tea, feeling like a Freudian cliché.

"These next Patrons are staying in Jane Austen so that's where I'm off to next," the Librarian was saying, sweeping another reminder about the annual Board meeting off the oak surface into the trash with one dismissive arc of her hand. "And I've already retrieved *these* two, if you can take them and hide them?" Directing the Gallerist's attention to a pair of teenagers curled up in big chairs by the fireplace nook. Boy and girl, both black-haired and pinch-faced, brother and sister from the look of them.

"I can help," I said at once, putting down my cup, but the Gallerist was already addressing the Librarian.

"I'll take these two but I can't hide *all* your ducklings for you. This would go a lot more smoothly if you'd email the Programmer."

"Over my dead body will anyone email the Programmer," the Librarian stated.

"I know *you* won't. Which is why I already did."

"You backstabbing French cretin—" the Librarian began, overrunning my inquiry of "Who's the Programmer?"

The Gallerist cut us both off with an indescribable and very French gesture that involved shoulder and wrist and a flick of the chin all at once. "We need help with more than hiding Patrons. These cards—" Pointing at the latest two squares of red. "There is something off. The attack two hundred years ago, it didn't happen this way. It should have come by now—why do you simply keep getting more and more warnings?"

The same thing that had bothered me, and from the crease in the Librarian's brow, it was bothering her too. "Perhaps they have tried to attack, whoever *they* are, and failed," she said, more to herself than either of us. "The safeguards we put in place two centuries ago must be holding."

"Then why do you keep getting warnings?" I asked. "Why is nothing else happening? What are they waiting for?"

Whoever *they* were. Was it really a coalition of angry spouses and partners and parents? Or something else?

"I need to check a few things," the Librarian said, black eyes flicking down some invisible list. "I need to test the wards, the margins. But my Jane Austen Patrons—"

"They can wait an hour," said the Gallerist. "You're exhausted—I know how margin-travel takes it out of you. Let the Library restore you for an hour, and use the time to check the wards and margins. Check *everything*." The Librarian opened her mouth to argue, shut it with a scowl. "An hour," the Gallerist said persuasively, and I had to admire just how deftly they were handling the Librarian. If I had a centuries-long friendship like this one, would someone come to know me that well? "Your Jane Austen Patrons will be safe for another hour, *je t'assure*. The clock would be chiming at us and the books would be panicking if anyone was truly getting close."

"I can help," I said again, straightening.

"She can," the Gallerist agreed with a smile. *"Alix est très serviable."*

I stood there trying to look whatever *serviable* was. "I can help you check these wards, whatever they are. Or retrieve your Patrons from *Pride and Prejudice*, or wherever they're staying in Austenland—"

"I do not need you traipsing unattended through the works of Jane Austen, Miss Watson. I do not need you *underfoot*." The Librarian waved an irritated hand, barely seeing me. "I need to think. I need to see what I'm missing here."

The Gallerist stepped forward, casting a glance at the nervous-looking brother and sister. "Let me settle these two, then—"

"Yes, yes. Stash them away somewhere safe. And Alix, go—do something. Do something somewhere *else*. Just give me an hour. I need to think," she muttered again, and began to rummage under the big oak counter.

The Gallerist drew me off with a whisper, before I could feel more than a smidgen of hurt at being sent out of the way like an underfoot toddler. "Leave her be for an hour. She'll drill down on this attack, who's behind it, and probably have it solved by the time you come back."

"Should I come to the Gallery with you, help you settle those two?"

"Something tells me they will take longer than an hour to place. Siblings, they never agree on anything." The Gallerist arched an eyebrow at the dark-haired brother and sister, who were having a hissed argument in Spanish. "I would wait here—just keep yourself busy and out of her way." A smiling look at my blue gown. "Don't you need a different costume, if you're headed to Austen next?"

They had a point. "At least your Gallery does free costume changes," I muttered, heading for the Wardrobe Department's crowded racks.

"The Astral Gallery didn't have their budget slashed by five percent at every annual Board meeting for the past six years," the Librarian called back testily over her shoulder.

"Just give her an hour to work her magic," the Gallerist repeated to me, probably not being metaphorical about the *magic* part, and headed toward the two teenage Patrons who were now looking decidedly worried. "Come along, ducklings . . ."

I hesitated, looking at the costume racks. As usual, nothing to fit me. I bit my lip, looking at the Librarian now rummaging among a stack of ledgers at the oak counter. "I'll be back soon," I said, making a decision. "An hour—" But I doubt she heard me as I disappeared back out into the Boston Public Library.

"Czarina?" Beau blinked, opening the door of Brummell's. "Back already?"

Right. It felt like about three weeks had passed since I'd been here getting fitted in my blue gown, but from Beau's point of view it had been less than twenty-four hours. Enough time had passed in the various book worlds while margin-traveling (not to mention my time in the Astral Gallery, and I had no idea how fast or slow time passed there) that I'd emerged into the Boston Public Library about midmorning the day after I'd last entered it. "Hi," I said, out of breath from jogging three blocks in all that blue moiré. "I need to swap this out for a different dress."

"Don't tell me something's wrong with that one. That dress is one of my finest creations and you are gorgeous in it."

"No, no, nothing's wrong with it. The, um, costume party I was going to? My friend called and said they've changed themes." I managed a rueful chuckle, a little eye roll. "It's Jane Austen–themed now. Can I swap this dress out on my original IOU? And can it be quick?" I added, checking the clock on the wall.

He scrubbed a hand over his face, waving me inside the shop. He was still in the same clothes I'd seen him in last—the taut breeches, the brocade vest, the billowy-sleeved shirt—and there was a crease on his cheek as though he'd dozed off with his head on his sewing table. "Sure. Okay. Regency, got plenty of stuff in that line in back . . ."

"I'm sorry," I said, belatedly registering his weariness. He was what, a month from the movie premiere of *Belle*? He didn't have time to be catering to someone like me who wasn't even a *close* friend, much less a rich client or one of his usual glamorous posse with endless legs and *y*'s in their names. "Look, I shouldn't have bothered you. I can get a costume somewhere else." I wasn't sure where, but I was really just killing time anyway. Giving the Librarian space to *work her magic*.

"Over my dead body are you getting some rayon-blend horror off Amazon." He was already heading to the back, wheeling a bulging rack out from the wall. "Teal velvet, no . . . white muslin, authentic but simplistic . . ."

"How do you have so much stuff in my size?" I couldn't help asking, as he threw a yellow voile gown across the nearest table, nixed a black velvet, looked consideringly at a printed silk organza. Because in my experience, being a size 22 meant you got the dregs when it came to clothing options.

"I costumed a body positivity–themed *Pride and Prejudice* in college," he said. "All different figures to work with; taught me a lot about dressing people outside your standard double-zero models. No pay, but I got to keep the best of the costumes." Holding a red velvet spencer up against me consideringly.

"You made all these by hand?" I rubbed the velvet between my fingers. "Just you?"

"Everything in this shop is by me. Someday I'll have a team: embroiderers, seamstresses, clerks, but for now . . ."

"When do you sleep?" I joked.

"What's sleep? You want red-carpet commissions before you're thirty, you gotta hustle." He cast a glance at the sheeted dress form that came close to loathing. "I haven't slept more than five hours a night since I was about fifteen and getting into historical fashion design, but for the last month, I swear it's been more like two hours a night."

"And here I thought it was all those glamorous parties that put the circles under your eyes," I teased, stepping up onto the dressmaker's dais. "You and your influencer friends in all those Instagram reels, all the VIP tables and bottles of Cristal . . ."

"You want to know what those parties are really like?" He pulled the measuring tape from around his neck and passed it around my ribs, measuring a Regency waistline. "I get waved under the velvet rope at ten p.m., snap a few pics at the VIP table for Insta because the shop account needs social media content, bolt half a glass max of that Cristal, and then duck out. I upload everything to Instagram and TikTok in the Uber on the way home, and by ten forty-five I'm back to embroidering crystal stars on gauze for some socialite dressing as Arwen for her boyfriend's *LOTR* birthday bash." Holding up a swatch by my face. "I don't have *time* for parties, Alix. I just make it look like I do on social media."

"So when do you finally get to"—I looked around at the shop and all its glittering signs of success—"enjoy all this?"

"Hell if I know." That cynical tilted smile again, his hands stilling briefly against my waist where he had the tape overlapped. "Maybe after *Belle* . . . In the meantime, don't believe everything you see on my Instagram feed. Or anybody's Instagram feed. Perfectly curated bullshit, most of it. Now, some proper Regency stays, nothing will hang right without the correct underpinnings . . ."

Twenty minutes and I was transformed: fine muslin in pale lavender skimming over my hips, one of those little rib-hugging spencer jackets in deeper indigo, matching reticule, a straw bonnet with broad blue-violet ribbons and cream feathers curled around the crown. I'd never thought Regency was a good look on anyone who wasn't wand slim, but Beau laced and pinned until the fit was perfect, and I couldn't resist a delighted grin as I gazed at myself in the mirror. I looked like I'd stepped out of *Pride and Prejudice*, ready to promenade Bond Street and go for an ice at Gunter's. I looked like I matched Beau, in his impeccable breeches and waistcoat. He'd always looked so impossibly glamorous to me that he might as well have been a different species—now, framed by the mirror, we looked like a *Bridgerton* spin-off.

"When I was a kid I liked to think about past lives. Who had I been, what had I looked like, what had I worn . . ." Beau's voice was warm on my shoulder; he stood behind me adjusting the angle of my bonnet. "Trying on a historical outfit is about the closest we can get to walking back in time, I always thought."

Oh, honey, no, I thought, wishing I could tell him about margin-traveling. He'd have swooned for all those seaside muslins in *Dracula*, the lace-swagged dinner gowns in *Jane Eyre*, the feather-laden hats in *Sherlock Holmes*. I glanced at the clock and saw that I had twenty minutes to get back to the Astral Library in time to make my hour deadline—but still couldn't resist tilting my head to watch the feathers on my bonnet dance. This place had its own ability to hold time in place, freeze a beautiful moment in a mirror so you longed to stay inside it forever. "Maybe I was a Regency viscountess in a past life," I mused.

"And maybe I was one of Beau Brummell's dandies." I could hear the smile in his voice. "Maybe we waltzed at Almack's—"

"And scandalized the ton?"

"Look at you with the Regency slang." He grinned, watching me transfer my few belongings—*Dawn Treader* paperback, a few odds and ends—from the blue moiré handbag to the indigo-weave Regency reticule now hanging at my wrist. "I thought you were a fantasy girl through and through."

"Listen, I read everything. I think Jane Austen could have stuck in a few dragons to liven things up, but that doesn't mean I haven't read—Whoops," I added as the crumpled bumper sticker from my childhood bedroom door slipped out of my hand mid-transfer.

Beau picked it up. "*'They Got the Library at Alexandria—They Aren't Getting Mine'*?"

"My mom's," I said, smoothing it out as I took it back. "From when she was a library page . . . Pretty much the only thing of hers she left me when she skipped town."

"Where is she now?"

A shrug. "I don't really know. Last time I saw her she was headed for LA." I wasn't counting random hallucinations in Cole paintings or Conan Doyle stories.

"I'm sorry," Beau said simply.

I shrugged again. Like any foster kid I'd had The Dream: the fantasy that whatever loser parent threw you to the mercies of the system, they'd finally clean their act up—ditch their taste for bad boyfriends or slot machines or meth—and swoop back into your life with hugs and apologies, home-cooked meals and parent-teacher conferences and good-night kisses, forever and ever amen. For me that dream had been dead a long time. Random hallucinations aside, my last maternal sighting had been her handwriting on a card arriving two weeks after my thirteenth birthday: *Love you heaps, see you soon!* And that was it. I'd made a few attempts to look her up over the years—searched for her name on social media, reached out to those of her old friends I could still remember—but only hit dead ends. Either she'd changed her name or fallen off the map. Or died . . . which gave me such a queasy feeling, all I could do was shove it away, hard.

It doesn't matter where she is now, I reminded myself, stuffing the bumper sticker into my reticule. *Alive or dead, she never chose you. But the Astral Library did.* "Thanks for letting me swap dresses, Beau. Do I owe you a cleaning fee for the other dress?" I asked, hoping he'd say no. The grip Libby Bibb probably still had on all my bank cards . . .

"Discount me a free hour when you do my data entry." Beau examined the hem on the moiré gown where it lay folded over a chair, and I cringed—I'd tried to be careful, but margin-traveling through fictional worlds could be a grubby business. "You said you hadn't gone to your costume party yet—but I'm seeing mud spatters here, and it didn't even rain yesterday."

"I'm sorry—"

He waved that away. "Historical clothing replicas are for having fun in, not sticking in a glass case. I'm just wondering what kind of night you had that this dress came back twelve hours later with mud spatters, orange dust—this is *country* dust, not Boston dust"—I thought of *Tom Sawyer* and those Missouri roads; the stone dust I'd picked up from Thomas Cole's ancient Rome—"and seawater droplets," Beau finished, pointing out dried salt residue where ocean spray from the pier at Bram Stoker's Whitby had splashed my hem. "Where did you go last night, czarina?"

It was pure impulse—mad, crazy impulse born of the fact that I couldn't explain, couldn't stay (fifteen minutes now to get back to the Library!), couldn't do anything but duck his very reasonable question. And maybe it was because for once I didn't look like I belonged to a different species from Beau. I stood on tiptoe, placed my hands on his impeccably garbed shoulders, and brushed my lips to that curious, beautiful mouth.

"Beau Sato-Jones," I said once I pulled back. "I truly, sincerely, honestly wish I could tell you."

"Alix! There you are, I've been worried about you. Are you sure you're—" Elizabeth, my BPL boss (ex-boss?), broke off mid-sentence, blinking through her purple-framed glasses at the sight of my Regency finery. "Did you change *again*?"

"Afraid I can't talk right now." I'd managed to duck Library Security on my way back into the BPL—Chester and his aviator shades were off duty, leaving his counterpart Chad at the security desk, and Chad wouldn't get off his ass unless you lit it on fire or took his Cheez Whiz away. I tried to steer around Elizabeth into the barrel-vaulted hush of the Reading Room—my hour deadline to return to the Astral Library was ticking down to the last minute, and I couldn't help fearing the Librarian had already left me behind to go margin-traveling again—but my former boss about-faced and came along with me, brows creasing.

"Are you sure you're all right, Alix? The way you're coming and going outside of your work hours, and these costumes—"

"Jane Austen party!" I said brightly, swinging my reticule. "You know Chad didn't even notice this getup? HR has *got* to hire some better Library Security than Chad and Chester; you know people call them Tweedledum and Tweedledumber?" I called them that, anyway. Chester had not been amused. Chad just didn't get it. "Really, you don't have to worry about me. I'm totally fine, right as rain. Just off to my Austen party, so—"

"You know, that's one writer I've somehow never gotten around to reading." Elizabeth shuffled a clipboard, a walkie-talkie, and a stack of paperwork in her tattooed arm, still not looking 100 percent convinced at my sudden reversal into good cheer. "I've seen the *Pride and Prejudice* movie, of course—"

"Elizabeth," I groaned. "Seeing the movie doesn't count. And she wrote other things besides *Pride and Prejudice!*"

"I never remember what. *Emma*? Wasn't there a movie of that too?"

I could practically hear the Librarian sniffing, *Really, is that what a library degree is worth these days?* "Must dash," I said, picking up my pace, ignoring all the stares from the Reading Room studiers at my feathered bonnet and muslin skirts. I wondered if all those eyes could see the mark of a man's hand at the back of my waist, because I could practically still feel it burning there: as brief as the kiss I'd planted on Beau had been, he'd had time to caress one lean, long-fingered hand across the small of my back—no hero on the cover of a seventies Avon romance novel could have done it better. I'd kissed the most beautiful man I'd ever met, and he'd kissed me back. My smile was so wide I probably looked deranged; no wonder Elizabeth still seemed concerned.

"Alix, if you need help—"

I sucked in a gasp, looking over her shoulder. "That man over there, he is pulling his pants down; is he trying to urinate on the books?"

"Wait, what?" Maybe my boss was a little vague on Jane Austen's backlist, but she was *not* putting up with anybody defiling her territory. She whipped around and went straight into a jog, neck craning over her walkie-talkie. "Library Security, someone get Library Security—"

The minute her back turned I dove for the bookshelves and fumbled for my Library card. It wasn't the same set of shelves I'd originally traveled through, but the door obligingly opened up anyway—even as Elizabeth was hissing, "Chad, get *up here!*" into her walkie-talkie behind me—and all but yanked me inside.

Where I walked into a fight.

In the big leather armchair nearest the oak counter, the Gallerist sat with long black-booted legs crossed, looking supremely amused. The Librarian stood nose to nose with a new arrival, shouting her head off.

"—miserable condescending tech-head *booby*—"

"*Nafasam*," the man intoned, clapping a hand over his heart. "You wound me."

"Don't you *nafasam* me," the Librarian snarled, jabbing a finger into his chest. She nearly had to go up on tiptoe to do it; the man was over a head taller than she was. Tall, Black, burly, stubble silvering along his jawline, decrepit jeans and a *Star Trek: Next Generation* T-shirt.

"That's the Programmer," the Gallerist called over to me, sipping from another of those robin's-egg-blue Wedgwood cups. "Don't worry, they shout like this every time they meet. *Un petit gâteau sec?*" Waving an elegant hand at the tray on the counter.

"Thanks." I swiped a cookie off the plate, melting at the taste of fresh-baked shortbread—the Library nixed any sensation of hunger or need to eat the moment you passed through its doorway into astral limbo, but it still provided such a nice line of snacks. You didn't need to be hungry when you curled up with a book to want a cup of tea and a plate of something tasty, after all. You just needed a book, and then the Library thoughtfully provided the tea and the tasties. This particular bit of tasty was lemon-lavender shortbread, utterly delicious and piping hot like it had come right out of the oven, and I wondered briefly where the Astral Library did all this baking. Did lemon-lavender shortbread just magic itself out of the ether, or was there a tiny kitchen somewhere staffed by more ghosts? Were there culinary ghosts just as there were book ghosts, baking their way through all the cookbooks they hadn't had time to try while still alive? I put that thought away for the more urgent matter at hand. "Has the Librarian checked the, um, wards? The safeguards?" She'd said she needed time to think, to drill down on what exactly was threatening her Patrons. "What did she find out?"

"Look, love," the man in the *Star Trek* T-shirt said, breaking into the Librarian's diatribe before the Gallerist could answer my question. His accent was English, leaning toward Cockney rather than BBC. "Much as I enjoy trading insults, I've got a defrag I should get back to. Unless you need my help?"

She just gave him a withering look.

"You do, don't you?" He grinned, ruffling a hand over the back of his head, and caught sight of me for the first time. "And since when did you pick up a mini-me, Shahrzad?"

"Your name is Shahrzad?" I asked at the same time the Librarian snapped, "She is not a mini-me, she is my *Page*, and I haven't acquired her, I simply can't scrape her *off*," and the Programmer laughed as he came to envelop my palm in his. "You hide people in . . . video games?" I ventured a guess, shaking his hand. First an Astral Library, then an Astral Gallery, then—What? An Astral Server? An Astral CPU?

"Bang on," he said, sounding cheerful. "Fancy being a wench baking sweet rolls in *Skyrim* or a sorceress slinging spells in *The Witcher*, I'm your man."

"I'm picking up a couple of Patrons living in *Sense and Sensibility* and *Sanditon*," the Librarian said witheringly. "I doubt they want to hide out in *The Witcher*."

"I'll tuck 'em into *Ever, Jane*," he said cheerfully. "What, you think Austen fans don't game?"

"*Ever, Jane* closed down during the pandemic," the Gallerist observed, crunching through another bar of shortbread.

"Not in AGNIS, it didn't—"

"Agnes?" I asked, lost.

"AGNIS. Astral Gaming Network Interspace System," he explained.

"Trust a tech-head to require an unnecessarily complicated acronym," sniffed the Librarian.

"Trust a Luddite not to move with the times—"

They were off and sniping again, and I turned back to the Gallerist. "That brother and sister who were here when I left—"

"Tucked into a lovely little Van Gogh café," the Gallerist reassured me. "They'll be safe until they can return to their books."

"Are they going to want to go back to their books?" A question that had been preying on me since resettling Stephanie and Sarah and Larry in their various paintings. "If their husbands or parents or whoever they're running from have proved they can *find* them in their books, aren't they going to want new ones?" Or to leave the Library altogether . . .

"That will be up to them," the Gallerist said simply. "We can offer sanctuary to our Patrons—and protection—but not miracles."

"Do not make me Shush you," the Librarian was snapping up at the Programmer, who clapped a hand to his heart as if stabbed.

"Don't invoke the Shush, Shahrzad. Not with the books already scared." The Programmer glanced upward toward the volumes still flapping around the ceiling, and I could have sworn I saw the green glass windows shiver in their panes at the *S*-word, which was very much capitalized in the way he delivered it. I had no idea what a shush did here, but I wasn't sure I wanted to find out. It's terrifying enough when an ordinary librarian shushes you, much less the Astral Librarian.

"I have work to do and Patrons to rescue, so if you wouldn't mind Control-Alt-Deleting yourself back to your defrag—"

"Alt-F4, thank you very much. If you have any Patrons you need me to hide—"

"You are not stashing any of my Patrons in one of your bloodthirsty game worlds. Please find somewhere nice and *tame* to hide them, where they won't get their heads swacked off by sword-happy paladins—"

"You didn't always disapprove of my bloodthirsty game worlds, Shahrzad. In fact, I remember a certain weekend I took you to the West Weald in *Elder Scrolls IV* and you had too much Argonian Bloodwine and took a hand ax to—"

"Not. Relevant," the Librarian gritted out.

"Or what about that little getaway to *Assassin's Creed Odyssey*; is that not relevant either? You, me, the lemon-scented breezes, sun rising romantically over the Parthenon. The sunburn on your—"

"Don't you dare!"

"Not to mention the mosquito bites on my—"

"Hey!" I raised my voice, and they both cut off, looking over at me. I drew a deep breath and addressed the Librarian. "What did you find out about who's behind all this? Checking the safeguards, the—" I waved an encompassing hand. "Everything. What's happening? Who's mounting the attack?"

The Librarian's snappishness faded like mist; she took off her rectangular glasses and pinched the bridge of her nose. "I don't know."

"You don't?" She was the Gandalf, the Aslan, the Glinda. She was supposed to know everything.

"The wards are intact. The safeguards are in place. No book worlds have been intruded upon, no attempts have come against the Library itself. Just more of those." Indicating the red cards scattered across the big oak counter.

I tried to wrap my head around that. "Has there been any explanation from the Library Board?"

"Another notification about the annual meeting." The Librarian nodded at another crumpled ball of paper on the oak counter. "Nothing else."

"Isn't that odd?"

The Gallerist spoke up. "Not necessarily. My Gallery Board is always behind the time; they might as well be a collection of Fourth Dynasty mummies." A very cynical, very French snort. "And since when have you ever heard of a Board of Anything that was useful in a crisis?"

Valid point, but my unease was rising and I could see theirs was too—the Librarian's, the Gallerist's, the Programmer's. "I—I suppose it's good there's been no attack," I said, trying to find the silver lining. "Gives us time to dig them out, whoever *they* are—"

That was the moment another red card shot out of the book-drop slot next to the big oak counter. Instead of dropping to the floor the way the first one had, it shot across the room directly toward me. I threw a hand out to bat it away, but it slashed across the side of my palm before finally spinning to land below the huge globe in its bronze stand. I stared at the side of my hand, which now beaded blood from a paper cut. A deep, nasty one, like the edges of that blood-dark card had been sharpened.

"Um." I held up my hand, trying very hard not to drip on Beau's pristine muslin confection of a gown. "Are we sure these red cards are actually warnings?"

The Librarian looked at me, her dark brows winging upward. "I beg your pardon?"

"I mean, do we really know if they're warning us about the problem, or if they *are* the problem?"

"As long as they are informing us of Patrons potentially in danger, our foremost priority must remain fixed."

"But—"

"Tell me, Miss Watson, is *sanctuary* a word you take lightly?" Her question wasn't rhetorical; she asked it and then stood waiting for an answer. I opened my mouth, then closed it again. "I do not take it lightly," she continued when it became clear I wasn't going to reply. "In centuries past, the offer of sanctuary meant safety—from being forcibly removed, from bodily harm, from death. That is what I offered you when you arrived here. That is what I offer any soul who comes through Library doors. Someone—we do not know who, we do not know why, we do not know how—is trying to violate the Library's sanctuary and endanger those under its protection." Her dark eyes behind their rectangular glasses glinted. "I am the Librarian. I can do *nothing else* until they are made safe."

"But—"

"I want as badly as you to know who is behind this and what they are planning. But any Patrons being threatened must be secured first. In other words, Miss Watson, when a shark attacks a cove full of swimmers, you must get the swimmers safely out of the water before taking on the shark."

She looked so imperturbable, this little woman with her gray bun and her sensible shoes and her tablet, that I felt instantly foolish. Maybe she didn't know absolutely everything that was going on here, but she was still the Gandalf, the Aslan, the Glinda. I'd read enough fantasy to know that if you're on a quest and you *aren't* the grumpy elder with the magic and the centuries of experience, it's better to shut up and pay attention to the person who is. "Hear, hear," I mumbled, just like Bilbo Baggins to Gandalf.

"We've dawdled long enough," the Librarian announced, giving another withering glare to the Programmer, who just linked his arms behind his head and grinned at her. "We've already got stops to make in *Sense and Sensibility* and *Sanditon*, now another in . . ." Inspecting the new card, which the Gallerist had fished out from under the globe and handed over. "Goodness, *Wuthering Heights*. Come along, Miss Watson."

"Take care of her, eh?" the Programmer said softly to me as the Librarian went rummaging in a new book to find our entry point. His grin had faded to something more serious. "Shahrzad plays it cool, but margin-traveling is a lot more exhausting than it looks. She's about done in."

I wanted a moment to think about that, because all around me the Library was showing signs of unease: the books weren't full-out panicking and flying off their shelves but they were rustling uneasily; the huge globe was spinning in its stand and the moving seas engraved on its sphere were roiling in bronze storms; the old-fashioned paper cutter had raised its long arm and was chopping downward over and over in an ominous rhythm. *Chop. Chop. Chop.* It sounded like a guillotine. I wanted a moment to pause, to *think*, but I didn't get one. The Librarian threw down the book in her hands and stepped into it, I grabbed her elbow, and once again we were off—to one last ominous, crunching sweep of the paper cutter.

Chop.

12

The red cards were finding us faster. One swirled down on us from the roof of the Delaford house in *Sense and Sensibility*, slicing the back of my neck as I stood in the front drive with a series of ladies in Regency frocks twirling their parasols and waiting for the footmen to bring out picnic hampers. "Ow—" I managed, barely, not to swear, slapping my neck as though a wasp had stung it.

"Are you quite well, Miss Watson?" asked a kindly looking girl I was pretty sure was Elinor Dashwood. "Perhaps the air is too cold—"

"Elinor is always believing everyone too cold." Her sister Marianne laughed, looking so incredibly young and flyaway with her lively little face and sunburned nose that I couldn't believe she'd be getting married at the end of this book. She didn't look mature enough to lead the revolution in a YA dystopian novel, much less get married. "Take care, or she will be fitting you with a flannel waistcoat like some old graybeard, and dosing you for every species of ailment that can afflict the old and feeble!"

"Miss Watson is hardly old and feeble, Marianne," her sister chided. "She is six-and-twenty—"

Marianne's blink clearly said that anyone of six-and-twenty had one foot in the glue factory and the other in the grave, but I headed her off before she could deal my ego any blows by saying so. "I'm quite all right, Miss Dashwood, Miss Marianne," I said, tucking the red card behind my back, and though I'd been hoping to angle a private word with Elinor Dashwood and tell her it was really a little early to start writing herself off as a hopeless old maid at nineteen, I extricated myself and beelined for the Librarian, who was busy with a middle-aged Patron who'd been inserted into the Austen party as one of the Jennings' cousins. I'd barely handed the red card over before another spun through on the wake of a messenger arriving on horseback (I was pretty sure we'd arrived at the part of the book where Colonel Brandon gets bad news and the Delaford picnic is canceled) and this card managed to nick the Librarian across one temple, opening another paper cut.

"Was that one aiming for your *eye*?" I hissed as all the Regency ladies (who had of course missed the card) fluttered around the messenger in a sea of muslins and fringed shawls, Colonel Brandon looked grim, and the plot went on unfolding right behind us.

"It's just a warning card, Miss Watson. It's not sentient." But her brows were drawn tight as we pulled our newest Patron between us around the side of the house and prepared for another margin jump.

"My poor nerves just can't take this," the woman in peach voile and straw bonnet moaned, sagging against me. "If either of you has any smelling salts—"

"Oh, buck up," I snapped, batting her lace parasol out of my eye.

"You weren't actually born in the Regency period, so don't expect a goddamn fainting couch."

"Bitch," she said, sounding suddenly a lot more modern.

"Call me all the names you want, just pick up your feet!"

Three more red cards found us on the seafront promenade in *Sanditon*, where the Librarian collected an elegant fortyish Black woman in jonquil-yellow muslin taking the air in a fashionable barouche, and I picked up three more serious paper cuts and a flutter of foreboding in my gut that would not be stamped out. The damn woman from *Sense and Sensibility* wouldn't stop whining, those cards wouldn't stop coming, and the pretty seaside expanse that was Sanditon looked thin around the edges as if the book world was starting to fray. "Nothing's *fraying*," the Librarian said when I ventured as much. "If it looks less fleshed out, that's because *Sanditon* is an incomplete book. Austen died before she wrote more than a fragment, so don't go getting our Patrons in a panic thinking that their book worlds are breaking down."

That only soothed my disquiet a little, because the Librarian looked so *weary*—by the time we took our newest pair back to the Library, my unease had racheted clear up past my stomach and into my throat. The Gallerist took the whiner and led her off with soothing pats and a lot of talk about taking a country weekend in a Leighton painting; the *Sanditon* woman took one look at the Programmer and drawled, "Honey, I'll go wherever you want." Leaving me the only one on scene to observe the way the Librarian gripped the oak counter for balance, and the way the long emerald-green windows seemed to have darkened like the circles under her eyes. If the Library was attacked now, I didn't lay good odds on her being able to withstand it. Whatever *it* turned out to be.

"You need to rest," I said, and got a bracing look.

"Not with four more Patrons to find and protect." The Librarian glanced at her next card, then at my little spencer jacket and bonnet. "It's cold where we're going; do you want a cloak from Wardrobe?"

"I'll be fine," I said, really wanting to say *Stop*. Because the Library globe was spinning faster on its axis and the paper cutter's lethally long arm was still rising and falling with a guillotine-like *chop chop chop*, but my uneasily thrumming fear wasn't any match for steely, centuries-long determination, and before I could blink we had fallen onto a crossroads under a lowering gray sky. A stone pillar loomed where the dusty road branched, and the way my nerves were twanging I half expected to see a dead body splayed under it, but there was only a series of worn, carved letters on each rough-hewn side. "That way," the Librarian said, taking off down the road indicated simply *WH*. The tablet had done its work again; her green cardigan had become a fur-lined green traveling cloak over a Regency walking dress and sturdy boots. "Pick up the pace. It's a fair walk to Wuthering Heights from here."

Wonderful, a gothic novel. Just the thing when you're already feeling edgy. *Don't* you *start reaching for your smelling salts, Alix Watson*, I scolded myself, heading after the Librarian and wishing I'd grabbed a cloak after all. I had no idea what time of day it might be here; the clouds rolled overhead low and charcoal colored without so much as a stray beam of sun; the moors unfolded all around us in a patchwork of distant crags, sullen brooks, tangled bracken, and stunted trees that seemed to cringe from the cold, biting wind. I'd read *Wuthering Heights* as a teenager and never thought it was particularly romantic—not the ambience, not the house, not Heathcliff, who let's be honest was a stack of red flags in a frock coat rather than any kind of worthy book boyfriend—and now that I was *in* the book, the general atmosphere was not improving my teenage opinion. Shivering in my spencer, I wondered what Beau would make of all this. *Give me Almack's,* I could almost hear him say, *Almack's and a quadrille and some Regent's punch.* Right now I agreed with him—especially when I saw another red card sailing out of the sky.

I halted right where I was in the middle of the road, watching it arc downward. "This is wrong. This is all wrong. We are in the middle of nowhere"—batting the card to the ground before it could slice down the Librarian's arm—"with these things spitting at us like darts, and—"

She picked up the card and kept going. "We are not in the middle of nowhere, we are in the middle of Emily Brontë's nowhere, which means Wuthering Heights is just that way."

"This cannot feel right to you!" I cried.

"Miss Watson—"

Another card came down, only this one didn't drift or even arc—it *sliced,* coming sideways in a vicious whistle, straight at my face. I threw up my arm but it dodged, that goddamn thing *dodged,* and as I dazedly raised my fingers to my cheek, I felt the long cut down the side of my face from temple to chin.

The Librarian broke off, staring at me. Still numb, I picked the card up in trembling fingertips and flipped it over, showing her. It was blank, no Patron's name, no book details. Just a razor-edged warning with my blood on it.

And suddenly I heard a thrum like a thousand papery wings, just as I whispered, "I think this is a trap."

The red storm whirled out of the dark sky like a cloud of blood-colored card-stock birds. Thousands of them. I had time for one shout before they were on me, slicing, darting, pecking. *They're just cards,* I couldn't help thinking stupidly, *cards from a card catalog*—but these were swirling around me like hungry shrikes. Dots of blood welled on the backs of my hands as I swatted and batted; sharp edges slashed my legs through my thin muslin skirts. Beau's beautiful hand-embroidered hems, slashed to ribbons in a matter of seconds; my plumed bonnet pushed back off my head and then the exquisite agony of my scalp being pricked by a thousand needle-sharp points.

I tried to run, but my foot caught in a tangle of bracken and I fell to my knees. I tried to crawl but there was nowhere to crawl to—we were trapped out here on this vast menacing moor, not a soul in sight, nowhere to shelter, no one to help. I batted about me wildly, opening my mouth to shout again, and a card flew straight between my teeth. It sliced the corners of my mouth and then the inside of my cheek with a taste like iron and ink, and I just snapped. Half choking and half screaming, trying to bite down on the fluttering thing, trying to wrap my arms around my head, trying to *run*—

And then I felt the Librarian's hands swatting them off me, felt the softness of fur-lined wool as she pushed me down, crouched over me, and swirled her cloak over us both. The drum of papery wings receded and my ears roared; I spat out the crumpled remnants of the card still squirming half alive between my teeth like a paper rat, and gasped in the sudden darkness. The Librarian's body blocked out the light; her cloak shielded us both. But that horrific paper storm was still roiling; I could feel the winces go through her as the cards flew at her, slicing and tearing at her cloak.

I don't want this, something in me wailed, *I didn't sign up for this*— but hadn't I? I'd wanted an adventure, and adventures had teeth. I'd gone off the edges of the map to where the warning said, *Here There Be Monsters*, and like any stupid girl in a book I'd paid no heed. No one ever does, because we all think the book is about us and the monsters will eat someone else. A card found its way under the edge of the Librarian's cloak and zipped across my ankle, drawing blood, and I couldn't hold back a helpless, snarling sob of pain.

Pressed above me, the Librarian exhaled. "Well, shit," she said, surprisingly calm considering the circumstances. "I was hoping I wouldn't have to do this."

She drew a long breath in as though bracing for a gale, and then she rose so quickly I tumbled onto my back in the moorland grass. The Librarian threw her arms wide as she straightened, scattering the red cards, her cloak rippling out like wings on either side—and I stopped trying to shield my face and just stared.

Her cloak flared upward, and just kept flaring. Up, up, and the green woolen folds suddenly had a jeweled glitter as they extended and lengthened, as her short plump figure lengthened with it and her tablet fell to the ground. The edge of her skirt narrowed and whipped like a tail—because it *was* a tail, I observed stupidly, and that wasn't a cloak flapping anymore, it was *wings*. Her long inhale became a deafening, bone-rattling roar, and the cyclone of scarlet cards bunched together in the air like frightened birds. A mistake, because she launched herself straight for them. In the split second it took for her wings to propel her off the ground, I saw the final vestiges of the Librarian fade away—her matronly brogues splitting into gleaming claws, the soft wrinkles of her neck undulating into glittering emerald scales—and a great green dragon took to the sky.

She tore through the cloud of red cards like an unholy maelstrom, jaws snapping, claws flying. Scarlet shreds of card stock winnowed down like blood rain, and I forgot I was bleeding from a hundred paper cuts as I watched her wheel and shriek and roar in the sky overhead.

But those little red bastards re-formed and swirled, what was left of them, and they dive-bombed her in all directions. Too many of them, too many and too small—the dragon's head slewed to one side as a storm of cards arrowed straight for her eyes, and then all the grass in a hundred-foot radius flattened as she buffeted higher in a couple of wingbeats and let out a shriek that echoed across the entire moor. My hair blew back from my face, my hands clapped to my deafened ears, and the cards scattered this time instead of bunching. The dragon wheeled and dove, straight for me, and I couldn't help it—I screamed. Trust me, it's what you do when a dragon dives right at you like a missile.

A sudden hush. My ears ringing. My eyes watering as I forced them open. The green dragon crouched on the flattened grass, one wing lowered in my direction like a ladder, golden eyes fixed on me . . . still framed, I saw with a jolt, by prim rectangular glasses.

"Grab my tablet, will you?" said the Librarian.

So many thoughts jumbling in my mind, so many words fighting to get free, and somehow the ones that spilled out first were "How on earth are you still wearing glasses?"

"Because I'm nearsighted in *any* form, Miss Watson." *You idiot*, her tone implied. "Hop on, will you? We haven't got all day."

I was bleeding, I was terrified, my heart was hammering as I ran to scoop up her fallen tablet and heard the papery hiss of the cards gathering in the air overhead. But terrified or not, it was with the fierce smile of a long dream wakened that I gathered my shredded skirts and scrambled (a little girl scrambled, a little girl whose mother had left her behind with a crumpled bumper sticker and a paperback book and a dream of all-capital-letters ESCAPE) onto the dragon's back. I hung on for dear life as those wings beat on either side and the Librarian launched into the air, endless moors falling away beneath us as I shouted, "Fly, *fly*, FLY!"

13

There I was. Flying. On a dragon. *Flying*, those great green wings beating steadily to either side of me, the wind raking through my hair as Emily Brontë's brooding moors fell away beneath us. At first I saw villages dotting the landscape below, white-ribbon strips of road, distant towns sketching the horizon . . . And then it all seemed to fade away somehow, and we were flying over a vast, undulating landscape stretching out changelessly in all directions. Not ocean; the ripples below were ivory pale. Not sand; the lines were too straight to be dunes. Then the entire landscape *folded* beneath us, rolling over like an endless wave, and I realized it was a page turning. A page in the book of the world, or the book between worlds, or the book that held all the worlds.

"Margin-traveling," the Librarian said beneath me, her smoky-pitched voice carrying through the wind without any difficulty at all since it was now resonating through the cavern of a huge scaly chest, "takes considerably longer in dragon form."

"I'll take your word for it. Um. Okay, still adjusting. This is—it's a lot." And I was still devoting a fair amount of effort to not falling off here. In fantasy novels it always seems easy: heroine leaps onto dragon's back and up up up and away she goes, long locks billowing picturesquely in the wind. But my hair kept getting in my mouth, my thighs were near to cramping I was gripping so hard with my knees, and I was hanging on to two ridges of her neck crest for dear life as I tried my best not to drop the green tablet wedged under one arm. "What happens if I fall off?"

"Try not to do that."

"Gotcha." My sweaty palms slipped on her neck crest, and I swallowed. "Is there any chance you can, ah, smooth out this ride?"

"Sure, let me just downshift into third," she snorted but let her wings go wide, sending us from a swooping climb into a soaring glide, and I began to breathe a little easier. I let go long enough to slip the tablet into the reticule still looped miraculously over one wrist, and realized the green scales flexing under me were softer than I expected—not horn or chitin but that hard, pebbled, slightly jeweled-looking leather used for seriously expensive bookbinding. I leaned down to touch the wing crest anchored under my foot, and it felt like a book spine: hard but flexible. Her claws and scale tips glittered gold like a book's gilt edges, and it wasn't hide stretching thin and iridescent between her wing joints, it was *vellum*, like an ancient illuminated manuscript. "Because you're not just any dragon," I breathed. "You're a book dragon."

The Librarian snorted out a small black cloud that I realized wasn't smoke but ink. Of course it was. "Where do you think the expression *bookworm* comes from?"

The Astral Library

Bookworm. Bookwyrm? I remembered some of her very first words to me when I asked if the term *Librarian* was a title or a calling: *I've been petitioning the Library Board to change it to Book Dragon.* "How long have you been able to do this?"

"The Library grants dragon privileges after the first hundred years or so."

"The Library, not the—the Board?"

"Yes." A brief pause. "The Board regards it as a waste of resources."

Another flap of her vellum wings, another long soar. Below us, a vast page turned over again—I could just about see the shadows of words tossing and turning on its surface like waves. Did paragraphs make up the tides here in this in-between margin space? Did words make up the rivulets and eddies?

"We aren't going back for the Patron in *Wuthering Heights*, are we?" It wasn't really a question.

"No. I don't believe she's in danger. I think you were right, Miss Watson. The cards were turned from a warning system into a trap. The goal was not to threaten my Patrons, but to exhaust me in my efforts to protect them."

I should have been pleased to be proved right; pleased that my instincts had panned out. Instead, I gulped down another wave of fear. It's not pleasant, finding yourself mid-adventure and realizing your Gandalf figure had the wrong plan all along. Gandalf, Aslan, Glinda, they're supposed to have all the answers—here mine was admitting she didn't.

"Where are we going now?" I ventured.

"The Library. I'll need to recover. This"—a ripple down the glossy sequined leather of her long spined neck—"it takes a lot out of me."

"If I ask why, will you tell me to ask the Library Board?" I said, attempting a joke.

"There is a lot right now I would like to ask the Library Board," she said grimly.

And we flew on over an endless parchment sea.

I don't know what I was expecting the Astral Library to look like from the outside—a spired castle on a crag? A sprawling palace stretching endlessly into this limbo of astral pages?—but I had no chance to see it. As soon as the Librarian began to glide downward as if toward a landing, the cloud appeared. A flutter of red dots swirling below like a blood-mist whirlpool, hiding the Library from view.

"Shit, are we—" I began.

"Hang on," the Librarian said, and I barely had time to clamp my hands around her neck spines and my body along her back when she let out another bone-ripping roar and screamed straight for the center of that ominous scarlet flock. I saw her hiss out another black cloud, a fine mist of ink that boiled and spat like acid wherever it touched red card stock, and for a moment I saw the thronged cards flutter back and thought we'd blast straight through to safety. But they swirled back with a vengeance, slicing and stabbing as badly as before—only there were so many *more* of them now than the cloud that had trapped us out on the Brontë moors. The Librarian threw herself into a corkscrew of a dive, whirling, snapping, biting, spitting her poison ink, down down *down*, and I just hung on for dear life.

I saw the cloud of cards divide, arrowing in long streamers on either side of us like a line of tracer bullets, aiming for her wings. I saw the taut vellum webbing pierced in a thousand places, saw the wind rip through—her left wing tore all at once, no longer knifing the air but fluttering brokenly through it, and we slewed sideways. One of the Library's long emerald-green windows loomed, and I buried my head in her scaled back an instant before we hit.

A shrieking splinter of astral glass, jewel shards exploding outward in all directions, and then the dragon and I impacted the floor in the center of the Library like a nuclear cloud blooming skyward. Her lashing tail whipped the massive oak counter to splinters; one flailing wing sent the bronze globe flying. All around me the books were screaming, taking off toward the vaulted ceiling. I lost my grip and tumbled down the length of her slashed, ruined wing, which she somehow managed to curve under me so I skidded across the floor rather than smashing headfirst into it. The moment I was down, her wing wrenched free and the dragon lurched upright, still roaring her rage toward the broken window. The bloodred wave was re-forming outside, readying to come through, and one card nipped between the jagged green edges and went straight for the dragon's eyes.

Her jaws snapped. Not fast enough. I saw the razor flick of the red edge as it knocked her glasses aside and sliced across her left eye.

"No," I screamed, "*no*—" And as I scrambled upright I swung Beau's hand-embroidered reticule with the tablet inside and swatted that little red fucker right out of the air. I stamped on it, felt it wriggling under my shoe like an eel, reached down regardless of those sharp edges and tore it into scarlet confetti. I could feel the Librarian's shadow on my back as she drew herself up, dragging one ruined wing, shrinking, dwindling. Barely a heartbeat passed before the juddering flail of wings and teeth and tail resolved itself back into the form of the little old woman in her green cardigan. Standing there snarling—one arm hanging useless and one eye a well of blood—up at the broken window with the scarlet cloud a hair from flying through.

She inhaled all the way down through her entire body to her toes, as she brought her finger to her lips.

'SHU

SH!" roared the Librarian.

The entire Library seemed to leap. Every window went dark at once; every book flew from its shelf. Half the volumes hurled themselves to the floor, piling into a circular wall around the Librarian and me; the other half flung themselves against the broken window and sealed it behind a barricade of leather and paper. The clock gave a tremendous *clang* and I heard a sound in my bones like a massive gate swinging shut.

And then a silence in the shattered space, like nothing I'd ever heard in my life.

"Well," said the Librarian, finger dropping from her lips. "That should hold 'em awhile."

A flicker of movement caught my eye at the head of the stairs to my right, but I didn't have time to look—I barely had time to catch the Librarian as she swayed and fell. "Ma'am—!" It was more of a controlled collapse than a smooth lowering to the ground. I barely managed to stop her head from cracking against the hardwood floor, my knees hitting the boards a second later. "Oh God—" Her eye was slashed to bloodied ruin; her arm was clearly broken. She was covered in cuts and gashes, bleeding everywhere. "Lie still, let me—"

"Get off." She still managed to sound irritated, swatting me as I tried to wipe the blood from her wounded eye.

"We need to stop this bleeding."

"Just let me rest. The Library will take care of me. It'll just—take—a while . . ."

"Uh, Alix?" A voice behind me, a voice I knew, but I could not look away from the Librarian, not for anything.

"Who is doing this?" I cried, trying to mop at the blood flowing down her face. "*Who?*"

And then there came the extremely prosaic sound of a machine spitting out pages.

Dazed, I looked around till my eyes found the book-drop slot where the first red card had come winnowing out, a harbinger of doom. It was now spitting out flyers, one after the other, like an industrial copy machine. Already they covered the floor like snow. I climbed over the waist-high book wall and picked one up. The same flyer I'd seen on and off for the last two days, usually crumpled up and sailing into the wastebasket.

ANNUAL BOARD MEETING: TWO DAYS!

For the first time I read the block of text below the title.

Three years ago, the Library Board voted in toto to request a detailed report as to the proposed restructure of the Astral Library bylaws. We have not at this date received your report or any other response to our communiqués as far as this aforementioned restructure, or Bullet Points 3a–12c of the last Library Board Annual Meeting (see minutes), and request immediate deputization of all acquired facts and figures in advance of the next Annual Board Meeting or else more stringent measures and/or involuntary retirement options will be deemed necessary in the essential modernization of the ALBM (Astral Library Business Model) . . .

It went on and on, an entire page of bureaucrat-speak that made my eyes cross. "What does this mean?"

The Librarian's voice was barely a thread issuing from her battered lips. "It means they must have passed a vote on those *stringent measures*."

"Who's *they*?" I nearly shrieked.

"The Library Board." She was clearly sliding fast into unconsciousness, falling headlong off the cliff, but she got the words out. "They've been trying for years to take the Library away from me by bureaucratic means. Now I'm guessing they've decided to employ *involuntary retirement options.*"

"*What?*" I cried, gripping her hand. "*What?*" But there was no answer, and behind me I heard that diffident, familiar voice again.

"Alix?"

I scrambled to my feet, whipping around. The Programmer—the Gallerist—I'd forgotten all about them after they'd departed with the last batch of Patrons to hide in paintings and games. *Please let them have come back.* Because I could really use a calming, centuries-old presence here to tell me what the ever-loving fuck I was supposed to do next.

But the figure standing hesitantly at the head of the sweeping staircase wasn't the Gallerist *or* the Programmer. It was a living, breathing, broad-shouldered fashion plate in a skintight claret-colored frock coat, impeccably tied cravat, breeches, and tall boots, silk top hat and elaborate silver-mounted walking stick in one gloved hand.

"Alix?" said Beau.

14

I was trying to find something to say that wasn't a complete cliché, still thumbing my way mentally past *How did you get here?* and *What are you doing here?* when Beau began to laugh in short, hiccupping bursts.

"Jesus," he said, looking from me to the clock with its complete lack of time-telling numbers to the books hovering against the ceiling like frightened birds. "I'm either hallucinating from lack of sleep, or I'm prematurely starting that nervous breakdown I've been promising myself once the *Belle* premiere is over."

I sighed. "Afraid it's a little more complicated than that."

He let out a whoop, startling both me and the books. "I beg your pardon," he said to us both, bowing with an elaborate swoop of silk top hat, and then he hopped onto the curving mahogany banister and slid down it all the way to the bottom of the stairs with another whoop. The whoop turned into a "*Whoops!*" as he tumbled off the banister and hit the carpet flat on his back, where he elected to stay, eyes and boot tops pointing at the ceiling. "Floating books," he mumbled. "Floating books and Czarina Alix. Did you just fly through that window on a dragon, czarina? Or did I imagine that part?"

"Hold that thought," I said, and turned back to the Librarian. In the sixty seconds my attention had been distracted by a Regency fashion plate walking through the door, the Library had somehow conjured up a deep leather chaise lounge and formed it up underneath her so she was resting more comfortably. I went to my knees, heart knocking, and felt for a pulse in the side of her throat. Slow, very slow, but steady. "Ma'am?" I whispered, but not so much as a flicker of an eyelash. I looked at the slash across her eye, but it had already clotted. So had my own various paper cuts and slices, I realized—they still hurt but they were scabbed over. If the Astral Library took care of your appetite while you were inside its walls, maybe it helped with your injuries too?

Just let me rest, the Librarian had said. *The Library will take care of me. It'll just—take—a while . . .*

Jesus, how long was *a while* in a place where time didn't actually pass? Was I about to be stuck here for the next hundred figurative years, watching her snooze like Sleeping Beauty?

Get it together, I told myself, unfolding the lambswool blanket the Library had thoughtfully provided along with the chaise lounge and tucking it in around the Librarian's still form. *At least she's not dead. She's alive, she's stable, and those goddamn cards can't get in.*

At least I didn't think they could. But what about when the Library Board made its next move? If it really was the Library Board behind all this . . .

"Czarina?" Beau's voice floated over, still dreamily bemused.

"Why is that terrifying paper cutter chopping up and down all by itself like a guillotine?"

"Beau..."

He propped himself up on one elbow, looking at me. "And what did you do to my dress?"

I winced, not daring to look down at the shredded muslin hanging in ragged strips around my legs. "Dragon ride plus murderous card catalog?"

He nodded slowly, scrubbing a hand through his hair. Being Beau, it gave him sexy bed head. I'd been wearing a bonnet so long, I just had hat head—and I'd lost the bonnet. I tried to pat my hair back behind my ears as Beau's dark eyes traveled from the clock to the crashed globe to the books plastered up against the broken window. "This is a much more elaborate breakdown than I was anticipating," he said at last. "The detail work is just amazing here. I'm walking around in the Guo Pei of embroidered fantasy worlds..."

"What's the last thing you remember?" I asked.

"I was at a party at the Boston Public Library." He sat up on the floor, propping his elbows on his doeskin-clad knees. "You know they rent out the gardens and fancier rooms for weddings and fundraisers and stuff like that? It was this big influencer birthday bash I swore I'd go to six months ago. I didn't want to go—Jesus, I can't even *afford* to go, I need to finish the lining on the bodice of the *Belle* dress, I'm so behind. But I need something for Insta that isn't just me frothing at the mouth at the idea of stitching one more goddamn channel, so I suited up and went to put in a fifteen-minute appearance. It was awful. Fairy lights all through that gorgeous Italianate courtyard filled with people getting drunk on Cristal and taking selfies..." He trailed off for a moment, looking so exhausted he might drop off right here. He had just a touch of silvery eyeliner along his lashes, echoing the small silver ring in one ear, and that flick of silver gave his blink a sleepy dragonfly glimmer. "You sure I'm not dreaming?" he mumbled.

"I'm betting you found a door?" I prompted.

"Right." Giving himself a little shake. "The Abbey Room and the Sargent Gallery were all done up with crystals and chrysanthemums—the only room no one was in was the Reading Room. Well, there was a guy doing a line of coke off what looked like a first-edition Yeats, but he went weaving out and I just sat down at one of those long tables—they had them all done up with white cloths and candles—and I just couldn't move. It's been so long since I got to sit and do *nothing*. I knew I needed to snap a few pics and head back to the shop and get to work, but I just sat there blinking at all those shelves of books and thinking about the very first historical costume book I was able to find when I was a kid. Just some sort of basic fashion retrospective, but if you're a kid from Texas who's already getting beat up because your jeans are a little too skinny, well, you get your hands on that book and you imagine walking through those rows and rows of brocade and satin. Like centuries are going by, but in fabric. Chalked Roman togas and lacquered samurai armor giving way to Indian sari silk and medieval furs and those fabulous multidimensional Tudor velvets..."

I could see we were going to get lost for a while in all those historical fabrics if we weren't careful. "Focus, Beau. What happened then?"

"I went through an open door." He shrugged. "I thought it was the door back to the Abbey Room, you know the one with the wall paintings of Galahad and the Round Table? But I ended up in here—and there were books flying everywhere and a dragon crashing through the window, and I thought, *Wow, I definitely fell asleep at the party*, and then everything sealed up with this huge crash, and..." He rubbed a hand through his hair again. "Yeah. Here we are."

The Astral Library

I chewed my lip a moment, wondering. I hadn't exactly pegged Beau as the kind of reader desperate enough to flee into a novel. But maybe *desperate* mattered more than the novel part. Mattered enough for the Library to give him a door—and a hand.

Or maybe the Library knew the one who needed a hand here was me.

Or maybe, a little bit of both.

"Wait a minute." Looking suddenly alarmed, Beau pointed over my shoulder at the chaise lounge with the Librarian under her lambswool blanket. "Who's that and how did I miss that she was lying there and is she *dead*?"

"No. She—"

"And where did the *dragon* go?"

"Try to relax. And listen up." I patted his shoulder. "It's monologue time."

I very quickly had a lot more sympathy for the Librarian's constant state of irritation. Having to explain the rules of a magical world to people over and over, every day of her job? No wonder she bit my head off when I asked so many questions. I was already out of gas trying to do this *once*.

As soon as I got through to Beau that this was a real place, not a dream or a hallucination, he very nearly went ahead and had that nervous breakdown he'd been talking about: "What do you mean I can't get out?!"

"I think you slid through right before the Library sealed everything shut," I said, following him up the stairs as he wrenched at the handle of the door he'd walked through. "We're sort of, um, in emergency lockdown." Thanks to one really epic *SHUSH*. I cast a glance at the Librarian but she was still as motionless as Snow White in her glass casket. If Snow White were old, Iranian, and battle wounded rather than young, white, and epically dumb.

"Alix, Jesus, I've got to get out of here. That lining on the *Belle* dress, if I don't get it done tonight I'm fucked. I'm so behind—"

"Beau."

"It's all down to the next few days. Final fitting's in a week; if I screw this up, I'm finished." He was pacing up and down in front of the door now in long agitated strides. "I swore to my dad I'd—"

"*Beau.*"

"—pay him back and if I don't, my brothers, Jesus, they'll never let me hear the end of—"

"*BEAU.*" I grabbed him by his immaculate claret sleeve and yanked him to a halt. "Calm down."

"When in the history of saying *Calm down* does anybody ever *calm the fuck down*?" he yelled. "Alix, it may not sound like much to you, but this premiere commission is going to sink me if I don't get it done, and I can't afford to lose even half a night's work, and how long have I been here already? *How long?*"

"Time stands still here, Beau. You go back out that door—*whenever* you go back out—it'll be the same moment you left."

That kicked off an entirely different overreaction as he stared at me one long wild-eyed moment, then yanked me into a hug, kissed me on each cheek, let out another whoop, and went back to striding up and down again, mumbling, "I get a break, I can actually get a goddamn break? Jesus, I need a break..."

I plunged into the rest of it then—the book worlds and the painting worlds and the game worlds, who lived in them, who the Librarian and her colleagues were, and exactly how things had started going wrong—but I wasn't sure how much of it was getting through. Beau ended up sinking down with his back against what remained of the huge oak counter, munching from a huge bowl of caramel popcorn the Library had helpfully served up at his elbow, mumbling, "I don't have a hundred yards of silk gauze to hem tonight. I don't have to finish the sleeve tabs tonight. I don't have to complete the goddamn spine embroidery tonight . . ."

I decided to let it all sink in before telling him about the attack on the Library, and went back up to the door at the head of the stairs. Still sealed, and with a stonelike solidity that meant the door panels didn't even rattle as I gave a thump with my fist. It might as well have been a painted door on a granite wall, and I had a feeling it was going to stay that way. The raft of books sealed over the broken window was still holding firm; I couldn't hear so much as a flutter of those damn cards from the other side. The Librarian was still motionless on her chaise lounge.

"What do I do, Dennis?" I asked the ghost, seeing *War and Peace* hovering in its usual space where he drifted reading, but he only ruffled a page nervously and edged farther back down the Library shelves. Other ghosts hovered behind him, barely more than flickers of motion clutching their own books, but none of them said a word.

Well.

I retrieved the green tablet from the carpet where it had fallen when I came crashing off the dragon's back, taking a moment to remember the password phrase. Sarah J. Maas, right. "'Libraries are full of ideas—perhaps the most dangerous and powerful of all weapons.'"

The tablet's screen remained stubbornly dark.

"Oh, come on," I begged.

It gave a pissy blat.

"'I ransack public libraries, and find them full of sunk treasure.' What, you don't like Virginia Woolf?" I demanded as the tablet blatted again, sounding even more offended. Maybe it didn't like the idea of being ransacked. Couldn't say I blamed it. "Okay, what about Erasmus? 'Do not be guilty of possessing a library of learned books while lacking learning yourself.'"

A sulky electronic snort this time. The tablet evidently didn't want to be chided. I gave it a shake, about to threaten it with a system update, but then I felt a breath at my shoulder as Beau spoke. His voice had dropped half an octave into a velvet rumble that curled my toes up like walnuts. "'My paradise,'" he quoted, voice lowering still further into a bedroom whisper, "'is a library.'"

The tablet gave a seductive buzz in my hands and opened right up to its home screen. I pushed down a little whimper of my own, clearing my throat instead as I looked over my shoulder at Beau. "Who, um, said that?"

"Karl Lagerfeld. The man had a library of over three hundred thousand volumes." Beau grinned at my expression. "What, you think fashion and fiction don't overlap?"

Words scrolled across the tablet screen:

Welcome, Alix

Provisional status: Page

"So, a magic tablet," said Beau. "Gotcha. What does it do?"

"As little as possible," I said, swiping past the welcome screen to the email icon. If I could only get a message to the Programmer or the Gallerist. They could tell me what to do here—

Access denied. Email function accessible to Librarian (status) only.

How to reverse shush, I typed into the search bar.

The Astral Library

Access denied. SHUSH protocol accessible to Librarian (status) only.

Library Board evil? I typed.

Access denied. Library Board bylaws and member list accessible to Librarian (status) only.

"Effect of meat grinder on library tablet?" I snarled, typing.
Pending, said the tablet, practically LOL'ing at me.
"Who's the Library Board?" Beau asked, having watched my search-bar typing. "And why are they evil?"

"I don't know." I sighed, and somehow found myself curled on the bottom step, leaning against the carved mahogany balustrade as I told him the rest of the crisis that had stranded me here with the books in a hysterical flock just under the ceiling and the Librarian unconscious on a sofa. "All along, she's given me the impression the Library Board is her boss. The higher authority. The good guys, or at least the guys on her side. Only now they've suddenly turned out to be the bad guys, the ones coming after her all along." Not enraged slavers, not pissed-off husbands and fathers. Her own bosses. "And I don't even know who *they* are."

Beau shrugged one elegant shoulder. He was sitting on the step above mine, long booted legs stretched out—he'd never looked more *Bridgerton*. "Does it matter?"

"Of course it does! How can you fight something when you don't know what it is? If it was another dragon coming at us, or a villain from literature, I'd at least have an idea where to start." What I'd give to face the White Witch from Narnia, or Smaug from *The Hobbit*. Captain Hook from *Peter* fucking *Pan*. At least with them I knew their weak points. "And since when is it plausible for the villain to be some . . . faceless corporate board?"

"Oh, honey." Beau laughed. "Don't you have student loans?"

"Foster kid here. You think college was ever a possibility for me?"

"Touché." He gave a salute. "Well, speaking as a guy with nearly six figures of student loan debt, let me tell you it is *entirely* possible for a faceless corporate board to be a force of complete and utter evil."

I raised an eyebrow.

"Who hikes student loan interest rates up so high no one can ever pay them off? Faceless corporate boards. Who shuttles kids like you around from one foster home to another? Faceless boards. Who closes libraries down?" Beau held up one of the flyers that papered the floor with its paragraphs of bureaucratic twaddle. "Boards."

"But we were *attacked*. Violently." Picking up another of the flyers. "The Librarian was half blinded. I could see that happening because of a coalition of slavers, or a cadre of abusive parents and husbands, but a board vote?"

Beau pointed at his own face—that brown, beautiful, intriguing mix of a face. "I'm part white, part Black, part Japanese, part Pakistani, and all bisexual," he said. "Just reaching for the very, *very* low-hanging fruit when it comes to the history of those latter population segments, I give you slavery, Japanese internment, colonization, and chemical castration. All, at some point, legal and accepted—and how? Because a lot of men claimed the right to sit around a table and bring exceptionally evil things into practice, while pretending to be polite, civilized, and moral human beings. Boards, committees, legislatures"—Beau's hand encompassed all of them, and more—"can be the ultimate gaslighters and normalizers of the inhumane."

I gave a silent salute and *touché* of my own.

The Astral Library

He went on. "So—what are you going to do?"

"I don't know if there's anything I *can* do. I'm a Patron with provisional Page status—this wasn't supposed to be my fight, it was supposed to be my way station on the road to a new life." My breath hitched in my chest, and when I looked down I realized my hands were trembling. I couldn't stop staring at the Librarian, thinking how that chaise lounge looked like a bier. "And now the place is a wreck and she's been laid out cold and—"

"Hey. Hey." Beau's voice was soft. "Breathe. Just breathe. In and out."

I breathed in and out. His hand rested on my ankle, a soft touch tethering me to the ground. I breathed in and out till my hands stopped shaking, remembering how the Patron named Stephanie had had a panic attack in the middle of *Jane Eyre*, how Sarah and I had soothed her.

Sarah. Something pinged me there, something to do with the resourceful brunette we'd relocated from Sherlock Holmes to Thomas Cole's Rome, but my disjointed mind couldn't quite grab hold of it.

"Better, czarina?" Beau's voice was so calm.

"I need the Librarian to wake up," I said, and was glad to hear my voice was no longer wobbling. "I don't know what to do, but she does. I need her to *wake up*."

"Okay," he answered. "What do we do to make that happen?"

I looked at him. "*We?*"

"I've been in this place less than half an hour, and I already know I don't want to see it shut down." He smiled. "And I've been sewing my life out on a red-carpet gown twenty hours out of every twenty-four for the past two months—I need a break, and since time stops here, I can actually afford to take one. So how can I help you save the world?"

I chewed my lip again, looking down at the flyer in my hand... *or else more stringent measures and/or involuntary retirement options will be deemed necessary in the essential modernization of the ALBM (Astral Library Business Model)...*

And the clock began to chime again—that same series of fast, urgent strikes that had first tipped me off that something bad was coming down the pike for the Astral Library. *Bong bong bong bong*, getting louder and louder, and the books began fluttering and flapping all over again.

"What's happening?" asked Beau.

I looked at the window, but the book shield was still holding—the cards weren't breaking in, so what was it? I put my hand on the nearest stack of books to quiet them, but they wouldn't be quieted. A flicker of movement at the corner of my eye, and I turned in time to see another official-looking sheet of paper slither out of the book-drop slot.

Dear Alix,

We know your in there, and we're here to help! This is an internal matter, we're deeply sorry the Librarian chose to involve you. If you have been granted provisional Page status, you should be able to unlock the Library for us when the Board arrives soon for the Annual Board Meeting—instructions forthcoming. We appreciate your cooperation!

Best,

Library Board President

"Who's the Library Board president?" asked Beau.

"No idea." I imagined a jowly, self-righteous, three-martini-lunch type in an expensive suit. Or maybe some prissy PTA-mom type with a blond bob. Either way, it felt oddly comforting to imagine a face at the head of this faceless Board. I had an enemy—*enemy*, singular. And I'd have known they were my enemy even if they hadn't tried to blind the Librarian and paper-cut me to death, because if there's one thing any ex–foster kid knows, it's that adults who lead with *We're here to help!* very rarely are.

Plus—my eyes went back to the first line of the note: *We know your* in there. And the comma splice in the sentence right after it! "Anyone on a library board should know how to spell," I muttered, thumb-typing a question into the tablet. And finally, it kicked up an answer I wanted to see.

> Book margin-traveling and costume changes now granted to Page (status).

"Thank you, you beautiful bitchy machine, you," I breathed, and typed a few more quick questions. This wasn't going to be pretty, but I didn't need pretty. I just needed fast. Grabbing the Library Board president's note, I turned it over and scrawled a note of my own with a pen from the splintered counter.

Beau was gently shifting the cushion under the Librarian's wounded arm so it supported her elbow better. "What are we doing?"

"What do you feel like?" I yanked a book off one of the endless shelves, opened it up, and tossed it down on the floor just as the Librarian had done when the Library's first alarm sounded. For what I was going to do next, I needed a handy list of books I knew very well—down to the chapter, plot point by plot point. Fortunately, that made a long list. Thumbing mentally through it, I asked, "How about some F. Scott Fitzgerald for starters?"

"Wherever we're going I could use a drink." Beau snatched up his top hat. "I could murder a gin rickey."

"Me too." I turned and looked at the books, fluttering anxiously all over the place. "You'll look after her?" I asked, and smiled to see the way that circular parapet of books drew itself closer around the chaise lounge. "Right. You do your part, I'll do mine."

"What is your part?" Beau asked as I strode over to the book-drop slot.

"Diversion," I said, and crammed my note through.

Dear Library Board President,

    Go fuck yourself. You want to talk to me, come and get me. Bring something scarier than your pissant card catalog this time, you comma-splicing hack.

                        Best,
                        Alexandria Watson
                        Page of the Astral Library

And I grabbed Beau's hand and jumped into limbo with him, feet-first into another book.

15

A loud *POP* made us both flinch, but then I felt a shower of spray and bubbles, heard a shriek of drunken laughter, and realized it had been a champagne cork. A woman buffeted past me, soaking wet, smelling of chlorine and French perfume, waving a champagne bottle overhead; as I watched, she ran straight through a crowd of men in tuxedos and with a shriek of laughter leaped into a huge sapphire-blue swimming pool. "Welcome to West Egg," I said, snagging a crystal coupe the size of a fishbowl off the nearest silver tray. I'd girded myself for a wave of post-margin-traveling exhaustion, having seen the Librarian look increasingly gray as we jumped from book to book, but what I primarily felt was ravenous thirst.

"Wow." Beau was looking around him with the same wide-eyed bemusement that had probably been on my face when the Librarian whisked me off to Sherlock Holmes's London. He should have stuck out like a sore thumb in his Regency togs, but somehow he didn't—partly because the Astral Library seemed to exude a slight dampening effect on margin-travelers in the way eyes slid away from us rather than lingering, and partly because this was a party for Beautiful People and Beau was definitely one of the Beautiful People even if he wasn't in a 1920s suit. Besides, everyone here was too tipsy to blink overmuch at a man in a cravat and a top hat. "Where are we again?"

"Jay Gatsby's mansion." I swigged half my champagne and parked another coupe in Beau's hand. As planned when I'd opened up the Astral Library copy to chapter 3, we'd been plunked down in the middle of the first Gatsby house party: a big marble pile of a house screened in ivy, lights blazing into the hot velvet night from every window, vast emerald lawn dotted with buffet tents and swarming with men in black tie and flappers in sequins, most of them falling-down drunk on Prohibition gin. I raised my voice to be heard over the orchestra on the terrace, sawing out ragtime as a cluster of shrieking women jitterbugged. "You know, the book we all had jammed down our throats in tenth-grade English? Cross-examination of post–World War One American values, the battle of the new and intoxicating against the shadow of the Great War and its attendant horrors? One man's struggle to never, ever admit that sometimes the girl gets away and you should just move on? My English teacher gave me a C for saying that in an essay."

"*The Great Gatsby*, got it. Why exactly are we here again? Why not just stay in the Library?"

"I don't want the Library Board thinking about how to break in and get to the Librarian. I want them distracted by trying to find *me*. Which I think they will, which will give her time to heal and wake up, and then—"

"*Beading,*" Beau yelped, and nearly tackled me. For a moment I thought he was going for a kiss, and I'd have gone for one right back, but it was my shoulder strap he was examining. That was when I remembered the tablet had upgraded me to costume change privileges along with the ability to margin-travel. My shredded Regency skirts and little velvet jacket were gone, and in their place— "Burgundy silk crepe with jet beads," Beau was muttering, examining the stitching on the underside of my shoulder strap. "What are we, 1922 from the mid-shin length? Looks like a Vionnet from the bias cut—"

"Focus, Beau." I steered us round a marble nymph with a basket of oranges in her arms, clapping a hand to my head as something tickled my ear. A long plume, it turned out, fastened to a sequined bandeau around my hair, which was now set in tight finger waves. I could even feel rouge on my lips; this makeover was top to bottom A-plus work and I wished I had a moment to appreciate it because who doesn't appreciate a good makeover in a book? But I didn't think we had time to hunt for a mirror so I could ogle myself. "We need to figure out if we're being followed—"

"Seriously, the Astral Library does quality stitchery." Beau had his nose parked practically between my shoulder blades now as he examined the beading on the drape of my new dress's back. "Did they put you in a bandeau brassiere or go for the more figure-flattering corset to achieve the period silhouette?"

"You don't get to examine my underwear for historical authenticity, sorry," I said, yelping as the summer breeze plucked at my skirt. Flapper-style underpinnings were a lot, um, *draftier* than the Regency stays I'd been wearing two minutes ago. I stood on tiptoe in the rhinestone T-strap pumps that were now pinching my feet, craning to look over the dancing, drinking throng. "I know it's a real mosh pit out here, but we've got to keep an eye out. Someone's going to be coming after us. Or some*thing*," I added, thinking of the card catalog from hell.

"We've got this," Beau said, swigging more champagne, sounding entirely too breezy, but he was still swamped with I'm-in-a-fantasy-world giddiness and hey, I got that. He hadn't had time yet to see just how dark the shadows were. Hadn't stumbled headfirst into a nineteenth-century opium den. Hadn't watched weeping prisoners stumbling in chains behind a victorious Roman emperor. Hadn't watched a cloud of razor-edged cards try to blind a dragon. "What if those card things come for you again?" Beau asked, evidently reading my mind.

"I don't think they will." A deep twang in my gut was telling me that, and generally I trusted that twang—any foster kid does, when you're sizing up a new set of carers and trying to figure out fast if this dad appreciates teenage girls a little too much, or this mom gets mean after a bad day at work. No, my gut was telling me the Board wasn't going to attack me in quite the same way they had the Librarian. "I don't think they want me weakened or down for the count the way they did her," I said, feeling my way through it. "They know she's incapacitated—she can't open the door for them, so I'm the only one who can. Therefore they can't afford to take me down too. They just want me scared and pliant so I'll *Open Sesame*, and I can't do that if I'm bleeding out in West Egg from a million paper cuts. So they're going to send something else other than the cards, something to bring me back and make me humble."

"And Alix Watson does not do goddamn humble," said Beau.

"Correct."

"Attagirl." He grinned, snagging some little oyster patties off a passing silver platter and passing one to me. "So, what do we do now? Any

The Astral Library

chance you can petition your tablet there to include me in the costume changes? Because I could really do with a little early-twenties menswear here. Some wide lapels, silk pocket squares, cuffed trousers—"

The tablet. I dug it out of the beaded art deco clutch that had replaced my Austen-esque reticule, but it was frustratingly blank.

"Suppose I should be happy I didn't get stuck in plus fours and a golf sweater," Beau was musing. "The twenties has a lot to answer for when it comes to normalizing sportswear as day wear. If you ask me it's a direct line from plus fours at Prohibition lunches to Patriots jerseys at the office."

A ripple in the crowd across the long stretch of velvet lawn—I saw the arrow of it, making its way up the slope. Not the kind of ripple that followed a waiter staggering along under a huge platter of caviar and toast points, or the one that followed a particularly athletic dancer flailing away at the Charleston—the ripple of a shark sliding underwater, the crowd giving way around it and re-forming with oblivious smoothness. The ripple of something that didn't belong here. *There you are*, I thought, parking my empty champagne coup on the marble balustrade. "Be ready to run," I told Beau.

"What—"

"Alix Watson," a voice intoned under the brassy blare of the orchestra playing Al Jolson. "Please come with us." No, not one voice—two. Two dark figures came knifing out through a pack of tuxedo-clad men whinnying over their flasks, and for a moment I thought the world had slipped sideways and I'd fallen out of *The Great Gatsby* into the Boston Public Library. Because it was Chester and Chad, Tweedledum and Tweedledumber, in their Library Security uniforms and badges, Chester's ironed knife sharp and Chad's with a Cheez Whiz stain. "What the hell?" I breathed, forgetting my entire careful plan, because I hadn't expected to see something—some*one*—I actually knew.

"Who are they?" Beau asked, taking a step forward with his silver-handled walking stick at half guard, and with a click the world slipped back into focus.

"Library Security," I said, because of course the Library Board would send for Library Security if they were dealing with a runaway Page, and Library Security took the form I was most used to seeing it in. This couldn't actually be Chester and Chad from the BPL—for one thing, nobody here seemed able to *see* them except Beau and me, and for another they marched toward me in a perfect synchronized lockstep they'd never have been able to achieve in real life, like a pair of glassy-eyed chess pawns. "Alix Watson, please come with us," they droned again in unison.

"Follow me." I yanked at Beau's sleeve, plan snapping back into place, but he was already stepping in front of me.

"Absolutely not, Mall Cop," he began, and Chester—or whatever it was that looked like Chester—shouldered him aside with surprising force. Beau crashed down hard, and when he sprang back up he had grass stains all down his doeskin breeches.

"Alix Watson," Chester intoned, stepping around him, "please come—"

"Okay, shit-brick," Beau said, twisting the silver handle of his walking stick and unsheathing a length of gleaming steel.

"You've got a *sword*?" I heard myself bleat, even as I backed around the fountain to put the spray in between myself and Chester.

Beau ignored me, leveling the blade straight out at Chad, who was still advancing, Cheez Whiz stain and all. "She's not going anywhere with you and neither am I, so walk your poly-blend ass back to—"

Chad never stopped, just walked straight into the blade. I saw it punch through the breast pocket of his wrinkled shirt and straight out the back, no resistance. "Come with us," he was still saying mechanically as he crumpled down, and the silver-sequined woman doing the tango past us didn't even seem to see the body as she swirled by, and neither did the waiter who stepped serenely over the tangled legs in their polyester trousers, and I had a crazily distinct image of a dark-suited man presiding from the balcony on the second story high above us whose eyes drifted blankly over the violent little play that had exploded on his lawn, in the middle of his party. Even Jay Gatsby didn't register us here, Beau or me or Library Security, just went on gazing out over the champagne-soaked hordes toward East Egg, looking for Daisy Buchanan.

Then Chester seized my wrist, and his grip was like cold, greasy stone.

"Alix—" Beau's eyes were wide and horrified, looking at the body on his blade. I threw myself away from Chester—I had satin evening gloves on, and I felt a pearl button on my wrist go *pop* as I yanked my entire hand out of the glove and stumbled back away from him.

"You will come with us," he said, dropping the glove, and I threw myself around the fountain to grab Beau's gabardine sleeve as he still stood gazing at the thing he'd stabbed.

"It's not real," I yelled, praying I was right, and I was: as Chad slid off the blade, he dissolved. No blood, no glazed eyes, nothing but empty clothes fluttering to the flattened grass . . . And as I watched, even those started to dissolve in the crush of rhinestone-buckled pumps and polished oxfords tangoing and jitterbugging all around us.

"Alix Watson, please come with us," Chester said, voice mechanical as his stride as he came around the fountain. The real Chester would be so proud: he'd finally managed to scare me.

"What the—" Beau began, and I yanked him deeper into the crowd, pulling him into a run.

"They're, um, simulacra. Or something," I jerked out, keeping my grip on the tablet and aiming for the thickest part of the crowd as we pelted down the grassy slope. No time even to take a fleeting moment's satisfaction at being able to work a really top-class word like *simulacra* into ordinary conversation; I just kept running. "They aren't human. They're just constructs, or at least that's my best guess. They're here to get us back to the Library and make me open it."

"So they can't hurt us?" Beau managed not to trip over his sword even at full sprint, still looking incredulous that there was no blood on the blade.

"Oh, they can hurt us." My wrist felt like it had been clamped in a vise from Chester's grip, and I was pretty sure I'd have an indigo-blue bruise in about an hour. "Pick up the pace!"

"Where are we—"

"Keep up! And why do you have a *sword*?" Dodging past a pair of waiters staggering along between a mattress-size platter of oysters on ice.

"Sword cane. Popular in the eighteenth and nineteenth centuries for any gentleman wishing for a discreet—"

"Know how to use it?"

"Sure. Stick 'em with the pointy end; isn't that what they say in *Game of Thrones*?" And he turned and lunged full extension at Chester, hurtling after us down the grassy slope. I had a distracted moment's admiration for the picture he made—there's really nothing like a man plunging his sword into the gut of your enemy to get the old heart fluttering—but this time the blade didn't go into Chester, who sidestepped it with a hard shove while still intoning "Alix Watson, please come with us." The shove sent Beau flying three feet into a marble cupid, which promptly crashed over.

"They learn," I yelled, grabbing a champagne bottle from the nearest giggling feather duster of a flapper lurching past me toward the swimming pool. "They know the sword's dangerous now, so they'll avoid it." They didn't know about champagne bottles, though, because Chester didn't try to duck as I swung the bottle with an overhead smash like Serena Williams serving at Wimbledon. He went down as the bottle flew spinning out of my hand, but I didn't see him start to evaporate into the ground so I guessed he wasn't down for good. I'd have hit him again, but the bottle had rolled behind him out of reach and he was already getting up. "Come on," I panted, yanking Beau to his feet, and we were flying again down to the bottom of the lawn and out through a pair of ornate gates where a series of flimsy-looking twenties roadsters were slowly weaving out with loads of inebriated party guests.

"Okay," Beau gritted, managing to sheathe his sword cane even as he examined a torn flap in his pristine sleeve. "Now I am goddamn pissed."

"Send the Library Board a bill. This way—" And we dove into a stand of trees just outside the Gatsby estate, right next to a roadside ditch.

"What are we doing? Is there a plan?"

"Yep." I craned my neck. The car should be coming up just about now . . . and so was Chester. I stepped out from the trees and waved to get his attention.

He changed course at once, marching along the edge of the ditch toward me. "Alix Watson—"

"Please come along, yes, I know. You're the one who needs to come along, Chester. Right—about—here—"

And a snazzy little roadster shot through the gate, clipped the column, swerved wildly, and plowed right at us. I stepped neatly back, the grille caught Chester, and the car flipped nose-down into the ditch with Library Security pinned at the bottom.

"Heh," I cackled, peering down into the ditch and seeing the dissolution of those polyester pants under the crumpled hood. "Got him."

Beau was staring at me. "What—how did you know—"

"There's a car crash in chapter three of *The Great Gatsby*." I hitched up my garters, which were starting to slide down my silk stockings. "A minor character named Owl Eyes drives his car into a ditch"—there he was scrambling out of the roadster now, spectacles draped over one ear, drunkenly complaining—"and it's all a lot of foreshadowing for the fatal car crash at the end of the book when Daisy Buchanan drives over her husband's mistress. A little heavy-handed on the parallels, I always thought, but handy for slowing down the Library Board's stooges. Most things go splat if you shove 'em in front of a speeding car."

Beau didn't look all that much more enlightened. "You just happen to remember the particulars of chapter three of *The Great Gatsby*?"

"Look, I'm not equipped to be the Chosen One in any novel. I don't know kung fu, I can't sling spells, I don't even have a cool hidden sword like you—" Gesturing at his cane, which once again looked like a humble silver-handled walking stick. "But I am crammed with book trivia up to my goddamn *ears*, and if the Library Board wants to send their simulacra thugs after me, I can keep shoving 'em in front of Daisy Buchanan's roadster, or off Huck Finn's raft into the Mississippi, or into the mouth of the French guns in *War and Peace*. I can do that as long as the Librarian needs me to, until she can heal up and take on the Board. I'm not too impressive in most ways, but book ways"—I brandished the tablet like a shield, with its infinite catalog of Astral Library volumes at my fingertips—"do *not* fuck with me."

"You," Beau breathed, a grin starting to break over his face, "are such a nerd."

"Says the man who gets all misty-eyed over bias-cut Vionnet," I retorted, and fired up the green tablet. "Come on. Because something tells me Library Security is going to be back."

16

They were.

Chad and Chester 2.0 showed up the moment we margin-traveled into *Bleak House*, a book I barely remembered except that it had a scene where an alcoholic ragman dies in his shop of spontaneous combustion (really, Dickens?). "Alix Watson, please come with us," Beau and I heard voices intoning as we descended the stairs of the London rag shop, before Beau could even start examining the cut of the plum-colored Victorian walking suit that had swapped out my Gatsby flapper finery. Chad and Chester were already marching across the jumbled shop floor as we came down, that same Cheez Whiz stain and those same aviators coming at us in lockstep, as if we'd never left them variously squished and stabbed in *The Great Gatsby*.

A reflexive leap of fear fluttered in my throat but I pushed it down, because I'd timed this just right when I bookmarked the page to jump into. A strategic dash across the shop to the bedroom of

Dickens's unfortunate Mr. Krook, where a curl of smoke was coming from under the door, a yelp as I twisted the too-hot doorknob and flung the door open, and then a well-timed double shove from Beau sent Chad and Chester 2.0 straight into the inferno that had just spontaneously kindled there. A slam of the door and that monotone recitation of "Alix Watson—" abruptly snuffed out, not in screams but in silence. I imagined their Library Security uniforms catching fire and then billowing down to the floor like empty sacks, and shivered.

"Hasn't spontaneous combustion been pretty well debunked?" Beau wondered, still breathing hard. "Scientifically speaking?"

"Not when Dickens wrote *Bleak House*, it wasn't." I was still wondering exactly what Chad and Chester *were*, or to be more exact, what Library Security was when it wasn't dressed like something from my memories. Where was it now, stuck out in some nebulous parchment sea like the one I'd flown over dragon-back with the Librarian? I imagined the vast page turning over, the tidal eddies of words and paragraphs swirling, giving birth to Chad in his stained shirt and Chester in his aviators all over again. The two of them emerging from the pages like monsters, but dripping words instead of water . . . "Better get out of here," I said, shaking off the uneasy image. "I don't know if they can find us twice in the same book, but I'd rather not have to margin-travel in a hurry." It had taken me absolutely forever, jabbing and swearing at the tablet by the light of a West Egg moon, to jump us from Fitzgerald to Dickens correctly.

"How many versions of Chuck and Charlie—"

"Chad and Chester."

"—do you think we're going to have to keep dispatching?" Beau neatly avoided tripping over the hissing cat who streaked across the crowded shop floor. Give Charles Dickens credit where it's due: he had some shifty plot twists like spontaneous combustion, but at least he didn't kill off the cat. "How many times can they come at us?"

"I have no idea." I'd already asked the green tablet as much, but it just made cranky electronic noises at me. I started pushing buttons on the touch screen—the Librarian had made it look easy, jumping from one book to another, but I had to navigate the search function and the selection bar and a pop-up that kept asking if I was *sure* I didn't want to bookmark this chapter, and I was fairly certain the tablet was just screwing with me, but I couldn't afford to piss it off. "Please-please-please, just *work*," I begged, and pages folded around us again.

Chad and Chester 3.0 found us in *Treasure Island*, where we managed to shove them off the deck of the *Hispaniola* into the heaving sea. Versions 4.0 took quite a bit longer to find us in *The Bride of Lammermoor*, long enough that Beau and I had a chance for a few hours' rest in the Highland heather before we had to engage in a little cliffside scuffling and shove the pair over the side of a Scottish crag. "You are the only person I have ever met who's read Sir Walter Scott," Beau panted as the tablet whisked us off to our fifth book. "*Nobody* reads Sir Walter Scott. The only reason I . . ." His voice trailed off as he got a gander at our new surroundings. I was too busy doing a full-body squirm at the slithering feel of my clothes dissolving around me into a different period outfit, from the underwear (*hello there, new corset*) to the sudden weight of heavy skirts. "Czarina, you didn't!"

I straightened my new plumed beaver hat over my equally new velvet mask. "Welcome to *The Three Musketeers*. Plenty of palace guards around here we can shove Chad and Chester into once they show up." Library Security very definitely kept learning with every creative new way we dispatched them—they now knew about swords, cars, fire, cliffs, and oceans—but I figured they didn't know yet about French pikes.

"Take my arm, milady," Beau said with a deep bow. "From the looks of things we're in the Hôtel de Ville in Paris, the king's masked ball. The party of the year."

"You're always at the party of the year," I retorted, taking Beau's arm and trying not to gape around me. This Alexandre Dumas shindig put our recent Gatsby bash to shame: the branching candelabras overflowed with fine beeswax candles; the fountains in the corners overflowed with champagne; the courtiers parading past overflowed with pearls and diamonds. I smelled perspiration that had been covered up with perfume rather than deodorant; I smelled wine and hair oil and hot wax; heard the whisper of satins and the sibilant hiss of gossip. Somewhere around here Milady de Winter was plotting devilry, d'Artagnan was thundering off to return the queen her diamond studs in the nick of time, and the book plot was unfolding, but this was a bubble of pure beauty. Not the kind of bland, Disney-fied beauty you saw flat on a screen in a costume drama—the three-dimensional kind, full of sweat and verve and life. I saw a pair of courtiers flirting up a storm without uttering a single syllable; I saw a footman surreptitiously swigging out of a champagne bottle while the aristocrats who underpaid him weren't looking, and I couldn't help a huge smile.

What a miraculous thing a book was, when you stopped to think about it: whole worlds springing to life from nothing more than squiggles on a page.

"I need a tabard," Beau whispered. "I need a plumed hat and a lot of needle lace." He'd managed to swipe a mask from somewhere; it didn't hide his Regency attire, but the Library was doing its usual job of making us semi-invisible to all the courtiers with whom we were pressed into this big ballroom. The French king was tut-tutting his way across the marble floor toward his queen, the sinister Cardinal Richelieu oiling along behind . . . Beau's eyes, I saw, were wide behind the mask's eye slits, drinking in every flare of silk and glitter of crystal. "I'm in Paris," he said softly. "I always wanted to go to Paris."

"Sorry it's not the version with Givenchy and Yves Saint Laurent on the Champs-Élysées."

"No, no, it's this version I always wanted to see. Dumas's version. I'd take a trip to modern Paris too, sure, but I always wanted to see the Paris that had royal balls and lace-topped boots and swashbuckling."

"Beau Sato-Jones." I looked at him behind the feather fan, which was also doing a nice job of hiding the green tablet. "Don't tell me I've found your favorite book!"

"When I was nine, I persuaded my two older brothers to dress up with me as the Three Musketeers for Halloween." His smile was tilted. "The one time they were ever willing to dress along with me."

I started to ask why when his eyes drifted over my shoulder and he went stiff. "C and C incoming."

I turned with a swish of satin skirts, seeing the familiar arrow of motion as French courtiers moved unconsciously out of the way of Library Security coming straight for us. "Right, I'll draw them off toward the nearest royal guards, and then you quietly—"

But Beau was not in a mood for quiet. He threw his mask aside, drew his sword from his walking stick with a flourish of what I could recognize as an invisible musketeer's tabard, howled, "*One for all and all for one!*"—and charged.

"Well," I said afterward, "I'm sorry we won't get to see more of Dumas's Paris while we're in town."

We were in the clink, sort of. Even the Astral Library's veiling anonymity couldn't entirely hide from the king's guards that a fight had broken out on the fringes of the ballroom floor, so after a royal pikeman dispatched Chad and Chester 5.0 down to empty suits (that caused a certain amount of muttering, followed by complete amnesia), everyone had looked up to see Beau (disheveled, grinning, sword in hand) and me (disheveled, dismayed, corset busk in hand) and decided we needed to be marched from the premises before the king's ballet was disturbed. We'd probably have ended up in some dank cell shackled to a rack if things went by strict historical accuracy, but the guards seemed to get hazier and hazier on who we were the farther we got from the ballroom, so we finally got stuffed into what looked like an unoccupied anteroom and locked in with a mutter of *We'll see what the Cardinal has to say about this.*

(No trouble on my part understanding the seventeenth-century French. Accelerated linguistic osmosis for the win!)

"I think you may have lost your sword," I told Beau. The royal guards hadn't had any trouble confiscating *that* before he could conceal it inside its innocuous cane sheath.

"A small price to pay for king and country." Beau was still fencing up and down the little anteroom with the sheath. "*Vive la roi!*"

"Let me margin-travel us out of here," I said, getting out the green tablet, which everyone's seventeenth-century eyes had skipped right over, but Beau turned mid-parry.

"Can't we stay a little longer? I don't want to skip out of Dumas's Paris just one chapter in."

"You want to stay locked in a closet?"

"I'm betting we can see the dancing from here . . ." Beau pointed up at a knob near the top of the wall. Pulling a cushioned bench over, he hopped up and gave an experimental tug. A panel slid to one side, and he crowed, "Ha, I was right—I bet the servants use this to spy on the courtiers. We've got a prime view and the king's ballet is just kicking off."

I hesitated. I *was* tired—margin-traveling was getting to me, even after the rest we'd had in Walter Scott's Highlands—and even if this was just a stuffy little anteroom, there was a tray on the nearest table that some maidservant or footman had clearly stashed away for later, with a bottle of Burgundy and an entire platter of little almond cakes. My stomach growled under my boned stays, and I realized that outside the Astral Library's suspension of appetite, I was hungry again. Besides, it wouldn't hurt to know how fast it took a resurrected Library Security team to catch up with us *without* jumping to a new book. "I'm in," I said, grabbing bottle and platter.

"Milady!" Beau handed me gallantly up onto the bench, wine and cakes balanced somewhat precariously on the ledge under the sliding panel, and soon we were watching the French court dance below in a mesmerizing swirl of music and masks and velvet, swigging Burgundy straight from the bottle and cramming down sweet almond cakes. I couldn't help humming through a mouthful of marzipan, swaying to the rhythm of the music. "Did I mention that I love the new threads?" Beau said as my billowing satin skirts brushed against his legs.

"Thanks." I was all huge sleeves and cleavage and pearls this time around: beaver hat with curling cream feathers, some sort of tabbed doublet in tawny velvet with pearl clasps, gold satin petticoat billowing down to my embroidered slippers. "Have to admit the stabby thing in the corset is handy." Dipping a hand down my bodice, I managed to extract the long strip of carved ivory that stiffened the front of my stays—it came to a decent point, and I'd managed to stab Chester 5.0 with it right before the royal pikeman reduced him to an empty shirt.

"It's not a 'stabby thing,' it's a busk. Helps keep the shape of a seventeenth-century bodice . . . and ladies gave them to their lovers sometimes, as a favor." Beau squinted at the etchings on mine. "Oooh, you got one with dirty carvings. That's definitely a threesome carved into the back side of—"

"Hey, now. Stop ogling my X-rated underwear." I wedged the busk back down my bodice and rested my arms on the ledge again. "Nice to get a bit of a breather, I have to admit."

"C and C have been finding us pretty fast." Beau frowned. "How exactly are they tracking us from book to book?"

"I have no idea. I'm making all this up as I go along."

"I know I haven't been here all that long, but is it starting to feel personal?" Beau saw my questioning look and elaborated. "I mean, I don't know how these warnings were targeted before, but it was all aimed at the Librarian, and we can assume they *know* the Librarian. Now everything's aimed at you—how is it they know so much about you, right down to your personal vision of what Library Security looks like?"

"Well, we can assume they have access to the Library's files on Patrons—"

"Can we? You said the Librarian kept things pretty locked down. How do they know?"

I chewed my lip, thinking. Had someone been feeding the Board information on me? Was that why I kept imagining my mother in this book or that painting, images of her being slipped in just to unsettle me? But who would be doing it? Not the Librarian, and I had equal faith in the integrity of the Gallerist and the Programmer—they both gave the impression they'd fall on a sword rather than betray the people we were trying to protect.

The people we were trying to protect . . .

"I wonder," I said reluctantly, not liking the idea one bit, "if it might be a Patron."

"Who?"

"There was one I met from the world of Sherlock Holmes . . ." Smart, resourceful Sarah who had soothed the hyperventilating Stephanie out of a panic attack and shepherded teenage Larry along with a sympathetic hand, but who had looked me in the eye and said, *I'd let that entire place burn down, and this one too, if it meant keeping myself safe from Ty.* Briefly, I told Beau about her. "I liked her, but she said point-blank that she'd throw anyone and anything under the bus to save herself from her husband. If the Board somehow got hold of her and asked for information on me . . ."

Yes, I could see her giving it. If it meant she could stay free and stay hidden.

"But how much does she know about you?" Beau pointed out. "You only met her a day or so ago."

She knew I was a foster kid; knew about my mother—I could hear myself tramping along through a pea-soup London fog, saying, *I walk into the world of a book, just like every reader has wanted to do since the dawn of time, and all I can do is fantasize about finding my mother. How much of a bad Freudian cliché is that?* Sarah knew quite a lot about me.

"This is all just speculation," I said, blowing out a frustrated breath. "I don't even know if the Board can make contact with our Patrons in hiding, so it's probably nothing." I didn't like to think that someone the Library had offered sanctuary to might betray us all, so I did my best to shove the thought out of my mind. Not like I could do anything about my roiling suspicions, anyway.

Beau passed me the bottle of Burgundy and I took a long swallow, looking back down at the dancing still going on below. Patterns like flowers, coming together and breaking apart again in this quiet pocket of untamed time . . . The French queen was so graceful, a swan in blue satin. "I could stay here forever," Beau said.

I smiled, forgetting Sarah and my ugly suspicions in the dreamy bliss of his expression. "What made you fall in love with Alexandre Dumas?"

"Some movie adaptation I caught on TV as a kid. I wanted to run around in lace cuffs, getting into sword fights . . . And it was more acceptable, you know?"

"Than what?"

Beau's eyes were still trained on the dancing, but his smile faded. "My older brothers always dressed up as Batman or Superman for Halloween, or their favorite football player. I always wanted to be something fancy, a Disney Prince or the Cavalier from the *Nutcracker*—something *gay*, they always teased me. So I came up with the Three Musketeers, because it's fancy but it's still badass. The tabards and the swords make the lace collars and the feathered hats just *not gay* enough, right?" A snort. "So my brothers dressed up with me, and the three of us ran around all night getting into sword fights."

"Did your brothers do that a lot? Tease you?" For some reason I remembered a girl in my sixth or seventh foster home, a year older than me, the one who called me *fatty* and made oinking noises whenever I picked up my fork. I probably would have ended up with a nice little eating disorder if she hadn't tried to stab another foster kid with a pair of pinking shears and gotten her bitch ass moved out, thank God.

Beau shrugged his elegant shoulders. "My brothers were pretty good to me. Always beat up anybody who picked on me at school.

But then they'd turn around and say, *If you didn't act like a fag, nobody would pick on you*—that kind of thing."

"Didn't your parents shut that shit down?" My experience of parenting wasn't exactly standard, but didn't parents usually referee the kids, prevent the teasing? Wasn't that a parent's *job*?

"My dad was a running back at the University of Alabama. Roll Tide!" Beau pumped a fist, mockingly. "He loves me, not saying he doesn't. But I wanted a Singer sewing machine for my thirteenth birthday rather than anything from Dick's Sporting Goods, so I puzzled him. Still do. And he's, you know, a manly man with a nice little wife and three boys at home, so he just . . . finds it easier to turn a blind eye whenever a guy turns up on my Instagram feed. I post a pic arm in arm with someone like Ysabel or Tyesha or Marleigh, my father will be on the phone in twenty-four hours asking me if I'm bringing her home for Thanksgiving. I could post a pic actually lip-locking with Deryk or Rhys or Marcus, and suddenly Dad's stone blind."

I kept my eyes trained on the spectacle below: a courtier in silver satin surreptitiously adjusting the pasted-on beauty spot below one eye in between complicated passes; a dwarf attendant aiming a look of suppressed loathing at the woman whose train he was carrying. "Your mom do the same thing? Not acknowledge the boyfriends?"

A shrug.

"But they've still got to be proud of you," I persisted, not entirely sure why I was pressing this except that . . . well, someone like Beau was supposed to have it all, right? Sure, he was stressed out and overworked, but he was still the gorgeous, confident, independent product of a childhood spent in an actual house with a yard, his parents neither divorced or absentee or routinely feeding the grocery money into the slot machines. If *Beau* didn't have it all, what hope was there for anybody? "I know you're stretched to the limit right now, but you've still got your own business, half a million Instagram followers, a movie star about to wear your dress on the red carpet. That's success any way you want to define it."

"Because my dad lent me the money to start the shop." Beau took a swig from the bottle of Burgundy. "He didn't get why I wanted it, but he was trying so hard to be fair. Because he loaned my brothers money too, when they each got married and bought houses, so he was going to do right by me even if he didn't understand why I wanted it, and I got the same deal: start paying it back in three years." Pause. "That was nearly three years ago."

"And you're worried about paying?"

"Of course not!" He flashed me the practiced, dimpled, easy smile I'd seen so often before the tumultuous last two days—the smile that said *Hi, gorgeous, ain't life grand?*—and jumped down from the bench, apparently losing interest in the dancing below. "I'm the guy who's Made It! The guy who has all his books in the black. The guy who can start paying his dad back without batting an eyelash."

"*Are* all your books in the black?" I took his extended hand and hopped down from the bench in a billow of satin, remembering that tidy QuickBooks account I'd been hired to set up at the start of our acquaintance. He'd been cash-strapped back in those days, but everyone was when just starting out a business. Surely now—

"Why are we talking so much about me?" Beau released my hand but took his time doing it. "Why can't we talk about you? Because I'm not the most interesting thing in this room—you are."

"Don't be ridiculous; you know my life. It's a patchwork of disasters. *I* was a patchwork of disasters before all this"—gesturing at the book world around us, the Astral Library beyond that—"happened."

"Oh, honey, no." Beau smiled a sweeter, sadder smile than the dimpled stunner he'd just flashed me. It kept the dimples hidden but creased his eyes and his cheeks in mesmerizing parallel lines. "Under the surface we're all a patchwork of disasters."

"Some of us more than others." I shrugged, trying to sound flippant. "I don't know who my father is, and my mother didn't want me. Get kicked out into the world with a start like that, you're guaranteed to be a fuckup."

"Your mom's the fuckup for missing out on your life. Not you."

"You know I keep *seeing* her? In a book world, then in a painting world . . . I feel like any time I slow down enough to take a look around me, she could pop up. Only so far, it's never her."

"It could be." Beau tilted his head. "What if she disappeared into a book, and that's why she left you?"

"I thought that too. I asked the Librarian but she said she couldn't tell." I tried to smile. "Apparently even the Astral Library has HIPAA violations."

Beau pointed at my tablet. "Could that tell you?"

I looked down at it. "I'm afraid to ask."

He hooked one finger through the long strand of pearls around my neck. "I'm here for you, Alix."

"It'll just tell me no," I said.

He waited.

I took a deep breath and typed my mother's name into the search bar. Hit Enter.

Access denied.

I wasn't really surprised to see it. Not surprised, but disappointed despite myself—disappointed enough that tears pricked the corners of my eyes. "Dammit, I'm going to ruin this lovely court makeup job that came with the dress." I tried to smile, tried to blink the tears away before they could fall. "See? Told you I was a fuckup."

"That's the last thing you are." Beau twirled his fingers through another loop of my pearls, shortening the distance between us. "You should see yourself, dancing between book worlds like a magician, spinning doors out of pages. You are seriously impressive, Alix Watson."

Because the Astral Library had chosen me, sprinkled some of its stardust on me. "It's this place, that's all."

"I don't think so." Tilting his head, gaze on me unblinking. "I think it's you."

Maybe he was only trying to cheer me up, distract me from my disappointment over not seeing my mother's name in the tablet . . . But I still felt the wild urge to take a risk. "Are you flirting with me, monsieur?" I asked, the sound of the music from below still swooping and swirling in the air.

"You tell me, czarina."

"I thought you only flirted with aspiring models who can't spell their names. Should I start signing myself *A-L-Y-X*?"

"Don't you dare. And if you can't tell I'm flirting with you right now, I need to up my game."

"Oh, I think your game is fine."

"Seduction: the only sport I've ever been good at."

"Since when is seduction a sport?"

He wound another loop in my pearls, drawing me closer. "It is if you do it right."

"You're good at other sports," I said, feeling my mouth go dry. "Where'd you pick up all those sword moves?"

"Tae kwon do, when I was fourteen. Get stuffed into enough lockers by enough football players, the idea of learning to flip people over your shoulder starts looking pretty good. I had a lot of staff training with a *bo*." A lazy smile. "It translates pretty well to a sword."

"What else translates from tae kwon do to *The Three Musketeers?*" I managed to ask, heart pounding away behind my carved busk.

"Dexterity. Endurance. Patience." Three more loops of my necklace were sliding down his wrist now. He began walking his fingertips up the strand pearl by pearl, climbing toward my neck. "Learning to take . . . your . . . time . . ."

Things like this don't happen to me, I couldn't help but think. *Things like this only happen in books.* But I *was* in a book, quite literally. I was in a book, and a beautiful man was flirting with me, climbing his touch slowly, so very slowly, up toward my throat like a prince climbing Rapunzel's hair hand over hand up toward the tower window. Until Beau's fingertips reached the top and curved around the back of my neck, and then he leaned down and unhurriedly kissed the space just below my ear, first on one side, then on the other.

Then he looked at me through those long lashes, and grinned like a devil. "Where next, milady?"

I hadn't ever taken tae kwon do and I hadn't ever learned patience either. I grabbed the broad Regency lapels on that wine-colored frock coat and pulled his mouth down to mine.

He was like falling into a world of velvet, being swathed in satin, spun into gold thread. All that diamond glitter on the surface of him, and I'd never imagined such a soft blaze of warmth beneath it.

"Hello there!" a cheerful young man's voice exclaimed. "Locked in, are you?"

Bad timing, d'Artagnan! I wanted to shriek, because that's clearly who this was: the young hero in dusty riding leathers, sparking and fizzing because he'd just completed his chapter 20 quest for queen and country. Adorable, if I didn't currently want to throttle him. Beau unhooked his fingertips from the neckline of my velvet bodice and I untangled my hands from his linen stock, both of us breathing a trifle unsteadily as we looked toward our rescuer.

"Sir." Beau must have realized who we were addressing, because he swept a bow that dripped chivalry and gravitas. "If we might beg your assistance? We labor in service of a very great lady, and are pursued by those who would threaten her. Your assistance in this matter—"

"Say no more," cried d'Artagnan, and he bowed over my hand with a flourish of his plumed hat and a flash of the eyes that somewhat dispelled my urge to choke him. "I am to the streets of Paris myself, and I will light your way, my own service to a very great lady just dispatched."

He was practically leaping off the tapestried walls as he led us out of the anteroom and down a series of corridors, like a big bouncy puppy with a sword and bucket boots. At first the floors beneath were marble, then plainer stone as we found the servants' passages, and all the while d'Artagnan yattered deliriously about his ladylove— "Beautiful as a summer moon, her eyes like diamonds and her skin like pearls! I pledge my love to her until my dying breath!"

"He's gonna be banging Lady de Winter in another hundred pages," I muttered, throwing a load of satin skirts over one arm as I trotted to keep up. "Some fidelity!"

Beau elbowed me, grinning as he fingered his neckcloth. "You destroyed my cravat, you jezebel. You know how long it takes to tie a cravat *en cascade*?"

"I'll destroy your whole ensemble if you give me fifteen minutes and a little privacy," I purred back with a swoop of my eyelashes. I'd never been much for flirting, but with that kiss fizzing in me like Dom Pérignon and this extravagant gown billowing around me, I was swooping my lashes like Scarlett O'Hara. I even gave a little flutter of my feather fan, starting to see the point of all these historical clothes

The Astral Library

as an aid to passion. A man tugging one finger through the complicated lacing of a bodice raises the pulse a lot more than feeling one wrench at the laundry-mangled hooks of an old Walmart bra, and the frustrating sensation of Beau's lean form up against mine with all those layers of broadcloth, damask, satin, and linen between us just made me yearn to peel him *out* of them . . .

I couldn't help but start meditating what book we might margin-travel to—what book had a convenient fainting couch to hand where we could do a little more exploration under all these layers after we dispatched Chad and Chester—but a bell tolled somewhere outside the palace in the dark Paris night, and I thought of the broken clock in the Astral Library with the Librarian lying unconscious beneath it. Could she be waking yet? How much time had we bought her, jumping between books? Was the door holding against the Library Board?

I spoke up, pitching my voice under d'Artagnan's excited chatter. "Beau, I think we should go back and—"

"Alix Watson," a familiar, monotonous, dual-voiced drone sounded up ahead. "Please come with—"

"Monsieur d'Artagnan," Beau called out at once. "Our enemy approaches. If you and I might fend them off while my good lady here"—indicating me with a sweeping gesture—"makes arrangements for our escape—"

But as soon as the striding duo of Chad and Chester (version six by now? Seven?) came around the corner, d'Artagnan let out a delighted howl of "*Leave them to me!*" and flew to the attack.

"Damned if I will, sir, a Sato-Jones leaves no fray without a blow struck!" Beau howled right back, flourishing his walking stick, and soon there was a brisk fight ranging up and down the stone corridor of the Hôtel de Ville. Chad and Chester definitely knew to dodge the swords by now, and they were doing so with surprising speed, but Beau was using his walking stick as a quarterstaff to great effect. All that tae kwon do had clearly paid off—he moved through a series of geometrically precise passes, *thwack thwack thwack*, putting Chester on the ground and then whirling to the rescue of d'Artagnan, who Chad had pinned to the ground after sliding past a disemboweling lunge. "Not today, you acetate horror show," Beau yelled, neckcloth flying, stick whirling over his head in a complex figure-eight before coming down with a smash across Chad's neck. "*All for one and one for all—*"

And I realized maybe I had something more than a crush on Beau, something more than the desire to peel him out of his frock coat, because my heart squeezed in my chest—literally squeezed to see him grinning and shouting and knight-erranting all over instead of flashing that sequined shield of a smile that hid all the pain and complexities underneath. That unruly muscle in my chest, squeezing and trembling under my tawny velvet bodice and boned stays and ivory busk with the threesome etched on it.

"*My hero,*" I sang out to him like any damsel worth her stuff, and as d'Artagnan bounded to his feet with a whoop and he and Beau engaged Chester between them, I swiped the green tablet open and thumbed us back to the Astral Library.

17

*G*ood news: The Library was rebuilding itself. The massive oak counter had somehow resurrected after being whipped to splinters by the Librarian's lashing tail when she was in dragon form; the huge bronze globe was back in its stand though it had yet to resume spinning; all the broken green glass had re-formed itself whole and uncracked from where the Librarian and I had crash-landed through the window. No sign of Chad, Chester, or the Library Board.

Bad news: the Librarian still lay on her couch motionless as a waxwork. The horrible fear that she had stopped breathing clawed through my stomach, but Beau said, "Look—" and dug a vintage art nouveau compact out of his damask waistcoat pocket, flipping it open and poising the mirror above her faded lips. Holding it up, he showed me a faint mist of breath on the surface.

"Okay." I straightened, claws in my stomach easing a little but only a little. She looked shrunken somehow, old instead of ageless.

Her wounded eye was covered by a bandage now, her arm wrapped in some sort of sling, and I wondered briefly how the Library had applied the first aid—a book, fluttering and flapping above her torso? One of the ghosts, Dennis with his eternally floating copy of *War and Peace*?

The Library will take care of me, the Librarian had slurred as she slid into her coma. *It'll just—take—a while.*

How long was *a while* in a place where time didn't pass in the normal way?

"I was hoping she'd be showing signs of waking up so she could..." I trailed off, not quite wanting to admit that the end of that sentence was *tell me what to do*. About the Library Board—who had sent another flurry of red-bordered notifications through the book drop, I noticed. About Chad and Chester, Library Security, who might not be able to wedge their way in here, but were undoubtedly waiting to pounce the moment I went margin-traveling again. About my terrible suspicion of Sarah, tucked away in her Thomas Cole painting, and whether I was onto something there or completely off base. About *all* of it.

Tell me what to do, I begged silently, but there was only the quiet tick of the Library's clock, the anxious fluttering of the books, who sounded like frightened birds, Beau looking at me expectantly like he thought I knew what I was doing.

Well, fake it till you make it. Right?

"She'll wake up at some point," I said firmly, like it was a foregone conclusion. "In the meantime, we'll just keep on leading Library Security away from the Library. Jump into another book and keep jumping." It had worked so far, hadn't it? "How do you feel about *Gone with the Wind*? Is that public domain?" Plenty of new ways to bump off Chad and Chester there, if so: marauding Yankees, burning cities—

"Absolutely not," Beau said. "No antebellum bullshit. I'm a shade too dark to blend in at the Twelve Oaks barbecue."

"Point taken. *The Arabian Nights*? Shove Chad and Chester off a flying carpet?" I began swiping on the tablet again.

"Can we get something to eat first? I was starving hours ago, and those little *Three Musketeers* cookies didn't really take the edge off now that—" Beau paused. "Wait, why am I not hungry anymore?"

"It's the Library," I said absently. "Time doesn't pass here, so you don't really experience hunger or thirst or the need to pee."

He cocked his head. "But we did when we were in *The Great Gatsby* and *The Three Musketeers*?"

"Yes, time actually passes in books. You pass a week there, a month, a year, it actually counts."

"But not when we leave the Astral Library and go home, right?"

"No, it does. Time in books is time in the outside world too. Which makes me wonder if our world isn't just a book too, on somebody's shelf," I added, still looking for *The Arabian Nights* in the tablet's catalog. "Come on, I know it's in here—".

"Wait." Beau's voice sounded suddenly tense. "How much time have we spent in all those different books?"

"Um." I paused, trying to think. Only an hour or so in *Gatsby*, less than that in *Bleak House*. Longer in *The Bride of Lammermoor*; we'd taken some hours to rest in the shelter of a craggy outcrop, letting Chad and Chester exhaust themselves striding around the cliffs for a while as I dozed off the margin-traveling weariness and Beau kept watch. How long had that made it, by the time we headed for a few more hours in Dumas's Paris? "Eight hours, maybe? Oh, *there it is*—" I clicked on the listing for *Arabian Nights* and began swiping chapter headings. I felt a flutter of tattered cloth around my knees and realized I was back to wearing the shredded Regency dress from

Beau's shop—what costume change would the Astral Library give me once we jumped through the margins to Scheherazade's world? "I really hope I don't end up in some harem pants outfit. Feels just a bit culturally appropriative on a basic white girl like me—"

"Alix. Have we lost *eight hours* on the outside, by jumping around all these books?"

I looked up. Beau's face was taut, all the creases and crinkles of his heart-stopping smile wiped utterly away. "Um. You didn't realize that?"

"Eight hours. Shit." He ran his hands through his hair. "*Shit*. You told me that whatever time it was when I came in here, I'd come out again and no time would have passed!"

"Yes, if we'd stayed in here. But it's different when you start traveling to books." I *knew* I'd told him that at the beginning, when he arrived. I repeated it now, as close as I could remember to how the Librarian had explained it to me. "In a book, time moves forward just the same as it does in our world. Go from here to a book, spend a year in the book, then come back to the Astral Library, you're a year older. And if you go back to your original life outside, time will have advanced there by a year as well."

"You didn't tell me that." His voice was getting louder. "You only said time didn't pass!"

"Beau, I *did* tell you—"

"You hit me with a fire hose of information—apparently I didn't catch every single detail, okay?" He reversed toward the stairs that swept up toward the big ornate door. "But you knew what a time crunch I've been in, and you didn't think to say something when time actually started passing again?"

"I was a little busy keeping us one step ahead of Library Security." I heard my voice rising too, as I followed him. "Beau, listen, this isn't a disaster. It's just eight hours, and time's paused again now that we're inside the Library. You can make up the work you missed—"

"Alix, I don't have eight hours to lose. I'm so behind—if I don't get the dress done in time, I am screwed." Beau stopped at the foot of the stairs, turning back toward me. "I don't get the exposure and commissions from the premiere, I can't make my rent. I can't pay my dad back, my brothers will be lining up to say *We told you so*—"

I blew out a breath. Less than an hour ago we'd been kissing—how had we gotten from there to snapping at each other? "Beau, I'm sorry you didn't realize you were losing time, and I'm sorry I didn't think to remind you. I'm still figuring out how everything works here, myself. But you can make the time and the work up. We'll find a way to bring that damn dress *here* to work on, if you like; you'll have all the time in the world then to get it all done."

I think it would have been all right—the corners of his mouth softened just a little, he took a half step toward me. But the book-drop slot spat out another red-bordered sheet of paper that came sliding across the floor toward our feet, and we both saw the greeting across the top:

TO BOMONT SATO-JONES FROM THE LIBRARY BOARD!

Beau bent down and picked up the page. "How does the Board know my name?"

"Well, you did just spend the last eight hours helping stab, drown, and defenestrate Library Security," I said, trying for a smile—but I saw the color drain from Beau's face as he read the notice. "What does it say?"

He thrust the page at me and took the stairs up to the huge Library door two at a time.

Dear Mr. Sato-Jones, the page read:

>Please be advised that your trespassing on Library grounds, and in serious violation of bylaw 3.92.111, Paragraph J, Sub-Paragraph 113c, in the act of giving aid to Ms. Alexandria Watson, who is illegally occupying the premises. Please remove yourself from the Library or its very likely we will be forced to take legal action.
>
>Future communications from our legal department will be sent to your place of business, Brummell's on Newbury Street. We have already been in communication with the landlord and understand you are in arrears as to rent—

There was another six paragraphs of legalistic droning, but I dropped the notice because Beau had bounded to the top of the stairs and started wrenching at the door handle. "How the hell do I get out of here?"

"Beau, wait. Don't fly out in a panic." I tried to make a joke of it. "They can't even spell *you're* or *it's* correctly; don't let people like that try to scare you—"

"Yeah, well, it's working. They're scaring me. I have to get back." Aiming a kick at the door panels. "Make this place cough up a key."

"You're just going to run away?" My voice scaled up; I nearly fell over my tattered skirts as I ran up the stairs after him. "That's what they want. You don't run from people like that, you—"

"Fight them? With what? I'm a *fashion designer*, Alix, not a goddamn knight. I only stayed here at all because I needed a break from my sewing machine."

That's the only reason? a small, hurt voice asked, somewhere deep down. I pushed it aside for now. "You can't let the stupid Library Board blackmail you into—"

"Yes, I can." He cut me off. "Because the shop, it's all I've got. If I lose that—"

"I know it's all you've got," I shouted. "I know it's your dream, I know it's your whole life, but we also have a woman in a goddamn *coma*." I gestured wildly back at the still figure of the Librarian. "A woman in a coma and a library in danger."

"And what's a dress shop compared to that?" He folded his arms across his chest. "Is that what you're thinking? It's *just a dress shop*. It's *just clothes*."

"Don't go putting words in my mouth—"

"You thought it. Everybody does. *Look at him and his silly sewing machine, get a real job.* Doesn't matter that I've built my life around a craft I love, a craft I've put thousands of hours into learning, a craft I'm damn good at. Doesn't matter that I've got a business I'm trying not to let get sucked down the drain along with every penny I own. Doesn't matter in the long run because when the chips are down, it's *just clothes*."

"Oh, fuck off! I didn't say any of that and you know it!"

We stood glaring at each other, my hands doubled up at my sides, him standing with arms folded. I swallowed my anger, because it wasn't anger that was making me flare up like this, not really. It was fear.

"Beau," I said, much more quietly. "It's terrible that the Board is trying to get at you this way, but—" But what? He stood there, face set, not looking at me. I reached out to touch his gabardine sleeve. "Please don't let them scare you off. Don't go. I'm just trying to save this place."

And I'm scared to do it alone.

"Yeah, well, I've got to go home and save *my* place." He looked down. "Can you please let me out of here?"

I swallowed around the boulder suddenly lodged in my throat. "Okay."

But I didn't need to go hunting on my tablet for an Unlock code. The Library knew when it wasn't wanted. The door opened by itself, just a hair, showing a sliver of library I wasn't familiar with—Beau's local branch, maybe. The handle rattled under his hand, an inquiring sound: *You're sure about this?* But Beau yanked the door open the rest of the way, speaking over his shoulder without looking at me. "Come by Brummell's and let me know how it all turns out, all right?"

"Beau—"

"I've gotta go," he said again, and the man of my dreams walked out of the Astral Library without looking back.

Well, I wasn't giving up that easy.

I needed help here, and I wasn't giving up on the one person I'd been able to enlist as an ally since the Librarian went down. I was going to crack this tablet, get past all the *Access denied* pop-ups on the email function, and find a way to get Beau a message. Tell him to bring that goddamn *Belle* dress back to the Library and work on it with time in limbo until he was done—he could keep watch on the Librarian while I went margin-traveling to lead Chad and Chester away again. He could finish his commission *and* help the Library—it wasn't an either-or. He could choose both. Dammit, I was going to make sure he chose both (*me, please choose me, Beau, I really want you to choose me!*) and I was going to do it *now*.

I blew out a breath. "It's a plan," I said aloud to the Library, and headed to the Wardrobe Department to change back into my old jeans and the T-shirt I'd put on what felt like a million years ago for my shift at The Bump 'n' Grind (more comfortable than a tattered Regency walking dress and spencer). I didn't dare head into a book world yet with Library Security breathing down my neck, but I could hunker down in here to crack the tablet. Get messages off to the Gallerist and the Programmer as well as Beau, because I refused to play Lone Hero here. For one thing it was a real cliché; for another it was unnecessary. There were people both inside and outside this strange, magical plane who could help me, if I could just find a way to rope them back in.

"All right, tablet, you and I are going to have ourselves a negotiation," I said, coming out of Wardrobe and swiping the little green machine off the counter. But the clock gave a soft chime, and when I looked up, I saw another piece of paper drift out of the book drop.

I braced for another of those nauseatingly bureaucratic, politely menacing, poorly punctuated communiqués from the Library Board, but this one wasn't on official letterhead, and it wasn't typed out either. It was handwritten in a breathless slantwise cursive, and I knew that writing like the back of my hand. I'd seen it so many times when I was a kid: on grocery lists, on day planners, on library cards. On that last birthday card I'd received at thirteen, saying, *See you soon!*

My mother started this letter without salutation, as though we were just picking up a conversation we'd abandoned ten minutes ago. Or as if she was writing so fast, she didn't have time for greetings.

> Alix, honey, *where are you?* I've been trying to catch up with you from book to book, and you keep slipping out of reach. I don't dare stay in one place too long with the Board trying to find me. Are they trying to get their hooks in you too?

A line drop there, making my stomach drop too, like I'd stepped off the edge of a cliff. I kept reading, realizing distantly that my hands were shaking.

> I'm sorry I was gone for so long. I was in a book—it's a long story, but time passed differently there, and the Board . . . well, they're bad news. I don't need to tell you that. But you shouldn't have to face them by yourself. I can help—I know a little something by now about how they operate, God knows.
>
> I don't know where you're going to pop up next, the way you've been running book to book, and the Library's sealed up like Fort Knox. So I'm waiting in the Boston Public Library—the Reading Room. Your favorite place.
>
> Let me help you, Alix. You don't have to do this alone.
>
> —Mom

Her handwriting. Her voice. Her words—I could *hear* her in my head, the breathless rush of her voice when she was worried. The entire inside of me tumbled and roared, bells clanging in my brain, hands still trembling. I'd been right—all along, I'd been right. She *had* disappeared into a book; I *had* been seeing her in one book world after another. And now she was waiting outside. Waiting to explain. Waiting to help.

I wasn't alone.

My mouth opened in a silent gasp, and I stumbled dazedly up the green-carpeted stairs toward the big door. I wasn't thinking clearly, wasn't thinking much of anything except that I needed to get out of here.

I wrenched open the door and ran out of the Astral Library into the familiar book-bound space of the BPL Reading Room. The sanctified hush of it in the morning light streaming through the windows—it had to be before opening hours; the room was empty.

Almost.

A woman sat at the very farthest table on the other end of the Reading Room, back turned toward me, head bowed.

My lips parted, letting out a cracked whisper. "Mom?"

Hardly feeling my feet beneath me, I began to walk down the central aisle. My heart thudded. I raised my voice so it echoed off the high barrel-vaulted ceiling. "Mom?"

She started to turn. And then I ran smack into a doughy wall of chest covered by a poly-blend uniform shirt with a Cheez Whiz stain.

"Alix Watson," Chad intoned. "Please come with me—"

It was just reflex, I swear. I'd dispatched Chad so many times by this point, I moved on instinct as soon as I felt the clammy touch of those surprisingly strong fingers. I wasn't thinking as I shoved him hard with both hands. I wasn't thinking that we weren't in a book world anymore; that this was the *real* world in the very real Boston Public Library.

I realized it in a split second of horrified comprehension right before Chad fell heavily backward, head striking the corner of the nearest reading table.

No slow collapse of empty clothes this time. There was a sound like a wet sack of cement hitting a brick hearth and an ear-splitting howl as a very real, very corporeal man hit the floor. I faltered back in utter horror as a drench of shockingly crimson blood spattered across the floor from a split in Chad's scalp, as Chester came running in his knife-edged uniform. The *real* Chester, not the simulacrum version that had been chasing me from Dickens to Dumas. "Alix Watson, you are trespassing on Library grounds outside of public hours of operation and have assaulted a member of Library Security."

I couldn't tear my eyes away from Chad, groaning on the floor, clutching his bleeding head. I'd done that. I hadn't distinguished truth from fiction and now a man was on the ground gushing blood.

Mom, I thought, and looked around wildly. But the woman rising from the table at the far end of the Reading Room and coming toward me with a click of heels wasn't my mother. It was just a clerk, some middle-aged library staffer with a puzzled face—puzzlement quickly turning to horror as she saw Chad on the floor bleeding, and began to scream. I recognized her vaguely from my shifts shelving books here as a page—I knew her, and she definitely wasn't my mother.

My mother wasn't here.

Inside the cage of my ribs, my heart knocked like a coffin lid.

Chester was dragging me along by the arm now. I didn't protest. *Mom*, I kept thinking, *Mom*—and then, absurdly, *Beau*. What I'd give to see Beau charge the length of the Reading Room to my rescue, swinging his sword cane. But Beau was on his way back to his shop, long gone.

I looked at the note in my hand. *Let me help you, Alix. You don't have to do this alone.* Still my mother's handwriting, still her voice. But where was she?

Chester bundled me down the Reading Room, clearly thrilled at the chance to do some actual manhandling. I had one last nightmarish glimpse of the spray of Chad's blood on the floor.

What had I done?

"Alix Watson," Chester boomed, dragging me out, "I am placing you into custody for violent criminal assault."

18

I expected to be frog-marched down the Grand Staircase past the stone lions on their pediments, through the bronze doors sculpted with the figures of Wisdom and Knowledge, and shoved right into the waiting handcuffs of the Boston Police Department. Instead, Chester dragged me down a side corridor to the Abbey Room with its checkered marble floor and Renaissance paneling and inlaid ceiling, shoved me inside with the requisite steely *I'm watching you* glare, and slammed the door. I stood there in the ornate chamber, which used to be a book delivery room and was now rented out for wedding receptions and corporate fundraisers, stomach churning sickly as the lock turned over, wondering how long I'd have to wait before the BPD arrived to haul me away. A library page knocking a security guard on the head might not be that high priority. Maybe I'd be here for hours.

The room was set up with round tables covered in red cloths; clearly some kind of event was planned for later. I sank down at the nearest one, mostly because my knees didn't want to hold me upright anymore. "Shit," I mumbled under my breath, but this was so far beyond cursing. I looked at my mother's crumpled note and stuffed it into my pocket. I didn't know where she was, if she'd ever been here at all or if it had been some kind of trap—I was leaning toward trap at this point—but over the sick stutter-step of my heart at seeing her handwriting, an even more terrifying drumbeat kept thrumming: *Violent criminal assault. Violent criminal assault.*

How much time did you serve for that? No chance I'd get off, even as a first-time offender who'd never clocked so much as a parking ticket—I'd been caught red-handed, dead-to-rights guilty. Maybe a decent lawyer could get the charges knocked down to community service, but how was I going to afford that with my bank account frozen and Libby Bibb stealing my identity? (Let *her* go down for assaulting Chad, if she wanted my life that badly.)

Violent criminal assault. I didn't even know if that was the real term for what I'd done or if it was just something Chester had heard on *Law & Order*. Whatever bargain-basement public defender I was assigned would have to fill me in on that. And afterward? I didn't think I was going away for life just for shoving a man into a reading table and giving him a whack on the head, but no matter how minimal the sentence, what kind of job was I ever going to get again with a jail stint on my record? Or maybe I wouldn't have to worry about what came after jail, because maybe I wouldn't be getting out. If Chad was badly hurt—

He's not, I tried to tell myself, *you didn't push him* that *hard. He wasn't even knocked out.* But the wet-cement smack of his head striking the table (glancing blow, it had only been a *glancing* blow!) kept reverberating sickly through my head, and my hands wouldn't stop shaking. My next library card was going to be for a goddamn prison library. Could the Astral Library find me there, open a door from inside cell stacks? Would it even want me anymore?

Yes, I tried to tell myself. The Library had chosen me; it wasn't going to un-choose me because of a desperate mistake like what had happened with Chad. The Library understood the desperate and the lost; that was almost the first thing the Librarian had told me. If I could just get out of the Abbey Room before the police arrived, get back to the Reading Room, I was sure I'd see my door fly open in welcome. Maybe one would even open up for me from here—

But when the door thudded open, it wasn't the Astral Library I saw as I scrambled to my feet. I didn't see any Boston Police Department uniforms either. A much more familiar and much more welcome figure walked into the room, jeans and purple-framed glasses and a full sleeve of flower-vine tattoos showing from her short-sleeved blouse. "Elizabeth," I exclaimed, almost falling on my boss. "I'm so sorry, if you can let me explain—"

She held up a hand, and my words dried up. My slightly funky boss who prided herself on being a cool librarian and not the old bun-wearing shushing kind, who tried to get me extra hours and sounded genuinely sorry when she couldn't, who traded tattoo stories with me—was she really going to send me off in a cop car? Hope rose cautiously because she was smiling as she looked at me. "Alix, please have a seat." Waving a hand back at the red-clothed table by the ornate Abbey Room fireplace.

"I didn't mean to hurt Chad," I burst out, sitting. "I swear I never meant—"

"Of course you didn't," she reassured me, sitting down opposite and laying her clipboard on the table. "Chad's fine, just a bump on the head. I know you, Alix, and you couldn't hurt a fly."

That should have been reassuring—certainly the news that Chad wasn't headed for the emergency room sent a lurch of relief through me—but somehow it wasn't. How well *did* Elizabeth know me, if she thought I wouldn't hurt a fly? I wasn't really very nice. Any kid from the foster system came out with teeth, usually well-sharpened ones.

But I wasn't going to point that out to someone who held my future in her hands. I was just going to sit here looking harmless and penitent. "Please don't turn me in to the cops, Elizabeth. *Please.* I'll do anything, I'll—"

"Yes. I know you will." Her smile widened at this point to an absolute beam, and that was even less reassuring. In fact, it started my stomach clenching all over again. "So let's have a chat, you and me. I've been trying to run you down all day, but really, you've been *very* hard to catch up with."

"Why have you been wanting to talk to me?" I managed to ask.

Her eyes twinkled through her purple-framed glasses. "Because I'm the president of the Library Board."

That moment stretched out into a little infinity all its own. Me, sitting there staring stupidly at my boss, the tiny details piling up in my brain because I couldn't—wouldn't—let the big picture come fully into focus. The smell of wood polish in this room, the bigger smell of old books that permeated all libraries through every wall and ceiling panel, the smell of the chemicals that had been used recently to restore the fifteen antique panels that lined the walls, depicting Galahad and the Grail Quest. Galahad himself, single-minded and dense in his red cloak, striding through adventure after adventure from his Perilous Seat at the Round Table to the Castle of Maidens.

Not as dense as Alix Watson, who had thought she was on an adventure but hadn't realized it was a trap. And now here I was in the heart of it, steely teeth closed hard around me.

The Astral Library

"I don't suppose you actually have my mother here?" I heard myself say, sounding eerily polite. Feeling the crumpled note in my pocket, the handwriting that I would have sworn on a stack of Bibles was hers.

"Oh God, no. What do you take us for, kidnappers?" Elizabeth laughed. "Your mother's married now, living in San Diego with an eight-year-old—"

I recoiled in my chair like I'd been slapped. "I don't believe you."

A shrug. "She wasn't hard to find, Alix. She runs an online shop, Bookish Notions, makes earrings shaped like tiny bookstacks, that kind of thing. I ordered a few kitschy little trinkets off her; she does her own packaging and writes her own receipts, so it wasn't hard to get a feel for her handwriting."

"I'm pretty sure forgery is a crime," I managed to say.

"All for a good cause!" Elizabeth twinkled at me. "We had to hook you out of that Library *somehow*. And really, a twenty-six-year-old with abandonment issues, it wasn't too hard to guess you'd come running for Mommy if Library Security had trouble nabbing you."

That hurt, even through my enveloping shock. How easy I'd been to manipulate. A forged note and a few manufactured book-world sightings . . . or maybe the Board hadn't even been behind those. Maybe I'd been imagining Mom all along, because I was just that desperate and needy. Elizabeth made a note on her clipboard, and I couldn't stop staring at this woman who had pulled the wool over my eyes with such ease. "Are you like the Librarian?" I heard myself ask, still somehow sounding polite. "Hundreds of years old, with a magic tablet and the ability to turn into a dragon?"

"Oh, no. Just an ordinary woman doing an ordinary job—all the regular Library Board members are. We're all a lot more in touch with reality than these old fossils like the Librarian. Much better for the Library if she retires and lets the younger generation run things, am I right?"

No, I thought. *Not in the slightest.* "If you're the head of the Library Board and in charge of all kinds of—of astral programming or whatever—what are you doing working in the Boston Public Library?"

"Using this as a base to dig out the Librarian, of course," Elizabeth replied cheerfully. "Not to speak ill of her, because of course the old dear is quite an institution, but I don't mind telling you she has been a *headache*."

"She's in a goddamn coma." I felt the first red flickers of rage starting to burst through my shock. "You sent your hell-fiend card catalog on her trail. You broke her arm and tried to *blind* her."

"Come on, she wouldn't be in this position if she hadn't refused every attempt at a more reasonable negotiation. The Board invited her input at any one of our meetings, but even when she attended she completely refused to discuss modernizing the Astral Library."

I remembered the Librarian's smoky, cynical voice: *They've been trying for years to take the Library away from me by bureaucratic means...*

"I don't see why the Astral Library needs modernization." I tried not to jut my jaw at Elizabeth. "It seems to be trucking along just fine the way it is."

"Alix, every system needs a periodic overhaul. Look at this old heap." Waving a hand at the Abbey Room, at the Boston Public Library beyond it. "Very picturesque, but a twenty-first-century library should be run along a business model rather than just operating as a book depository. Ideally a modern library should be one-quarter books, one-quarter computers, one-quarter tertiary media, and one-quarter monetized programming—"

The Astral Library

"A library isn't a business," I tried to say, even as my outraged brain shrieked *Only one-quarter books?!* but Elizabeth was in full flow.

"Take spaces like this, now. What library needs a lot of Edwardian murals about fusty old knights?"

"Victorian murals," I said before I could stop myself. "Edwin Austin Abbey was commissioned to paint these murals in 1893; that makes him Victorian, not Edwardian. And that's if he was English, but actually he was American. And it's not just any fusty old knight; the murals depict Galahad and the Grail Quest, which is all about the ceaseless search for what is longed-for and unobtainable except for those who strive and make themselves worthy. Which is actually the perfect metaphor for a library, since it serves people who strive after knowledge. But you didn't actually know any of that, did you?"

A brief flicker of annoyance crossed Elizabeth's cheerful face. "You only know it because you read it on Wikipedia."

"No, I read it here in the BPL. I saw the murals and asked the library staff about them, and they gave me books and I read the books and got even more interested and ended up going down a whole rabbit hole about Arthurian myth and symbology. Because that's what people like me do when we can't afford college but we can afford a library card." I folded my arms across my chest. "Which is the entire *point* of a library, it would seem to me."

My boss tilted her head to one side. "You're a bit of a fossil too, aren't you, Alix? Young as you are. Well, given your upbringing, I suppose that's understandable."

I wasn't going to talk anymore about my upbringing, not with her, not after she'd weaponized it against me. "What is it you brought me here to talk about? I'm pretty sure this isn't about me shoving Chad into a reading table." I was starting to wish I'd shoved him harder. Into Elizabeth, off a cliff.

"Isn't it obvious?" Elizabeth flipped to a new page on her clipboard, all business. "You need to open the Astral Library for me tomorrow, when the Board convenes for the annual meeting to discuss the Library's future."

I opened my mouth, but she held up her hand to forestall me.

"Let's skip the part where you tell me to go to hell, Alix. You open the Astral Library tomorrow morning, and not only will all criminal charges against you be dropped in regards to the violent assault on Chad—"

My stomach gave a queasy roll hearing those words again, *violent assault*.

"—but you'll get your life back. Your online identity, your debit card, your bank account and all thirty-six dollars and eighty-two cents left in it. I'll even throw in your mother's current address and phone number."

It wasn't wholly unexpected, but I still sat there like I'd been sucker-punched. My frozen bank account; my stolen life. I looked at Elizabeth and something else slid into place. "You wouldn't also happen to go by Libby Bibb, would you?"

"My little joke." She smiled. "Libby, like for librarian? Clever, right?"

"Not really, no."

"And Bibb, like for—"

"Bibliophile, yeah, I get it."

"You really have quite a vocabulary for a girl who never went to college," Elizabeth said, sounding vaguely surprised.

"Yes, I'm a sesquipedalian at heart," I said. "That means someone who likes big words, in case you don't know. I figure you don't. You really have quite a limited vocabulary for someone who went to college. You ignorant bitch."

Another flash of annoyance, but she covered it with an indulgent look. I couldn't believe I'd ever thought this woman was cool, or that cool was something a librarian should aspire to be. Right now I'd settle for the old-school kind with glasses and a bun and a *shush* that could level city walls, who called books to her hand like falcons and whose oath was to the sanctuary she guarded and not some bunch of bureaucrats with clipboards. A librarian who wasn't a Board member, but a goddamn Book Dragon.

"What kind of librarian are you?" I heard myself asking, voice starting to rise. "Why have you got the Astral Library in your crosshairs this way? Sending Library Security around like your own private army, attacking the Librarian—*why*? Are you one of those book burners who wants to ban every book they don't like, all to Save the Children? One of those people who thinks libraries are corrupting our national moral fiber?"

"God, no." Elizabeth made a dismissive little wave. "These book-banning types are a *bit* over the top. We have one or two on the Library Board, and goodness, but they take themselves seriously!" Chuckle, chuckle. "But they're having a moment right now in the national conversation, so I've found it's easiest to just give them a seat at the table."

I stared. "And who are you all going to invite to your book burning in Copley Square?"

"Don't be so dramatic, Alix. I'm just doing my *job*—an ordinary woman doing an ordinary job, remember?—and I was hired to make sure that the Astral Library moves with the times. Institutions have to change, or they won't remain relevant. That's true of any institution, in any field. And in any field, someone has to see which way the wind is blowing and what kind of rules need to be enforced. I'm just here to enforce the rules." She gave a bright, meaningless smile. "Not have opinions about them."

No fanatical gleam in her eye; no grand ideology propelling her down this lunatic path. Just a rule enforcer with a clipboard. Well, any dictatorial movement needs plenty of those—can't get it all done with frothing fanatics, after all. Gotta have the ones with their well-organized clipboards who say afterward, *I was just doing my job.* I looked down at my hands, spread flat before me, and folded them very precisely so I wouldn't fly across the table and bitch-slap Elizabeth right out of her purple-framed glasses.

"So why me?" I couldn't help asking. "Why go to all that trouble wrecking my life? What did I ever do to you?"

"Alix, this isn't about *you*. From the beginning, we never meant any harm to *you*. I said you'd get your life back no harm done, didn't I?" She moved to pat my hand, but I slapped her away. She tutted at that. "Don't be violent, Alix. Violence is never the answer."

"Except when you're slicing up the Librarian and me with your death cards, right?" I raised my eyebrows. "What, no corporate comeback on that one? Go on, then. Go back to telling me why you ruined my life, Libby Bibb."

She exhaled a little sharply but continued. "Given the Librarian's lack of cooperation about allowing the Board entry, alternative methods of access were explored. A focus group was convened, and it determined the best method would be through one of her Patrons."

"You use the passive voice an awful lot when you drop into bureaucrat-speak," I noted. "'Alternative methods were explored'; 'a focus group was convened.' Does that make you feel like none of the consequences are actually your fault?"

She smiled again, but I could tell I was pissing her off. That cushioned complacency was fraying around the edges, and it gave me a spurt of savage satisfaction even as she went on. "I was inserted here at the BPL to find a candidate who could gain entrance to the Library. A bookworm with an underprivileged background, minimal education, few family ties—"

"You can just go ahead and say *loser*," I said. "That's what you're getting at, isn't it?"

"—and as soon as I met you, Alix—!" A little *voilà* gesture. "Of course, it takes a great deal for someone to walk away from their whole life and head off into a book to live. Really, a very impractical plan. So it was felt—"

Stop with the fucking passive voice, just stop it stop it STOP IT.

"—that we'd need to apply additional pressure. Some financial urgency. Just to make sure you'd take the Library's offer." Elizabeth sat back as if to say *There now, isn't that reasonable?*

"So you stole my entire life," I said. "Probably voted on it at your last Board meeting, right?"

"You can have the meeting minutes if you want to review the vote," my boss said. "It's all entirely aboveboard." A little smile. "'Aboveboard,' for a Board vote. That's funny, isn't it?"

"Hilarious." My fists were clenching and unclenching in my lap, under the edge of the red tablecloth. Red cloths to match Galahad's red cloak in all these Victorian murals that marched around the Abbey Room, and I wished Galahad would march in here with his sword and sweep me out of the Perilous Seat in which I'd so unexpectedly found myself. Or better yet, Beau with his sword cane. But no one was coming to rescue me, not today, not ever. "One thing I can't figure out," I said at last. "You saw me and thought, *Here's the perfect deadbeat bitch to get a foot in the door to the Astral Library*—"

"Alix, please don't use words like that." Her smile had curdled.

"The Library Board has a very strong stance against abusive language and pejorative—"

"Shut the fuck up, *fräulein*. What I want to know is how you figured the Astral Library would open a door for me exactly when you needed it to." I gave a smile of my own, thin and edged. "Because I've been a deadbeat bitch—sorry, deadbeat loser—my whole life, and I only just got the magic invite. So how did you know the Library would choose me now?"

Elizabeth stared at me a long moment, then went into a peal of laughter. "Oh, you think you were chosen? Oh dear." Another succession of chuckles banishing her annoyance; this was just too funny. "The Librarian has shut us out of most of the Astral Library's inner workings, but she hasn't been able to keep out *all* the modern updates. The Board has full access to all the information on who the Library extends its invitations to. Getting access to the invitational process wasn't exactly a walk in the park, considering we didn't have access to the Library itself, but—"

"But what?" My heart was thumping away in my chest, tolling like an alarm bell. "*What?*"

"The Library didn't choose you," said Libby Bibb. "I submitted your name."

19

I don't remember being escorted out of the Boston Public Library. I must have left by the newer entrance because I found myself dazed and blinking on Boylston Street, not in Copley Square. The Boylston Street entrance leads to the modern addition to the library, which looks like a municipal parking garage crossed with a health insurance headquarters, rather than the Copley Square entrance, which leads to what looks like a gracious and storied bastion of learning. The modern addition is utilitarian and blocky, the kind of library where someone like Elizabeth wants to work. A library that is updated and modernized, and only one-quarter books.

You'd think Elizabeth would have kept me locked up until tomorrow morning when the rest of the Board arrived, but no. She knew who she was dealing with; she knew this deadbeat loser in leaky pleather boots wasn't going to give her any more trouble, so she cut me loose with a final twinkly little warning. *Do remember, Alix—if you're thinking of ducking out tomorrow morning, heading back to the Library, and disappearing into your favorite book as a way to avoid the Board? We'll just send Library Security to retrieve you, and you can't evade them forever. So really, dear, don't try.*

I'd nodded numbly.

Off you go, then. Entirely restored to complacent good cheer, now that she knew she'd broken me. *Get some sleep. Big day tomorrow!*

I thought of the lumpy sofa that smelled of Brandon's weed and Laurel's cotton-candy vape, and I could have gone back—I was reasonably sure I wasn't going to have to look for a new living situation, after all. Elizabeth had promised to float me a small loan (to be paid back, of course, deducted from my pay as a BPL page) so that I could make it worth Brandon's while not to get rid of a third roommate after all. I was getting my life back; I'd be able to access my bank account again and I wouldn't have to move, and all it would cost was my integrity.

I should have gone home and gotten some rest because I'd have to be back here bright and early to meet Elizabeth and the rest of the Board, but instead of heading for the T station I stumbled up Boylston toward the Boston Public Garden. Not a place you go if you grew up in Boston, because it's always jammed with tourists, but I went there anyway and made my way down the green pathways and around the swan boats, past the pond that froze over in winter. All the way to the quiet corner where the bronze sculpture stands of a mama duck and her waddling offspring, the monument not to a war hero or a politician but a book: *Make Way for Ducklings*.

My mom read me that book when I was little.

I stood there staring at the mama duck, and I did what I'd been dreading. Took out my phone with the cracked screen and did a search for an online shop called Bookish Notions.

As Elizabeth said, it wasn't hard to find. A cute website in purples and blues, curly script, neat online catalog for book-shaped earrings, book-shaped key chains, book-shaped stickers and paperweights and coffee mugs. Based out of San Diego, my mom listed as owner—new surname; no wonder my earlier online searches hadn't found her. There was a phone number.

I'd never felt so numb in my life as I did when I dialed it.

A woman's voice, just a little breathless, answering on the third ring. "Bookish Notions, may I help you?"

I stood there, breathing silently into my phone.

"Bookish Notions, may I help you?" Slightly more impatient now. "If I can—sweetie, stop that, you'll break it." Scolding, but with a laugh in it. And I heard a child's voice in the background: *"Moooooom, you said you'd read to me—"*

Gently, I hung up.

Maybe it was another of the Library Board's tricks; someone impersonating my mother. But I didn't really see Elizabeth going to quite those lengths once she already had me on the hook. It was probably real—the online store, the San Diego number, my mother's new life. Complete with a kid just the age I'd been when she walked out on me. Sounded like a girl.

I wondered if she'd read her new daughter *Make Way for Ducklings*. Mom had always been a good reader: did all the voices, the gasps of astonishment and the cries of joy and the shivers of fear. She could curdle my blood with her rendition of *Where the Wild Things Are*, but she'd never let me go to sleep afraid. She always finished up with *Make Way for Ducklings*, so I'd go to sleep nestled in feathers and a mother's (duck's) love.

She shouldn't have been such a good reader, not if she was going to leave me. A shitty mom should be shitty all the way; should leave you with nothing but bad memories so you can cut the cord dry-eyed. What business did she have reading me all those books and doing all the voices, if she was just going to dump me into foster care because a lousy boyfriend with a tech start-up didn't like kids? All so she could somehow end up married to a guy who evidently *did* like kids because she'd replaced me with a newer model?

I stood there staring at the bronze mama duck and her scurrying bronze ducklings, thinking: *My mother didn't choose me.*

And the Astral Library didn't choose me either. It just got hacked, the way that my life got hacked when a Board vote convened a focus group to determine the best means of accessing a magic library, and really, I should have known. Nobody chooses me. Not my mom, not any of the fantasy worlds I'd been reading about since I was eight, not Beau, and certainly not the Astral Library. I didn't belong there. I never had. I was the walking example of life's undefined—I might as well not exist.

A huge ugly sound burst out of me, too guttural to be a sob, too low to be a scream. A woman in an Atlanta Braves cap gave me a startled look and hurried her toddler along. *Good for you, lady. Keep your kid safe; it's what the best moms do—or really, it's just what adequate moms do; it's the bare minimum of parenting, but some of us don't even get that.* I swiped at my eyes, and realized my bag was still hanging on my arm—the reticule Beau had given me, eons ago. Not much in it but a set of keys, the old bumper sticker from Mom, and my ancient copy of *The Voyage of the Dawn Treader*. I wanted to hurl the book into the pond, because I never should have gotten myself hooked on stories that promised magic doors. I'd finally gotten a magic door and it had turned out to be an illusion. The worlds that lay behind it weren't for me—the only door in my future led back to ten-hour shifts doing data entry, probably for finance bros in Hugo Boss suits who said *Smile, honey!* I stared at the book, but I'd have to backtrack through a horde of tourists if I wanted to hurl it into the pond, and I'd probably be cited for littering, so I kept on stumbling out of the Boston Public Garden toward the T station.

But I never made it home.

There was a little free library on the corner one block west of my apartment building. Nothing cute like you'd see on Instagram, with a shingled roof and a jaunty sign saying TAKE A BOOK, LEAVE A BOOK!—mostly it was a dumping ground for old textbooks and ancient Stephen King paperbacks missing their covers. I'd once scored a beat-up copy of *A Court of Silver Flames* there, though, so I always gave it a hopeful once-over. Even now I checked mechanically, wedging the warped door open and flipping past a Boston Conservatory workbook on entry-level music theory and a few Colleen Hoovers. My hand found the splintery wood at the back, and then suddenly it wasn't there anymore; suddenly my fingers were scraping air and smelling parchment, and it really was true that the Astral Library could open a door from any library in the world, because it yanked me in through a little free library nailed to a listing post in Southie. One moment I was standing on wet concrete on a street corner near a Dunkin' Donuts, and the next moment I was back at the head of those sweeping stairs, looking at the emerald-green windows and the endless shelves of fluttering books.

"You dumb library," I said aloud to those sentient, beautiful walls as I came down the green-swarded stairs. "You just invited a Judas back into the fold. You should have rescinded my library card." But the books just rustled, because thanks to Elizabeth and the Board and their hacking job, I'd been illegally added to the guest list. I'd be left on it till I handed over the keys to the fucking castle.

And the Librarian still lay on her couch, chest barely rising and falling under the lambswool blanket.

"Please wake up," I heard myself saying softly, gazing down at her. "You'd know what to do, wouldn't you? You've been fighting the Board for who knows how long; you'd know how to Aslan your way out of this. You'd even forgive the traitor, just like Aslan did."

She lay there, arm still wrapped in bandages, the slash across her eye now healed to a thick stripe of a scar. She looked like a sleeping pirate queen, one who'd been recently wounded in battle.

I made a hopeless stab at the email function on the green tablet again, hoping against hope that I could get a message out to the Programmer or the Gallerist. They'd help out, they'd know what to do . . . But the tablet just blinked at me: *Access denied. Email function accessible to Librarian (status) only.* Just like it had the first time. I threw the tablet down and found myself sinking to the floor beside the Librarian's chaise, listening to the huge clock tick loudly like a drumbeat to nowhere.

"What do I do?" I asked.

She just lay there, breathing. Books rustled all around us. By the fireplace I could see the ghostly outline of Dennis hovering with *War and Peace*, not even reading it, just nervously flipping the cover open and shut. Flip, flip. Behind him I could see more floating volumes, more of the library ghosts clutching their unfinished books.

"Could I just stay here forever?" Not open the door for the Board tomorrow; live here on Darjeeling and lemon-lavender shortbread and caramel popcorn. Never go into a book, because as Elizabeth had threatened, Library Security would follow me to any world I entered; never go back to the world where I'd started out because Elizabeth owned my identity and my bank account and my life. Just stay here, in stasis, forever.

"She'll find another way in here," I answered my own question, running my finger across the ageless wood of the polished floor. "That Board will locate themselves another loser with no money and no spine, wreck their life so that when they get invited into the Library they'll jump for it just as hard as I jumped, and fall just as hard as I fell once Elizabeth reels them in. She'll get her foot in the door, one way or another. And then what happens to you?" I asked the Librarian.

She lay so still. If you didn't look closely, you'd think she was a waxwork.

"Elizabeth didn't really say what would happen to you once the Board has their hooks in the Library. She made some noises about retirement . . . Can you even survive without this place?" Looking around these walls. "Will it survive without you?"

These walls. These emerald windows. These beautiful, wild books.

"What's going to happen to this place?" I screamed up at the vast vaulted ceiling. My howl echoed through the endless shelves, echoed and then died away, and that's when I wept. I wept surrounded by distressed books and anxious ghosts and a Librarian about to be sheared of her dragon wings, and I didn't know if I'd ever felt more alone.

What's your dream library?

Every bookworm has one, after all. Maybe yours has sweeping spiral staircases double-helixing around each other, or an enameled art deco cage of an elevator. Maybe yours has the austere stone walls of a medieval castle, or the gilded swirls of a rococo palace, or the columned tranquility of a Greek temple. Probably your dream library features a ladder. We all watched *Beauty and the Beast*, after all, and dreamed of being Belle sailing the length of a bookshop on a rolling ladder.

My dream library was the Reading Room at the BPL, so that's how the Astral Library presented itself to me: the barrel-vaulted ceiling, the long windows, the marble busts, and the endless shelves. Only unlike the BPL, the Astral Library went on forever into the distance, the shelves stretching out into infinity, holding all the books of all the worlds that were ever written or ever would be written.

I wanted to see the rest of the Library, if this was going to be the Library's end. I had no confidence that the evil goddamn Board was going to let this place continue in its current state, so if this was its last night remaining fully and completely itself, I was going to see it all. I was still crying a little as I got up from the Librarian's side and began to walk down the endless line of books.

At first it all just stretched on, shining oak shelves and impassively staring busts, barrel vaulting and emerald windows. It took a long time before I realized that the library wasn't stretching ahead of me in a straight line; it was on a very, very faint curve—the curve of the earth, the curve of an infinite horizon on a fantastical sea like the ones I'd dreamed about as a kid, where the water ran sweet instead of salty, where dragon-prowed ships beached at the edge of the world and elves carried themselves off to die. The windows weren't opaque green glass anymore, they were growing clearer with every pace of my heartsick feet, and when I pressed my nose to one wavy, ancient pane, I could see the endless ivory roll of the parchment waves outside, eddies of words casting up against the window in fragments. *Quest* broke in a spray of letters across the glass and slowly slid down the window; I followed the *Q* with my fingertip until it dripped off the glass and back into the eddying foam of words below, and then I kept walking.

The ceiling, changing above me—intricately carved vaulting to time-worn, smoke-blackened beams almost close enough overhead

The Astral Library

to graze with my fingertips, then to white and gold swirling panels enclosing plump cupids who fluttered between clouds passing books to each other, then to ultra-modern glass skylights letting in buttery bars of sun. The floor, changing under my feet—ancient stone slabs sloped toward the middle by the passage of a thousand thousand years of feet; then Byzantine mosaics laid in uncountable tiny swirling tiles to look like bookstacks beneath my worn boots; then wine-colored Persian carpets so deep I sank nearly up to my ankles. The shelves, changing from carved oaken stacks to deep chests piled one upon the other to asymmetrical cubbies built from gleaming alien alloys.

The books themselves changing: massive hand-illuminated things bound to their shelves with loops of gilt chain; then scrolls of papyrus on ornate carved spindles; then clay tablets lettered thickly with cuneiform. Modern mass-market paperbacks with shiny movie poster covers; leather-bound gilt-edged volumes trailing ribbon bookmarks; slim electronic e-readers teeming with title lists in Times New Roman; marble columns etched in story murals winding toward their pediments; sandstone walls covered in hieroglyphs; tiny futuristic e-chips that vented their stories in three-dimensional holographic displays. A million tragedies and triumphs stretching to infinity, a million what-might-have-beens, a million beginnings and a million endings—but all of them still *stories*. Stories on parchment, on rice paper, on scraped unborn-calf skin vellum; stories scripted into pixels or stitched into silk or incised in stone by chisels. All stories, regardless of form, and every one of them alive.

They fluttered as I passed, as if in greeting: paper pages rippling, clay tablets clattering, woven panels of story tapestries moving in a windless breeze, holographic figures bowing. And this time when I looked out the nearest window at the parchment sea with its slow ripple of pages turning over like waves and its foaming eddies of words, I saw in the glass's reflection a glimpse of other library levels even stranger than this one. Libraries fathoms down under the word-ocean, where barnacle-encrusted humpback whales with vast heavy-lidded eyes stored books of songs; beehive libraries where pages were packed into hexagonal cells smelling of honey and wax and pollen; libraries of nothing more than air and breeze where the four winds collected stories from all corners of the earth and piled them on pink-tinted clouds, waiting to see if they'd hold together long enough to find a reader or blow away again in a storm shower of words raining back down into the parchment ocean.

And in the reflection of another window, I even thought I saw—just for a moment—the long-vanished Library of Alexandria. The pale marble columns, the lost scrolls in their tidy rows, the serene-faced statues of the nine Muses, the graceful green gardens where figures in chitons and togas strolled, and over it all the pale, tapering spire of Alexandria's great lighthouse, flashing its mirror to every horizon of the world: *Here there is knowledge. Here there is the cure of the soul.*

I could *feel* the crumpled sticker in my tattered reticule: *They Got the Library of Alexandria—They Aren't Getting Mine.*

I'd never turned around and reversed direction in my slow pace through the Astral Library's halls, and the path under my feet had never varied from its long bending curve, but I was somehow back right where I'd started: under the barrel-vaulted ceiling so much like that of the BPL Reading Room, looking up at the great door with its sweeping staircase. Slowly I moved past the bronze globe, the anxiously fluttering books, the Librarian in her enchanted slumber, crossing to the huge oak counter. I could feel the drum of my own heart inside the cage of my ribs as I picked up the green tablet. I was still signed in: *Alix Watson, provisional status: Page.*

The Astral Library

I looked at the Librarian, who had shielded me under her wings and flown me across the word-sea to offer me sanctuary. I looked at the tablet and I didn't try any sweet talk this time; didn't try to guess what might unlock its capricious heart. I just looked at it, the same emerald color as the windows of this place, and told it something true:

"Maybe you didn't choose me. Maybe you wouldn't *ever* have chosen me. Maybe I don't belong in the Astral Library, not really." A deep breath. "But even if you didn't choose me—I choose you."

And my heart rang like a bell as the screen lock dissolved with the message *Full Librarian access granted* and the Astral Library gave up its secrets.

20

"Do you have a plan?" the Gallerist asked.

Full Librarian access meant I could message the other branches. I couldn't make heads or tails of half the contact list (what exactly was the Banned Books Directive? the Cloud Codex? the Wordsmithing Forge?) but I'd managed to shoot emails off to the Gallerist and the Programmer, and they'd both come at once at my message flagged *Urgent*. They arrived not by the main door but through the stacks, and I wondered aloud if they'd hitched a ride in on that Arnold Böcklin ferry boat from the *Isle of the Dead* painting.

I installed an encrypted VPN tunnel between here and the Kaer Morhen library in The Witcher 3, the Programmer had answered me. He now stood leaning his broad forearms against the back of the Librarian's couch, looking somber in decrepit jeans and an even more decrepit *Fallout: New Vegas* T-shirt, but listening to me intently. So was the Gallerist, standing tall and elegant by the bronze globe in a lot of supple French cashmere and a Hermès scarf, asking me if I had a plan.

I swallowed, feeling with a spasm of panic that people like this should not be looking at me for the plan. I was not the person with the plan. I was the person looking for someone else—an adult, or at least a more responsible, more experienced, adultier adult than me—to provide the plan. But right now, that option was off the table. "I do have a plan," I gulped, and outlined it.

They didn't laugh in my face, which was nice of them. Neither looked exactly enthusiastic either, but not much about the situation we found ourselves in called for pompoms and confetti. "I'll take Shahrzad, then," the Programmer said, touching the Librarian's hand with its emerald ring, and I wondered if he'd given it to her—wondered how many decades he'd had to know the Librarian to even learn her name, much less be invited to use it. "I'll tuck her away with the healing acolytes at the Temple of Kynareth in Whiterun. If anyone wants to get at her there, they'll have to fight their way through every side-quest in Skyrim first."

I nodded. I didn't want the Librarian anywhere near Elizabeth or her Board members when it came time to let them in. Which I was going to do: I'd already emailed Elizabeth through the tablet that I'd returned to the Library but would admit the Board as promised when they arrived tomorrow morning (well, morning for them; a few changeless hours for me). I was trying not to find Elizabeth's lack of response ominous.

"I'll make calls to the people you mentioned." The Gallerist checked off a list in their little leather-bound notebook. "I can't make guarantees that anyone—"

"I know."

"You're sure you don't want us here?" the Programmer wanted to know. "Backing you up at the Board meeting?"

I did. Desperately. Having the Gallerist's elegant unflappable presence at my back, the Programmer's faint Cockney drawl and broad arms, would be distinctly comforting. But— "If I have written statements from the two of you, that should do. According to the bylaws, anyway." I'd been crash-coursing myself through everything the tablet could teach me about the Library Board and the annual meeting rules of operation. There were a lot of them. (Aren't there always, when it comes to bylaws?) "I wish I could have you both here, but you should be looking to your own domains. If the Board wants to take control of this place, they might want the Astral Gallery and the—" Oh, hell, I couldn't remember what the Programmer's domain was called.

"AGNIS," he said. "Astral Gaming Network Interspace System."

"Right. Well, go back and start raising your defenses, both of you, because I have a feeling this"—waving one of the annual meeting notices—"is only the beginning."

"What are they planning to do to this place?" the Gallerist asked, looking around at the anxious books.

"I don't know," I said honestly. "I really don't. Elizabeth kept lapsing into all this bureaucrat-speak. 'Essential modernization' and 'updated business model' and 'monetized programming.'" And I felt a moment's blunted anger at the Librarian for isolating herself here with her Patrons and her live books, rather than taking this on before it became the juggernaut now bearing down on me.

"'Monetized programming?'" The Programmer blinked. "What are they trying to turn us into, alternative arts?"

"Maybe a bit of modernization wouldn't be so bad." The Gallerist sounded like they were trying to convince themselves as much as me.

"Elizabeth thinks the ideal library is only one-quarter books," I stated, and we all traded dark looks. Dennis the ghost jostled a decanter of brandy on the nearest table with a clatter of crystal as if suggesting we all have a good stiff drink, but there wasn't time. The Gallerist sighed and headed out in a flutter of Hermès silk and the Programmer soon followed, bringing the Librarian behind him on a raft of anxious, floating books that carried her like an airborne gurney. And I was alone, but I wasn't really alone.

Can a bookworm ever really call herself alone when she's surrounded by books?

"For the last time," I asked the green tablet, "can I really not just morph into dragon form? Because I could take Elizabeth and the whole Board out in a few good chomps if—"

But the tablet rolled out a big unblinking *NO*, just as it had the first, second, and third times I asked. There were some things apparently even full Librarian status could not grant access to right away—the Librarian had said it had taken a hundred years or so for her dragon to come in. Which frankly was a real shame. If I could access myself some wings, fangs, and claws, I'd munch Elizabeth down with a bottle of hot sauce and sleep like a goddamn baby afterward.

Because now that the shock had worn off and the bleak reality of the fight I'd chosen was dawning, something else was rising in me and that was *rage*. At Elizabeth, for the casual just-doing-my-job way she'd exploited my precarious little life and its various buried traumas so she could get her foot in the door of a world that didn't want her; at the Library Board, who had blithely voted to maim the Librarian all because she'd declined to cooperate with the people who had voted to steal everything I owned or was. Rage at *all* of them.

But rage wasn't going to give me dragon scales and dragon teeth, so I bid that particular fantasy goodbye with a pang of regret, and pulled a chair up to the big oak counter. "All right," I told the green tablet, swiping over to the drop-down menu for Library history, "we'll do this the hard way."

I'd never actually peeled the backing off my mom's old curling bumper sticker—every home I'd ever been to, I just stuck it up with a thumbtack because I knew I'd probably be moving on soon. But I peeled the backing off now and smacked that sticker front and center across the long oak counter:

They Got the Library at Alexandria—They Aren't Getting Mine.

And I pulled up *Library History* on the tablet and sank into the bylaws to prepare the Library's defense. Because if you want to beat a lot of bureaucrats at their own game, be prepared to beat them with words . . . And maybe I was a loser who'd never gone to college, a foster kid who'd largely educated herself with a library card, but I was a pissed-off sesquipedalian bitch crammed to the gills with words.

I had a dozen pages of notes and was halfway down the silver pot of perpetually hot coffee the Library had thoughtfully parked at my elbow when I heard a knock. "Is that the Gallerist sending their written statement over, Dennis?" I called to the ghost, who had put down *War and Peace* so he could hover at my elbow all evening like a spectral secretary, periodically bringing me texts on Astral Library history and refilling the plate of lemon-lavender shortbread and Girl Scout Thin Mints at my other elbow. "If it is, thank them for me and take their statement along with the Programmer's. If any more come in—"

"Who's Dennis?" a familiar voice called, floating through the

Library door panels, and my head snapped up so fast I nearly gave myself whiplash. I stared a moment, then I pushed back from my chair and stumbled around the long oak counter, almost tripping over my pins-and-needles feet as I ran up the staircase and flung the door open to reveal—

Beau Sato-Jones.

Not Beau as I'd ever seen him before, I realized in a split-second head-to-toe glance. He'd always been dressed in some exquisite hand-tailored ensemble, a walking advertisement for his shop in a Regency frock coat and Hessian boots, or a Japanese yukata with stenciled willow trees, or a reproduction of the gold brocade kaftan worn by Czar Nicholas II to a Winter Palace costume ball—but here he was on the Library's doorstep in a heather-gray T-shirt and old jeans, looking rumpled and hollow-eyed, not so much as a single flick of eyeliner at his lashes. This was Beau stripped down to brass tacks, exhausted and rumpled and struggling to hoist an enormous box under one arm, saying quietly, "Can I come in, czarina?"

I yanked him in fast, before Library Security could appear. Though he hadn't entered through the BPL—behind him I saw a sliver of dingy metal book stacks belonging to some underfunded branch library, visible in the barest glimpse before I slammed the door shut. "Where did you walk in from?" I asked, and then directed my second question at the Library itself, demanding, "I thought we were in security lockdown, and here people are waltzing in and out like Kenmore station at rush hour?"

The tablet blatted at me crossly from the counter as Beau answered my first question. "I came in at the shitty little branch library near the fabric store where I stock up on thread and beads for the shop."

"Why?" I made myself ask, throat suddenly thick. Because he'd stamped out of here pretty heatedly, without a backward glance.

He shrugged, still juggling that huge white box. "I just went into the library stacks and . . . thought really hard about this place. I felt pretty dumb doing it, but I guess you could say it worked—I asked nicely, and it listened. The door just opened up between two sets of shelves."

"No, I guessed that part—the Library issued you an invitation once; it clearly kept you on the list if you were willing to come back." I swallowed. "I'm just—not sure why you'd *want* to come back."

Beau's tired eyes flickered. "I try to act like a gentleman, not just dress like one," he said. "And I wasn't even halfway back to my shop before I knew that a gentleman wouldn't have left you here to defend this place alone."

"I get why you left, Beau. The Board threatened your livelihood." His business, his whole life, everything he'd worked for. Elizabeth had threatened my whole life and everything I'd worked for, and I'd folded on the spot.

"They threatened you too," Beau said, reading my mind. "But you're still here."

I looked at my pages of scribbled notes, Dennis hovering ghostily with the coffee and cookies, the books fluttering. They'd drawn closer to me over the hours, I realized. "The Library Board convenes here in the morning for the annual meeting. I'm letting them in—I don't really have a choice—and I'm going to defend the Library. I don't know if I can win, but I'm going to try."

"Some fights are worth starting," Beau said. "Even if you think you'll lose."

I gave a wobbly smile and filled him in on everything—my confrontation with Elizabeth, the note in my mother's name—before disjointedly hashing out my plan. It was sounding weaker every time I went through it. Beau just nodded. "How can I help?"

I nearly broke down crying. "Just—be here for me. Be here to see me through it, because no one ever does. Everything hard I've ever had to face, I end up facing alone."

"Not today," he said simply.

The words resonated through the air, through the Library, through my bones. *Not today.*

Beau had chosen the Astral Library. Beau had chosen me.

"So I have to ask . . ." He looked me over, my old jeans with the rip in the knee, my coffee-splashed T-shirt. "You aren't wearing *that* to face the Library Board, are you?"

"I hadn't gotten as far as my Board meeting ensemble, Beau," I said, managing to sound wry when all I really wanted was to fall on his chest and blubber. "I don't think it matters what I wear."

"Oh, honey, no. They think you're a loser, some spineless jellyfish who can be strong-armed into doing their dirty work for them? Fuck that and fuck them. You show them something different, something they don't expect, and they'll sit down to that meeting feeling off-balance. Show them you're not a jellyfish *or* a loser. Walk in there as a goddamn queen."

"And what would a queen wear to an annual board meeting?" I asked, eyeing the big white box in his arms.

He parked it on the floor and lifted the lid, releasing a waft of scented tissue paper. "I've got just the thing."

The knock at the door, at what I presumed was nine o'clock sharp the following morning in the outside world, was every bit as officious and obnoxious as you'd expect a knock from the Library Board president to sound. Not particularly patient, because mere mortals don't keep Board presidents waiting. I did. I waited till she knocked again, even less patiently, and then a third time, and then I gave Beau the nod.

Whatever Elizabeth and the cadre of suits at her back were expecting to see as the door flung open, it wasn't Beau in his jeans and T-shirt, lounging against the carved doorjamb like an off-duty supermodel.

"'Sup, dipshits," he said with his most devastating smile. "You must be the mouth-breathing asswipes trying to destroy this place."

"You must be Mr. Sato-Jones . . ." Elizabeth looked him up and down. "Must say I'm disappointed. I hoped we'd made our position clear in our last communication."

"Oh, are we being polite? Apologies, ma'am." He swept her a bow worthy of the Prince Regent's court. "*Entrez,* dipshits."

He made Elizabeth step around him as she headed down the stairs—and I saw her blink behind her glasses when she saw me.

"The *Belle* dress," Beau had said simply, unveiling his masterpiece. "If you're an actress playing everyone's favorite bookish Disney Princess, what do you wear to the premiere of a gritty feminist fairy-tale retelling but—"

"A book dress," I finished, barely breathing as he lifted it out of its box. A book dress—I couldn't think of any other way to describe it. Beau had unpicked the cover bindings from a dozen nineteenth-century books, bindings of soft jewel-like leather with faded gilt titles in French and Italian and Latin, and sewn the spines tightly onto a boned corset so the book spines fluted together out from the waist and upward around the breasts. He'd laced it with ribbon bookmarks embroidered in quotes by everyone from Marcus Aurelius to Yeats to Beyoncé, and fashioned flowing sleeves out of tissue-thin gilt endpapers crumpled and distressed to the texture of silk gauze. The big sumptuous skirt that touched the tops of my shoes was made of old book pages weathered to a color like mellow gold, fluted and fluttered to overlap together on a hooped backing so the printed page lines in more French and Italian and Latin rippled with my every movement like the books were about to take flight. "Oh" was all I could say, drinking it in.

He'd taken a discarded trunkful of nineteenth-century volumes destined for a dumpster, picked them apart, and put them back together with lace and rattan, boning and ribbon, gold thread and silver thread and crystal beads as tiny as stars. He'd taken a library and—with care and craft and genius—made it into a miracle.

"There's no way a dress for a Hollywood actress will fit me," I'd breathed, looking at the frothy page-turning confection of it, but it had. The actress starring in *Belle* was no size-zero waif like most starlets; she was one of those body positivity types who snapped at journalists when they asked if she should really be shooting nude scenes at a size fourteen—still a lot smaller than me, but Beau had added a placket and some extra lacing to close the gap at my back. He spent close to an hour stitching me into his masterpiece, recruiting Dennis and the rest of the library ghosts to *pin this, hold that, fold here, fluff there*, all of them fluttering around me like devoted minions reverently robing a queen for her council of war, and God damn, but I liked the feeling. Beau finished the last stitch half an hour before the Board arrived, not saying a word when I finally looked at myself in the mirror. He just gave the small, pleased, private nod of a creator who is very well satisfied with their work.

Elizabeth didn't look quite so pleased. "Oh, Alix. *Such* a drama queen," she said, giving a little laugh as she came down the stairs. But I'd noticed the flicker behind those purple-framed glasses when she saw me standing cold and regal at the foot of the stairs, my shoulders rising out of those gilded book spines like a fortress, the vast flowing skirt making me look a foot taller than I was, my book page hem fluttering even as the entire Astral Library fluttered its books around me from floor to ceiling. My hand rested on the big bronze globe.

(*You want to project power even in stillness*, Beau had told me. *Take the ground out from under them immediately. With the globe it's very Queen Elizabeth I in the Armada portrait, just without the huge lace ruff like a dog collar because ruffs are* not *a good look even on a queen.*) I did not move to greet my erstwhile boss when she descended the stairs. I waited while she came to me, half a dozen suits trailing in her wake, and I stared her straight in the face. I did not look like some spineless loser with thirty-six measly dollars in her checking account. I did not look like a drama queen. I just looked like a queen—like I ruled this domain and everything in it.

"Elizabeth," I said at last. "Board members." Nodding to the men and women behind her, my face unsmiling. "As acting Librarian of the Astral Library, I formally pronounce that the annual meeting of the Library Board is now in session."

21

$\mathcal{B}$oard meetings: after fifteen minutes you fear the boredom will kill you; after half an hour you're actively hoping it will.

"And that concludes the reading of the quarterly report," a woman in a pink cardigan said happily after droning for a solid quarter hour in one long, unbroken sentence. She looked like an ambulatory muffin, the overly frosted kind, and she had a voice like a bumblebee on helium. "There is only one item on today's agenda, which would be the modernization of the entity known as the Astral Library. Do we move to discuss?"

"I so move," said a broomstick of a man with a face like a wet wipe. There were eight of us: seven Board members and me all seated around a long table that the Library had grudgingly conjured, along with a handful of supremely uncomfortable metal chairs. I had a plushy leather throne of an armchair at the head of the table, but the Library clearly had no interest in making our guests comfortable.

Dennis floated a pot of Darjeeling and the familiar blue Wedgwood cup over to my elbow and I sipped, not offering any to Elizabeth opposite me at the foot of the table. Beau also had a teacup where he stood lounging with superb grace against the bronze globe, and he was making sure to slurp from it with obnoxious loudness at regular intervals as he watched the proceedings.

"I have a complete list of titles I would like to cross-check immediately with the Astral Library's catalog," a sheep-faced woman volunteered at once, waving a packet at least fifty pages thick. She had Coke-bottle glasses and a baby-blue sweatshirt that said *Support Your Local Library!* and something told me the irony was completely lost on her. "Titles deemed inappropriately salacious or profane for a library space where children could potentially be exposed to—"

"Not now, Darla," Elizabeth said, businesslike, and the woman subsided resentfully. "The primary matter before the Board today is the Astral Library's current model of operation."

"If you can even call it an operation. Does it have any use at all?" said a very pretty brunette in a sleek designer suit who had been nodding like a bobblehead at everything Elizabeth said. There were titters around the table. I could feel my blood start to heat in my veins, and there was a corresponding rustling from the books on their shelves.

"I think we can skip the discussion and call for an immediate vote on the basis of Subsection 3339567—" Elizabeth began, but I interrupted her.

"Excuse me, but the meeting's host must levy approval of any vote that would summarily conclude the meeting. I so exercise my rights as host and call for a full discussion of the matter at hand."

They looked annoyed at having to hear me out. I looked around the table, refusing to back down, until Elizabeth finally shrugged. "Discussion will proceed."

"If we're being picky about hosts, I question if we must demand the presence of the Librarian," Pink Cardigan continued, sounding peevish. "Since she would be the usual host—"

"She's recovering from your attempt to have her blinded," I said. "And while we're on that subject, I would like to enter a complaint into the record under Article Five, Subsection C, registering my belief that the Board has acted with complete fucking barbarism." I smiled. "If you'll pardon my French."

"Using that kind of language is utterly inappropriate in a library setting where children might be unduly influenced," sniffed the woman named Darla with the Coke-bottle glasses.

"Just what authority do you have here?" Wet Wipe asked me before I could retort, *See any children around, lady?* "Miss Watson, if you have any right to speak for the Librarian—"

"I'm so glad you asked. Under Article Two, Amendment Seven, the Library may appoint an internal representative to speak on its behalf if the Librarian is incapacitated and unable to perform her duties." I gave Beau a nod, and he passed copies of the bylaw around the table. The book-drop slot had acted like a copier for me, spitting out what I needed, and I had an entire stack of papers ready to be deployed. "I would also like to invoke representational privilege to address the Board first, as per Amendment Fourteen."

They didn't look too pleased that I knew my bylaws. I saw shiftings and mutterings, and little notes being taken—of course these people were notetakers. All except for Elizabeth, who had recovered that beaming smile of hers, and it made me feel queasy, but here I was. Beau gave me an encouraging look, and I plunged in.

"I was hoping I could lead you all on a tour of the Astral Library so you can properly understand it," I began. "You've debated this place's future, but none of you have ever seen what it is." I was convinced that no one who walked the shifting halls of this place the way I'd done last night could ever vote against it. "If I could just show you—"

But all around me I saw shaking heads. "Unnecessary," Elizabeth said. "We've all been briefed on the full functionality of the Library and its capabilities."

"The Library keeps entry and exit logs—I *know* none of you have ever been here, because before today you always held the annual meeting off-site. Are you claiming expertise on a place you've never once visited?"

"We have been briefed—" Elizabeth began to repeat, but broke off at a loud slurp from Beau. She cast him a brief irritated glance, then looked back at me. "Proceed to your next point, Alix."

No tour. Disappointing but not unexpected. I took a fortifying slug of Darjeeling and moved on. "You ask what the Astral Library's usefulness is, in its current model. I would like to offer testimony from those the Library has aided." I had written statements from both the Gallerist and the Programmer, detailing the work the Librarian had done in making the Library a sanctuary as well as a repository for knowledge, and I passed copies around the table—but I had something else up my sleeve. Taking a deep breath, I rose and smoothed the front of my vast book skirt. "Beau, will you please escort our witnesses forward?"

He was already moving down the endless length of the library. A short pause as the Board looked on impatiently, and then the sound of footsteps—so many footsteps. Beau at the head of a small crowd, holding the hand of a little girl in braids and an apron. Behind them were familiar faces: Larry in his Huck Finn overalls; Elaine in her garnet-red pleats and dark glasses, small smile hiding her fangs; Sarah back from the Thomas Cole painting in her twill dress and cameo worn from Sherlock Holmes's world, not the villain I'd imagined she might be, just a scared woman hoping to go home to 221B Baker Street. Behind them, so many more: Masako in her Heian court silks; the elegant Black woman the Librarian had plucked out of *Sanditon*; a weathered-looking sailor in a salt-stained coat with a spyglass in the gold-braided pocket; yet another woman in a Regency spencer and bonnet . . .

I was shocked by how many had come. When I'd put out the call to the Library's Patrons, and had the Gallerist and the Programmer get word back to those we'd sheltered in games and paintings, I'd expected written statements. Those had arrived too, sifting down through the book drop like snowflakes—but then the knocks had started. And the Patrons had come—grim-faced, angry, scared—to tell me they would testify in person.

I stepped forward, extending a hand to the little girl with the braids and the apron. She looked different from the waif with the bruises on her arms and the West Virginia twang whom I'd watched the Librarian usher into *Anne of Green Gables*—even just a short time in her book world had put roses on her cheeks, filled out the hollows under her eyes. Beau gave her hand an encouraging squeeze, and she stepped toward me. "You're safe here," I told her, putting an arm around those thin shoulders and turning her toward the long table. "Remember, you're under sanctuary. Just tell them what you told me."

She took a deep breath, one I could feel resonate from her shoulders down toward her brass-toed boots. "I'm eleven years old and I live in *Anne of Green Gables* with the Gillis girls, and I think I would be dead if I hadn't come here. My dad was—" She stopped.

I squeezed tighter around her shoulders. Last night when we'd gone over her testimony I'd taken her hands and said, *You don't have to do this*, and she'd jutted her chin and said, *Yes, I do*. So I just squeezed as hard as I could now, throat thick, and she said in a rush, "My dad was beating me up and my mom was letting it happen, and the last time he wasn't happy hitting me with his belt so he got a plank from the shed. He hit my head so hard I blacked out, and now I'm living in Avonlea making raspberry cordial and I'm supposed to go to the church picnic on Sunday. Please—" She gulped. "Please don't make me go home."

The silence around the table was absolute. One or two of the Board members looked down at the table.

"You're very brave," I whispered to the girl, and the books rustled at that. She nodded, swallowing, and Larry in his Huck Finn overalls stepped forward next, jaw jutted at a pugnacious angle.

"I didn't have much of a library where I was, because I lived in a compound outside Billings that was just a hair shy of a cult and they didn't believe girls should read anything but Scripture, and they *really* didn't believe that you could be born a girl and actually be a boy. Like me. But there was a Bible room with a lot of tracts and books about hellfire, and that counted enough to offer me a door, and if I hadn't gone and decided to live in *The Adventures of Tom Sawyer*, I'd be married by now to a man who was sixty-three years old and already had two wives barely out of middle school." All the fight went out of that taut jawline all at once. "I tell you now, I'm not going back. You try to drag me out of this place and send me home, I won't go. I'll throw myself in the Mississippi first, or off that castle wall of the painting I was hiding in."

"You won't have to go back," Beau told the boy, offering a fist bump, and Masako in her fluttering court silks stepped up next.

"I had no opportunities where I was, nothing at all, no kind of future, and now I'm a poet at the court of Lady Fujitsubo in Heian-period Japan..."

And then it was the man with the gold-braided coat and spyglass, a navy vet who'd been on the verge of killing himself thanks to post-deployment PTSD, until the Library offered him a door and a life spent sailing the high seas with Long John Silver. And the shorter woman in the Regency spencer and bonnet: "I couldn't have children in my world, and now that I live in *Pride and Prejudice* I have a beautiful little boy named John Fitzwilliam after his father—you take me out of my book, I'll never see my son again." One by one they stepped forward, gave their stories. Stories I'd heard in the night as they'd arrived, as I asked them if they were sure about testifying. Stories that tore my heart to shreds.

"These are just a few of the people the Astral Library has helped," I said at last, as Sarah gave a terse account of the husband who'd beaten and belittled her until she fled into Arthur Conan Doyle's London. "There are more. So many more." I held up another sheaf of papers, written statements from more than a hundred Patrons who hadn't come in person but had answered the call, and looked from face to face around the Board table. I saw flashes of sympathy, interest—I was getting through, I knew it. "I ask you to pay our Patrons their due respect by reading these."

> I was bullied every day at school and I was failing all my classes and about to run away from home. Now I help rescue French prisoners from the guillotine with the Scarlet Pimpernel...
>
> I solve mysteries with Hercule Poirot...

I live next door to the March sisters in *Little Women* and I got to help decorate for Meg's wedding . . .

"On the first day I came here," I said as the Board leafed through pages of testimony, "the Librarian told me that the Library offers sanctuary to booklovers in need. People who are desperate, who have nowhere else to go but between the pages. People who are fleeing something: an abuser, a bad life, a lack of choices. Here they have choices—"

"This child living in *Anne of Green Gables*," the woman named Darla interrupted, looking accusingly at the girl who had testified first. "If her parents come looking for her, the Library Board could be held legally liable. Charges of kidnapping could very well be levied!"

I saw the girl shrivel inside her gingham apron, and stepped forward to put myself between her and Darla. "Her father was beating her with a plank and her mother was letting it happen. *Fuck* her parents. She belongs here, as long as she feels safe."

"Of course we're committed to protecting the children. Which is why I feel we should turn our attention to this list of books deemed inappropriate for underage readers." Behind those thick glasses, a feverish gleam was lighting up Darla's eyes. *Book banner*, I thought. Or maybe book *burner*. "If we can examine the Library's catalog and begin pulling all titles deemed—"

"All in good time, Darla," Elizabeth said, and I remembered her words in the Boston Public Library about book-banning types: *I've found it's easiest to just give them a seat at the table*. Well, if this shiny-eyed drone started pulling volumes off *my* shelves . . .

"I think the real point," Elizabeth was saying, "is that no underage Patron belongs here, regardless of home circumstances. Libraries can't be interfering in private family matters; that's a job for Child

Protective Services. I move to add an age minimum to the Patrons this facility has extended doors to."

One or two Board members looked uncertain but— "Seconded," said the pretty bobblehead in the designer suit. "And in the case of these various women who walked out of marriages—" She made a vague wave at Sarah and the others like her, without actually making eye contact with any of them. "Do we really have the right, legally, to withhold information if their husbands make inquiries? As their legal next of kin, these men are entitled—"

"Are you serious?" I sputtered. "You don't all agree with that, do you?" Hunting for the faces that had looked sympathetic just a moment ago, but they looked down at the table as murmurs began rising from the others.

"—might well open the Board up to lawsuits—"

"—unnecessary legal risk—"

"—accusations of overstepping—"

I fought to keep my voice even. "I'm telling you this place helps people in danger, and you are worried about *lawsuits*? Look me in the eye, all of you, and tell me out loud that you'd rather have a little girl beaten with a two-by-four because it spares you some inconvenience. I want that entered in your goddamn *minutes*."

Some shifting and muttering at that, but Elizabeth just blinked at me through her purple-framed glasses. "Public institutions have to remain controversy-free, Alix."

"I thought the point of a library was to court controversy when necessary." I looked at them: Elizabeth, Darla, Pink Cardigan, Wet Wipe, the Bobblehead, the two others—a man with a mouth like a pickle, a harried-looking human mouse who had been tasked with taking the minutes and barely looked up from her tablet. "Libraries exist to help their patrons. If we don't do that—"

A few chuckles ran around the table. "Alix, that's a very old-fashioned viewpoint," Elizabeth said, sounding indulgent.

"Then what?" I moved back to the table, laying my hands flat on its gleaming surface. "What does your new, modernized, twenty-first-century library exist to *do*, exactly?"

"It protects children from—" Darla began.

"Shut up about *the children*. You're using *the children* as an excuse. I'm asking what your electronically advanced, shelf-culled library actually provides. Aside from clipboards and meeting minutes and salaries for people like you?"

Silence. None of them looked shifty or uncomfortable now—they just looked blank, as if I'd spoken in Latin. One or two throats cleared, and then the man with the mouth like a pickle spoke up. "I think we should address the matter of Darla's list, especially as it intersects with the Astral Library's standing operation known as the Banned Books Directive. I for one am uncomfortable knowing that so many books deemed problematic have been specifically collected by this institution."

"If you want to talk about legal liability—"

"A strategic cull of the volumes listed as controversial would seem to be in order—"

"The children!" Darla bleated.

"Who are you, Goebbels in a library sweater?" I snarled. "What are you going to do, make a pile of books in the courtyard and strike a fucking match?"

"Alix, really." Elizabeth tsked. "I've already told you about the Board's stance against abusive language."

"Right. What's your stance on book banning?"

"Public institutions have to remain controversy-free," she repeated serenely. "If that means that not all books remain forward-facing in today's climate—"

"What kind of goddamn librarians *are* you?" My temples were starting to throb. The books were definitely rustling more loudly on their shelves, the huge paper cutter was starting to raise and lower its long sharp arm in that ominous guillotine, *chop chop chop*, and the bronze globe under Beau's elbow was spinning faster on its axis. He gave me another encouraging look, but behind him I could see the Patrons shifting and whispering among themselves. The *Anne of Green Gables* girl was crying silently under the arm of Masako in her layered court robes; Larry stood tall and taut and furious; Elaine the vampire had gone so still inside her garnet silks that she looked like a statue—or like she was going to shift into bat form and swoop off into the ceiling.

"I'm not sticking around for this," Sarah said, picking up her skirts as if about to stalk off back to Sherlock Holmes's London or her Thomas Cole painting or anywhere that didn't have the Library Board arguing her future.

"Sarah, wait." My Patrons had put themselves on the line; I was damn well going to keep fighting. "Give me a moment," I said to Sarah, the very first person I'd met inside a book world, the one I felt I'd maligned even if she'd never know how I'd once imagined she might be selling out her fellow Patrons. I owed her better than that, and when she jerked out a nod I turned back to the Board, smoothing my hands over the book spines of my bodice. The pages of my skirt rustled, and the Board looked up—in that dress I was impossible to ignore, and I took a deep breath that filled up every stitched word of it.

"I think you've all forgotten your purpose," I began, feeling my way down the path of words I was so desperately trying to parse here for these suited skeptics. "A library isn't an ivory tower; it's a place for real people with real needs. Varied needs, complicated needs. A library is not a business. It isn't about turning a profit—"

"Good luck keeping the doors open if it doesn't," Elizabeth said with one of her merry peals of laughter. I looked at her a moment as the Board tittered and my Patrons rustled behind me. Then I moved in a huge cloud of skirt to the oak counter where the paper cutter was chopping at air and put my hand on the arm's long handle so the machine stilled. I don't know if the contraption was already about to give or if the Library knew what I wanted and gave it to me without so much as a screech of metal, but one yank and the paper cutter's long arm came loose: a handled, one-sided blade with a lethal single edge like a cutlass. I came back to the head of the table and without any ceremony at all gave my makeshift sword a whirl in one hand like the Pevensie kids readying for the Battle of Beruna, and then slammed it down into the polished surface of the table. The paper-cutter blade sliced into the wood like butter. I released it to stand there, vibrating in the middle of the table, and the Board's tittering cut off like I'd sliced *them*.

"I'm still talking," I said.

For the first time, Elizabeth and Darla the book burner and all the rest regarded me in complete silence. No note-taking, no shuffling feet, no little whispers. They looked *shocked*, of all things. They were allowed to come here and threaten me and my Patrons, but apparently I wasn't allowed to push back. *I* was the one who had to keep my voice down, keep my language nice, keep being deferential.

Fuck that.

"You have all forgotten what a library is supposed to be," I said, looking from face to face over the quivering hilt of my library sword.

"It isn't a business. It probably doesn't turn a profit. It isn't *about* profit. A library—and I mean any library, even the most roach-infested underfunded branch in the worst part of the worst town you can imagine—is a sanctuary. It's one of the only places left where you can walk through the doors and draw breath and *stay*, without needing to buy something, without having to justify your presence. It's where kids go when their parents are nowhere to be found, and they want to feel less alone. It's where women go when their husbands aren't safe to be around, and they need to research what their options are. It's where students go when they can't get peace and quiet at home for their studying, and people looking for work can search job boards and fill out applications. It's where people who don't have a computer or whose phones are broken can go look up when the next N. K. Jemisin is coming out, or who their favorite celebrity is dating, or whether Fermat's theorem has been solved, or whatever it is they're asking themselves in the dark of the night. A library is where you should be able to find the books that people are trying to ban, and exactly why people are trying to ban them. It's where people educate themselves when every school they've ever attended has failed them. It's where people are *safe*, or at least they should be." I drew a long breath. "Without libraries I would probably be dead. A great many people would probably be dead. They are *sanctuaries*. Cathedrals used to be sanctuaries, but that was only for people who believed in the same things, the same god—people who weren't too different. Libraries are sanctuaries for everyone, no matter how different.

"And this library—" I looked upward, along the beautiful barrel vault of its ceiling, where the books still fluttered like anxious birds. "This is the library of libraries. The one where all the library ladders in the world start. The one where *all* the books are. The strongest place in the world, strong enough to hold out a thousand mobs, but you people can destroy it with the stroke of a pen. You take away this library's ability to offer sanctuary, you strip its shelves of the books you don't want causing controversy and strip its Patrons of their protection . . ." My voice trailed off. "Well, I don't know what will happen. I truly don't. But I assure you, it will be *nothing* good. Because every tyrant of the world, from the sacking of the Library of Alexandria until now, cements their rule by targeting knowledge. They do it with guns or they do it with book bans and board meetings, but that is where it starts.

"And you don't want to find yourself on that side of history."

22

The silence fell all over again. My eyes stung. I couldn't see the Board's faces through the blur in my lashes, so I looked at Beau. He returned my gaze with a fierce nod. Behind him, so did Sarah.

"What about membership options?" Elizabeth said brightly, looking around the table. "A tiered paid membership offering the Astral Library experience on a level-by-level basis. Tours of book worlds offered at the highest price point, tours of the Library itself for mid-level members—"

"I like that," the pretty brunette bobblehead said. "The system needs to be monetized, we can all agree on that."

"Haven't you listened to a word I've said?" I cried, but no. They had not. I'd poured my heart out, every drop of eloquence I could summon, and I might as well have been talking to a pile of bricks. Maybe I'd gotten through to one or two on the Board—some were looking uncomfortable, refusing to meet my eye, but they were still clearly going to fall in with the party line. So much for the last-reel stirring speech that always worked so well in the movies. Pink Cardigan and Pickle Mouth were discussing membership price points ("$69.99 per month for Platinum Members, $49.99 for Gold Members, with a five percent fee raise every two years, or could we get away with eight percent?") and Darla had bustled her sheep face and her fuzzy blue sweater over to the nearest shelves so she could scan the titles for books to cull, and I could see where all this was going. The Library Board wasn't going to argue with me. They were just going to ignore me, as they carried out every last one of their threats.

"Alix?" Larry said in a small voice. "What are we going to do?"

I looked at his pinched face, trying so hard not to show fear, and I didn't know. Because I'd given it my all and it still looked like I wasn't going to be able to stop him from being returned to his Montana cult, or Sarah to the husband she so feared. Or stop this place from becoming a theme park with tickets for admission, where the only people allowed to enter a book were the ones who could afford to fork over $69.99 per month for the privilege.

"All the Patrons living in books would have to be relocated," Elizabeth was saying, completely ignoring the cluster of men and women and children standing right there listening to her pass mandates on their existence. "Can we all agree thirty-days notice is sufficient?"

"Oh, more than sufficient. Doesn't it feel a bit like freeloading, when you come right down to it? Really, who are these people and who's subsidizing them to live in our books on our dime?"

"It isn't your dime," I tried to say. "You can't monetize magic.

And you are not going to talk about my Patrons like they aren't *right here*—"

"I think I'd better get our people out." Beau drew me away from the table, his whispered voice gone taut. "Back to their books, their paintings, wherever. Maybe they can go into hiding—"

"*Fahrenheit 451*," Darla cried out from the nearest wall of shelves, pulling a volume down and brandishing it. "A book like this, full of vulgar language, in a library setting where children could be corrupted by—" The book snapped at her fingertips. She responded by wrenching it open and flattening it against the wall. It was still trying to fight its way free when she produced a big red stamp and banged it down on the fluttering title page. I had just enough time to see the bloodred word DISCARD before the book fell limply to the floor like it had been shot.

"Did you just kill a *book*?" I cried as Darla stepped over the volume and motored on to the next shelf. Elaine gave a hiss that exposed every one of her fangs as that blue sleeve brushed past. On my other side, Wet Wipe was droning about special price points in the membership plan for Board members. I couldn't think fast enough to know which way to turn. My head was pounding and Larry's chin was wobbling like he was trying hard not to cry and I couldn't *think*.

"As for the Librarian, what is the plan for her replacement?" the Bobblehead was saying.

"Well, she's really at retirement age, isn't she?" Wet Wipe answered. "A suitable exit bonus for her long service, but really, a woman of her years should be putting her feet up. Which of course leads us to the question of who would step up to guide the Astral Library through this crucial transition period—"

"A lengthy job search would have to be convened," harrumphed Pickle Mouth, "and surely a focus group should be canvassed—"

"Oh, we can dispense with that." Elizabeth twinkled. "I'll take on the job myself!"

And that—as Elizabeth claimed the Librarian's place and Darla sent another book winnowing to the floor with her red *DISCARD* stamp—was when the panic and desperation churning in my corseted middle began solidifying back into fury, hard as a diamond.

I stormed back to my place at the head of the table, shoving my chair out of the way so hard it flew over backward and hit the floor with a resounding crash. All faces spun in my direction for the second time. Even the minute-taking woman looked up.

"There is no way in *hell*," I snarled, "that I am letting you do this."

"Really, Alix." Elizabeth looked amused. "We've been very fair here. You've added your contribution for the record; we've heard you out. And it's very commendable, you representing the Library with the Librarian out of commission—Patty, enter into the minutes an official thank-you from the Board to Ms. Watson for stepping up to fulfill duties for which she was never adequately prepared. But it's time for the discussion to move forward now."

"Elizabeth—"

"If you further disrupt the meeting, we will be forced to call Library Security and have you removed." She overrode me. "Which would, of course, jeopardize our agreement about dropping charges of violent assault against poor Chad back in Boston."

The other Chad stepped forward at her side, right alongside Chester—not the real-world human versions I'd once found so annoying, but the blank-eyed simulacra that existed in this limbo between worlds and could neither bleed nor back down. I should have felt fear at the sight of them, but I didn't. The rage just billowed higher. "Get those bloodless abominations out of my face," I snapped, and behind me I could feel the rising rustle of the books. "You haven't destroyed this Library yet, and until you do I'm in charge here, not you."

Elizabeth sighed. So put-upon, so patient, as she made a check mark on her clipboard. "Chad, if you can escort Miss Watson from the Library. Chester, you can begin the eviction process for all Patrons currently present—"

Chester was closest to Sarah in her Victorian print dress and cameo. His hand locked around her elbow before she could jerk away, but she brought her free hand up in a resounding *crack* against his ear. It didn't appear to faze him at all. "If you will please come with us—" he began to drone.

Chad started toward me, I started toward Sarah, and Elaine showed her fangs again in a silent hiss, but Beau got there first. In one yank he freed the paper cutter's arm from the table where it still stood embedded like the Sword in the Stone, and pointed the razor tip straight at Elizabeth. "Lady, you tell your bullshit poly-blend zombies to back off or I will *feed* you that clipboard." Taking a step closer so the sword's edge fluttered the collar of her blouse. "Edgewise."

Chester dropped Sarah's elbow at a nod from Elizabeth but then took a synchronized step with Chad in the other direction instead, toward me. Elizabeth drew back around the edge of the long table, out of lunge reach even for Beau's long legs. "Alix, please don't make this difficult."

"Discard," Darla was muttering, flourishing that bloodred

stamp. "Discard, discard, discard—" Books were dropping to the floor like victims of a firing squad. I turned back to my Patrons, speaking low and fast.

"The minute the fighting starts, you run back to your books and you hide there. I'll hold them off as long as I can, Beau and me both—" Beau was already raising his library sword and I lunged for the silver pot of tea with a semi-hysterical thought of sending a boiling arc of Darjeeling right at Elizabeth, but neither Beau nor I had the chance to strike.

Behind me I'd been hearing the rising rustle of the books—all at once it rose in a kind of papery roar and I saw a dark swoop of flying shapes moving almost too quickly to track. One entire wall of the Astral Library's books rose like a wave and hurled themselves at the twin drones that were Chad and Chester.

The *splat* as they were crushed to the floor under a hundred-weight of leather bindings was sudden, savage, gelatinous, and final.

For a moment the Board just stared at the angry heap of volumes where Library Security had been standing . . . and then the books began to pull out of the pile, shaking themselves off a little bit, rustling their pages as they moved back toward Beau and the clustered Patrons and me, and circled around us like a castle's moat.

"They'll be back in just a moment," Elizabeth said, looking at the gluey spot on the Library floor where Chad and Chester had been standing.

"You sure about that?" I asked. "This isn't a book world; this is a whole different plane. The Library makes the rules here."

"That is simply ridiculous." Her voice rose. "A *library* does not

The Astral Library

make rules for itself. The Board makes rules for it, and—Alix, will you call those things off?"

"No," I said. "In fact, I think we're just getting started."

Because the books were rising behind me now like a wall. Not just the ones that had attacked Chad and Chester, but *all* the books. Every shelf in the Library was emptying, every volume flocking to my back. And I could hear that angry rustling just growing louder and louder.

I looked at the enormous cloud of volumes swirling and rising behind me, and then I looked back at the Library Board. I smiled, and I could feel that it was a smile with an edge, like a glint of light off a dragon's fangs. Because I was suddenly remembering what the Librarian said had happened to that group of slavers two hundred years ago, when they tried to force their way into the Library.

The books ate them.

"Uh-oh," I said softly to Elizabeth with her clipboard and Darla with her lists and all the rest of them with their pages of notes. "You people made the books mad."

"That is ridiculous," Pickle Mouth said, and then he yelped when a hardcover copy of *Bleak House* snapped at his shoulder like a viper. He stared as the book flew to join me, trailing a swatch of tweed from Pickle Mouth's sport coat.

"Oh, they're *definitely* mad," I remarked.

"Or they just have standards," Beau replied. "Tweed in April?"

"Shouldn't have got out that *DISCARD* stamp," Sarah said venomously.

"Alix," Elizabeth snapped, "call off the books."

"I don't know how," I said with complete honesty. The rustling at my back, it was only growing louder. Angrier. "What makes you think anyone can control stories, Elizabeth? They take on a life of their own, once the author sets down the pen. Stories are not obedient. Even old well-loved favorites sometimes grow teeth."

"Don't be ridiculous," she said in a clipped voice.

"It's a *magic library*, you fucking idiot," I said, and she rocked back as though I'd slapped her. "Yes, you're an idiot," I repeated. "Call yourself a librarian. You don't know a thing about books. You don't even know what Jane Austen wrote other than *Pride and Prejudice*. You come here to a magic library thinking you can control it with your bylaws and committees?"

I'd thought I had to be the one to fight for this place—me, or the Librarian, or *someone*. I hadn't quite realized until this moment that it could fight for itself. That maybe all it needed was a general.

"The thing you seem to have forgotten about sanctuaries," I told the Library Board, "is that they are allowed to defend themselves when they are violated. Defend themselves, and the people they shield. Did you think you got to waltz in here and make threats, maim my boss, blithely lay out your plans to ruin all these lives, and we somehow weren't allowed to fight back?"

I could tell from the look on their faces that this was exactly what they thought. Of course it was. Consequences, damage, harm—those were things they had the privilege of dealing *out*, not ever dealing *with*.

"Alix," Elizabeth said in that oh-so-reasonable voice, "no one here is looking to harm—"

"Yes, you are," I cut her off. "Just because you people are dressing it up in bureaucracy around a board table doesn't mean you aren't looking to inflict damage, you goose-stepping hypocrites. But here's what you don't understand." I smiled at her again, the smile she didn't like. "When you crossed this threshold, you came into uncharted waters. Haven't you ever seen the warning on old maps, when the waters grow deep? *Here There Be Dragons.*"

"Absolutely not." Elizabeth slapped her clipboard down on the table. "This place needs order, and it needs modernization, and it needs *monetization*—"

"Good luck with that," I remarked.

"You have outstayed your welcome, Alix." Elizabeth started around the table toward me, bright red patches of anger flaring high on her cheeks. "You have been a very disruptive presence to the annual Board meeting, and I am going to have you removed from the premises."

Beau moved to intercept her but stopped at the quick shake of my head. I let her come past him to me—let her give me the short, sharp shove I'd gotten from so many people in my foster-care childhood. The mean little shove of a real bully; the shove that had sent me scurrying over and over, since the age of eight, back to my dream life in the pages of *Voyage of the Dawn Treader.*

But this time that shove didn't budge me an inch. I stood there rooted in my book dress, a column holding this barrel-vaulted roof up, and she rebounded off me like a swell of the parchment sea outside. I lifted my hands on either side of me, palms up, and behind me I felt the books—every book in this library—rise in a dark, furious wave.

"Leave this place," I said softly. "Leave now."

"I am the *president* of the *Library Board*," she seethed, and shoved me again.

Wrong decision.

Like I'd seen the Librarian do when this place was under attack, I inhaled all the way down through my entire body to my toes and brought my finger to my lips.

'SHU

SH!"

Even before the word roared from my throat, the books behind me had sprung. They lunged like a great shadowy whip, curling down around Elizabeth and wrapping her up, hiding her from sight. The storm of book-bound violence hurled into the air as the Board shrieked and the Patrons gaped and Beau gripped his papercutter sword, and the entire Library seemed to shriek too. Every green window flashed dark; the clock gave a tremendous *clang*; the globe spun madly on its axis; and with a howl I felt in my marrow rather than heard with my ears, the Astral Library flung the president of the Board through the dark glass of the nearest window and out into the void.

I thought I'd hear a scream, but there was nothing. Not a sound as the parchment sea of stories below swallowed her whole.

My heart thudded and my mouth burned, as if I'd shouted a word made of fire. Part of me wanted to be sick, to say, *I didn't want that to happen*. But the books didn't care what I wanted. They simply defended themselves when threatened. This was the Astral Library, and here there be dragons.

So I looked back at the rest of the Library Board, standing frozen and horrified around the long table. Light was slowly returning to the room, the dark windows shading from ebony to emerald to peridot. The glass from the window where Elizabeth had been flung headlong twinkled unbroken again.

"Well, we can't have this," Darla shrilled, shattering the silence so suddenly everyone in the room flinched. "We simply cannot have this kind of thing, not in a space where *children* could be exposed to—" She flapped her hands, not even finishing that sentence. "All these books will have to be discarded, and as for you—"

The Astral Library

She came straight at me with her stamp raised like a dagger, and I wasn't for one moment afraid. Not with the books clustering ferociously over my head like a cloud of furious birds. But before the books could strike, Elaine did.

She moved in a blur of otherworldly speed, an arrow of garnet-red taffeta. The abused woman who had fled into Bram Stoker's England and remade herself as a Bride of Dracula flashed down on Darla like a swooping bat, battening down right above the collar of that baby-blue sweater with its curly lettered *Support Your Local Library!* And the *DISCARD* stamp clattered to the floor as the vampire drank the book burner dry.

Then she stepped back from the husk on the floor, patting her lips, and the little girl in the pinafore who had escaped to *Anne of Green Gables* composedly handed her a lace-edged hankie. "Thank you," Elaine murmured.

I felt even more dry-mouthed and just a little sick. But I hadn't picked this fight with the Board; they'd started it themselves, and now they were staring ashen-faced at the consequences. I moved around the long table to its head, taking my time, marshaling myself. Overhead the storm of books was dissipating, most floating serenely back to their shelves, others congregating in satisfied little groups under the ceiling, some coming back to check on me. An ancient leather-bound *First Folio* of Shakespeare's plays nudged under my hand like a playful pony and I gave it a stroke, sending it back to its shelf with a whisper. The Board flinched, watching it soar away from my hand.

Beau righted my fallen chair, and I took my seat in an enormous rustle of skirt, looking around the table from face to face—Pickle Mouth, Pink Cardigan, Wet Wipe, the Bobblehead, the secretary.

"You are all free to leave," I said at last, quietly. "But if you keep gunning for the Library or its Patrons, you have seen that we will fight back."

Not one person met my eyes.

"Right." I drew a deep breath. "The motion to monetize and modernize the Astral Library is hereby voted down by unanimous count. And I declare the annual Board meeting at an end."

23

I guess I'd been expecting to hear something poetic or heroic or moving when the Librarian finally opened her eyes and rejoined the land of the living, but the first words out of her mouth were "Where the hell am I?"

"You're back!" I shrieked, almost dropping the tea tray I'd just maneuvered through the door.

"Don't you dare drop my Darjeeling," she said ominously, regarding me one-eyed around the bandage that still crossed her forehead. It looked even odder now because she'd morphed out of the slumbering human form I'd left her in: the sight that currently greeted me was that of a green-scaled dragon in a head bandage lounging across an oversize four-poster bed, tail lashing crossly, claws flexing across the sheets as she stretched her long neck from side to side. Somehow she wasn't too big for the bed, or else the bed and the entire room around it had grown to accommodate her scaly form. On the other hand it was a very large, very grand room. "Where am I?" she asked, looking around at the damask-hung walls, the Savonnerie carpets, the marble-topped washstand, and the antique writing desk.

"Downton Abbey," I said, setting the tea tray down on a satinwood occasional table. "Specifically, *Downton Abbey: Mysteries of the Manor*. Did you know the show got a video game?"

The dragon stared at me.

"The Programmer hid you in a game to recuperate while we sorted out the Library Board. You started out in *Skyrim*, but once the danger was past I thought you might like something a little more luxe than the Temple of Kynareth in Whiterun." No offense to the Temple of Kynareth, which was a perfectly nice wooden-timbered place staffed by a very helpful priestess and acolyte who kept dosing the Librarian with healing potions when they weren't tending their altar and trying to get me to go on a quest to heal the dying Gildergreen tree. But the flagged stone floors were arctic, the local wind god kept sending regular blasts through the drafty hall, and all in all I wanted to tuck the Librarian under something a little warmer than a few wolfskin blankets while she recovered from her coma. "So I asked the Programmer if he had anything a bit more comfortable," I went on, "and here we are." In a first-person puzzle game set at the most famous fictional English country house ever to grace the TV screens of Anglophiles everywhere.

"I've visited the Programmer's games before," the Librarian said, eyeing the outfit the Astral Library had given me when I popped through the encrypted VPN tunnel to check on her. (Early 1920s afternoon dress in crushed rose-pink velvet topped by hip-length loops of pearl beads—I fit right in around here.) "Are we going to get subsumed into some kind of side quest?"

"No, the main game leaves us pretty much alone. Downton Abbey has been ransacked by an intruder and gamers are trying to restore the stolen objects and find the culprit, but we're at the top of the house, out of the main areas of play." I'd gotten used to the feel of being inside a game, which was very different from being in a book or a painting. The world around me had a slightly flatter, more two-dimensional feel, and objects sometimes visually popped at me as if they were urging me to start collecting them and join the scavenger hunt—a sort of *Quest starts here!* nudge from the world around me. And the conversations tended to happen on repeat with the NPCs (non-player characters, as I now knew to call them). "Every time I come through, Carson the butler stops to ask if I want a bite to eat sent up to the room, and I say yes, and he has the same line about *these sad days we find ourselves in, what is the world coming to,* and later Anna the lady's maid brings up the same cream scones, raspberry jam, watercress sandwiches, and Victoria sponge. But it's delicious. Let me tell you, you haven't lived until you've eaten Victoria sponge in actual Downton Abbey."

I'd told the Programmer as much after my first few visits, and he grinned and said I really needed to get into gaming. *Downton Abbey's only the start. You want a fantasy world, longships and castles and gryphons flying overhead? I can hook you up with that.*

But that was for later. Right now there was the Librarian, actually *awake* and glaring at me, and oh, how I'd missed her glare. "Why did you shift back to dragon form?" I asked, pouring out a cup of tea and doctoring it up with two sugars, just the way I'd seen her take it back in the Library. "I thought it took a lot out of you to change form, and you should be conserving your strength." No matter how much absurdist delight it gave me: the sight of a green-scaled dragon lounging in an English Stately Home among the hunting prints and Minton china, the end of her twitching tail rattling the fire irons.

"I didn't know if I'd be waking up straight into some kind of battle." The Librarian flexed her injured wing out to the side, careful not to smash out the window on the other end of the room, then delicately peeled off her eye bandage with one claw. "Wing's better, but the eye's still not good for much. Might take a few decades to heal fully. How long have I been out of action?"

"It's been just over a week since I had you moved here." I perched on the edge of the bed, passing over her Darjeeling and proceeding to fill her in on everything. She listened unblinking, claws folded around her teacup and saucer, one eye still painfully sealed closed, the other long and golden.

"Hmmm," she said at last. "I owe you a thank-you for taking on my duties in a time of crisis, Miss Watson. You did very well indeed."

"I'm not sure how much I was really needed," I confessed, unable to stop myself flushing. How much I'd wanted her approval, and here I was downplaying everything now that I'd gotten it. Because really, what *had* I done for the Library in the end? "It defended itself."

"It's not always aware when it needs to do that. Hence the need for a Librarian."

"Well, I'm happy to pass that title back to you once you're feeling fit. I was only ever granted Acting Librarian status, anyway." I slid her green tablet across the counterpane, then hesitated a moment. "The Library Board . . . do you think they'll be back to cause more trouble?" Because if I knew anything about bureaucracy, it was just how hard it was to win against it. Throw a Board president out the window, they'd just come back with another president and a new bylaw.

The Librarian made another *hmmmm* sound deeper in her throat, closer to a growl. "Perhaps. But not, I am guessing, for a *very* long time. And when they do try to make a run at me again with a meeting memorandum, I shall be more prepared. I have been"—and here her claws flexed against the sheets ever so slightly—"a bit head-in-the-sand about it all."

I wanted to ask her how she'd let it get so far. Why she hadn't taken them on earlier. But I couldn't figure out how to phrase it so it wasn't an accusation. She answered me anyway, clearly reading my thoughts.

"I did try to take them on, in the early days. They kept boxing me out. And they were all so *ridiculous*, with their quarterly reports and their stamps and their fussy bureaucracy, it felt impossible to take them seriously. So I left those odious drones to their asinine meetings and assumed they'd leave me to do the real work." She prodded painfully at her scarred eye. "Appropriate, perhaps, to be nearly blinded when I was clearly already blind."

"Never underestimate bureaucrats," I said with about as much feeling as I'd ever said anything in my life. "Just because they're odious drones doesn't mean they can't also be evil bastards."

Another growl from her, this one sending smoke curling up from her snout. She wanted to know about the Patrons then, and I was able to reassure her that Larry and Masako and Elaine (bless her fangs) and all the rest of them had been restored to their chosen books. I'd enlisted the capable Sarah to help me escort everyone home, waving her off last of all back into Sherlock Holmes's London. I was going back next Tuesday (her time) to meet her for lunch at the Langham hotel.

A knock on the door—Anna, right on schedule with the scones. "Fresh out of the oven, miss," she said just as she always did, and then deviated from script by peering around my shoulder to where the Librarian's green-scaled tail was just visible, coiled around the bedpost. "Is the dragon awake yet?" she asked, sounding interested.

"Um. You can see the dragon?"

"Of course I can see the dragon," said Anna. "I'm guessing a hack import from *Skyrim*?"

"You know about video games?" I couldn't help asking.

"Well, I know I'm in one, but I'm not sure Mr. Carson's quite caught on. Gets a bit repetitive, honestly—I wouldn't mind a visit to somewhere more exciting. I talk to the gamers sometimes about the other games they play." Anna looked briefly wistful. "But at least it's a lighter workload here, just running around helping the gamers rather than doing all the housework. A house this size, there's a *lot* of housework. Enjoy your scones, miss—" And off she went to go assist the gameplay. I brought the tray in, shaking my head a little, and heaped a scone in jam and clotted cream for the Librarian, who was still clearly thinking about the people I'd left behind in the Astral Library.

"What about your Mr. Sato-Jones, what's his status?"

"Well, he's not a book-world candidate, truth be told. He doesn't want to leave the world he's in; he just really, really needs a break. So he's sort of been living in the Astral Library Wardrobe Department." He'd taken it over with his sewing machine and Newbury Street workshop supplies, at my invitation—I'd led him there, still in the book dress, after the shambles of the annual meeting and said, *Time doesn't move here—take the room over and get this dress finished the way you need to.* Beau was bringing the dress to LA soon for the final fitting before the premiere of *Belle*, and who knew if it was really going to fix every problem he had (the shop's past-due rent, the loan to his dad) but it was now finished down to the last crystal bead, and he'd had all the paused time in the world to do it.

Though I'm not sure how I'm going to feel, lacing an actress into it, Beau told me two nights ago as he packed it up in its enormous box to take back to Newbury Street. *It's always going to feel like your dress, czarina. That moment I watched you stand there in the middle of the Library, with the books rising up behind you like wings . . .* He leaned in, dropping a kiss on the side of my neck. *You looked like a Book Dragon.*

Now I looked at the real Book Dragon, curled in her green scales on her four-poster bed, eating a scone and sipping from a flowered teacup balanced between her claws with incongruous delicacy. "What's next for you?" the Librarian asked me, her one-eyed gaze unnervingly piercing over the teacup's rim. "Have you chosen a book to live in?"

"I don't . . . think I want to go live in a book anymore." I fiddled with my slice of Victoria sponge, finally putting the flowered plate down. "Do I even have a right to go to one? I mean, the Library didn't actually choose to invite me. The Board hacked the system and put my name in."

And to be honest that still hurt—just a little. Maybe the Library had given me full access later, when it needed me to help deal with the Board, but I had been the only person it had on hand. Being picked from a pool of one during a crisis isn't the same as being chosen for yourself when there's time for real consideration.

"Oh, Alix," the Librarian said in her smoky voice, "what utter rot."

I blinked. "Pardon?"

She put her teacup down, giving a full-body shake that traveled from her head to her tail tip, and at the end of the shiver she was back to her normal self—just a round little woman of seventyish years, with a gaze considerably older than that, decorously garbed in a long-sleeved linen nightgown but still giving me an exasperated, dragonish glower over the counterpane. "The Board may have put your name in because they saw an opportunity in you. But do you think a crude hacking job like that can make the Library do *anything* it doesn't want to?"

"Um. Yes? I mean, because it worked. I got my invite that same day."

"Because the Library saw your name, took a look at you, and *chose you*. You silly girl."

"It—it did?" I wobbled.

"If it hadn't wanted you," she stated, "you would never have found a way in. It chose you to be a Patron, as it chose so many others. And then it chose you again as a champion, over all the others it's ever invited over its threshold, because you were the one above all who proved you wanted to fight for it. Oh gods," she said at the look on my face, "please tell me you aren't going to cry."

I was absolutely going to cry. I dug a starched linen handkerchief out of my period-appropriate Library-supplied handbag and blubbered for a bit as the Librarian sat there rolling her eyes and slathering more raspberry jam on her scone.

"So you don't want to go live in *Around the World in Eighty Days*?" she clarified when my flushed, sodden face emerged from the handkerchief.

I shook my head, blowing my nose. When I first entered the Astral Library I'd wanted to dive headlong into a book and never come out—leave my entire disappointing world behind me forever. Now I wasn't so sure. I didn't want one book world; I wanted *all* of them. I didn't want to leave my world behind either. The regular world had the Boston Public Library Reading Room, which I was going to miss. It also had the Boston Public Garden and the sculpture monument to *Make Way for Ducklings*. And it had Beau, who had dressed me for the fight of my life and had then undressed me afterward, his fingers unpicking every single lace, tie, and button without once lifting his mouth from mine.

Leave all that behind?

But I didn't want to leave the Astral Library behind either. Or the live books who had for a brief moment flown at my back like wings.

"Alix," the Librarian asked me from Downton Abbey's best guestroom four-poster, "would you like a job?"

EPILOGUE

One year later

The new Patron was going to be just fine, I could tell—she'd taken in my rundown with barely a hitch, and she already knew which book she wanted to live in. "*Phantom of the Opera*," breathed the lanky chorus singer who'd walked from a dinner theater production of *Les Mis* into the Astral Library via a company library of musical theater scores. "I've always wanted to live in Belle Epoque Paris!"

"You're aware the book world won't look exactly like the musical, right?" I asked, steering her toward the big oak counter, where the Librarian was finishing up an irritated memo to the Programmer. "For one thing, no one's going to go around bursting into song—"

"What have we here?" My boss looked up, swiping a pencil out of her gray bun where she'd jabbed it—she looked considerably more dashing these days even in her cardigan and tweed skirt, since Beau had made her an entire wardrobe of sequined eye patches to wear over her scarred eye. Today was the deep emerald-green eye patch, which made her look like a pirate queen if pirate queens were dressed by Galliano. "New Patron?" she rasped.

"Read in and ready," I replied, and gave the new arrival's arm a squeeze. "*This* is the Librarian."

"I thought you were the librarian?"

"Nope, just a Page." I'd be a Page for decades, and I was fine with that. It took time, learning the ropes of a place like the Astral Library. I was still barely wrapping my head around the concept, introduced last week, of the Cloud Codex (apparently that's where the whole idea of downloading to the cloud comes from). And don't even get me started on the Wordsmithing Forge. (A smithy where the muses who inspired poets and novelists actually beat metallic blocks of words out into sentences on anvils with hammers. *I work for Kate Quinn*, one haggard-looking muse said, dripping sweat onto her blacksmithing apron, *and that bitch runs a* sweatshop. "Kate who?" I'd asked, but the muse just went back to hammering and swearing.)

I passed the newest Patron off to the Librarian for any clarification on her new existence and marked the transfer off on my sapphire-blue tablet. (Much less touchy and temperamental than the Librarian's; it only changed the password on me when I used the wrong *your* for *you're* while taking notes too fast, and really, who could blame it?) After that, I headed for the Wardrobe Department. "You've got a new Patron to dress," I called, swinging through the doors. "She's heading to Belle Epoque Paris circa *Phantom of the Opera*."

"I've got a dress at the shop inspired by Emmy Rossum's mourning outfit from the *Phantom* movie." Beau materialized from behind a mannequin where he was draping a turn-of-the-century evening gown for another Patron set to head into a Henry James novel in two days. "Inspired by, but more historically accurate. Less cleavage, more pleating and tucking." He had one of his Brummell suits on, pearl-gray waistcoat and billowy-sleeved shirt and skintight trousers, and my God, was he a snack. I was *so* over modern clothes that could just be yanked off in a few tugs. All that exquisite frustration when you had nine hundred mother-of-pearl buttons to undo and period corsets to be painstakingly unlaced and intricately tied cravats to be unwound . . . Let me tell you, it's *highly* underrated.

"Come here, you." I reached for the measuring tape around Beau's neck, using it as a rein to draw him in for a kiss. I wasn't the only one who'd been offered a job around here: Beau had taken over the Astral Library Wardrobe Department. *Because these sad racks of old theater costumes are just depressing*, he'd groaned, getting one look at the room where our Patrons were made over before heading into their book worlds. *Sending people off to their new lives in slapdash cotton-blend replicas? Oh, honey, no. Besides, it feeds my soul, doing real period stuff and not just movie-costume stuff.*

You wouldn't think Beau would have time to dress the Astral Library's Patrons, not with all the new commissions he was getting after the star of *Belle* landed on a dozen gushy best-dressed lists following her red-carpet walk at the premiere—but he could afford to be picky about the commissions he chose these days (not to mention hike up his prices). And with his sewing machine and workshop now living in the Astral Library, where he commuted with me every day through the BPL Reading Room stacks, he had all the time in the world to get the historical details right when working in a room where time didn't pass. All the time he needed to finish a dress, pull together a historically accurate outfit for a new Patron, get a nap in, and head back to his shop, where it would still be morning and he could photograph his newest creation for social media or head to one of those glitzy events his latest few hundred thousand Instagram followers couldn't get enough of on his feed.

I broke the kiss, gripped by a sudden clutch in my stomach—the lurking awareness that this couldn't go on forever, this enchanted time where I had the Astral Library *and* the Boston Public Library, the Librarian's world *and* Beau's. Sooner or later I'd have to start spending more and more time in this world so I could take over from the Librarian, whenever she was ready, and Beau would have to decide if he wanted Brummell's on Newbury Street and the world he'd been born into, or the Astral Library Wardrobe Department and me. But that decision was just a melancholy shadow on the horizon for now, so I let it go with a long, steadying breath.

"Thought I'd go to the Boston Ballet tonight," Beau was saying, not noticing my sudden shaft of foreboding. "Opening night of *Firebird*, and the costumes are supposed to be out of this world, very Persian inspired. Want to come, czarina? Wear my latest?"

"If I get back from my afternoon appointment in time, yes, please." Because his latest was a creation fit to banish any attack of the blues: a stark black skirt with a complicated cage of a bodice in sapphire-blue silk satin he'd fitted high and tight around my neck and down to my wrists, but left completely open down the back, from the nape of my neck to the base of my tailbone—all to showcase the line of iridescent blue that had started coming in down the line of my spine. Most people thought it was some kind of bedazzled tattoo when they saw it, but it wasn't. It was scales.

"Your dragon form's coming in," the Librarian had said matter-of-factly when I pulled up my hair to show her the sapphire flash at my nape. "Don't get too excited, you won't be able to full-form shift for at least another eighty years—" But, hell yes, I was excited.

The Astral Library

Eight-year-old me wanted to jump on a dragon's back and fly, fly, fly. Grown-up me was going to do the flying herself.

I gave Beau another lingering kiss and swung out of the Wardrobe Department, stashing my blue tablet at the long oak counter and running a fingertip over the bumper sticker, which the Librarian had, to my surprise, allowed to remain stuck to the front like a proud-flying flag. My mom's bumper sticker finally finding its home, just like me. She wasn't ever going to see it, and I didn't think she was ever going to see me either. I'd done a lot of quiet thinking over the last year, wondering if I should try to make contact with her out in San Diego . . . I'd decided no. Maybe someday I'd feel differently, but right now I thought I'd leave her to her Etsy shop and the family she'd picked over me. Her loss, not mine.

Though I thought I'd keep a long-distance eye on my little half sister, just in case Mom ever decided to walk out on her too. If that happened, she wasn't going into foster care like I had.

Dennis flew at me as I turned toward the library door, brandishing his latest book angrily. "Yes, Dennis, I know *Fourth Wing* ends on a cliff-hanger. Let me get you the sequel." Dennis fluttered along agitatedly behind me as I went to the shelves; *Iron Flame* flew down to my hand as soon as I raised it, and I concealed a grin as I passed the book over. I'd persuaded Dennis to give Tolstoy a rest, and now he was plowing through all my favorite fantasy series. (You should have heard the spectral gasping and muttering when he hit the spicy bits.) At this rate Dennis was never going to get back to *War and Peace*, much less finish off his TBR stack and ascend to wherever it is ghosts ascend. But, maybe that was just fine. Some people would rather spend eternity reading than go to heaven anyway. I'd gotten to know all the library ghosts by now, the more reticent ones who didn't corporealize: Ethel, who was trying to catch up on all the Reese

Witherspoon Book Club picks; Sajidah, who had just gotten into sci-fi and was plowing through Ursula K. Le Guin . . .

I left the Library and hopped the T out to the Boston suburbs for my afternoon appointment. I'd been hoping the Librarian would take it on, but she'd thrown the ball back into my lap: *Your proposal*, she'd said, *you spearhead it. Besides, I've got my hands full restructuring the Library Board.* All the old members who had come to the annual meeting had been summarily fired (one or two just fled), and she was in the process of restructuring the bylaws to make sure the Library was protected, not just from external dangers but from internal bureaucracy . . . But that left me alone with my proposed new plan, which made me equal parts proud and terrified.

"You said you were from a library initiative of some kind?" The ponytailed woman who let me into her home office had a keen gaze behind glasses with blue-green frames. "What's that got to do with my books?"

"I love the whole series," I couldn't help saying. *The Five Queendoms* by G. R. Macallister: one of my favorite fantasy worlds with its ruthless sorceresses, its resourceful queens, its warrior women, and its world of magic rites and desert sands—a world I'd have loved to visit, but it wasn't in the public domain, because G. R. Macallister herself was alive and standing right in front of me.

Hence the new program I'd proposed to the Librarian. *Can't we get around copyright issues if we have legal permission from the author to utilize their books as living worlds for our Patrons?*

I had Zoom calls next week with Eloisa James, Julia Quinn, and a whole slew of historical romance authors, because hist-rom provided *just* the kind of prettied-up world (low on the violence and bad dental hygiene, heavy on the royal balls and handsome men) that I could imagine hundreds of readers wanting to escape into. And I'd emailed the C. S. Lewis estate, heart in my throat, asking for a meeting. They hadn't answered yet . . . but might I one day get permission to walk through a door and see a lamppost gleaming in the middle of a snow-hung forest? Might I one day walk the deck of the gilt-prowed *Dawn Treader*, where the waves rolled sweet all the way to the utter East?

I hoped so.

But for today, I had my first face-to-face presentation to get through.

"What if I told you," I said to the wordsmith in front of me, "that you could visit the world you write about? If readers who loved it could visit it . . . or even live in it?"

I expected skepticism. I expected laughter, derision, outright disbelief. But writers are a different breed, aren't they? Their heads are already off in the clouds, those clouds I saw drifting past the Astral Library's green windows every day, sweeping in words from distant winds and collecting stories from all corners of the earth and raining them down gently into the parchment sea. Writers already know the sound of those winds bringing them stories. Writers already know about far-off worlds lying just a tornado ride or a wardrobe door away from our own.

G. R. Macallister's eyes gleamed, and I knew she was seeing the world she'd written: its citadels piled with scrolls, its bone-beds and arcane sacrifices, its matriarchal women who dueled and clawed and fought to make their own fates. I couldn't wait to lead her there, and I felt sure I'd get the chance because that gleam in her eye told me she was ripe for the invitation—the invitation every bookworm child wants to hear when they devour stories and get lost in library stacks, when they dream of sailing the length of an endless bookshelf on a library ladder like Belle.

I smiled and asked, "Have you ever wanted to live inside a book?"

Author's Note

My mother was a librarian and my father read aloud to me incessantly before I could read myself, and those two facts have shaped everything I came to be. I grew up running around libraries; books were the building blocks of my entire world, and my happy place was the huge old-fashioned claw-foot bathtub in the children's section of the library where my mom worked: padded out with quilts and pillows, it could fit four little girls with their *Baby-Sitters Club* paperbacks or two exhausted moms with babies in slings and the latest Debbie Macomber. That bathtub was magic. It turned exasperated adults with mile-long to-do lists into giggling kids again, ditching their shoes and their afternoon errands for an hour of indulgent me time with a favorite novel. Children understood instinctively that the bathtub could fly and it might at some point rise off the floor and whisk you away to your favorite book world.

I believed in book worlds as a little girl because fantasy was my gateway drug: some of the very first books my father read aloud to me

Author's Note

were C. S. Lewis's Narnia series and L. Frank Baum's Oz novels. I spent a lot of my childhood poking my head into wardrobes looking for a door to Cair Paravel (I was very interested in the idea of being made queen of a land full of fauns, dryads, and talking mice) and had I lived in tornado country I undoubtedly would have walked myself straight into a twister for my one-way ticket to Oz. My father and I had read our way through both series and moved on to King Arthur and the Round Table by the time I hit first grade and began learning to read for myself—as soon as I realized that I could be my own dealer for this particular addiction, I had a library card application slapped down on the counter with my name crookedly crayoned across the top. I ran up library fines in double digits, I sneaked into the adult section to get my hands on books people said were too mature for me (and came to absolutely no harm because of it), I got in trouble at school for reading under the desk in my more boring classes . . . and somewhere along the way, I became a storyteller myself.

I write books set in the real world, usually the past, but I have never lost my childhood love for fantasy worlds. It was a pleasure to pay tribute to my favorite fantasy authors in this book: sharp-eyed readers will catch references not only to Narnia and Oz, but to the worlds of N. K. Jemisin, Ursula K. Le Guin, J. R. R. Tolkien, George R. R. Martin, Tamora Pierce, Jeannie Lin, Anne McCaffrey, Leigh Bardugo, Ayana Gray, Rebecca Yarros, Sarah J. Maas, Rick Riordan, Lev Grossman, and G. R. Macallister. I also enjoyed paying tribute to some of my favorite classic novels, by the likes of Jane Austen and Charlotte Brontë and Alexandre Dumas; and my favorite painters, such as Thomas Cole, Edmund Blair Leighton, Arnold Böcklin, and Claude Monet. Especially sharp-eyed readers may catch a crossover cameo in Thomas Cole's painting *The Consummation of Empire* to my ancient Rome novel *Lady of the Eternal City*!

Author's Note

Like any reader, I have fantasized about being able to live inside the worlds I imagine so vividly while reading. The idea of a magic library that opened up those kinds of doors came to me a few years ago, and as soon as my imagination conjured it up I knew it looked like the wondrous Boston Public Library Reading Room (or Bates Hall, as I have never heard anyone but a tour guide call it). As a college student I spent many hours in that reading room, setting my laptop up at one of the long reading tables beside the jewel-green lamps and hammering away at whatever book I was currently writing. No magic door ever opened for me there but really, the Boston Public Library—and all libraries—are magic enough all on their own. As Alix says with such passion, they are far more than just repositories of books. They are living, breathing spaces for living, breathing people, and all the messy, complicated problems people carry on their backs: one of the few public places where a purchase is not necessary if you wish to linger, a refuge for children and the unhoused, a place where information and free access to it are elevated over all.

And libraries are under attack, now more than ever. They are chronically underfunded, their vital programming and services continually slashed by budget cuts. Frothing-at-the-mouth book banners are always waving lists of books they want culled from the shelves of their local libraries. And subtler threats come from bureaucratic board member types who trade a lot of catchphrases about *essential modernization* and *the need to remain relevant in a changing world* and *monetization as the key to the future.* Some of these changes are necessary as well as well meaning—institutions do need to change and adapt if they are to survive. But some are not well meaning at all, and threaten to put libraries out of business or change their entire purpose for existing: there are people out there who genuinely believe a modern library should only be one-quarter books.

Protect your local libraries. Support them, fund them, use them,

Author's Note

vote for measures that will ensure their survival against the book banners, the budget cutters, and the board members. Libraries are beacons in the dark. Don't let them go out. They got the Library of Alexandria—don't let them get yours.

I owe enormous thanks to the many people who helped in the writing and production of *The Astral Library*. My editor, Tessa, and my literary agent, Kevan, who didn't bat an eyelash when their historical fiction author proposed writing a fantasy novel. The wonderful team at William Morrow: Amelia, Deanna, Kelsey, Madelyn, and my publicist, Julie, who I invariably address as Khaleesi the Mother of Dragons for her ability to breathe smoke and make problems disappear. My wonderful critique partners, Stephanie Thornton, Lea Nolan, and Stephanie Dray, whose feedback helped me hone an ungainly rough draft into something worth reading, and marvelous fellow author Rene Denfeld, who writes with such sensitivity about children in the foster system and advised me how to fine-tune Alix's background and character. The spectacular Greer Macallister, who let me put her in the book along with her sensational matriarchal fantasy series, *The Five Queendoms*—if you haven't picked up the first, *Scorpica*, and reveled in its ruthless queens and desperate sorceresses and heroic Amazons, then you are seriously missing out. While you're at it, check out the Instagram page of French fashion designer Sylvie Facon, whose jaw-dropping creations—antique books unpicked and restitched into couture gowns—inspired Beau's book dress.

Thank you to my husband, Stephen the Overseas Gladiator, an inveterate gamer who helped me flesh out the idea of the Programmer and the Astral gaming worlds. Thank you to my much-missed father, for getting me hooked on fantasy in the first place. And thank you most of all to my mother, who started me out along this path by showing me what a real Librarian (capital *L*) is supposed to be.